Bloodsoaked

Richard Champagne

Formatting by C. S. Cooper
www.cscooper.com.au
Paperback ISBN: 979-8-9992315-0-5
Hardcover ISBN: 979-8-9992315-1-2

On the Fringes

Monsters have always existed.

Since the first humans walked the earth, creatures that defied imagination and logic have preyed on them. Supernatural horrors of an imagination run rampant and given form. They exist on the fringes of humanity. Parasites that latch onto people to survive. They are stronger. They are faster. And they are more resilient. They are predators of man that walk among their prey.

Legends tell of them. Savage man-beasts that prowl untouched forests. The dead who hunger for the life blood of the living. Spirits of the deceased too tormented to go to their final rest. Men whose desire to control the very essence of reality exceed their own earthly grasp.

All of those myths and more are real.

The world as it exists today is a lie. There is a hidden world—the real world—lying just beneath the surface. A world of power. A world of control. A world of evil and depravity. There, the monsters of legend subsist. They use us as cattle and pawns in their battle with each other for control of humanity and its resources. And they have done so for centuries untold, undaunted and unchallenged. To them, this is the way of things.

But, there have also existed those who refuse to

tolerate them.

Even from the earliest days, there were those who fought back. Men who would not sit idly by and let the monsters have their way. They learned to control their fears. To grow stronger and fashion their bodies, their minds, and their very souls into potent weapons against those creatures of myth. They trained for decades at the highest peaks and deepest jungles before spreading throughout the world. Fueled by their faith, these few men hunted the demons that hid in the shadows, bringing justice to them, one beast at a time. Though their numbers have always been small, they continued to travel the lands, freeing those they came across from the grasp of unnatural evil.

For untold generations, these men toiled unseen by the world at large, handing down their teachings from master to student. Alone, they walk the back alleys and forgotten roads, hunting the things that go bump in the night. They stand at the fringes, pushing back the evil that should not be, fighting the myriad nightmares that torment mankind from the safety of darkness.

These brave men have no scripture, no monuments, nor any stories to be sung. They hunt not for fame. Nor for glory or for riches. The hunt is their calling—their duty. They are known only for their deeds and only by those whose lives they touch.

This is one of our untold stories.

Prologue

Friday, July 15th, 1980. 11:47pm

Friday, July 15ᵗʰ, 1980. 11:47pm

The little boy cowered under the bloody bail of hay.
     The storm had begun an hour after nightfall and hadn't let up since. A million raindrops drummed on the roof of the old barn. The air inside was cold and crisp from the moisture. The block and tackle swung wildly from the winds. Occasional flashes of lightning burst through the loft window, illuminating the dirty interior a split second at a time. Despite the weather, most of the animals slept soundly. They always slept soundly. Especially the sheep—nothing ever spooked them. Even when Dad and Uncle Jimmy would shoot their rifles, the animals didn't care.
     The cow carcass next to the hay pile reeked. Legions of flies buzzed around the gaping hole in its chest.
     Earlier that day, one of the farmhands found the thing dead in the grazing pasture. A massive tree branch had pierced its ribs, standing upright like a flag marker. The cow was still breathing when Dad and Uncle Jimmy came to look at it. The gunshot had echoed for miles. They had to store the remains in the barn so the coming storm wouldn't damage it. The boy had heard a few of the farmhands whispering that it was some

kind of a warning.

Dad said that they would bring it to the butcher's shop in the morning. The boy hated that idea. Tomorrow was his birthday. He was excited. 10 years old! Double digits! And on a Saturday, too! They were going to have a party at his favorite restaurant in town and everything. Of course, Mom said his stupid sister had to come. She was going to ruin it—she always started fights with him.

Lightning struck. The boy shut his eyes, fighting the tears. The heavy storm was loud, but it did nothing to drown out all the screams.

A stranger had visited the farm that afternoon. The boy never saw anyone like him before. He had long, gray hair, and his face was covered with crazy-looking scars. The man wore a big purple bathrobe-thing over his grubby clothes. Dad said he was a hitch-hiker that was passing through, but Uncle Jimmy said he was a crazy jap—whatever that meant.

The man talked with Dad and Uncle Jimmy for hours, well past his bed time. The boy sneaked out of bead just as the man was leaving. He did his best to stay quiet, but the stranger saw him hiding under the stairs. And for just a second, he looked at the boy with scary eyes. They were yellow—and they glowed in the dark!

It scared him, but he didn't run away. He just stared in awe at the old man. Something about him seemed to root the boy in place. Then the man's freaky eyes went back to normal, and he left.

The scary men came to the farm a few hours later.

It started with gunfire. Not the big booms like Dad and Uncle Jimmy's hunting rifles. These were different. Faster. Everyone on the farm started shouting. The lights went on. Mom ran into his room in a panic, waking him and his sister. She was scared and crying. He'd never seen her like that, except that one time when he broke his leg.

He heard more guns as they ran down the stairs. And more shouting. Angry shouting.

And screams.

Mom reached for the front door, but the thing exploded off its hinges and knocked her to the floor. Lightning flashed, silhouetting the dark figure of a large man. The floorboards creaked under his dripping wet boots. Another crack of lightning made his eyes gleam, and for that one heartbeat, they were red like blood.

Mom crawled backwards on her elbows. She shouted for them to run. His sister tugged at his arm, finally uprooting him from his fascination. The big man snatched Mom's nightshirt and picked her up like one of his toys. She screamed like he'd never heard before, terror that should have frightened the boy, but he only stared at the dark man, his hands balling into tiny fists.

And then the man bit her under the chin. Her terror immediately ended. The boy had never seen so much blood like that. Never felt so much anger. His sister pulled him away and ran for the kitchen door.

The rain came down like a blizzard outside. The grain silo was on fire. But the barn wasn't. He saw more scary men running around the farm. They were shooting big, loud guns into all the buildings and laughing. Some of the farmhands ran out with tools, but the scary men shot them. The others disappeared into the wheat fields, screaming in terror. Some of the scary men chased after them.

Still holding hands, his sister headed for the big blue barn. They slipped through the tiny crack in the doors, and together, they pushed them shut. He followed her under the bail of hay while the guns and the screams continued. Neither dared speak a word in case any of the evil-looking men heard them.

Eventually, the chaos died down. Then talking.

It was muffled and distant, dulled by the constant

patter of rain on the hollow ceiling. Every so often the talking would stop and everyone screamed. He recognized the voices of the farm hands, Uncle Jimmy and his girlfriend, and Dad. He didn't hear Mom. A gun would go off, and all the screams would stop . . . and one of the voices. The cycle of talking, screaming, and shooting repeated until there were no more voices left. And then there was just rain.

The boy finally grew tired. His sister had already cried herself to sleep next to him.

Gunfire—lots of it—woke them up. Different yelling accompanied the noise. His sister exchanged looks and climbed out from under the hay. He grabbed at her foot, but she shushed him and went to the door. Pushing hard on the handle, she cracked it open. A second later a big hand quickly dragged her screaming through the door. Her voice drowned in the ongoing chaos outside.

Finally, tears rolled down the boy's cheeks. He didn't cry when they bit his mother. Nor did he cry when he heard the screams from his father and uncle or the farmhands. But when his stupid sister's voice faded into the night, that's when the tears came.

The gunfire finally stopped a few minutes later, and the yelling ended soon after. The boy quietly sobbed. He didn't want to think about it—to acknowledge the truth. They were all gone. The farmhands. His parents. His sister.

The barn door creaked open.

Lighting flickered again, outlining a dark figure in the doorway. Rain dripped from a curved sword in its hand. The boy held his breath, covering his mouth shut with both hands. The figure stepped into the barn, quiet. The boy scooted further under the hay, willing himself not to be noticed.

"Boy?" the figure called out.

It's eyes flashed, and two bright yellow orbs

slowly swept across the building. It was that stranger from before. His purple bathrobe fluttered behind him. He took a few steps inside. Not a single strand of straw covering the floor moved under its foot.

"Boy?" the voice called again. The pair of yellow eyes fell on the hay pile. The stranger flicked the water off his sword and tucked it under his robe with a metallic click. His eyes stopped glowing and he approached the hay pile.

"Boy?" he said, his voice softer. "It is over."

The boy looked up. The stranger was kneeling before him. The man extended a rough hand wrapped in wet cloth. Slowly, the boy took the stranger's hand. The older man pulled him out of the smelly hay pile and stood him up straight.

"What is your name?"

"Ethan Ward," the boy sniffed. He wiped his nose with a pathetic snort.

The stranger's eyes seemed to penetrate him, judging him on something he couldn't possibly see. His jaw flexed once before he spoke again. "Your family is gone. Do you have somewhere to go? An uncle or grandfather, maybe?"

Tears rained down like the storm outside. "No," he squeaked.

The stranger put his hands on Ethan's shoulders. "Friends who can take you?"

He shook his head. Ethan didn't have any friends at school. His classmates all made fun of him and his sister. The stranger looked out the door with a heavy breath.

"Stay here."

He stood up and left Ethan in the barn. The boy sat down, alone for the first time in his life. Time lost meaning as he cried. Winds howled through the open door, breaking up his sobbing and the dreary drumming of rain on the ceiling. The stranger finally returned holding a filled knapsack in one hand and Ethan's school bag in another. Both were filled to the brim. His uncle's sheathed hunting knife was tucked into the stranger's waist band. He dropped the school bag at Ethan's feet.

"My name is Takuan. You will bury your family; then, you will come with me."

Ethan looked up to the stranger. His face was hard as stone. A massive gash split the skin over his right eye from forehead to cheek. Blood seeped out, but the stranger paid it no mind. He took Ethan's hand and lead him out of the barn.

The boy's tears disappeared in the rain.

Night Was Black

Monday, February 24th, 2003. 3:31am

With a gnarled stick of charcoal, an old, emaciated man carefully drew out a perfect circle on a dark marble floor. Within that circle, he connected five red candles with sharp vertices, delicately inscribing phrases at each intersection. He quietly chanted each phrase several times before moving on to the next. When the pentagram was complete, he took a mixture of white dust and ash from a nearby basin and cast it into the circle. Kneeling next to the finished circle, the old man chanted louder. The candle flames pulsed with each uttered syllable.

London Bray leaned against one of the workstations in the darkened alchemy lab. He watched his old friend, Oberon, conduct the ritual with a marked detachment. Mysticism like this was never his forte. London had always preferred a more hands on approach to getting what he needed.

With a sigh, he slipped a hand into the pocket of his tailored suit. In the reddish half-light, he checked the time on a gold pocket watch worn smooth from use. The watch closed with a soft metallic clap. It was just past three-thirty in the morning. Oberon had requested his presence tonight to discuss a special favor, but it was getting late, and he still had many things to tend to before that damned sun came up.

London had been friends with the old mage for well over a century now. They had first met in Normandy years after the fall of Napoleon. He was only a neophyte then, having gone through the changes barely a decade before. London had just inherited an old family property in America and was preparing to take possession when he had encountered Oberon. During their trip, the two Englishmen struck up a conversation that had lasted the entire night. They pontificated on the state of the Empire to the nature of sea travel, celestial navigation, and the metaphysical elements of creation. Oberon had tried to initiate London into the ways of magic during that voyage, but the intricacies of the mystic arts simply eluded the old soldier.

His inability to fully grasp the systems of magic did not hamper their growing friendship, however. After London had assumed control of his family's home, he allowed Oberon to add a few well hidden rooms to its ongoing construction. Over the years the two formed a small following of like-minded friends in the burgeoning American city of Free Port. There, they studied and sought power, both mystical and physical. Oberon jokingly referred to them as his personal flock, but London knew what they were—his cult. And he was in charge of the cult's protection.

Next to him, Alexander fiddled with a trench lighter. The young man had been his number two for a decade now. He had impressed London with his strong force of will when he joined his private security company. He rose rapidly through the ranks, displaying a level of creativity and initiative surpassing everyone else. When London offered the man a *special* promotion, Alexander did not take long to accept it. Unfortunately, his newly minted protege did not share

London's appreciation of Oberon's practices.

The chanting grew louder and louder, and the flames blazed brighter and brighter. Alexander's eyes darted around the laboratory, searching for anything to focus on other than the arcane rite unfolding before him.

The small flames surrounding the old man shed light like tiny bonfires now, their red glow illuminating more of the circular room. The intense flickering outlined workstations bearing complex distilling equipment, jars of strange substances, and dozens of specialized tools. Beyond them, a row of tall boilers stood watch against the curved wall. A latticework of pipes from their tops snaked across the domed roof into a row of glass stasis chambers filled with bubbling liquid behind a wall of glass panels. A massive mechanical armillary dominated the center of the lab, quietly ticking away on a bulky set of gears.

The chanting reached a crescendo and the candles suddenly snuffed out all at once, covering the room in darkness. The bitter scent of ozone and sulfur filled the void. London's keen ears detected the swish of Oberon's robe when he stood up. With a snap of his fingers, a small reddish-purple flame appeared in the old mage's hand. Stepping around the ritual circle, Oberon calmly walked over to the closed door. Fluorescent bulbs bathed the alchemy lab in a harsh, clinical white.

Oberon closed his fist, smothering the mystic flame.

"Is that it?" London asked.

A satisfied grin curled at the edges of Oberon's gaunt face. Dark rings colored the bags under his sunken eyes, his thin salt and pepper hair curled at the collar of his robe. Coarse electric light painted the old mage with a deathly pallor as it did to London and the rest of their kind.

"Almost."

Alexander raised an eyebrow watching the old

man brush his hands clean of the fine dust he had sprinkled earlier. He leaned back on a workstation like his mentor and disturbed one of the glass jars. It clinked against similar ones arranged on the table.

"Do not touch that!" Oberon barked. He immediately yanked the man away from the table with a strength far greater than his bony frame belied and cautiously went through each jar, delicately placing them back in their original position.

"Damned oaf. Any one of those could have killed all of us had they broken!"

Alexander glared at Oberon. "What're you talking about? I barely moved it."

Oberon stiffened at the remark.

"Speak to me like that again, and I will personally insure that the punishment will be long and painful."

London put a heavy hand on his protege's shoulder, preventing the man from offending his friend and host. Alexander snapped a glance at him. London nodded to the door.

"Go. Wait for me at the lift," London said evenly.

With a lingering sneer, Alexander marched out of the lab, slamming the behind him. Grumbling, Oberon began collecting the spent candles and placing them on an empty table.

"I understand that your man is still new to our practices, London, but you need to do something about him. His attitude is a severe problem."

London held back his rebuke. "I will consider that the next time such a thing happens."

Oberon wiped away the charcoal design.

"There should not be a next time. Such dissent should be stamped out swiftly and permanently, even if that means starting over with a new man."

London tightened his jaw. He had invested ten

years in Alexander—he was not about to let all that effort go to waste.

"I will deal with him on my own terms, Oberon. Now," he ran a hand through his shortly cropped blonde hair, "What do you need of me?"

The mage regarded London with a hard expression, but the edges creaked into a pained facsimile of a genuine smile. "The primary ritual will take place eight nights from tonight. The rite you just witnessed will produce us a subject—one with the proper soul required for our purposes. But in the meantime, I need to prepare the vessel and the altar for said subject's arrival. And for that, I will need blood."

"How much?"

"Seven bags worth," Oberon returned immediately.

London shrugged. "Easy enough."

"But they must be young."

He crossed his arms. "How young?"

"Adult sized." Oberon slipped the robe from his thin shoulders and hung it on an iron hook. He opened the door next to it. "Too small and it would take more than seven to fill the vessel and prepare the altar. Also, they must be pure."

Oberon interrupted London's followup question before he could open his mouth.

"Very pure, London. They must be in excellent health, have a good physique, and—above all—they must be virginal."

London followed Oberon out through the joining hallway and into a large wood-paneled foyer. An old woman in a traditional maid's outfit busily dusted a large bouquet of white flowers on a round table nestled in the rear of the room. She spied Oberon approaching and quickly curtsied when he passed by. Though she moved with practiced fluidity, London noticed the subtle creak in her joints. He halted by the gold encased mirror.

"Virgins?" London quickly opened and closed his pocket watch with a sharp *clip-clap*. "Oberon, you do know that the youth of today is far more promiscuous than they were in our time?"

The old mage gave him a dismissive frown. "I know that. Spiritual purity would be better for the ritual, but it will be far easier to find seven virgins in this city than half as many youths with actual faith. You have been handling the primarch's logistical operations for eighteen years now. I think you are more than capable of fulfilling this request along with your usual duties."

Oberon snapped his fingers, and a wizened butler appeared from the corner of the room with London's overcoat draped over his arm. The servant smoothly unfurled the heavy garment and slipped it over London's suit. Once done, the servant bowed and silently melted off to the side.

"Yes, yes, thank you for the compliment," London said, settling the coat onto his broad shoulders. "Anything else?"

The mage nodded. "One last thing: this—all of this—must remain absolutely quiet. The primarch cannot know of it."

"Of course I know that."

"No, London. Decades of research and preparation will finally culminate in one week. We cannot raise any suspicions, lest everything we have worked for will be lost. We already lost twenty years because of the primarch's short-sightedness."

London put a hand on this friend's shoulder and smiled, the scar above his lip twisting his mouth into a sneer despite his best efforts.

"Do not worry. Everything is in good hands."

With a curt nod, London turned and left. He found Alexander relaxing in the opulent hall by the lift, idly playing with his lighter next to the two gold doors. He pushed off the wall when he saw London approaching and tagged the down button. The two stepped into the lift and headed to the garage level.

"Well? Did I miss anything?" Alexander asked.

"Hmpf. You know your attitude nearly cost you your life?"

The younger man scoffed. "That old asshole was off his rocker."

London gave his protege a hard look.

"Reign in your mouth, Alexander. I give you leeway to speak freely, but that only applies in private. Do not speak to elders with the same tongue, nor disrespect them. Understand?"

Alexander rolled his eyes. "Yeah."

"Care to try that again?"

"*Yes, sir.*"

"Better."

The elevator continued down.

Alexander dug out a cigarette. "What was the spooky light show for?"

"He needs a special woman."

The younger man shot London a sideways glance. "All that for a woman? Why not just go to Old Town and say 'Yes' to the first one he sees?"

"A woman, not a *whore*."

"Same difference," Alexander scoffed.

London rolled his eyes. "The ceremony next week requires a woman with the right metaphysical requirements. The second half of it would fail otherwise."

"Didn't the primarch ban all that 'woo-woo' shit back in the Eighties after the war?"

Clip-clap.

"Yes."

Alexander slipped the cigarette between his lips. "You know it's our heads if he finds out?"

"He won't."

The lift dinged, and the doors parted, revealing the garage level. Alexander instantly lit his cigarette once inside the concrete cave. "How many pickups do we have tonight?"

"Thirteen."

"Thirteen?! He's fucking crazy! It's almost dawn."

"Agreed."

"I fucking hate this pickup and delivery shit," he said, billowing a thick cloud of smoke from his nostrils.

They walked over to an all black Chevy Suburban. The engine turned on when the two approached. A man in a black tactical uniform sporting a large sidearm stepped out and opened the rear passenger door. The two men climbed in and buckled up. The armed man returned to his seat and the vehicle promptly took off.

Smoke swirled in the darkly lit cab as Alexander blew out another drag. "Remind me why that pompous suit turned us into glorified fucking garbage collectors?"

"Because it is the primarch's pet project, and he insists on it running smoothly. I am no more a fan of it than you are, but he *rewarded* me with the responsibility after the pogrom. So if we wish to end his reign, we must trust Oberon's plan."

"And what happens if all his magical bullshit fails?"

London quietly watched the buildings and street lights zip by.

"Hell, I imagine."

Clip-clap.

2 Living After Midnight

Tuesday, March 4ᵗʰ, 2003. 9:42pm

Panicked footfalls echoed in the grimy alley.

The waning light of the full moon cast dark shadows down the trash-laden back street. Clusters of garbage cans huddled against the sides of the brickwork canyon. Dirty vents and locked doors punctuated the walls at irregular intervals. Gutter pipes disappeared into roof ledges. A single huge metal trash bin in wheels stood vigil near the mouth of the alley. Bright lights poured in from the busy city. Cabs, buses, and other vehicles trundled across the distant thoroughfare. People criss-crossed the adjoining sidewalks going about their nightly business. A red city bus with silver stripes pulled to a squeaking stop in front of the alley mouth.

A man ran down the alley. He was pale with dark rings under his eyes. A thin sheen of terror coated his face. The end of his dingy brown jacket flapped behind him in his hurry. He clutched a tightly rolled paper bag under one arm. A single, smooth cut separated his old t-shirt with red blotches staining the edges.

Something screeched behind him. Daring a look back, a large black rat bolted from a pile of black trashbags, quickly chased by a mangy gray cat.

Barely relieved, the man hurried on.

Tonight was important. The beginning of their ascendance. He knew he shouldn't have stopped for that drink. It was going to make him late, but he was so thirsty. He couldn't show up on an empty stomach. The pale man didn't expect to be watched, however. All he saw was a flash of metal in the moonlight. It was all he could to do just to get away. He didn't even finish his meal, he just ran. For the first time since he started his new life, he felt true fear.

Something white hot fluttered out of the darkness and bit him in his calf. The pale man stumbled and tripped over a metal trash can. Clawing his way back to his feet, the man froze.

His bag!

"Fuck, fuck, fuck, whereisit?!" he sputtered.

The man frantically dug through the piles of bags, not bothering to check the burning pain in his leg. He loudly knocked over stacks of boxes and empty crates, looking for his precious bag. Finding it wedged between two crumpled cardboard boxes, he snapped the bag up in a flash and immediately checked the contents. Satisfied, the man barreled to the safety of the light.

Another trashcan fell in the distance.

The pale man ran faster.

Another thing bit his thigh. Like his calf it burned hotter like anything he had ever felt. He stumbled again, but kept from falling this time. The mouth of the alley was close. He could just make out the blank faces of the people walking by. The air brakes on the bus tooted and its diesel engine rumbled. He was going to miss it!

Without warning, the world suddenly flipped upside down. The pale man's head smacked the side of the big trash bin as he swung in the air. The pedestrians, the vehicles, the buildings, everything instantly turned fuzzy.

The man's stomach jumped into his throat. He looked down. A thick black rope wrapped around his ankle yanked him into the night sky in long spurts. Still gripping the bag, the man reached for the snare, his fingers hopelessly brushing against the knot. He noticed a bit of metal sticking out of his thigh. The thing was sharp and had four points. Blood and dust coated the point digging into his skin. Wasting no time, he ripped it out and sawed at the rope with its keen edge, snapping bits of fiber with each panicked swipe.

He suddenly stopped rising. The stone ledge of the old brick building hovered a few feet from his head. A dark figure crouched on top of it, holding the end of the rope. It was motionless. The pale man stared, mesmerized. Two pin pricks of golden light instantly blazed to life on the figure and something cracked the pale man in the face. The paper bag fell from his hand as did the bit of metal.

The figure snatched the bag out of the air.

"Going somewhere?" it spoke in a low menacing tone.

Before the pale man could speak, something sharp pierced his chest, and everything stopped.

The blackness suddenly ripped away. The twinkling facades of skyscrapers reached down to the sky below him. Above, the blue glow of street lamps bubbled over the edge of the roof. His tattered shirt and jacket lay on the gravelly ceiling a few yards in front of him. The world gently swayed back and forth. The man couldn't feel his arms or legs. Nor did the tips of his fingers. Even his eyes refused to obey his commands. He tried to move, but the mere thought sent jolts of agony through his body.

The twin golden pin pricks appeared in front of him.

The pale man tried to scream but nothing

happened.

As his eyes adjusted to the lack of light, he saw the shadowy outline of a man materialize behind those pin pricks. The figure wrenched out the thing in his chest with a wet *sucking* sound, and the agony instantly went away, returning all the feeling to his body. He promptly tried to move but realized his arms were tied tight behind his back. Looking down, his bound ankles dangled from the rung of a water tower.

A fist wrapped in boxing tape cracked him in the face. The strike burned like the sharp metal.

"Catch you at a bad time?"

The pale man spat blood in response.

"What's the matter? You didn't finish your dinner?" his captor asked, pushing him gently.

He said nothing.

"Why the hurry?"

"Fuck you!" he snapped. The figure smacked him again. A tooth went flying.

The shadow let him swinging for a moment. The burning pain from the punches lingered like the furnace-heat of a blow torch held inches from his skin. The fist appeared in front of his eyes with a metal cross hanging from it. It glinted in the moonlight right before the figure pressed it on his forehead.

Smoke rose from his sizzling flesh. He forgot about the pain in his legs or from the punches. Pigeons flapped away from the man's screams until the piece of metal pealed off with a puff of char. He panted heavily. He hadn't breathed like that in a decade.

"I'm gonna ask you some questions. If you give me a smart answer, you get this again." The figure brandished the metal again. "Understand?"

"What the fuck!?"

The metal burned another shape into his skin. The pale man instantly understood.

"Now. I've been watching you tonight. Right

before you stopped off for that drink, you were going somewhere in a big hurry. Where were you going?"

"Home," the pale man answered. He expected to get hit him again, but nothing happened.

"And where is home?"

He forced himself to stay silent.

An annoyed rumble escaped the glowing eyes. The figure snatched a lock of hair, and forced the devilish bit of metal against his cheek. Flesh sizzled like meat on a stove. Course rope tore at his wrists. He bobbed back and forth on the rope, sizzling agony rocketing up and down his spine.

The metal pulled away.

"Again. Where is home?"

The pale man glared at the shadowy figure while more bits of burnt skin flaked off the cross.

"Go   spit!"

The metal cross appeared again. The pale man quivered and tried to back away from it. "A mansion, a mansion, a mansion!" he blurted out.

The cross went away.

"What mansion?"

Still huffing his useless lungs, his mind raced. He couldn't betray the leader. He was kind to him. The leader took him in, showed him the light. He was going to give them all a new life, out from the shadows. He owed the leader everything!

The figure squatted down next to his face. The two golden pin pricks burned inches from his nose.

"What? Mansion?" the figure growled.

Malice dripped from the figure's words. He felt the hot breath on his forehead. He would not betray!

"What do you think will happen if I put this on your left eye?"

The pale man quivered. Moonlight reflected off the metallic cross as it neared his twitching eyeball.

"It's out of town!" he yelled.

The cross stopped in place. He willed his body not to so much as vibrate with the metal so close to him.

"Can you you be a bit more specific?"

The man squeezed his eyes and mouth shut. *Don't betray! Don't betray! Don't betray!*

"Have it your way."

The shining, room-temperature metal crossed the final inch. It melted through his eyeball and into the ocular cavity with a smoking squelch of pus and gore. Smoke rose and ash fell. He shrieked louder than he thought possible. Time dragged through each agonizing second as every nerve ending fried one by one, until the only thing he felt was barren cold.

The figure withdrew the cross and waved away the cloud of gray that used to be his left eye. A red tear ran down his other eye.

"You should see yourself. Got a crater the size of a golf ball on your face now. I wonder how long it would take for that to heal? Tell me, what was so important that you were in a hurry?"

His whole face was numb. He couldn't hear the shadow's voice over his suffering. With a loud sigh, the figure brought over the paper bag and made a big display of opening it and pulling out the contents. The pale man's lone eye immediately fixated on the purple bundle of velvet in the figure's hands.

"What's this?"

The shadow flapped out the cloth, revealing a hooded robe.

"Don't tell me you already forgot how this works? How about the other eye this time?"

The cross floated closer and closer to his twitching eyeball until something primal inside him snapped. The pale man suddenly didn't care about the leader anymore. He didn't care about himself, either. He just wanted to rip those two glowing eyes out and spit on whatever lay behind them. His entire body shook with rage, and he viciously snapped a pair of sharp teeth at the hand. With all his strength, the pale man pulled at his bindings. Some of the rope gave, but not enough to free his hands. Blood dribbled down his exposed back.

The figure punched him in the other cheek again and again, until the rage began to slip away. It grasped his snapping jaw and held him close. It's very touch burned.

"Where's the mansion, parasite?!" the figure demanded. "Tell me and it stops!"

"Deacon Hill!" His voice was guttural, almost beast-like. "Nothing you can do will stop us! He will call her forth, and she will remake the world in our image!!"

Bloody spittle hit the figure just below it's angry eyes.

"Who?!" it seethed.

The pale man spewed a wordless froth of zealous rage. He bounced wildly on the rope, his jaws snapping at the figure's finger tips like a chained dog lashing out an intruder just out of reach. A first struck his face again, but this time he felt nothing.

Somehow, the punch knocked some of the fury out of him, and his bestial ramblings coalesced into words. "Hair like the sun, born of death! A woman of nowhere! All will tremble when the leader calls upon her to bring us out of the shadows!! Those who defy us will be washed away in a cleansing—!"

A long slender blade flashed in the figure's hands and the pale man's head instantly separated from his neck. The hairy lump of flesh and hair and bone rapidly decomposed into ash before it touched the gravel. The rest of his body disintegrated immediately after, leaving the coiled rope flopping loosely with nothing to give it shape.

Ethan Ward pulled off his cloth mask, revealing

a shaggy head full of scars and stubble. Like the mask, his green shirt was faded and threadbare from too many wash cycles. His jeans had more holes and crude patches than actual denim, and his sneakers were more dirt than their original red. In a swift, practiced motion, he sheathed his sword in the scabbard slung across his powerful shoulders before digging out a weathered black sack from his road-weary leather jacket. He unfurled the long bag and slid the sheathed katana inside.

Ethan stared at the pile of ash at his feet while tucking the mask between his belt. "Born of death?" he quietly repeated.

For years, every heartless parasite he had dealt with bore some kind of superiority complex. Some were worse than others, but each one thought it was above the natural order. However, this felt leagues away from from the ramblings he usually encountered. And those fangs didn't carry around strange costumes, either.

Air brakes broke the silence.

He craned his head over the ledge. Another bus had pulled up to the sidewalk. A small crowd of people shuffled out of the big vehicle. A pair of homeless men stumbled out as well, only to be collected by two big men with hard faces and leather jackets. Ethan snapped another glance at the robe.

"Deacon Hill, huh?"

Gripping the bagged sword, he hopped off the ledge.

31. Got Mine

Kneeling next to a large oak tree, Ethan settled his ratty mask over his head.

Night had fallen over the massive derelict mansion in front of him. Light from the full moon cast weak shadows over the decaying edifice of the once great building. It stretched on forever to the left and to the right. A large decayed armillary stood vigil over a stone-lined fountain near the main entrance, unfolding into an overly long reflecting pool. Algae and other plants choked the lifeless black waters. On either side, a wide courtyard expanded outward, overgrown from a century and a half of neglect. Broken statues, errant trees, and wild bushes sprouted defiantly out of the sea of chest high wild growth. Behind him, a sprawling ancient, low-hanging oak trees surrounded the mansion grounds for a quarter mile in every direction. Thick, thorny bushes crowded the forest floor, growing around and through dead tree limbs, preventing all but the most determined foot travel The crumbling remains of a stone fence held the encroaching woods at bay, parting only for an old dirt road carving through the forest.

Nothing stirred in the cool, dead air.

Ethan made to move when the large double doors at the entrance suddenly swung open. A pair of big men in black tactical uniforms walked out of the mansion carrying automatic weapons with custom flashlights and laser sights attached to the barrels. The two men marched down the stone steps into the courtyard. The light beams from their guns bobbed up and down on the dirt path ahead of them. A second pair of men closed the doors behind the first two. They halted at the edge of the fountain and scanned the neglected property. The first pair continued out to the end of the reflecting pool, playing their flashlights into the treeline to Ethan's right. A third pair rounded the north wing, slowly making their way south. Chattering radios tucked into the men's combat webbing broke the night's silence.

For an abandoned mansion, the place crawled with fancy firepower.

With a deep breath, Ethan silently crept through the tall grass, barely disturbing the vegetation. Avoiding the armed patrols, he came to a stop at the edge of the grass a few yards away from the mansion wall. Ethan noticed one of the third floor window shutters hung on a single hinge. The window was completely open in the moonlight—no shards of glass or bits of wood remained in the frame. He quickly checked left and right. The three patrols obliviously scanned the grounds.

Gathering himself, Ethan leapt impossibly high into the air and latched onto an escarpment on the second floor. He bounded up to another one just below the open window and climbed in. The room was pitch black and empty. He closed his eyes. Concentrating on his breathing, Ethan centered his mind on his heartbeat and felt its energy. Focusing on that energy, he pushed that feeling beyond his body.

The new sense slowly stretched out into the room, searching for like energies in the immediate area. Finding nothing, he pushed the sense further. He detected nothing on the third floor, nor did he sense anything on the first and second floors either. Outside, he felt the faint energies of two men standing by the old fountain and a small handful roaming what must be the basement. Pushing further down, deep below the mansion, he felt it—a large concentration of cold. Dozens of bitter, frigid signatures packed closely together, and another one, warm and tart, slowly approaching them.

Ethan opened his golden eyes. That's where he needed to go.

With no one nearby, he drew an old flashlight from his jacket and panned the weak beam around the room. Shards of glass reflected on the floor. Faded strips of wallpaper hung from the walls, and pieces of plaster dangled from the moldy ceiling. The bulb suddenly flickered and dimmed. He whacked it a few times, vainly trying to coax more power out of the batteries. Before the light completely faded away, he saw footprints. Fresh ones, and they led from the window to the door. He wasn't the only who came this way.

Ethan knelt there for a minute and let his eyes adjust to the darkness. The full moon outside was perfect for sneaking in, but unfortunately, the boarded windows kept out the spare light. When enough of the interior finally bloomed into view, he relocated the footprints and followed them. The steps were wide enough apart to suggest a certain height and stride—not far from his, maybe a few inches shorter. They were narrow and long, meaning the owner had moved lightly on the edges of his feet. Whoever they belonged to was well trained in stealth.

He continued into the mansion, paying attention to his senses. The footprints wandered off into various rooms. A few items had been moved in each chamber, the dust ringing them having been disturbed ever so slightly.

Silently, he climbed down a set of wide, double-ended stairs leading to a large foyer on the first floor. A thin layer of dust and debris covered the ancient stone tiles. Slivers of moonlight splintered through the boarded up windows and painted the floor with uneven blue lines. Ethan stepped onto the rubble, disturbing nothing.

He immediately froze as a door creaked in the distance.

Boots—heavy ones—crunched the debris-laden floor. Ethan dashed under a wide archway, pressing himself a shadowed wall between the moonlight. Peeking around the corner, he saw another pair of men like the ones outside rounding a hall corner. Their flashlight beams illuminated the dirty ground by his feet. Ethan slowly reached back under his jacket and unsheathed a large, serrated bowie knife—an old keepsake from childhood. Holding the blade reversed in his hand, Ethan wound up to strike.

A radio chirped and the boots stopped. Ethan held himself and listened.

"Interior sweep complete. The subject has reached the tunnels. Please advise," one of the men spoke. His voice was low with a slight monotone.

A deep, garbled voice on the radio responded, "Maintain perimeter and make sure the subject doesn't double back."

"Copy, that."

Ethan focused his senses on the two men, feeling them about to move just before their boots crunched the floor. He exhaled softly, readying for the right moment. As the men passed the arch, Ethan shot out. He grabbed one from behind, forcing the big man to the ground with a kick to the back of his knees, and thrust his knife into the base of the man's neck. Blood spurt from his mouth, and the submachine gun fell from his hands.

The second man spun around when he heard the muffled gurgling. He saw his partner's body in Ethan's hands and immediately snapped his weapon to bear, bathing both of them in bright white. Ethan instantly yanked out the knife and threw it. The blade plunged into the man's chest, its impact knocking him off his feet. A dark pool slowly spread through the heavily cluttered ground.

Ethan remained there, focusing for any suspicious movement. When he heard nothing and sensed the same, he relaxed. He withdrew the knife and wiped it clean on the body before resheathing it under his jacket.

The subject reached the lower levels?

Were they talking about whoever owned those footprints? Was that the tart energy signature he felt earlier, or was there another party involved—someone he hadn't encountered yet? He considered dragging the bodies out of view, but with all the blood and debris on the floor, the trail would be easily found.

Besides, Ethan had a strange feeling that time was running short.

He quickly found the footprints and followed them further into the dilapidated mansion. The trail led down into the cellar and wandered less and less, the spacing between steps growing farther apart. The person was moving faster—he probably found what he came for. The corridors were tight and narrow in the cellar, lined on either side by thick vertical wood posts.

For the first time since entering the building, he saw light. Small sconces with lit candles hung from the posts. The flames fluttered slightly and all in the same, uniform direction. There was a cool breeze flowing through the cellar. And the footprints headed directly into it.

The trail led Ethan to a dead end room. It was a wine cellar. The footsteps led straight into a corner.

They shuffled around, pointing in all directions, but they didn't double back. The owner must have found something here. He looked around. A criss-cross pattern of empty shelves from floor to ceiling covered every wall in the alcove. A single candle hung from a nearby post.

Something wasn't right. The old scent of wine should be strong here, but it wasn't. And why was the breeze strong here?

Ethan placed his hand in various spots along the shelf-wall, hunting for the gentle wind. It was strongest in the lowest corner in the back, but the light didn't reach there. He reached for the candle from the old iron holder for a better look, but, instead of relinquishing the stick of wax, the entire thing bent down. A heavy thunk sounded from behind the shelf, and the whole wall jutted inward an inch. Cautiously, Ethan gripped the central shelf panel and pushed. Grunting, he heaved the wooden shelf into the wall. The false wall slowly ground open on ancient metal hinges.

A pitch dark tunnel yawned before him. It was carved from the dirt and rock and just wide enough for two people to stand side by side. The breeze howled from the passageway. Ethan concentrated his senses again, pushing them downward. The bitter cold presence was close now. The footsteps continued into the secret entrance as well.

This was the right path.

Retreating back a short distance, he snatched a candle off a different sconce. Now with a light, he entered the tunnel. Moments after, the disguised heavy door closed shut behind him. A thick iron ring attached to the end of a chain hanging slowly retracted into the ceiling as the door closed. The aged mechanism clunked louder on this side, locking it in place with a hefty thud.

The tunnel went on and on, descending even

lower than he had expected. He cupped the flame with
his free hand, shielding it from the ever-present wind.
Ethan began to question the tunnel's length by the time
he came upon a large spiral staircase. Though old, the
wooden structure was solidly built with thick struts
reinforcing each step from underneath, leaving the
center of the spiral empty. Moisture dripped from the
ceiling and pooled lightly on the ground below.

The howling grew louder and more distinct the
further Ethan descended. He detected a rhythm in the
noise. It fluctuated up and down and repeated every few
seconds, but it wasn't the wind. It was chanting—
rough, indistinct, and repetitive. He recognized words
and phrases in Latin, but there was something else in it.
Something strange and a sinister hidden within its
melody. Ethan swore he had heard words like that
before, long ago when he was a child.

Faint red and blue light bled into the second leg
of the tunnel. The chanting roared now—almost
deafening echoing off the solid rock. The walls and
ceiling grew wider and taller until Ethan saw the source
of the light: a pair of wooden doors, massive and
imposing. Easily over eight feet tall and almost as wide,
both were split into six huge sunken panels with strange
designs carved into each one. Eerie red light traced all
twelve carvings. The left door was cracked open and a
thick strip of blue peeked out from behind it.

Ethan snuffed the candle in the dirt and peered
through the crack.

A gigantic stone coliseum unfolded beyond the
doors. Ornate iron braziers hung from huge columns.
Arches swooped over every pillar on the wall, each one
topped with a skull motif carved into the ancient rock.
Decaying iron bars descended from the stone arches and
into the flagstone floor. At regular intervals, wide lanes
of stone carved stairs sloped down to a central dais. The
stairs were bordered by pairs of large raised plinths,

each topped with a tall iron torchiere. Blue flames lit the auditorium, casting a daemonic hue throughout the vast chamber. Orange fires blazed on four iron basins hanging from the ceiling by thick chains, and between them, a single shaft of matte black iron thrust down to the center of the dais. Iron spikes like thorns on a rose jutted out at regular intervals with a polished round barb adorning the tapered tip. Directly under the shaft sat an altar carved from black stone, permanently tilted at an angle like some ancient operating table. Leather straps dangled loosely from the sides, and strange red diagrams decorated the old stonework. Dozens upon dozens of hooded figures filled the spacious arena. Each wore a purple robe like the one he saw earlier, and all of them chanted in unison. Two more armed men guarded the dais.

In the center of it all, a man in an ornate robe led the crowd in their singing. His hood was down, revealing shoulder length, salt-and-pepper hair combed back and curling upwards near the collar. His brow was wrinkled with heavily arched eyebrows and a sinister widow's peak. His face was gaunt, and, like the man on the roof, his skin was pale. He held an elaborately fashioned knife high over his head. Gleaming red gems capped the carved golden handle and the blade was long and wavy. The man offered it to the iron shaft above him.

The whole scene exuded a palpable evil, nearly overloading Ethan's senses.

What the hell did he stumble into?

A woman's scream halted the chanting. Off to the side, another pair of the men in black grappled someone covered head to toe in some sort of black diving suit. A woman. The men lifted her up off the ground by the arms. The slender lady twisted wildly in their grip, her feet scraping frantically against the dusty floor, but to no avail. Ethan caught a glimpse of the

woman's feet before the men hauled her down the stairs.
The bottoms of her boots were soft, narrow, and long.

Those were her footsteps he had followed
through the mansion.

The crowd renewed their chanting while the man
on the dais extended a hand towards the squirming
woman, welcoming her. At the bottom of the stairs, the
woman jammed her feet against the raised dais and
fiercely pushed back with all her strength. But it didn't
last long. The other armed guards quickly snatched her
by the ankles, and together, they hauled her writhing
onto the platform.

The four men forced her onto the altar and
proceeded to strap her down despite her resistance. As
they worked, the woman slipped a hand free and struck
two of the men, but a third smacked her on the head with
the butt of his gun, dazing her. One of the men ripped
off her black hood and a pair of goggles, revealing a
shock of very thick and very long blonde hair. The
woman's face was awash with enraged terror. The
guard tossed the garments and then strapped her head
firmly to the altar. Finished, all four men left the dais
and stood at attention around it.

Ethan inched the door open and crept inside. He
crouched behind one of the plinths at the top of the
stairs, looking out into the giant arena. The place
reminded him of an ancient Greek amphitheater, like the
ones he had learned about in grade school.

Greek!

He slapped his forehead. That's what the other
words sounded like! The priest from his family's
church used to lead prayers in Greek sometimes. Too
bad he never learned it. Down on the dais, the robed
vampire raised a fist in the air and the chanting instantly
stopped. Only the woman's hopeless struggling broke
the silence. He spoke loudly, addressing the crowd with
his nasally Latin.

Ethan listened.

Did he just call her Kathleen?   Is that the woman's name?

More talking.   The leader went on forever, praising all those in attendance with all sorts of flowery language.   Ethan groaned.   He hated when parasites rambled on like this.   But, then he started talking about tonight's gathering.   And, unfortunately, he spliced in more Greek with his speech.   Ethan strained to pick out the few words he recognized.

Only one word from his old priest's prayers rang familiar:

Resurrection.

The crowd cheered at the word.   The robed man presented the knife to the crowd, and they cheered even louder.   He then turned to the woman and proceeded to cut her outfit from collar to navel while she fought against the straps.   He then pierced his palm with the tip. Dark blood seeped from the wound, and he drew something on her exposed skin with it.   The leader chanted again, genuflecting up towards the giant iron shaft.   In response the crowd repeated his words and began swaying in unison.   Once he finished, he approached the struggling woman.   She let out a horrendous scream until he put his bleeding hand over her mouth, silencing her terror.

Ethan sat back against the plinth.   The woman's scream echoed through his mind.   Her terror dredged up the memory of his sister being pulled through the barn door.   The image repeatedly paraded in front of his closed eyes no matter how hard he focused.   Her scream turned into the woman's below.   Her blonde hair grew to the length of the woman's below.

He had to help her.

No! I'm not here for this!

Ethan came here to investigate.   To listen in on this meeting.   Not to rescue some dumb woman.

But this didn't look like a meeting. And it didn't look like an initiation, either. This looked far sinister and very important.

Out among the swaying audience, ribbons of red light slowly materialized on the floor. He looked down at the dais. The robed man was bent over the woman's neck, his hand still on her mouth. The fight had completely left her now. The altar and the iron spire above it slowly lit up with patterns of red light.

"Oh shit . . . " Ethan muttered to himself.

Ethan dug out a small handful of paper slips from his jacket. Hastily scribbled Latin words covered every inch of them, back and front. He quickly repeated the written phrases under his breath until the script illuminated his old mask with a soft bluish glow of their own. Ready, he stuffed them into his jacket pocket and rose to his feet. He turned to the stairs and unsheathed the sword strapped across his back. The unearthly blue flames lining the walls reflected on the long slender blade of his katana.

Now of never.

Ethan sprinted down the stairs two or three steps at a time. He reached the bottom in seconds and loosed a cluster of metal throwing stars with his free hand. The fluttering pieces of matte steel rapidly stabbed the guard standing off to his left in a tight group on the man's upper torso. The guard let out a warning but only blood gurgled from his shredded throat. He lost his balance and fell backwards.

Still moving, Ethan swung down at the next closest guard, chopping the long, razor sharp blade neatly between the collar and neck, and yanked, slicing further into the man's torso. The body jerked violently before folding into a heap. The third guard noticed the attack and brought his black submachine gun to his shoulder, but he wasn't fast enough. Ethan closed the distance in a powerful leap, burying the blade into the guard's chest as he landed, the bloody tip punching through the black vest.

He glanced across the dais. The robed man hadn't budged and the audience still sang, but the last guard had caught sight of the sudden action. Before he could raise his gun, he staggered back a step. A black combat knife like the one he and his comrades carried protruded from his sternum. Before blacking out, he saw the masked man pulled his sword out the torso of the other guard.

On the dais, the robed man was still bent over the woman. Ethan couldn't aim for the neck without hurting her. Reversing his grip on the blade, he plunged the weapon clean through his chest. Black, viscous blood dripped from the weapon's tip along with flakes of gray ash. The robed man released the woman with a jerk as Ethan ripped the blade out. He then hooked an arm under the man's shoulder and tossed him off the woman, letting him roll off the dais in a tangle of purple fabric.

A collection of gasps broke through the crowd, ceasing the chanting.

The red lights suddenly winked out along the altar, the metal spire, and the surrounding arena.

Ethan quickly looked the woman over. Her neck bled and the man's dark blood smeared her lips and exposed chest. One of her hands was almost clear of the straps—had she a few more seconds, she probably would have freed it. Ethan sliced through the worn brown leather with a few deft motions. Her her chest heaved with fresh air.

Members of the crowd began throwing off their robes, revealing a mixture of high-class attire and basic shirts and jeans. Every last one of them was pale just like their leader. They climbed over the seats headed directly for him, shouting angrily. Ethan snatched a couple of the glowing papers from his pocket and winged them into the crowd. The slips arced on uneven patterns of blue light before slamming into the rushing wave of bodies. They erupted with bluish-gold flames and deafening thunder with each impact. Those caught in the blasts instantly burst into a flaming cloud of ash. The rest of the crowd recoiled from the blue-gold shockwave, creating a large gap all the way to the top.

Time to go.

Something metallic on her belt scratched against his face when he scooped the unconscious lady onto his shoulder. It looked like a gun, but bulky and misshapen. Bounding off the dais, he sprinted through the gap in the crowd, warding off the shouting mob with his sword as he ran. Reaching the top of the stairs, Ethan cast another handful of glowing slips into the crowd, further scattering the congregation with more explosions.

With the coliseum in flames, he wrenched aside the massive door and bolted down the dark tunnel. The door swung shut behind him, bathing the corridor in darkness. Pulling the last paper slip from his pocket, Ethan held it up and let the faint blue light illuminate the tunnel. He continued to the foot of the spiral staircase. Angry shouts echoed down the dark corridor, far behind, but not by much.

"Shit."

Foot on the stairs, something thumped on the dirt. It was the woman's gun. He set her down and pick it up.

In the wispy blue light, he got a good look at the thing. A large metal spike protruded from the muzzle, and a small winch hung under the barrel. Arching an eyebrow, Ethan fired it into the wall. The spike shot out with a *pop-hiss* and stabbed into the rock. A thin wire trailed the thing, drawing taut right after. Two small buttons—one orange, one green—on either side of the trigger guard blinked softly. Curious, he pressed the orange button. The spike immediately dislodged itself from the wall. Tagging the green button, the spike quickly retracted snugly back into the barrel.

Behind him, the shouting grew louder and louder. Ethan craned his head up at the hollow center in the staircase.

His mind worked quickly.

He placed the last strip on the ground and recited a few more words in Latin. Lifting the woman back onto his shoulder, he pointed the gun directly overhead and pulled the trigger. The spike impacted on the ceiling three flights above and the line automatically wheeled taut. Pressing the green button again, the gun yanked him and the woman up with surprising speed. In seconds they were at the top of the stairs. He pressed the button again, and the wheel unlocked. Ethan dropped, barely landing on the wooden platform.

He hooked the device on his belt and bolted down the upper tunnel. Yells echoing below him quickly were silenced by an explosion that belched blue flames into the stairwell.

Ethan quickly retraced his steps back to the first floor. Stopping in front of the main entrance, he raised his foot to kick it open when he heard lots of angry men barking orders on the other side. Flashlights splintered through cracks in the boarded windows. He spun around and ran back to the first room on the third floor. Looking into the courtyard, he saw more men in black hurrying to the main entrance.

The woman moaned painfully over his shoulder.

He laid her on the ground. Her pulse pounded rapidly, and her breathing was short and shallow. Her skin had grow pale now and was slick with cold sweat. Her forehead was so hot it almost burned his fingers off. He checked the wound on her neck. Though small, it wept blood onto her shoulder, some of it thick and black. Her dark green eyes had rolled into their sockets, and her face was locked in a rictus of pain. Moonlight reflected off the woman's long, blonde hair. It was a soaked and tangled mess, but glowed warmly in the subtle light.

"'Hair like the sun'," Ethan repeated.

While looking her over, he noticed her strange bodysuit reflected none of the ambient light. It had a rubbery texture with semi-rigid sections over the vitals, and it perfectly conformed to her lean, shapely figure. The thing looked custom-fitted and very expensive. Its supple material felt tough, yet, strangely, the robed vampire's knife had sliced through it and her undershirt with ease. An intricate diagram traced in blood covered her exposed chest, and a similar design encircled her neck wound. They looked like the symbols on the door panels he saw earlier.

Ethan tore off a section of his shirt and wrapped it firmly around her neck to staunch the bleeding. He had no idea how much she had lost and gave her 50/50 odds of seeing the morning.

The doors downstairs suddenly burst open with shouts and boots thundered through. He glanced out the window again. The courtyard was empty now. Someone called out the two bodies he had left earlier. Multiple sets of boots clambering up the old wooden stairs immediately after. Ethan unhooked the lady's gun from his waist and fired at the eve hanging over the window. The spike bit into the wood. Settling the woman back on his shoulder, Ethan quickly descended to the thick grass below. Whipping the big pistol, he snapped the spike out the overhang.

While the line retracted, he fell into a dead heat across the sea of grass and vanished into the treeline.

4 Would I Lie to You?

After three servings, Ethan was still hungry.

He sat in the rear booth of a diner. The main counter ran the length of the restaurant with worn chrome stools screwed into the floor in front of it. The cracked cream laminate counter buckled at the edges, revealing the decades-old hardwood frame underneath. Stoves, flattop grills, and other cooking stations covered the wall behind the counter. Thick layers of burnt grease and char drenched the old stainless steel backsplash above them. Metal cooking pots and utensils hung from hooks on the ceiling, their luster lost from years of over use.

A walled off row of booths took up most of the drab linoleum floor space. The counter ended at the opposite side with a small glass case displaying a handful of cakes and pies. A lengthy blackboard stretched over the cooking area with the menu and today's specials scribbled in different colored chalk. Off-white wallpaper covered the walls and a thick layer of age and vaporized grease covered the wallpaper. Perched on a shelf over the cash register, a faded boombox radio blasted reruns of *American Top 40*. Next to it, a big bland wall clock kept the time.

Savory bacon sizzled on the blackened flattop next to a rapidly curling strip steak. The lone waitress busied herself cleaning the cracked counter with a dirty rag. The skinny forty-year-old feverishly swirled the cloth on a stubborn stain that looked more like a part of the laminate than a dried up spill. Off to her side, the overweight cook leaned against an unused stove while he watched the meat. Every few seconds he stole glances at the waitress's backside. Only one other patron sat in the restaurant. An older man in a rumpled tan jacket nursed a cup of coffee and all but ignored his supper. He lazily perused a newspaper, carefully flipping pages between sips.

The diner was old and dirty and quiet, and it reminded Ethan of home. But as relaxing as the place was, he kept dwelling on last night. The lights, that giant spire, all those robed figures. What the hell did he witness? And that woman. What did they want her for?

Hair like the sun, born of death. A woman of nowhere. She will remake the world in our image.

Who was she? Her strange bodysuit was like nothing he had ever seen. It looked like an armored diving suit. Military maybe? Whatever it was, it had to be expensive. He had checked her for any sort of ID once they were safe from pursuit, but she had nothing, just a belt with a bunch of pouches holding odd looking tools and glass marbles. However, he did find a key-ring with a pair of car keys, a set of numbered house keys, and a small magnetic card with the name of a building on it.

And that building was a fancy skyrise apartment Downtown. She lived in a spacious loft on the top floor shared with two other apartments and a large, open air swimming pool. The woman's place looked very expensive and very bland. Ethan had laid her in bed and inspected the pattern drawn on her neck and chest. The bloody design singed his fingers when he touched it. He tried to wipe it off with a towel, but it refused to come off. Soaking the towel in cold water didn't work. Hard scrubbing didn't work either. Only when he examined it with his golden vision while cleaning did the bloody markings finally slick off, instantly breaking her fever. He put a fresh bandage on her neck and waited. An hour had passed when the lady thrashed about in bed in a grand mal seizure. Ethan quickly examined her again with his golden vision to see a cold and bitter energy quickly corrupting everything inside her. While shoving a wad of sheets in her mouth, the woman clamped her teeth onto his left arm. Having left his weapons on the kitchen counter, he had to punch her multiple times just snap her out of it before her bite sapped the fight from of him. Blood and spittle spilled all over the sheets when Ethan finally pried her off his arm. Woozy, he tumbled down the stairs and passed out moments after.

Ethan woke up hours later on the cold, dark marble of her living room. He had lost a lot of blood and had to find food to replenish his strength. He stumbled out of her apartment, snatching his weapons, her keys, and the woman's wallet on the way out. Her car was a fancy convertible, and he drove it to the diner, grabbing his big green duffel bag he had stashed on a nearby rooftop along the way. Staggering inside, Ethan fell into a booth, ordered steak and eggs, and told the waitress to keep them coming.

And so, he slowly recuperated for the last three hours.

His gaze wandered outside to her car parked across the street. People eyed the vehicle as they walked by. It was an old red Ferrari. A pretty car. Probably as expensive as her bodysuit.

Swallowing another bite, he thought about that woman. Her seizure bothered him. It was violent—as if her body was trying to wring out the foul energy growing inside. He had never seen a transformation like that before. None of what he had seen made any sense. Even after cleaning her wounds, that bloody diagram left a faint imprint on her skin—like it was burning itself into her.

After this plate, he would go back to her apartment.

This time with weapons.

Still looking out, Ethan watched another pedestrian approach the convertible. The lady wore a black, wide brimmed hat and a thick pair of sunglasses. Fancy-looking jeans and designer tennis shoes poked out from under her long brown trench coat. She nervously bent down and looked inside the vehicle. Cautiously, she reached inside but quickly pulled back. The lady shrank away, self-consciously covering her mouth. She hurried across the street, her pace quickening in the sunlight while yet relaxing once in the late afternoon shade.

When she walked up to the door, he saw her face. It was the woman from last night. The one who bit her. Walking in the sunlight.

What the hell?

A string of bells attached to the glass door jingled as she entered. Ethan went back to his meal, watching her from under his brow. She stumbled at the threshold, holding her nose in disgust. The woman slowly panned around the restaurant, taking everything in, until her gaze stopped on him. Hesitantly, she headed straight to his booth.

Ethan swallowed his food and slowly undid the strap of his knife.

How is she up so soon . . . ?

The woman stopped at the corner of his booth while he ate. She said nothing as if waiting to be acknowledged. After a few moments of silence, she slid onto the bench. The woman sat there and stared at him cutting another chunk of meat, his movements smooth and precise. She awkwardly rested her hands on the table, nervously flexing pale fingers into small, manicured fists.

"Who are you?" the woman finally spoke, careful not to open her mouth too much.

Ethan chewed another bite.

"I asked you a question. Who are you?" A mixture of enmity and dread hung from every quivering syllable.

Ethan looked at her. Her chin twitched, and she stifled a sniffle.

"Answer me, damnit!" she pounded the table. All the plates along with the napkin dispenser, the condiments, and the salt and pepper caddy bounced violently from the impact, surprising her. The utensils rattled so loudly, the other people in the diner all stopped and looked at her. She pulled her hat lower and scrunched further into the booth. Ethan saw light reflecting off her eyes darting back and forth behind her shades. He glanced out the window. The sun had finally started to set.

"There's still daylight outside." He remarked, his voice rough and even.

"What?" she snapped.

He finished chewing, "Strange that you're walking around outside before sunset."

She glared at him through the dark lenses. "Look, mister," she said, barely holding her emotions back. "I don't remember much of last night, or how I got home. I don't know how, but I know you were there. What happened?!"

His knife and fork clanked sharply on the table when Ethan put them down. She jolted from the sound like she expected him to react with violence, but instead he returned her stare, flashing his eyes golden for a beat. She gawked at the sight but quickly shut her mouth and pulled herself together. Ethan promptly returned his eyes to normal. He didn't want to spook the lady until he knew exactly what he was dealing with.

Besides, he already knew enough.

"What happened is you stumbled into something you shouldn't have," Ethan finally answered.

The woman swallowed hard, gazing at him. He noticed the new adhesive bandage on her neck. A small oval of blood had seeped through the center, well on its way to becoming old and brown.

Ethan went back to his meal. "How's your neck?" he asked mid-chew. "Had to use part of my shirt to stop the bleeding."

The woman remained silent. She rubbed at the bandage, worryingly running her fingers along its edge.

"What were you doing at the mansion?" he continued.

Her eyes darted around again. "I . . . um . . . A friend of mine sent me a message? Something there might get me in trouble with my . . . job, so I had to go there and find out for myself."

"Some friend. You always dress up like that for your job? The 'sexy cat-burglar' look sticks out a bit. Very flattering, though."

The woman scowled at him.

"Why did they call you Kathleen?"

Her expression broke for a split second. "I don't know," she immediately responded.

"You sure? 'Cause Lauren Fox sounds fake as shit."

The woman straightened up at the name. "How do you know my name?"

"Driver's license."

Ethan pulled a crumpled brown paper bag from beneath the table and slid it over. It held the lady's fancy wallet and her dark, over-sized pistol. She slowly checked the contents and pulled it onto her seat. He followed her gaze out the window. Steam rose up from the vents on the sidewalk outside. A middle aged couple walked past, both looking at the fancy convertible. The woman caught her reflection in the glass and slowly touched the top of her lips. White fingers with rosy knuckles rubbed a pair of subtle bumps, and her whole body went rigid. She began to shiver.

"I . . . remember parts of the mansion. The entire building was supposed to be abandoned, nothing but dust and cobwebs. I found a hidden tunnel in the basement. I remember singing. Strange singing, in . . . in a language I've never heard before. I saw a big door with lights. People in strange robes. I can't . . ." she buried her face in her hands, her voice cracking, "I can't remember anything after that!"

"Latin. Mixed with Greek."

The woman looked up, tears streaking from under her big glasses.

"That's what you heard."

Her jaw trembled. "Are . . . are you one of them?"

Ethan chuckled. "Hell no."

"Who were those people?"

He took another bite. "I don't think you wanna know."

"Please," she leaned forward with barely contained panic. The woman pulled her sunglasses off. Her irises were bright red, like a pool of blood glowing under a heat lamp. "What happened to me?"

Ethan blinked at the sight.

What the fuck?

He considered using his vision again, but the woman looked unstable, and he didn't want to start something with bystanders present.

Now that she was conscious, Ethan took a good look at her face. Her chin twitched faster, and she nervously chewed at the corner of her full lips. Tears welled up under her big eyes. Almost all the color had been drained from her skin, only a short strip of redness outlined the top of her cheek bones and the edge of her ears. Her thin eyebrows were dark gray now. Her long hair had been hastily tucked under her hat with thick strands of bright white loosely framing her slightly heart-shaped face.

Ethan took a long breath, his nostrils flaring as he exhaled.

"I've been watching them in this city for weeks now. Tracking their movements. Looking for their hideouts. They have their hands in almost every pie here: police, transportation, waste disposal. The fucking power grid. When I caught wind of their little gathering last night, I thought it might be a good way to see just how big their infestation is."

"Infestation?"

He ignored her question and continued.

"The place was crawling with heavily armed security. They were guarding the main entrance and watching the grounds. I had to get in through an open window on the third floor just to avoid them. But, I wasn't the only one to choose that point of entry, wasn't I?" he pointed to her, "because when I got inside, I found your footprints and followed 'em. You're not easy to track, unless you know what to look for. And I wasn't the only one who knew you were there—the guards were tracking you, too. I overheard them keeping tabs on your location. Turns out they were ordered to keep you from *leaving*.

"After dealing with them, I followed you to the hidden entrance and went down into that auditorium. The place was large and made of stone—like those ancient theaters you see in the history books. I got there in time to see the guards drag you down to the center platform. You were kicking and screaming something fierce while they strapped you down to a big black altar, and the crowd was cheering for it."

Her throat tightened. "They were cheering?"

"Cheering, chanting, I don't know. I couldn't make out most of the words—never learned Greek. But their leader called you Kathleen, and he thanked you for joining them. He said you were going to change the world in their image."

"What . . . image?" She rubbed her neck unconsciously.

Ethan paused for a moment to consider his words. "Vampires. That's about when he bit you on the neck."

Tears flowed down the woman's face. She sank into her seat, sobbing. Ethan tossed the distraught woman a napkin from the dispenser. The lady balled for a good minute.

"I remember pain," she spoke through the tears. "I couldn't fight it. It felt . . ." she sniffed, "it felt *so* good. I knew it was horrible, but I didn't want it to stop."

"Yeah, their bite does that. It has a euphoric effect." Ethan rubbed his arm. "I've run into people out there who crave it—even chase after it. Real freaks."

She wiped away her tears. "How did I get home?"

Ethan took another paper napkin from the table's dispenser and wiped his hands and mouth and tossed it on his plate. He signaled the waitress for the check.

"Like I said, I was there to scope out the size of their infestation. But, when they went to work on you, I decided to stop whatever weird ritual they were performing instead. I figured, maybe, if I could interrupt them, I might learn more about them. So, I attacked the leader."

"How?"

"I stabbed him with my sword," he said frankly.

"Your sword?"

He went on, "Didn't have time to finish him off, though. The crowd started coming after me. So, I cut the straps, grabbed your body, and ran for it. Ended up using that funky climbing gun of yours to get back to the surface. Neat gadget. Security was swarming after that. It took me a minute to evade them. No way I could take them on while hauling you around. When I got out of the woods and back to the road, I jumped onto the first bus that passed by. Eventually, I made it back into the city. You were in and out of consciousness during the ride, rambling about something or other."

"I was rambling?"

"You kept going on about sparrows or whatever. I didn't pay much attention to it. But you repeat an address a few times, and I found a set of keys on you with a building name, so I figured that's where you lived. Had to jump onto a few different buses to get you there."

She blinked. "Wait, you carried me into a bus?"

"No, not *in* the bus, *on top* the bus. I'm not about to drag you inside, all limp and bleeding from the neck, dressed like Halloween. Give me a break."

"Jesus . . . " she uttered.

He shrugged.

"Whatever. Believe me. Don't believe me. I don't care. When I got to your building, I dragged you through the parking garage and snuck you up to your place. That's how you ended up home."

She sunk further into the booth, broken. The woman barely noticed the waitress bringing over a to-go box and taking a credit card from Ethan. She absently stared into the formica while he stuffed the food into his duffel bag in the booth's corner.

"What do I do?" she mewled to herself.

Ethan leveled his gaze on her. Her eyes focused on nothing, and her lips twitched at the corners.

"My advice? Whoever Lauren Fox was died in that mansion, so you might as well act like it. Leave. Tonight. Grab your shit and get outta the city.

Disappear. Go to Canada, go to Mexico, go to fucking Japan—I hear it's nice this time of year. But do it today. You know about them now, and they know you know. These things thrive on secrecy, and you're a loose end to deal with."

Climbing out of the booth, he fished her car keys out of his jacket and tossed them on the table. She flinched when they slid against her hand.

"Oh, and by the way, I *borrowed* your car when I left your place. So, lady, whatever the hell you end up doing, forget you ever saw me. You'll live longer that way," he emphasized the last sentence.

Shouldering the big green bag, Ethan headed for the exit. He paused at the door and spared a look back. The woman was still slumped in the booth, staring at the table. A shame that all this had to happen to her. She was a pretty girl—the kind he'd seen on the cover of his uncle's old magazines. Ethan shook his head. Her circumstances reminded him of that night back on the farm. His life had been forever changed by vampires then, just like hers was now.

Seeing what had happened to her, he knew what he needed to do, yet for some reason, he couldn't bring himself to go through with it this time. The glass door slammed shut after him. The bells jangled violently and snapped off, falling to the floor.

He hoped she would take his advice.

Because, if he ever saw her again, he'd have to kill her.

She's Long Gone

"**Y**ou payin', honey?"

Lauren didn't want to believe vampires were real, but deep down she knew it was true. There was no denying it. The punctures on her neck. The awful burning sensation under the sun. Those hideous teeth. Her life was shattered. Lauren had made contingency plans in case she was ever caught, or if her identity was ever revealed. But this?? Had the whole world gone crazy? What could she do?

They turned her into a monster!

There was no coming back from something like this. Everything she knew, everything she had ever accomplished—all of it—was gone now. Escaping her childhood and forging a new life. Gone. Years spent learning her trade from the best. Gone. Making a name for herself, one job at a time. All gone!

"Excuse me? Miss?"

They even knew her name! Lauren hadn't thought of her old self in years. She had spent considerable time and effort burying that life. Her new identity was air-tight—the best that money could buy. Kathleen was completely gone now. A distant memory. How could someone have found out? And who was that man? He knew about those people under the mansion. And he knew something about what had happened to her. What else did he know? Did he know what to do about it?

"Miss, are you okay?"

Lauren swiveled her head up. Her cheeks were still moist. The waitress stood over her with a receipt and a pen in hand.

"You two had a fight or something, Miss, umm, Fox?" the waitress asked, reading her name off the credit card before handing it over.

Lauren shook her head numbly and took the card. Lauren Fox, American Express Platinum. It was hers alright. And the bill, too: $126.71 charged to her account.

"How much?!" An alien anger snapped forth inside Lauren, jerking her out of her fugue.

"Your boyfriend's been here for hours. Never seen anyone eat that much steak."

"That son of bitch stiffed me with the bill!?" Lauren barked. She scrambled out of the booth and hurtled for the exit.

"Hey!" the waitress called out. She pointed into the booth. "Ain't you forgetin' somethin' lady?!"

Lauren quickly ran back and snatched the brown bag still on the seat cushion. The lady waved the bill in front of her as she turned to leave. Lauren ripped the receipt from the woman's hand with surprising speed and quickly scribbled something on it, glaring daggers at her the entire time. The lady backed up, catching the ruby and pearl glow of her eyes.

"He's not my fucking boyfriend!" Lauren seethed and burst through the door, nearly breaking its hinges.

The setting sun above the skyline slowly sunk behind the western mountains. Its red-orange light shone brightly. Lauren wondered why dusk looked so different until the putrid stink of the city slammed into her. Exhaust fumes from dozens of idling cars, piles of decaying trash awaiting pickup, sewage vapor billowing from every grate—all of if instantly sent her gagging. Her eyes burned from the bright blue street lamps and the sea of coarse headlights clogging the streets in front of her. The grating cacophony of every bleating horn echoing off the buildings drove pulsing spikes through her ears.

She gnashed her teeth against the overwhelming pain. Hastily, Lauren slapped her sunglasses back on, muting the blinding lights. Most of the throbbing in her temples subsided much to her relief. Shoving a handkerchief over her nose and mouth, she stretched above the passing pedestrians. She wanted—no— *needed* answers.

Three blocks north she saw a green bag bobbing over the river of foot traffic.

There!

Lauren ran. She ran faster than she had ever run before, going through each long block in seconds. Pedestrians jumped aside from Lauren threading through the congested sidewalks at break-neck speed. So focused on catching him, she didn't realize her hat had fallen off. A long sheet of cotton-white fluttered behind her careening down the last block. He was about to turn into an alley.

She was close enough to grab him.

In a flash, the man spun around, yanking her into the alley by her outstretched arm and slamming her bodily against the wall. The impact knocked the wind out of her with a heavy grunt and tipped over a bunch of metal garbage cans. He wrenched her arm back and shoved her to the ground, locking her wrist high in the air behind her. The pain was tremendous.

"What the hell are you doing?!" he yelled at her.

"Let go of me!" Lauren demanded through gritted teeth.

"I told you to stay the fuck away. What are you,

stupid?"

Lauren struggled against his grip. He was strong, too strong, she thought. But something in the back of her mind squirmed at the notion of submission. She started to pull her arm away. Slowly, surprisingly, her wrist began to slip from his hand. He promptly twisted further, halting her resistance with a sharp yelp.

"You prick! What did they do to me!?" she growled through the torment.

When he didn't respond, she pulled again, and again his grip began to give. Suddenly, he released her wrist and backed up a few steps. Her hand whipped back and banged on the pavement nearly cracking itself. Lauren rolled onto her back and sat up, rubbing her throbbing joint. She glared at him, not noticing the bruise—and the pain—quickly fading.

"Go back to your fancy penthouse, lady. Got yourself a nice, boring life there. Leave me out of it."

He turned and walked down the alley. Lauren pulled herself up. "Hey!" she shouted after him. "What the hell did they do to me?!"

"Not my problem!" he yelled over his shoulder.

"Why won't you answer me!"

He kept walking.

"Get back here, asshole!!" she stomped on the ground.

Nothing.

Lauren grunted in frustration. She looked around the alley. She had knocked over a trio of trashcans when he shoved her against the wall. Ruptured bags of refuse had spilled their contents all around her. She bent down and snatched the closest object, a large work boot caked in a white, powdery residue. She reared back and chucked it. The boot sailed faster and farther than she had expected. Powder trailed the leather comet, and it bounced off his shoulder, nearly clipping his ear, and left a white bootprint on his dingy jacket.

The man stopped and turned.

"That got his attention," she muttered.

The man marched back to her, anger twisting his face. He was only a few inches taller than her, but far more muscular than some run of the mill vagrant. He reeked of days-old unwashed sweat and dirt. His clothes were full of holes—some crudely patched with other fabrics, others with duct tape or a soiled bandanna, and his leather jacket looked like it been dragged through miles of gravel. Scars covered his face—the largest one cut across his nose, separating two day's worth of stubble from his steel blue eyes. His dark brown hair was short and disheveled.

He stopped inches away from her. Lauren could practically feel the barely contained violence oozing from him. She fought the urge to run.

"Last chance," the man smoldered.

Swallowing hard, she said, "Why is this happening to me?"

"I have no idea," he seethed through a clenched, square jaw.

"Please," her voice quivered. "You have to help me."

"You are not my problem, woman!"

Lauren blinked at his response.

"Bullshit!" Lauren snapped. "What did those vamp—" she paused, uncomfortable with the word, "—people want with me? Why did they do this? Who am I to them?!"

His face hardened while she ranted.

"How can I go back to my life like this?! Can I still eat food? Am I going to have to drink, you know," she lowered her voice, fear slipping back in, "blood?"

The man rolled his eyes. "I don't fucking know! If it bothers you that much, close your curtains and make friends with a butcher."

That strange anger from deep inside leaped up and squashed her fear. "You know what? Fuck you! Who the hell do you think you are, stealing my car and stuffing your face on my fucking dime?! How do I know all this didn't happen because of you? You need to take responsibility for this and help me!"

The man instantly went rigid. She had no real idea if it was his fault, she was only throwing out possibilities in her sudden furor, but his fist balled into tight rocks at that last accusation. He glared at her with the burning intensity of a sun. Catching his boiling rage, Lauren went silent, ready to react when something behind her disrupted his rage. His anger vanished, and he suddenly snatchedr her by the shoulders. She battered his hands away only for him to grab her wrists and pin them against her chest.

He locked eyes her. His were distant and hard but hid a level of awareness that belied his bedraggled attire.

"Lady, I don't know what's going to happen to you. I don't care what's going to happen to you. But whatever you do, do it far away from me." He released her with the push and jogged down the alley.

Silenced by the abrupt exit, Lauren noticed a small crowd gathering behind her. Worse, she realized that her hat was gone. She knew no one would recognize her, but she had a feeling someone might call the cops soon. Lauren promptly snapped up her bag and ran down the alley after him. He turned left and disappeared around another alley. She skidded to a halt right before the edge. Slowly inching around the corner with her hands ready, Lauren carefully peeked around, expecting him to grab her again at any moment.

But nothing happened. The alley was empty.

"He's gone."

The back road went on for at least a hundred yards to the next street. Orange-yellow door lights dotted the walls on either side. A group of trashcans littered the area, none large enough to hide behind. A few fire escapes hung from the walls, but she didn't hear any clanking, and none of the ladders were extended.

She flapped her arms in frustration, "Where the hell did he go?"

Something banged off a nearby trashcan. She followed the sound to see bits of brick and tile falling from the roof. Tracking the direction, she caught sight of a red sneaker disappearing over the roof ledge.

No way he could have got up there that fast!

Thinking quickly, she drew the pneumatic pistol from the paper bag. It was a piton launcher. A 21st century version of a grappling hook and rope. It shot a razor sharp, carbon-titanium spike connected to a fifty meter spool of micro-fiber rope attached to a powerful miniaturized winch and a compressed air reservoir. It was a tool of a professional thief, illegal in thirty-seven states—including this one.

She pocketed her wallet and tossed the crumpled paper bag. Aiming just under the roof's edge, she fired. The pistol loosed a soft *pop-hiss* and the dense, needle-sharp spike rocketed upwards, trailing an expanding coil of fine wire in it's wake. The spike bit into the red brick, and the line immediately drew taught. Her hand tight on the grip, Lauren pressed the green button by the trigger guard, and the electric motor quickly pulled her up in a flash.

As she mantled onto the roof, Lauren spotted her reluctant savior running for the far side of the building.

"Hey! Stop!" she called out. He ignored her and kept going.

"He's not gonna to try to jump to the next roof, is he?" she thought aloud.

"Holy shit!" she exclaimed, reaching the end of the roof. Not only did he jump across the alley, but he handily cleared the thirty foot gap, effortlessly somersaulting at the peak even with that massive bag strapped to his back. He landed smoothly and kept going like it was nothing. She watched hopelessly as the man continued on. No way she could keep up with that.

Defeated, Lauren turned around.

She stopped in her tracks, remembering how she sprinted down the sidewalk earlier, easily as fast as an Olympic sprinter. Lauren looked at the pneumatic pistol in her hand and wondered. Could she make the jump?

Why not? Crazier things had already happened.

The man was about to reach the end of the other roof. She'd lose him if she didn't act fast.

"I am going insane," she intoned, backing up with her pistol ready in case she had truly lost her mind.

Lauren reached full speed in a flash. The roof edge came quick, too quick. She nearly missed the ledge at the last second. To her astonishment, Lauren soared across the gap. Her hair trailed behind her like a banner on an airplane. Not only that, she sailed high up in the air, just like he did! She couldn't believe it! It was impossible. It was amazing. It was—

Too short.

Eyes bulging with panic, Lauren came down too far to catch the roof's edge, screaming. The man looked back just as she vanished below the raised lip. For a split second, Lauren caught a glimpse of concern in his hard blue eyes, and she fired her pistol at them.

Lauren thudded hard against the brick wall with a loud grunt. She dangled from the piton launcher still locked in her grasp. Her vision spun and her shoulder ached. A dozen feet above her, the man's scarred and shaggy head appeared inches above the anchored piton.

"What the hell are you doing?!"

His voice pulled Lauren out of her daze. Fury blazed from her red eyes, and she hit the green winch button, quickly shooting her up the wall. He barely dodged Lauren tumbling over the ledge. She rolled end over end before coming to a stop in front of him, groaning. Her pistol clattered next to his bag. Chuckling, the man reached down only for Lauren's fist to smash into his chin, sending him reeling backwards into a pipe vent jutting up through the roof tile.

The man lay sprawled out. "Yep, definitely got their strength, alright," he uttered, shaking the ringing from his head.

Lauren drunkenly staggered over to him. Grabbing his hand, he made to get up, but she tossed him over her hip and back onto the ground, flat on his back. Holding onto his arm, she adjusted her grip to lock his elbow like she'd practiced hundreds of times before. Two could play at this game, and she was going to force the answers out of him.

But before Lauren could secure her grip, the man yanked her off balance and wedged a foot under her, sending her wheeling backwards with a solid kick. She bounced on the dirty tile and slid a few feet on her back. Lauren looked up to see him spring to his feet ready to fight. He wheeled his arms around making strange hand gestures before resuming his stance. She wasn't sure, but it looked almost like the air around him shimmied.

Lauren slowly stood up, facing the man. A short gust of wind blew between them. He stared at her, unmoving. Cautiously, she approached him, arms wide, making herself look as nonagressive as possible.

With a deep breath, Lauren said, "Okay, thank you for saving me the other night. I'm sorry for being a bitch just now, but I don't know what's happening to me, and you're the only person I can think to turn to. Please, I need your hel—"

She was a few yards away when he finally moved. In the blink of an eye, she was flat on her back with her right arm locked painfully around his left arm.

His very touch felt like fire—the pain was sharp and excruciating. He pinned her under his knee and held his thick, calloused fist above her face. She tried to free her right arm like before, but it was like moving a mountain. His eyes burned bright gold, and his face was grim.

"You have a death wish or something? I gave you one last chance to back off, and you *still* didn't listen." He reared his fist, ready to strike. "I knew I should have killed you when I had the chance!"

Her eyes bulged with fear. "Oh my God! I'm sorry! I'm so sorry, please don't kill me!!"

He hesitated, confusion playing across his eyes.

"Please, I've got no one to turn to!"

Lauren tried to move her arm but couldn't budge it no matter how much she tried. The confusion left his face, and he raised his fist again. Lauren closed her eyes.

"I just wanted help," she whimpered, her voice breaking.

"Help?! Lady, you are beyond help! You're just another parasite now, just like the rest of 'em!" he spat.

"But I haven't done anything!"

"Bullshit! You already tried to bite my arm off!"

"What!?!"

"You did this!"

He pulled up the sleeve on his left arm in front of her. It was covered in scars and callouses like his face, but in the middle of them all, she saw it: two large punctures just like the ones on her neck surrounded by a ring of small indents. The holes were healed over with fresh scar tissue, but the teeth marks were still present. Lauren looked from the arm to his face, horrified.

The man's eyes returned to their blue color, and he stood up.

"It happened after I got you home. After I treated your wound, you went into convulsions. I tried to hold you down, but you woke up and bit me—started sucking my blood right there. I nearly had to kill you to stop you. Sooner or later you're going to start doing that to other people."

Lauren finally put together what had happened. She had woken up in the early afternoon horrified to see blood staining her mouth and sheets. Rushing to clean it off, she saw her face, and how alien it had become, from hair, to skin, to teeth. And now, she realized now she knew the blood was his from the smell the moment she sat down in the booth.

He was right; she was a vampire.

How could she live like that, feeding off people like a monster? She could barely stomach beef.

"There's nothing that can be done?" she lamented.

"Only one thing I know of."

She sat up and watched him dig inside his bag. He tossed the takeout from earlier onto the ground. A few grenades clipped to a frayed military belt tumbled out next to them. He pulled out a cloth bag covering something long and slender. Untying the knot, he withdrew a long katana from it. The sword's red and black handle was well worn, but the blade looked lovingly polished and very sharp. She realized now what he had in mind.

Lauren slumped forward, defeated. Her instinct was to run, but how could she run from something like this? It was a part of her now.

"Why did they do this to me?" she asked bleakly.

"Don't know. Could have something to do with calling you Kathleen."

No . . . It couldn't be. Could it?

"My . . . My name isn't Lauren Fox." She craned her head over her shoulder. "My real name is Kathleen Mary Baxter."

The man shrugged, "And?"

"My father is Donald Baxter."

He shrugged again.

"Baxter Logistics? They're one of the biggest shipping companies on the eastern seaboard."

He thought for a moment. "Controlling a shipping company could have a lot of uses for their kind. They could use it to smuggle supplies, food . . . themselves. Still doesn't explain that big ceremony. That place lit up when their leader started on you."

"That's not how they make vampires?"

"No. They just do it."

Her mind raced. Something didn't add up. "Wait. How long does it take to become—you know—one of them?"

"A single night."

She watched him take a few practice swings. His movements were very smooth and precise, the blade sliced through the air with a sharp swish.

"Would sunlight kill one after that time?"

"They'd burn up in seconds."

"But I was walking around in the sun all afternoon. How could I do that and be one of them?"

He shrugged again and moved behind her, his eyes golden. "Something to do with that ritual, maybe. Doesn't matter. The thirst will get you in the end. Now, sit up straight. I'll make this as painless as possible."

Lauren threw her hands up, "Wait!! Something must be different. It has to! I mean, how can I walk under the sun all day and not burn!? That has to mean something!"

He arched an eyebrow.

"The sun didn't kill me! It, it . . . it just felt like a really nasty sunburn. That has to mean I'm not one of them! If that's not normal then there might be a way to reverse this."

His shoulders dropped a touch.

"Besides, don't you want to know what they wanted me for? We could find out together! We can help each other! I'm a thief—a good one! I can get into places that nobody can't. I can help you!!"

Tears glistened her red eyes. "Please, I don't wanna die."

As she looked up at him, his brow furrowed, and the katana flashed. She flinched, but nothing touched her. Risking a peek, she saw his eyes had returned to normal, and he spun the katana in a flourish with his left hand, resting the blade against the back of his arm. He held his other hand out to her.

"Give me your hand."

"Why?" Lauren asked, warily. Her eyes shifted from his empty hand to the sword.

"Because I'm asking you to."

Hesitantly, Lauren shuffled around and lifted her right hand up to him. He took it, gently this time. The man put a calloused finger against the bottom of her wrist and held it there, checking his old watch while keeping an eye on her. After a full minute, he pulled her to her feet.

"Your heart is still beating."

She stared at him guardedly, not sure what was about to happen. "Is that . . . a good thing?"

He let go of her wrist. "The heart has to stop before the transformation can begin. Only the dead can become a vampire."

"Are you sure?"

"I've watched it happen."

The man walked to his bag. He picked up the long cloth sack and smoothly sheathed the sword. She watched him carefully repack the large blade along with everything else. Lauren took a few tentative steps towards him.

"What . . . what does that mean?"

He picked up her piton launcher and shouldered the heavy bag. "I don't know what it means. But you're still alive."

"So, does that mean you're going to help me?" her knees nearly buckled.

"We'll play your game—for now. Go home Lauren. Or Kathleen. Or whatever the hell you call yourself."

The man tossed the launcher to her. She caught it with both hands. "What happens next?"

"When I need you, I'll find you. Do not make me regret this."

With that, he left Lauren standing there for the opposite end of the roof. He was about to jump, when she called out, "Hey! What's your name?!"

The man stopped and looked back.

"Ethan Ward," he yelled and disappeared over the edge.

6 Strange Times

*L*auren stepped back from the false wall. The needling, brooding feeling in the back of her mind urged her into the ancient stone-carved passage. It had been with her all week now, prodding and pressing her. Every night the presence grew heavier. Every dream showed her the same ever-progressing string of images: an old forest, an abandoned mansion, a dark passage descending deep under the earth, a rickety staircase, and a massive doorway that opened to—

Hesitantly, she stepped forward into the rough hewn burrow. One foot after another, Lauren trodded through the dark tunnel and down the creaking wooden stairs. Wind in the corridor carried a tune with it, sinister and low. The music grew louder and deeper with every step. Words hung on the notes, words in a language she had never heard before. They poured over her, filled her, pulled her forward. Their rhythm matched her heart beat, rising and falling with every thump.

As she came to the end of the tunnel, the week long dream merged with reality. A large pair of carved wooden doors loomed over her. Dark and fuzzy behind her thermal goggles, the other worldly designs on the door danced and wobbled. She pushed her goggles onto her forehead. The patterns sharpened and sloughed off their wooden panels, beckoning her. Each night, her dreams ended when she opened the mysterious door, thrusting her awake and lingering at the back of her thoughts throughout the day.

Lauren goggled at the door in front of her. She watched her arms reach out and push against the aged heavy frame of their own accord. Intricate patterns of red lit the rough hewn design from her touch. Red light traced the patterns of each panel, the glowing shapes welcoming her, waving her inside. Singing burst through the parting doors and swallowed her whole.

A massive stone coliseum unfolded before her. Eerie blue flames lined the walls above the arena with larger orange fires encircling the center. The domed roof came to a point where a long black spire lined with sharp-looking barbs. Countless purple robed figures with hoods over their heads filled the chamber. Each one of them sang the same persuasive rhythm in her heart over and over and over. At the center of the arena, a single man stood next to a black marble altar with his arms outstretched. He wore a more ornate robe than the others with the hood pulled back.

Lauren floated through the entrance, stopping inches from a set of stairs leading to the hoodless man. Her body swayed listlessly with the singing. The hoodless figure slowly turned toward her and called out. His words were old and exotic, but she heard something that had been dead and buried for a long time:

Kathleen.

The sound of her old name instantly snapped Lauren awake. She shook the mental fog away and instantly turned white with dread. Her gut twisted in knots as every the robed figure ceased their chanting and faced her in unison.

"Oh my God," she breathed, rigid terror creeping into her voice.

Slowly, very slowly, Lauren backed away. She

did not belong here and desperately wanted to be somewhere else. Suddenly, cold hands clamped around her upper arms and lifted her off the ground. Their grip chilled her, even through their hardened leather gloves and the thick, supple fabric of her suit. She yelled out in protest, pulling as hard as she could against their icy fingers, but the two men were unmoving, their faces impassive masks barely registering her struggle. They were dressed in shadow and blood dripped from their eyes. Her feet scraped helplessly on the stone floor while they hauled her down the stairs.

The robed man on the dais welcomed Lauren with a bony white hand. As the black heavies carried her to him, she jammed her heels into the platform's edge. Groaning from the strain, she managed to halt them. If only for a moment. The leader immediately gestured and two more men in black with red eyes grabbed her by the ankles. The four carried her writhing body onto the dais and threw her onto the stone altar, holding her down with unearthly strength.

Lauren screamed and fought. She managed to slip a hand free. Her flailing fist smacked two of them, but something solid slammed the back of her head and sent a shock rippling through her entire body. One of the guards ripped off the goggles and hood from her head, sending a handful of curved bobbypins flying. The others ignored her struggle and robotically tied her down with leather buckles, the final one forcing her head to the side, exposing the left side of her neck. Finished, the four men exited the dais and stood watch. Lauren fought to breathe through the tight bindings.

The hoodless man suddenly raised his hand. He was deathly pale with salt and pepper hair combed straight back revealing a sinister looking widow's peak. His eyes were sunken and a thin, manicured goatee surrounded his equally thin lips. Lauren fought against the straps, trying to wriggle a hand free while the man addressed to the crowd. The rapid thumping in her chest drowned out his words. He turned to her, brandishing a wavy, wicked-looking knife. Still speaking in that weird language, he dragged the blade down her torso, effortlessly slicing open her bodysuit from collar to navel like it was taut tissue paper. Her exposed sweat-slick skin reflected the blue and orange flames above her. The man then pierced his palm with the knife, drawing dark and viscous blood.

Panic set in. The pale man traced the icy fluid over her heaving chest and neck. She struggled harder to free her hand, and the old leather gave slightly. The pale man finished drawing, and invisible, icy tendrils lanced into her skin around the blood. He turned to the gathered crowd and raised his bloody hands upward, chanting louder. Lauren pulled at her right arm, desperate to escape. She felt the strap give again and pulled with all her might. The crowd chanted along with the man. As their voices rose, the blood on her body suddenly became hot and began to glow.

When he finished speaking, he turned back to her and smiled. She watched in horror as two hideous fangs extended from his yellowed teeth. When she screamed, he thrust his bloody hand over her mouth and held her jaw open with unimaginable strength. Cold, bitter liquid gushed into her mouth. She refused to swallow, but he pinched her nose until the back of her throat forced open. The frigid blood raced like fire through her body. Choking, Lauren's eyes were glued to the fanged maw descending on her exposed neck.

She fought violently against the loose leather, but her wrist was caught on the strap. If she could just get to her belt . . .

Lauren felt an acute, needle-like pain. Everything instantly went numb, and an explosive wave of ecstasy flooded her being. She mentally recoiled from the alien sensation, but its insidious bliss drowned every thought. Her eyes rolled into her head, and the horrible pleasure swept her away into darkness.

Lauren shot up in bed, drenched and heaving, clutching the side of her neck.

Nervous fingertips felt the adhesive bandage there, and, in a panic, ripped it off. It was still dirty from last night, the blood stain was brown and dry and old. She felt the exposed skin with her other hand. There were no puncture wounds, no scabs, not even the bump of scar tissue.

Nothing.

She looked at the bandage and threw the hellish thing on the wooden floor. On her nightstand, bright, blood-red digits cut through the gloom of her bedroom. It was five minutes past noon. The apartment was dark and silent. She had slept through the entire morning.

Reaching over, Lauren pressed a switch on the wall, and the all the window blinds in her apartment slowly twisted to filter in the bright, midday sun. She sat motionless in her bed, staring through the railing, the final moments of her nightmare gradually dissipating.

After retrieving her car from the diner last night, Lauren fell into bed, exhausted. But, emotionally drained as she was, she couldn't sleep. Everything that had happened that day kept circling her mind. The physical changes, the revelations from that scarred man, going from nearly dying to some sort of alliance. She had laid there in the dark for hours trying to process it all.

Lauren let out a long, ragged sigh and shuffled into the bathroom. After washing the sweat and dirt and sleep from her face, she absently stared at herself in the vanity mirror for a long minute. Her irises were completely red now. That was the first thing she had noticed yesterday. Looking closer, she saw that they shimmered, like flecks of pearl dust had been embedded in them. Her skin had lost all of it's sunny color. Lauren ran her fingers through her hair and inspected a handful of it. She had spent years properly maintaining her blonde locks—her last memory of her mother. Now every strand was as white as her bed sheets, and her eyebrows were now the color of ash.

She gargled a cup of mouthwash. Hesitantly, she bared her teeth, bracing herself for the sight. To her amazement, they were normal. Puzzled, she poked at one of the canines. When she woke up yesterday, they were long and sharp and repulsive. She traced a finger along the enamel. It didn't feel any different than her other teeth. Nor did the gums.

"Where'd they go?" Lauren morbidly thought aloud.

How did they work? Was it a reflex? Do they grow on their own? She shuddered. How was all this possible? Vampires were a myth, a boogieman used to scare kids or bring out during Halloween. How in God's name were they real?

Her stomach growled, and she rubbed her flat belly. Lauren hadn't eaten at all yesterday. The pure shock of everything had absolutely ruined her appetite. Throwing on a robe, Lauren climbed down the curved stairs to the rest of her home. She turned on the television and walked into the kitchen.

Lauren Fox was a health nut. She kept her fridge filled with expensive bottles of juice, organic fruits and vegetables, fancy cheeses, and lots of yogurt. She would joke to prospective employers that she was effectively a vegetarian in everything but name. It was a choice, really. Years ago, Lauren had cut out meat from her diet in an effort to clean up her digestion and reduce her potential profile on a job. Despite living next to famous local butcher shop, she didn't miss it anymore.

While grabbing a small variety of fruit, she stared at a single porterhouse steak for a hard minute. It was still wrapped in wax paper from the restaurant. Blood stained the sides. Recently, she had met with a client to discuss a job. He was an elderly gentleman who had wanted an old keepsake returned to him. Her fixer, Vassily, had vouched for the man, and he was willing to pay well for the service. She had secured a private room at the restaurant *Flouraisons* for their meeting. The job was simple enough: break into a commercial shipping warehouse, locate an antique book, and deliver it to him, without alerting any security.

Throughout the meeting, he kept raving about the steak he ate. She simply had to try it, he had told her. Lauren couldn't stand looking at the thing, however. The sight of blood had always made her squeamish. When she politely refused, he insisted and bought an uncooked steak for her to take home anyway.

That was three days ago.

Lauren hadn't even started the job yet. She was a professional—she always finished what she started, especially commissioned work, but during the entire meeting, all she could think of was that damned mansion.

Lauren slammed the door shut.

She had bigger things to worry about now than professional integrity.

She diced the fruit, tossed it in a blender, and zapped it into a thick smoothie. She looked for the biggest glass to pour it into before giving up and drinking straight from the pitcher. Half way through, Lauren noticed the midday news playing on the television. The anchors were going back and forth over some sort of traffic incident last night. At the top corner of the screen, the news channel displayed a blurry still image. Apparently, during a police chase, their helicopter had caught sight of a man leaping off the top of a bus.

"What the hell?" she choked.

Lauren ran into the recessed living room and turned up the volume. A female anchor spoke, "—of you just joining, during last night's police chase through downtown, our pursuit helicopter caught a daring feat of athleticism."

"That's right, Janice," her male co-anchor continued. "During the chase, our very own Channel 7 News-Chopper captured footage of a man *surfing* the top of one of Free Port's metro buses. As you can see from the angle, the unidentified man literally jumps from a bus heading south on 39th St to another bus heading east on Madison Blvd."

A distant and blurry video filled the screen along with the customary news logo graphics. The helicopter's camera centered on a white SUV dodging through traffic on the elevated I-65 freeway that cut through downtown followed by several police cars. At an intersection one block north, the tiny figure of a man carrying something dark over his shoulder leapt into the air from one bus onto a different bus waiting at a stop light. The clip lasted barely two seconds while the helicopter followed the fleeing vehicle.

Lauren fell into the couch. That man really wasn't lying about last night. One look in the mirror told her as much, but now everything he had said finally hit her. The world really had gone crazy.

"When you slow it down," Janice spoke, "it looks like the jumper seems to be carrying something. It's hard to tell from this distance, but it looks like the man is holding a large duffel bag with something yellow hanging from it."

"That was me he was carrying, you idiot," Lauren sullenly scolded the television, as if Janice could hear her.

"You know," the male anchor retorted, "That looks almost like a person being carried."

"Bingo, dumbass."

She turned off the television and tossed the remote onto the coffee table.

Lauren looked around at her sparse apartment. There were a few plants here and there, a pair of large flat couches, both an uninspiring shade of gray. The kitchen was gray, the polished marble floor tiles were some sort of black, and the rest of the furniture was bland and brown—all prefurnished. There were no pictures. No family photos, no personal shots of her on vacation or group pictures with friends. No decorations. Only the pieces of an unfinished wooden puzzle lay scattered on the square coffee table and a few little origami animals cluttered the writing desk in the corner behind her.

The home was clean, minimal, and cold.

Lauren Fox was a thief. Though she had displayed a lot of talent as a youth, it was later that she had honed her craft for real, and she had learned from the best. And the most poignant piece of advice she had ever received was never make friends. Don't create a life you couldn't walk away from at a moment's notice.

She was pretty sure her mentor got that from a movie, but it made sense. She would break the rule from time to time for a few small extravagances—namely her car—but her home reflected that mantra perfectly. Lauren had no real social life. The closest she ever got to it was occasional trips to the movie theater—alone. Boyfriends were out of the question. She allowed herself the occasional one night stand only when she was certain the tryst couldn't get back to her. Her life was carefully constructed and restricted. She would appear normal only when the job needed her to. It was lonely, but it was the world she had built for herself, and she was happy with it.

But none of that mattered anymore.

She had fallen into a new world. A crazy one where vampires were real as well as people with golden eyes who could jump thirty feet into the air. And what the hell was Ethan Ward if he wasn't one of them? By sheer luck, he had saved her from that hellish gathering—

Almost. Who knows what would have happened if he wasn't there.

She rubbed the left side of her neck. And to think, she almost didn't believe him.

"I never should have gone into that stupid mansion," she exhaled. "Place wasn't even abandoned."

Lauren sat up straight, suddenly gripped by a thought.

"I wonder . . . ?" she said, looking to the empty corner in her kitchen.

She walked over to the blank wall next to the fridge and pressed her hand on the bare marble. After holding it there for two seconds, the kitchen track lights blinked twice. A ceiling tile flipped down where a ladder, slowly and silently, dropped down inches from the floor. Lauren quickly climbed up and disappeared into the ceiling.

Light blue fluorescent lights blinked on, illuminating a small workspace. A tall steel safe and a handful of metal shelves filled with various specialized tools lined one wall, and a long drawer-filled workbench and cork-board occupied the opposite wall. Next to the bench, and a detailed city map separated it from a shallow wash basin and shelf full of photo processing chemicals and metal clips hanging from the shelf's edge. Behind the ladder, a human shaped paper silhouette was stapled to the bare wood wall with a handful of throwing knives wedged into the different bullseyes. A large computer station and a massive flat-screen monitor dominated the far end of the room along with a high-backed computer chair.

The room had originally started out as a jacuzzi extending from her bathroom. She had the tub removed and that half of the bathroom walled off and converted into a panic room. It was then heavily modified into its current form, hidden entrance and all. Afterwards, she paid for the records of it's construction to be "conveniently lost" at City Hall. She had also bribed the construction company and the building manager to lose all records of it as well. The construction manager tried to force Lauren to perform some embarrassingly "intimate" services, but fortunately for her, he had a few skeletons in his closet that weren't so well hidden. A simple reminder of their existence sealed the deal and preserved her dignity.

Lauren pressed a large white button on the exposed wall and the ladder retracted, closing the roof tile behind it. Concealing her workroom from the public cost her over three times the price to have it built. But, to her it was worth it.

She walked down the narrow aisle, sparing the barest of glances at the cork-board. Pinned newspaper clippings highlighting unsolved thefts in the Free Port metro area dominated the spongy wall. A few of them referred to a mysterious burglar the columnist dubbed "The Sparrow". Small origami birds hung from each clipping, and a few more littered the workbench. The last clipping caught her her eye for a long, pregnant moment. It was a five-year-old obituary for a Kathleen Mary Baxter. Her eyes hovered over a laminated ID card clipped to the obituary. An old pilot's license, issued 1996. She looked away.

Among all the unbelievable revelations from last night, one alarmed her most: someone had figured out her identity. It had been over five years since Lauren

Fox had started her new life in Free Port. The city knew her as a rich, trust-fund orphan born abroad and returning home. Financial documents, medical history, dental records, Social Security number—all forged by the best in the business. Lauren was as real as money could buy, and she had taken every precaution to safeguard that secret.

It wasn't enough, apparently.

She pulled her sneaking suit off the computer chair. A thick layer of dust and dirt covered most of it, and blood stained the collar and left shoulder—her blood. It was made with a special, rubbery fabric designed to baffle body heat and absorb light. The boots were a special blend of the black fabric, soft rubber, and plastics that bent easily and muffled footfalls while maintaining grip. It had other unique innovations, too. Flexible plates placed in sections of the torso and limbs helped reduce impacts, and her fixer had personally assured Lauren that the Kevlar lining weaved into the entire suit was virtually knife resistant.

She traced her hand along the cut bisecting the torso.

"Knife resistant my ass," she muttered.

Lauren draped the suit on the work bench and sat down at the console. Something piqued her curiosity. The big computer hummed to life with a soft green glow. Months ago, the Free Port Times had advertised that their entire back catalog of editions had been fully digitized and made available to subscribers on the Internet. They were very proud of themselves, boasting that over 70 years of daily articles were completely searchable online. The paper even ran a large piece detailing the process and how to use it.

"Well, let's see if I'm not the only one who stumbled into something she shouldn't have."

She ran a search: VAMPIRE.

Links to hundreds of articles popped up. Almost

all of them talked about Halloween costumes and the occasional film premier.

New search: VAMPIRE SIGHTING.

66 articles, again the majority about Halloween parties with a few police reports detailing teenage pranks gone wrong.

CANNIBAL ATTACK.

20 articles returned. Again about Halloween parties, mostly from fifteen years ago, coinciding with the *Cannibal II* film premier.

MURDER.

Too many articles. She thought for a second.

MURDER + EXSANGUINATION.

9 articles. A week ago, a string of murders hit Free Port City. The bodies of seven teenage girls had been found at the edges of the old Deacon Hill district, each one dead from acute blood loss. The coroner's report stated each victim had showed no wounds or any signs of attack or duress. Police theorized that the killer drained the victims' blood via medical means. There were no patterns linking the victims other than their sex, age, and cause of death. A county-wide manhunt was still searching for the killer.

DEACON HILL + MURDER.

23 articles. Aside from the previous articles, every few decades a mysterious body would turn up in the Deacon Hill area dating back to the founding of the city. Every victim had no identification on them nor were there any obvious signs of attack. Some were slaves, others were laborers that had been missing for days or even weeks. Lauren moved over to the city map and put a red push pin at the location of each body. The pins created a rough twelve mile circle around a single location in the district: Undergrove Manor. The same mansion as the other night.

She went back to the computer.

UNDERGROVE MANOR.

13 articles.

Undergrove Manor dated back to before the Revolutionary War. Belonging to the Bourne family, the mansion was built in 1763, and. It started off originally as a tobacco plantation, but in 1831, due to a tragic wave of deaths from rheumatic fever, possession was turned to Emile Berger, a distant relative still living in England. After accepting control of the plantation, Emile sold off the surrounding farmland and all the farming assets and slaves. With the money from the sales, Emile had commissioned extra construction on the main building. In two years Undergrove Manor had more than doubled in size.

However, the additions were never finished. During those two years, workers would disappear while on the job or simply went missing altogether. Also, many of them had complained of poor working conditions and worse treatment. Finally, with the disappearance of the construction foreman in 1833, the workers revolted and left the mansion in it's unfinished state. Shortly after, Emile Berger, who reportedly rarely appeared in public, went missing, too. At that point, the construction project and the mansion itself was abandoned.

For decades Undergrove Manor lay in total disrepair. Local legends sprang up of hauntings and sightings of strange lights and other unexplained phenomena. In late 1940 the city government tried to appropriate the mansion and it's remaining grounds for the creation of a munitions factory. Fortunately, the local historical society rallied support and blocked the attempt. After the war it was officially deemed a historical landmark.

In the following decades, the city launched several efforts to renovate and refurbish the mansion to turn it into a local museum. Each time, however, legal red tape and litigation dragged down the efforts before they could start. Eventually, the restoration projects were dropped entirely, and Undergrove Manor remained a dilapidated ghost house ever since. Police would occasionally search the mansion when investigating the nearby murders over the years, but they always found nothing.

While pouring through the articles, Lauren noticed something odd. The pictures of the Free Port City Historical Society president during the war appropriation hearings bore an uncanny resemblance to the only known portrait of Emile Berger. Not only that, the current president, London Bray, bore the same resemblance as well.

She opened a new window.

EMILE BERGER.

Lauren found a few links on the local historical society's website. Most of them were scans of hand written letters sent to and from him in his home in the north of Wales. One link brought up a painting of the man, dating back to 1817. The painting depicted Emile in a red British Army uniform drawing an elegant officer's sword next to a grand wooden desk. His cheekbones were rough and high with slightly hollow cheeks. A deep scar cut into his upper lip on the right side of his face giving him a permanent sneer. Emile had thin eyebrows that arched with small points near the bridge of his nose. His foreboding, gray eyes seemed to bear down at Lauren from the screen.

She pulled up another search window, covering the bottom half of the painting. Lauren found a local chat forum discussing local oddities around Free Port City. Several of the group members went back and forth about the nature of Undergrove Manor. There were as many theories as there were users on the forum. One user theorized that Emile was a serial killer and preyed on the construction workers, and that they eventually got their revenge on him in the end. The user went on saying that it was his ghost who had haunted the mansion, killing any who dared enter. Another user claimed that Ezekial Bourne, the last patriarch of the manor's original owners, was the real ghost in question. A lone theory said that the construction was actually finished, the worker revolt was engineered, and that the true purpose of the additions was to funnel ambient spiritual energy into the mansion for evil pagan rituals. The majority of the chatroom denounced the theory and said that the user should stop watching *Ghostbusters* so much.

Looking at the clock above the computer, four hours had passed, and despite having finished off the entire smoothie, her stomach still rumbled angrily. Odd. Smoothies always filled her up, even after a heavy workout. Lauren put the computer on standby. By habit, she checked the small security monitor by the ladder that it was okay for her to open the door. With everything clear, she climbed down to the kitchen.

Going back to the fridge, Lauren pulled out a host of vegetables to make a big, hearty salad. Half way through dicing the tomatoes, she stopped, her eyes drawn back to the fridge. She reopened the door and pulled out the steak.

She gazed at it awhile, wondering why she had done that. Hesitantly, she opened it and cut a small chunk. Though cold and moist in her fingers, it had a faint but savory scent. She took an awkward nibble. It was juicy and amazing. Lauren sliced off another cube and popped it in her mouth. She cut another. And then another. Soon, there was nothing left but bone and a long strip of fat.

Lauren stared lovingly at her red stained fingers, chuckling to herself. That old man was right!

Then make friends with a butcher!

Ethan Ward's words echoed in her mind while she licked her fingers clean. Giancarlo's Meat Market was only five blocks away.

She quickly threw on some clothes and hurried to the elevator.

In the Evening

*E*than crouched on the roof of the brick building.

His eighteenth birthday was coming up, and Sensei Takuan had finally taken the boy with him on a hunt. Was this some sort of gift? For years, Sensei made him stay hidden and observe while he confronted whatever supernatural freak they had tracked.

Last week, Ethan had finally grasped how to stretch out with his senses. After months struggling to expand his consciousness, he had finally moved past his own body and felt something beyond him. In the following days, Ethan extended his consciousness further and further, feeling the warmth of the trees and the animals in the forest where they camped. He marveled at the ebb and flow of life energies that connected the world and the living beings that inhabited it. He felt the heartbeat of nearby animals and could see how the energies surrounded them, too. Earlier tonight, he felt the energies of the people on the streets. Their heartbeats, their spirits—their auras.

And down below, Ethan felt the aura of the vampire. Stale and barren, the cold, negative presence of the animated corpse filled his newly developed sixth sense. Puzzlingly, the vampire's aura had a taste, too. It was bitter, like an old bottle of wine that had long ago rotted into vinegar.

The young man angrily fidgeted while he watched. Even after years of grueling training, he still wanted nothing more than to avenge his family's slaughter on the nearest parasite he could get his hands on, especially the one he watched. Ethan tightened his worn knuckles til they were bleach white. Takuan smacked him on the back of his head. He didn't say anything this time, but Ethan knew what was on his master's lips.

Stupid boy.

Takuan called Ethan that every time he had screwed up—usually after a jarring slap like now.

For the last few hours, they had shadowed the vampire's movements through the small city's downtown area. The parasite mingled with the night crowd like a wolf stalking through a heard of sheep. Sensei let Ethan take the lead. The young man had lost him once, but—fearing the harsh reprimand—he concentrated harder and quickly regained the trail one street over. They followed the vampire for blocks, eventually leaving the streets for the roof tops.

Finding their quarry in the middle of his unholy act, Sensei had to restrain Ethan to make him observe. Jaw tight to the point of cracking enamel, Ethan watched the repulsive act below him. The vampire sucked the life-blood from his victim slowly, its face twisted with delight. The victim twitched with every sip.

"See how the gaki takes his food," Takuan whispered. *Gaki.* That was what he called the parasites. *The hungry dead.*

"Why isn't the man fighting back, Sensei?"

"The bite of the gaki is subtle like poison. See how it subdues its prey."

Ethan focused on the man's face. His eyes and mouth contorted with pleasure and pain. The man's pupils were rolled into their sockets and fluttered from every gulp. Ethan's anger rose. Sensing his pupil's growing fury, Takuan put a firm hand on his shoulder, pushing him back down. Ethan looked to his master, desperate for answers.

"No. Tonight we watch," the old man stated quietly.

Ethan returned his attention to the crime against nature. He thought of the screams that night on the farm. Imagination finally filled the gaps of what had happened while he and his sister cowered in the barn. What had happened to her after they took her. He looked down at the vampire as if this was the creature who had taken her. He had no way to know if that was true, he had only seen one of them. But he wanted to believe it. He wanted to slake his rage on every blood-thirsty freak who stole his family.

But Sensei had a reason for bringing him here. He always had a plan—even when he didn't.

The vampire dropped the lifeless body onto the pavement. Blood stained the parasite's teeth, his inborn tools of both death and sustenance. He gazed at the dead man at his feet, licking the blood from his lips. The vampire stooped down and cut a small gash in his hand with a sharp nail. He then opened the corpse's mouth and loosed a steady stream of his own blood into it. The body quivered violently for a moment and then fell limp again. After that, the vampire stood up, the gash on his hand sealing in seconds. He picked up the body and left the alley.

With Ethan in tow, Takuan trailed the vampire to an abandoned warehouse in the outskirts of town. They entered the building from the roof and silently observed the vampire for hours. The parasite had placed the dead man in a wooden box in a secluded corner and climbed into one of his own.

Night turned to day. They stayed in place, taking turns sleeping, eating, and watching.

When night returned, the vampire rose to life. He left the building shortly, returning with an unconscious woman over his shoulder not long after. Ethan had focused his newly acquired senses on them. The woman was alive, barely—her heart rate was weak and slow. He then focused on the sealed box. While he felt the vampire's negative presence easily, he sensed something vague yet similar from the box, too. It was faint, but growing rapidly.

The vampire dropped the woman next to the box and sat down at a makeshift table with an old oil lamp on it and waited.

A short while later, the box began to rock back and forth until the man exploded out of it. Animal fury contorted his pale face. The woman on the floor had woken up as well, gradually coming to her senses. The enraged man swept his gaze around the warehouse, nearly focusing on Ethan and Takuan before his maddened eyes fell on the woman. Snarling, he leaped onto her and clamped his mouth on the base of her neck. She barked in terror as he restrained her before succumbing to his bite just like in the alley. Fresh blood dribbled from his lips while he gorged on the woman's vital fluids. Ethan watched her panicking aura fade to nothing. The woman's skin slowly lost its color. The man's fury dissipated.

Sated, the recently dead man stood up, his mouth smeared with crimson. Dread tugged at his face once he noticed the dead body at his feet. The first vampire took his confused, newly minted spawn by the shoulder and guided him out of the warehouse. They left the dead woman there on the dirty floor, with only a few drops of blood trickling from her torn neck.

Ethan turned to his master, distraught. "Why didn't we stop him, Sensei?"

Takuan's face was harder than stone. "Now you know how they breed."

For years, Sensei had drilled into Ethan's mind the importance of what they do. Takuan was one of a long line of hunters, dating back to the dawn of history (or so he said). They protected regular, unassuming people from the predations of the supernatural. Through stories handed down from his teacher and the teacher before him, Ethan learned how the creatures of legend fit into the world at large. Their actions, their strengths and weaknesses, how to defeat them.

And every lesson was punctuated with the reminder that no matter how tough or strong or fast the creatures of the night—the demons of the world—may be, they can be killed just like everything else.

Takuan climbed to his feet and handed Ethan a long and slender black bag. The young man took it with both hands. He slowly untied the end and slid the fabric back, revealing a sheathed katana. The scabbard was long and black with a red cloth cord tightly wrapped around the black rayskin handle. The gold/white handguard and pommel glinted in his scant moonlight. Ethan pulled the sword out of the scabbard and held it, feeling its weight and balance. The perfect blade shined brightly in the moonlight filtering through cracks in the ceiling. He sheathed the weapon with a satisfying click.

The wizened teacher put a reassuring hand on his student's shoulder.

"Now we go to work."

Ethan opened his eyes.

Wind ruffled his hair and buffeted his jacket against his broad shoulders. He sat on the roof of a bus with his green duffel bag across his lap. The sun was high and bright in the early afternoon. Trucks and semi-trailers dominated this part of the city with only a handful of commuter cars daring to brave the rough highway.

Rushing air stung his face. The bus traveled north towards Free Port's old industrial sector, but he paid no mind to it. That Fox woman's face kept distracting his thoughts. The terror and sorrow in her eyes when she begged him for help last night refused to go away no matter how much he meditated. He pitied her. That vampire in the ornate robe had done something grotesque to her, though he knew not what. She was desperate. He couldn't blame her. He'd be desperate, too, if had he been turned into a parasite.

It had been six years since he left Sensei. After avenging his family's memory in Cheyenne, Ethan had wandered for years, hunting and killing vampires as he found them. He came to know the parasites—knew how they lived, how they hunted. He knew their habits. Some vampires treated their prey with respect, taking care to drink only what they needed. Others simply glutted themselves whenever the opportunity presented itself. But it didn't matter how a parasite ate their meal, they were all abominations who tormented the living.

He should have killed Lauren Fox last night.

But he didn't.

Something felt different about her situation. A vampire's heart does not function. Nor could a parasite safely walk under the sun without burning to cinders in seconds. But hers still beat, and he had watched her walk through daylight without even a blister.

Was that the purpose of that abominable ceremony—to create a vampire with no weakness? And what did those insane ramblings he beat out of that parasite mean? There had to a reason for all of it. Maybe if he kept her around he could unravel that mystery. She did offer him her skills as a thief. He could easily find use for those talents in his line of work.

The bus exited the freeway onto a heavily traveled avenue below. The road was cracked and pockmarked from hundreds of trucks and trailers trundling back and forth every day. Ahead, men in dirty uniforms crowded the bent signpost of a bus stop coming up on the left. Beyond it rose a multi-storey public parking garage and a sprawling chemical plant. The road split the plant into two sections joined by a large series of pipes crossing overhead.

The massive brakes squealed to an ear-piercing halt, and it pulled up to the crowd. Ethan shouldered his bag and silently dropped down. The haggard-looking workers piled inside, all of them too tired to notice the dirty vagrant with a big green backpack suddenly appearing from behind the bus.

Living with Sensei had taught Ethan how to effectively live off the land—or the streets—when necessary. Time in cities accustomed him to living among vagrants. Hell, he often posed as one. But when he had entered this city, the first thing he noticed was the complete lack of homeless encampments. Even after a week of canvasing the metro area, he found absolutely no signs of them. Not under the bridges. Not in the subway tunnels. Not even in the occasional alley or rooftop. And yet, he saw them on almost every bus he rode.

Ethan turned north at the street corner while the bus returned to the freeway. Wind corralled dirt and refuse into small trash twisters. He tilted his head down, shielding his eyes from the floating particles. Walking along a tall chain link fence, Ethan spied a security truck lazily circling the plant perimeter. Gravel slowly crunched under its fat tires. He noticed the weary look on the driver's face. His puffy cheeks blew out smoke. Bent cigarette butts and crumpled fast-food wrappers clogged the dashboard. Beyond, graffiti defaced many of the massive pipes jutting up from the ground. Strands of thread-bare fabric clung to the coils of razor wire capping the property's fence.

Continuing on, a massive bus yard stretched out in front of him. A tall sandy brick wall surrounded the facility. The loud whining roar of large diesel engines moving around inside carried over. At the other end of the block, a pair of kids in oversized hoodies and jeans giggled while spraying graffiti on the brick wall while one of their number swiped at a pair of security cameras with a bent pipe. A uniformed security guard appeared through a break in the stone barrier. He yelled at the kids, prompting them to drop everything and run. The guard gave chase, his keys and equipment belt jangling with every labored footfall.

Ethan stretched out with his senses before the guard got too far. He felt the taint of vampiric essence on the man just as he disappeared around the stone wall. Concentrating, he felt more past the gate. He peered into the yard the thrall just left.

A small squat security office with a moving barricade stood next to the gate. Ahead, a wide boulevard cut through two collections of parked city buses all the way to a huge red brick building at the end. It was two stories tall and stretched out to the opposite ends of the yard with a bulging white roof. Six huge doors dominated the left side of the building, all but one with a municipal bus packed inside. Two men in matching sets of overalls guided a bus into the last empty lane. Once parked, thick pistons rose from the floor underneath, slowly raising it off the ground. After securing the big machine to the pistons, they went to work on it with tools from big red toolboxes and heavy plastic carts lined up between each vehicle.

With the guard chasing the two vandals, the security booth at the entrance was empty, so Ethan helped himself into the yard. He spread his senses throughout the area, until he happened upon a cold presence. Multiple ones in fact, scattered throughout the area. The two men working under the newly jacked bus; the rest of the mechanics in the garage; all of them carried the taint of a vampire. But among them, he felt a bigger presence. Very cold, very bitter, and dormant.

A vampire slept here. An old one.

A lair? he wondered.

The two mechanics chatted while under the vehicle. Ethan strolled up to the wall next to them. He leaned against the dusty brick and listened to them over the clank of tools.

"I heard you workin' again tonight?" one asked with a raspy voice.

"Yeah. Another double shift. I gotta earn my fix," spoke the second.

The first mechanic blew a cloud of cigarette smoke out the garage door. The cloud dissipated next to Ethan's face. "You know there's supposed to be a delivery tonight."

"Another one? Didn't they do one two days ago?"

"Don't know what's up with this one. And we're paid not to know, remember?"

"Yeah, I know. When's it s'posed to go down?"

Another cloud wafted out the door. "11 o'clock. Same time, every time."

"Like clockwork, huh?"

"You just remember to keep your eyes to yourself if you wanna get the juice."

"I know, I know. We see nothin'."

"Right." A spent cigarette bounced next to Ethan's shoe. "C'mon, let's get this piece of shit checked out."

Ethan eased an eye around the corner. The two men crawled back under the machine and proceeded to dismantle parts of the undercarriage, neither of them noticing his presence. Ethan reached down and inspected the cigarette butt. Sniffing the filter, he focused his senses on it. Through the tobacco scent, he caught the hint of vampire taint on the saliva still coating the tan filter.

Still holding the butt, he focused his senses into the garage. He felt the two mechanics. One had a weaker level of taint than the other—likely the one needing a "fix". Sweeping his senses further, he searched for the old presence. A bitter cold emanated from the back of the garage, somewhere up and to the left. He concentrated on the negative presence, focusing on its—

"What the fuck you think you're doing here!?"

The guard from earlier standing in front of him, his hand gripping a black Beretta on his hip. He glared daggers at Ethan, equal parts nervous and angry.

Ethan offered the cigarette butt to the guard. "Bumming a smoke."

"This is a restricted area." He tightened his fingers on the pistol. "Get your ass outta here!"

"Sure," Ethan smashed the butt under his red sneaker.

The guard eyed him while Ethan walked down the lane cutting through the parked buses, keeping a close pace behind. The gate immediately rolled closed after crossed the threshold. Ethan faced the guard standing safely behind the barricade.

"I see you around here again, you're gonna get a bullet. Got that, trash!?" the man threatened.

"Got it," Ethan said coolly.

What kind of delivery were they expecting. Drugs? Weapons? Was juice the vampire's blood? Whatever it was, a powerful vampire was here, and that alone piqued his interest.

He headed back to the bus stop, keeping an eye at the chemical plant. A cluster of the tall distillation silos towered near the edge of the plant's property line. Ethan bet he could see the whole bus yard from up there. Probably all the way into those big garage doors, too. He thought that Fox woman's climbing gun and fancy black suit. If she had the money to purchase something like that, then would she have some sort of long range cameras? If she was half as good a thief as she claimed to be, then she probably did. He'd have to grab her before coming back tonight.

Ethan returned to the bus stop. It was empty.

He didn't want to work with someone again— especially another woman. The last time that happened, it didn't end well.

Six months ago he had rescued a lady deputy. She was a rookie and dead set on helping him hunt down a particularly nasty beast. Girl wouldn't take no for an answer. Of course, she had no idea what she was getting into. Neither did Ethan, but, it had been so long since he had any kind of companionship, he decided to let her tag along against his better judgment. They got close during that hunt. Too close. It felt good to sleep in a comfortable bed for once—a rare occurrence given Ethan's line of work. And it felt even better to share it.

But getting close distracted him, however. He carelessly gave his trust to the lady, and when the investigation lead them to his quarry, Ethan expected her to follow his lead. But she didn't. And because he wasn't fast enough, the woman died a very gruesome death.

And now another woman he had saved wanted to tag along.

He knew the thief was telling the truth when she begged him—her heartbeat proved her honesty—but could he rely on her to listen and do as he said? And if he kept her around, would he be fast enough to keep her safe when she inevitably got herself into trouble? Would she even last long enough for him to learn what that ceremony was really about?

More importantly, would she try to drink his blood again?

Ethan grimaced.

He would have to be extra careful around this Lauren Fox.

8 The Thirst

*T*he five o'clock sun baked Lauren on the sidewalk.

Giancarlo's meat market occupied the ground floor of a five story tenement building dating back to the 1920s. It had been a fixture of Free Port's Midtown district since the Depression. Though modern supermarkets reigned supreme, Giancarlo's was still *the* place to go for many Free Port residents for hand-cut, raw, and cured meats. It was listed as one of the best food markets in the city for three decades straight.

Lauren had never been here before. She had passed by it many times but never paid the place any attention. At peak afternoon rush hour, a line had formed outside the entrance. She fought a losing battle for patience while it slowly churned through the door, her skin crawling miserably with every second.

When she finally entered the building, Lauren let out a heavy sigh of relief. She saw customers pulling a numbered paper ticket from a red ticket machine at the door and did likewise. Ticket in hand, Lauren witnessed just how popular the establishment truly was. Past the threshold the line had completely disintegrated into a writhing sea of shoulders and hair in the cramped sales floor. She spied a large digital counter hanging in the back corner displaying the current customer being helped. What little patience she had left melted when she glanced at her ticket. There were over twenty people ahead of her, and just getting through the door took over half an hour.

God, this is taking fucking forever!

Standing there among the crowd, Lauren withdrew into herself. She wasn't a meat eater. She knew she didn't belong here and desperately wanted to be anywhere else.

But the smell was absolutely *intoxicating*. A tidal wave of savory odors filled Lauren's nose. A pair of specialized slicing machines rowed back and forth cutting bundles of processed beef, pork, turkey, or chicken. A clerk busily filled entire trays with thick slices of beef dripping with blood. Dry-rubbed steaks and seasoned chops exchanged hands. The moist aroma of freshly cut meats floated out of the prep room.

The collection of smells made her light headed.

She craned over the mulling crowd on her tip-toes. Though her skin had stopped crawling, Lauren felt a new level of discomfort. Dozens of people shouting at once melted into an auditory slop of deafening white noise. Customers pressed against the glass counter took their time picking out product on display. Clerks explained the fine minutia of today's specials over and over again with rote enthusiasm. More than once, some old lady droned on with the clerk, giving the man her life story or something just as inane. All of it rankled her ears. Lauren hated mindless small talk, even when on a job. It reeked of anxiety.

Just like she felt now.

After an eternity, one of the clerks finally called out her number. Lauren shouldered her way to the counter.

"What'll it be, lady?" the clerk asked, busily moving something out of view.

A wide eyed Lauren stared into the glass counter.

"Umm, I . . . I've never been here before. How, uhh, does this work?" she fumbled.

The clerk glanced up at her and then at the mass of people behind her. "Tell me what you're lookin' for, ma'am, and we wrap it up for you. That's how it works."

"Okay. What do you recommend?" she asked meekly.

"Steaks are always popular."

"Oh. Uhh. Can I see them?"

"They're right in front of you, ma'am."

Turning her gaze back down, Lauren's hungry eyes took in all the different slices of beef lovingly displayed in front of her. She pointed to the juiciest pile, "How raw are these?"

The clerk scrunched his face at the question. "'Scuse me??"

"Would you step it up, girl!? Some of us've lives to get to!" an old lady rasped behind her. The old bat's breath reeked of medical cream and tobacco. Lauren heard a few giggles floating over the packed crowd. She blushed, pulling her black knit cap down further.

"How fresh are these?" she restated, pointing to the tray of boneless ribeyes with blood pooling at the bottom.

"Those were cut late this morning."

"How much for it?"

"$8.37 a pound."

"Can I buy them?"

"The whole tray??"

"Umm, yes? Please?"

The clerk shrugged and emptied the pile of beef into a steel bowl covered with a fresh sheet of wax paper on a digital scale nestled in a cluttered table against the wall.

"Okay, lady. That's about twenty-three pounds, at eight thirty-seven a pound, with tax comes out to . . .

," he punched in the numbers on a calculator, "$204.16. Cash or card?"

Stunned, Lauren fell silent.

"Hey lady? Cash or card?"

She blinked. "Cash—I mean card!"

The clerk nodded and began wrapping the meat in wax paper and boxing it up. An older clerk came through the plastic blinds with a tray of smoked sausage links and began hanging them from empty hooks behind the counter. Through the swishing plastic, Lauren saw one of the butchers take a massive haunch to a bandsaw. She saw blood splatter the stainless steel splash guard behind it. Her mouth watered.

"Um, sir? Excuse me," she leaned in as close as she could against the glass case. "Excuse me, what do you do with the blood?"

"The what?" the clerk asked.

"What do you do with the blood?" She pointed to the back room.

The clerk looked up and shrugged matter-of-factly, "We dispose of it."

"Can I," she lowered her voice, "can I buy some of it?"

"Nah, we stopped selling that."

"You sold it?"

"Yeah, but the local Health Department put a stop to it 'bout a decade ago."

"If you're just going to toss it, can I have some of it then?"

"Lady, we don't do that anymore," the younger man restated.

"I can pay you." She pulled out a wad of cash from her wallet. The older clerk watched Lauren while he finished hanging the links.

"What?! No!" the young clerk barked.

"I'll pay double for the steaks," Lauren said more forcefully.

"Look, ma'am, I can sell you the meat, but I can't sell you blood from the prep room!"

Some of the customers behind Lauren started shouting for her to leave. She shrunk a little where she stood. This was worse than small talk.

"Jimmy!" The older clerk walked over. "I'll handle this. Go help the next customer." Jimmy rolled his eyes and stepped aside as the older man looked Lauren over with a smile. "That'll be $204.16."

Defeated, she handed him her credit card. He quickly ran the card and handed it back along the heavy box of meat. She hardly noticed the weight. Lauren turned to leave when the older man called out to her.

"Ma'am. Don't forget your receipt." He held out the slip of paper patiently for her. "Please make sure the math is correct before you leave."

Huffing, Lauren grabbed the receipt from him and checked the slip in case this guy was trying to rip her off. As she ran through the math, she felt odd bumps on the little piece of paper. She flipped it over and her jaw dropped an inch or two.

There, scribbled in pencil, was a had written message: *Back alley.*

The older clerk winked at her and went back to helping customers. Something looked off about his face, but she couldn't quite place it. No stranger to secret messages and off-the-books transactions, she had seen her fair share of back alley deals. But every one of them was solicited in some way. This wasn't. The clerk saw her gawking in the middle of the throng of customers and flashed her a toothy grin. With an askance look, she quickly shoved her way out the store and hustled to the back alley.

When she arrived at the back door, the older clerk was already there, smoking a cigarette. He had the abattoir reek of blood about him, but she detected something else. Something pungent and musty, like freshly turned sod.

"You wanted the blood, huh?" he said between drags.

She forced herself to nod.

"You from the FDA?"

"What?" she blinked.

"You a fuckin' narc?"

Lauren scowled. "Do I look like a narc to you?" The butcher leaned in close and stared into her eyes. Lauren held her ground, but looked away when she remembered her new eye color.

"Okay. two-hundred bucks, like you offered."

"Is," she swallowed, "this normal?"

He held out his hand, scoffing, "Lady, ain't nuthin in our world is normal. You buyin' or what?"

She handed him the cash. He snatched the bills and handed her a bag with a large foam cup in it. It was cold in her pale hand.

"Ask for Greg whenever your *friend* needs this. No need to make a fuss next time, okay?"

He winked again. Lauren stared dumbly at him. The edge of his gray irises were ringed with a thick layer of red. The man stubbed out his cigarette and went back inside, leaving her alone in the building's shadow.

The sun had set by the time Lauren returned home. The television was still on, playing some sitcom rerun. She pulled off her knit cap, letting her white hair fall down. Examining a thick tuft, she realized she should do something about it. Usually, she kept a few bottles of hair dye around for disguises, but had ran out after her last job. She made a mental note to buy more the next time she went out.

Lauren set the box and bag on the kitchen counter. Who did that older clerk think her friend was?

Maybe vampires frequented the place for blood? Did he think she was one of them?

No. That couldn't be right, she was out in the sunlight. Or did he think she was some kind of vampire minion? Like Renfield from that Dracula movie a few years ago.

Are Renfields even a thing?

She unboxed the steaks while pondering what happened at the market. She had purchased a total of twenty-one ribeye steaks, each dripping with blood. Her mind swirled with all the different ways she could cook them. She could shave them and stick them in a stir fry. Slow cook them in the oven. They could be fried, grilled, cubed and stewed. Why had she never tried steak before? She had watched others eat steak and rave about it. Her last client certainly did so.

But, steak was more of a guy-thing. She'd never had any interest in it. Now, she wondered what type of potatoes paired well with ribeye.

Lauren stored half of them in plastic baggies and stuffed them in the freezer. The rest went into the fridge. All that was left was the styrofoam cup on the counter.

Staring at her.

"They make sauces with this, right? I could do that." she mused aloud.

No. Lauren wasn't much of a cook. She always preferred to eat out or make a big dumb salad. Like she could make a stir fry! Lauren could barely boil an egg. In her mind, the cooking was better left to qualified people.

"I'll just save it, I guess. For later."

Picking it up, she squeezed the cup too hard and some of the contents spilled over her hand and onto the floor.

"Crap."

Lauren put her hand under the sink. She reached

for the faucet but stopped. Haltingly, she licked it. The taste exploded on her tongue. She licked the rest of her fingers. When her hand was clean, she ripped the top off the cup and drank. Thick, chilled, and smooth, it flowed over her tongue and down her throat. Neither savory nor sweet, the flavor defied classification. It felt like Thanksgiving *and* Christmas dinner—gluttonous, filling, delicious. Satisfaction arced through her body, stimulating every nerve.

Tipping the pint up, blood dribbled down the sides of her mouth. Her skin rippled with goosebumps, and her eyes fluttered and rolled up from the soothing pressure welling up at the base of her head. The pressure throbbed with her heart and intensified every sensation. She felt her canines instantly grow long and sharp. She didn't care. Gulping the luscious beverage, an enlarged fang pierced her tongue. Lauren gagged, spitting up crimson liquid all over the cabinets and floor. Seeing the blood everywhere, her knees gave, and she collapsed into tears, a pathetic mess.

In the span of a day, she had gone from wanting a fruit smoothie to craving raw meat and drinking blood. And she had made a fool of herself trying to fulfill that craving. She had never eaten steak before, but now Lauren had twenty of them in her fridge, and she just guzzled a pint of blood illegally purchased from the same place.

Lauren was becoming a monster just like he said.

How long until this wouldn't be enough? How long until she craved something . . . *fresh*? She was a beautiful woman. How difficult would it be easy to chat up some guy in a bar, take him to a secluded spot, and bite his neck?

She cried harder at the thought.

Through her wailing, the intercom buzzed. She tried to ignore it, but it kept ringing. Lauren pulled herself off the floor, still sniffling. She snatched a paper towel and wiped away the tears, smearing the blood around her cheeks. Sniffling, she wobbled to the intercom.

Lauren pressed the talk button. "Hello?" her voice wavered.

"Evening, Miss Fox." It was Mr. De Vera, the building's doorman. "Umm, I have a gentleman here who says he needs to see you. Are you expecting anybody tonight?"

"No." Lauren wanted to be alone with her misery.

"He says he has business with you."

"I don't want any visitors right now."

"Understood ma'am. Guy's probably just another crazy homeless person. I'll take care of him."

No. Already??

She slapped the talk button, nearly breaking it, "Wait!"

"Yes, ma'am?"

"What . . . what did he want?"

There was a pause. Then, "He said you two have work to do."

"Does he have a lot of scars?"

"The guy looks like he's been dragged through hell. You want me to call the police, Miss Fox?"

"NO! I mean, no. Umm, send him up. Just give me . . . give me, like, five minutes?"

Lauren didn't wait for a response. In a panic, she wiped all the blood stains on the floor and the cabinets. She desperately didn't want him to see her like this. He'd think she was acting just like he predicted—that she was too far gone and would put her down. But if she refused to see him, he might suspect her and come up one way or another to finish the job. She had to work with him, if there was any hope to fix what had happened to her.

She frantically trashed all the blood-stained towels along with the cup and anything else lying around from the market. After, Lauren bounded up the stairs, quickly ripping off her stained clothes as she went. Chucking them in the hamper, she threw on an old v-neck shirt and jeans. Hurrying past the mirror, she glimpsed the smears of blood on her face. Worse, the fangs were still there.

"Oh, God! Please go the fuck away!" she pleaded while viciously scrubbing her face. Lauren swished a big swig of mouthwash, hoping she didn't accidentally bite herself again. In her haste she didn't even notice that her tongue had completely healed.

The door knocked.

Shit! "Hold on!" she called out after spitting, trying to mask her anxiety.

He knocked again.

"Coming!"

Lauren flew down the stairs. Barefoot, she jumped over the last few steps and straight across the foyer in a single, impossible leap. Lauren stared at herself, stupefied by what she just did, while Ethan a third time, harder and faster. Snapping out of it, she flung the door open so fast, the hinges nearly snapped in protest.

Ethan stood in the small hallway, his hand poised to knock again. The elevator doors dinged shut behind him. A slender black cloth bag hung across his back—she knew what was in it. He wore the same clothes as yesterday, only the shirt was red. She wrinkled her nose. His smell hadn't changed either.

Still winded, she quickly probed her teeth with her tongue. Grateful the fangs had gone away, she bore Ethan a normal, toothy smile.

"Hi!" she panted, cheerfully. "What's up?"

He said nothing.

"Find any bad guys yet?"

"You have a camera, right?" he sighed.

"Uh huh," she nodded vigorously.

"Zoom   lenses?"

She nodded again.

"Get 'em. And your climbing gun."

He eyed her standing in the doorway catching her breath. Her smile started to fade.

"Umm, now?"

"Yes, now. And you're driving."

9 Take Me Out

*E*verything was bright tonight.

They sped north through a the major thoroughfare not far from Lauren's apartment. It had taken her a few minutes to gather her camera equipment and pack it into a pair of black bags. Lauren begged Ethan to wait outside in the hallway, much to his annoyance. She wasn't sure if she could trust him with the knowledge of her secret workshop. Keeping it hidden—even from the one person who knew her real identity—was important to her.

As Lauren slipped past a line of cars turning into a parking lot, she reached into the glove box and retrieved her driving glasses. She couldn't explain why, but all the street lights and headlights heavily strained her eyes. Normally, the city's light pollution blocked out the sky on a clear night like tonight, but Lauren could see the stars. And not just a handful of the brighter constellations, but the whole damned galaxy of them!

This was weird.

A few tufts of white fell out from her black knit cap when she slid on the sunglasses. Her eyes instantly relaxed behind the dark lenses.

Her passenger was eerily quiet, his eyes closed with his cloth bag wedged against the center console.

The man had said close to nothing since they packed her equipment in the trunk. In fact, the only thing that came out of his mouth was the address to a municipal bus maintenance depot in Free Port's industrial center to the north and to get there quickly. The gave with no indication of what they were going to do there or why. He just slept. Even when she made a few aggressive lane changes, the guy didn't react.

Nearing the freeway, Lauren glanced at him again. She didn't mind silence—she was used to working alone—but this guy unnerved her.

"Sooo," she said loudly. "All that steak and eggs yesterday. Any good?"

Silence.

"You're welcome by the way. Ya know. 'Cause I paid for it."

Nothing.

"Also, I'm, uh, really sorry about biting you . . . that night. For what it's worth, I don't even remember doing it."

"Stop talking," he finally responded.

Lauren winced.

Yeah, he's still sore about that.

The V12 engine roared as she pulled onto the freeway. When Lauren bought the car years ago, the exotics dealer tried to talk her out of it. "The Ferrari Daytona is a man's car, Miss. You wouldn't want something this demanding," he had told her. "No power steering, no power brakes, manual everything. This is a car built for an enthusiast." He had tried to steer her into buying an ugly Mercedes Benz SLK, but Lauren had already fallen in love with the look and sound of the sleek Italian convertible. It made her feel like James Bond—well, Jane Bond if you wanted to split hairs. The smooth, simple red curves, the supple tan leather, and the throaty exhaust. It exuded the perfect blend of sophistication and reckless adventure.

Lauren had to own it—legally, of course. She pulled off quite a few jobs to gather the extra scratch to pay for its hefty price tag. Once she finally bought it, though, it had taken her a full month to get used to the heavy steering and pedals. But she didn't care. It was hers. The first thing Lauren Fox had officially owned. And the only thing that showed off her success to the world.

Tonight, however, the pedals and steering felt feather-light. In fact, everything felt feather-light now.

"Your name's Ethan, right?"

When he didn't say anything, she looked over. His eyes were still closed.

"Hey, are you asleep?"

"Meditating."

"So . . . you're awake then?"

She waited a beat in case he said anything— which he didn't. "So, how long have you been doing this?"

"Doing what?"

Lauren downshifted past a semi-trailer. "Uhh, hunting vampires?"

He growled something under his breath.

"How long?"

Ethan opened his eyes. She caught the angry glare he threw at her.

"You're nervous," he told her.

"Hey, with everything that's happened to me these last few days: the mansion, these changes, *you*!" she gestured to both of them, "you can't blame me for being on edge."

Ethan closed his eyes. "For a professional thief, you talk to much."

She fixed him with a hard glare. "Look, asshole, I've never dealt with anything like this before. What the hell can I expect if I'm supposed to help you?"

He opened his eyes again. "Fair."

Huh. Well, that's progress. "Alright. Where are we going?"

"I told you already. We're going to a bus garage."

"Yeah, but what's there *besides* the buses?"

"Possible vampire activity. Something is supposed to happen at eleven o'clock, and I wanna see it, but I can't get close. Might also do some prep-work for sneaking in later."

"Okay. That sounds doable. What's supposed to happen?"

He kept his eyes on the road. "I don't know."

"What do you mean you don't know?"

A scowl grew on his face.

"Two of the workers spoke of a delivery tonight—something they were bribed to ignore. They said they get paid with something called *Juice*."

Lauren threw him a sideways glance. "How do know they weren't talking about a drug deal?"

"Because they were thralls."

"What are thralls?"

"Minions."

"You mean like hired muscle?"

He thought for a second. "Sort of. Feed a living being a bit of vampiric blood, and you force that person to be a devoted servant for a time. Duration and strength of devotion is determined by the amount of blood given."

Lauren cocked her head at him. "So, like a Renfield?"

"A what?"

"Renfield. Ya know, from Bram Stoker's *Dracula*? He was Dracula's minion. A bit crazy, though. That guy was really unhinged. I think they stuck him in a mental institution."

Ethan ruminated on her example. "I suppose so. But, I haven't read that book in a long time."

"I meant the movie. The one with Keanu and Anthony   Hopkins?"

"They made another movie?"

Lauren quickly passed a slow car.

"Yeah, it was a big thing a few years back. I think there was a controversy about it because Keanu didn't have a good English accent. You didn't see it?"

"No."

She drove on for a few miles in awkward silence. After passing another exit ramp, she spoke up again.

"What's the layout of this place? Is it completely enclosed or open air?"

"Both."

"Did you notice any security measures? Cameras, alarm systems, guards, that sort of stuff?"

"I didn't see anything besides guards."

She grimaced. "Okay . . . Is the place fenced in?"

"Yes."

"How? Is it see-through like a chain link fence, or is it walled off for privacy?"

"Eight foot brick wall."

From the side of her eye, Lauren noticed Ethan looking at her with a raised eyebrow. "What? Why are you looking at me like that?"

"I thought you were nervous."

She shrugged. "I'm a thief. Sneaking into places is what I'm good at. It's what I do. And any good thief knows what she's getting into."

"Right."

"Good," she eased back into her seat. Looking back, she nodded to his bagged sword. "What's that for then?"

He turned to her. "In case I need it."

Her fingers tightened on the steering wheel. In case he needed it *for her*, right? she thought. "Let's get one thing straight: I don't like violence. I'm not a fighter. I avoid confrontation in my line of work."

Ethan turned back to the road. "Don't worry. We're not going there to take anyone out tonight."

Lauren hoped to hell he was right. Shifting gears, she drove into the night.

They arrived near the bus depot at a quarter to eleven.

After stashing her car in one of the middle levels of an empty parking structure, Lauren followed Ethan north to their destination on foot. They each shouldered a large black canvas bag from the trunk. A fully lit up chemical bottling plant stretched in front of the bus depot. The facility spanned three entire blocks of tangled pipes, mazes of scaffolding, and multiple distillation towers ringed with catwalks. Amber sodium lights sprinkled the entire complex, leaving few shadows save from under the bundles of pipes or the parts of the perimeter too far from the light towers. Multiple graffiti tags marked many of the structures despite the whole place being ringed by an eight foot high chain-link fence topped with loops upon loops of razor wire.

The place was nearly vacant—only a handful of security guards patrolled the perimeter either in a marked pickup truck or walking around the lone three story building off to the south.

Lauren crouched next to Ethan in the shadows between street lights. She clocked the roving patrol truck slowly creep by. To her surprise, she saw the guard clearly and sharply from across the street and the same distance past the fence. The glow of the truck's gauge cluster gave the heavy bags under the man's eyes a faint bluish-green outline. His face twisted, and the vehicle suddenly stopped. The man climbed out and approached the front of them. Lauren tensed, ready to run. As silently as possible, Lauren slipped a hand inside her coat.

Ethan halted her with a hand on her arm. His shadowed face was calm as stone. Through the darkness, Lauren saw the subtle shake of his head, and his eyes quickly flashed golden for a beat. Suddenly, she heard the clear sound of a zipper. Snapping her head towards the abrupt noise, she watched the guard begin to urinate. Lauren recoiled from the acrid ammonia stench that drifted across the street. After a full minute, the guard shook himself, zipped up, and ambled back into the truck. The truck drove off, and her shoulders loosened.

Once it passed out of view, Ethan, eyes now golden again, crossed the street and somersaulted effortlessly over the razor fence. He landed smoothly and immediately beckoned her over. She tossed him an incredulous look, but recalled her disastrous leap between buildings the other night. Was he expecting her to try that again? Ethan stood up and waved her over again with annoyed vigor.

With a deep breath, Lauren gathered herself and jumped. Much to her amazement, she sailed high over the coils of concertina wire with inches to spare. Unfortunately, she misjudged the fence and fell down hard a few yards ahead of Ethan. Lauren rolled twice on the loosely packed gravel before stopping.

Lauren dragged herself off the ground and brushed off random bits of rock from her black pea coat. It was an expensive jacket, but that quick roll in the rocks had torn open a hole in one of the sleeves. She sighed. Ethan said nothing and started moving. Biting back a curse, she followed close behind.

Bewildered, Lauren eyed Ethan while they ran through the shadowed plant yard. For years, she used a unique set of thermal goggles while on a job. The device helped her keep track of security patrols (like the one just now), locate laser trip wires, or simply see in the dark. She mourned their loss at the mansion, wishing she still had them for tonight. But now, her naked eyes pierced the shadows like a clear, sunny afternoon. Lauren could even see much farther with full clarity, too. Was this another change she was going through? What else was going to happen to her?

She glanced back at the security truck. With the driver-side window rolled down, she could still smell the man. Even through the exhaust and the sharp, chemical tang that blanketed the entire area, she easily picked out his scent. More disturbing, she could tell he had just eaten a greasy cheese-steak.

Lauren had a long history of being quiet and stealthy—she wouldn't be much of a thief if she weren't, but this man baffled her. Not only did he move just a silently as she, he didn't even leave any tracks! They were running full tilt on soft gravel, and he left absolutely no sign of having been there. When they paused for a security camera to pan away, she glanced at his feet. He didn't even sink into the crushed rock!

How the hell is he doing this?

She jumped slightly when Ethan tapped her shoulder. Lauren silently scolded herself: she was better than this. Over a hundred successful jobs, and now she was jumping at the slightest touch. The man pointed to a distillation tower overlooking the depot. His eyes were still glowing with that eerie golden light. The sight unsettled her, especially with her newly sensitive vision.

Swallowing her jitters, she nodded, and they quickly broke for the tower.

When they reached it, Ethan pointed to the top and mimed shooting with his fingers. Seeing what he had in mind, she pulled her piton launcher from under her coat and aimed. It was a long distance shot, but the spike found purchase with a muffled *tung*. When the line drew taught, she gave him a nod. Ethan hooked a thick arm around her waist, and together, they ascended, bypassing multiple stories of well-lit spiraling stairs.

Atop the tower, they commanded a superb view of the bus depot below. Though amber light bathed the plant and everything beneath them, the very top of it remained completely unlit—the perfect place to hide.

Lauren knelt down and removed the canvas bag from her shoulder. The gentle slopping roof was caked with a mixture of dust, dirt, and compacted chemical soot shorn thin by years of wind and rain. It left dark patches on her knees, and every movement kicked up a small cloud.

Taking the second bag from Ethan, she set both down and opened them up. She donned a pair of black gloves from her jacket pocket, careful not to dirty her bare hands on the tower or anything else. She dropped the launcher on the bag and retrieved a large SLR camera and a thick tripod. Next, she pulled a massive two-foot long telephoto lens from the other bag, attached it to the camera body, and then to the tripod before loading a roll of special high-speed film. Lastly, she handed a small pair of binoculars to Ethan.

Finished, Lauren knelt on the bag and peered through the viewfinder.

The depot stretched on forever. Over fifty red city buses with muted silver stripes—some old, some new—were packed into the massive lot with at least half as many dark blue double-length buses. Beyond the yard lay the maintenance building. Harsh flood lights bathed the building perimeter with a cold shade of blue. White light poured out of a half dozen open garage doors lining the facility. A handful of people moved around inside, working under and around buses raised on massive struts shooting up from the floor. Just like he said, an eight foot brick wall surrounded the entire facility. Fifty foot tall tower lights dotted the expansive yard and an adjoining unfenced parking lot. The primary entrance to the facility lay below them, directly in front of their tower. She tested the camera with a couple quick shots of the whole facility.

"Not a bad view you've found here," Lauren noted.

Chill northerly winds whipped around them, biting through her coat. She wrapped her arms tight around her to stop from shivering. Peering through her binoculars, Ethan crouched next to her, motionless. His jacket and shirt billowed loosely in the sharp breeze.

"You're not cold?"

"Cold only bothers you if you let it."

"Of course it doesn't," Lauren muttered, ignoring his condescending look. Grateful he was downwind, she said, "Okay, tough-guy, what are we looking for?"

Ethan swept the binoculars across the sprawling depot, "Until they show up? Strange activity. Anything out of the ordinary."

She slowly panned the big camera left and right. "You still want to sneak into this place later on, right?

"Yep."

"Okay," she said, thinking aloud, "where would the best place be to enter?"

"There's a security post at the main entrance" Ethan noted. "Single guard manning it."

"I see it." She snapped a couple shots, the camera quickly whirred, automatically feeding the next section of film. "No good. Multiple cameras at the post. Even if you could disable them or loop the live feed, the entrance itself is too wide. You'd be out in the open and easily spotted."

Ethan panned further north.

"I see a small gate along the west wall near the

main building."

Lauren took more pictures. "There's a parking lot right next to it. Looks pretty vacant, too, so there's probably not a lot of people here at night. Automated employee entrance, maybe? I see cameras there also. I'm guessing there's a code lock on the gate, or maybe a keycard system. Possible to defeat, but it's too well lit. Easier access to cover once you're through. No security guards there, either."

"Why defeat it when we can just jump over? I'm pointing out access points for reinforcements."

She suddenly remembered the fence earlier. "Oh. Yeah. Well, how would you get in?"

"The wall west of the entrance. No lights there. Could easily jump over unnoticed." Ethan pointed directly below them.

Lauren panned down to the street area. She couldn't see much through the shadow, which she took as a good sign. She felt along the bottom of the lens body and pressed a button, activating the built in starlight system. Her view bloomed with light, recoloring everything in various shades of green. The street lamp near the wall was out, but the bulb and pole looked intact. She saw a pair of security cameras along that stretch of wall, but one of them looked broken, and the other had torn power cables. The wall there sported a multitude of graffiti tags. On the other side, the one tower light in that section was also out. She took shots of the entire area.

"Okay, that could work. But it's a long way to the main building. I see a single guard walking around with a flashlight—foot patrol." She looked to Ethan. "If he's there on foot, there's probably an electrical issue in that part of the area. The cameras there are out of commission, too."

"Notice the graffiti," Ethan said. "It's all along the stone wall surrounding the yard. This area has problems with vandalism. Something to exploit."

"Such as?"

"That patrolling guard looks bored and distracted. Same as the one in the chemical plant. I saw him chase away some kids spraying graffiti early. Security here is probably used to dealing with them breaking cameras, too. Knocking out one or two of them might not attract much attention."

"Huh. Okay, yeah. Good point."

She turned the camera to the main building. Multiple skylights and ventilation stacks dotted the bulging rooftop. There was also a trio of access panels, locked and probably alarmed, but those wouldn't pose her any problems with the proper tools.

"For my money, though, I'd go through the roof. I see a couple points of entry there. No patrols or cameras, and security should be easy to bypass. The eastern side of the building butts right up against the street. We could scale the wall there. If we move fast, we can avoid any cameras or at least a cursory investigation if we have to damage one of them like you suggested."

"If you plan to do that, bring spray paint. Make a half finished tag so they think we ran off."

"Good idea."

She took pictures of the roof and the wall next to the street.

Lauren looked at Ethan from the side of her eye. The prospect of working with this man worried her. She had always worked alone on jobs—no need to rely on someone else keeping their word or screwing things up. But this guy seemed serious enough and noticed things she didn't. And, he could sneak around just as well as she could. He might be able to keep up with her.

Maybe.

But there was something unusual about him— more than just those creepy eyes. How did he know there was a vampire here? And how could he tell all the men were—what did he call them?—thralls? He was still a surly son-of-a-bitch like yesterday, but now he wanted her help instead of her head.

Lauren worked her jaw, still tasting a dreg of pig's blood on her tongue. The lingering flavor pleased her. She squeezed her eyes shut. She felt disgusted by that, and she didn't want to think about it. Just an hour ago, she had downed an entire pint of the stuff, not even thinking about it until it was all over her and the floor. What was she becoming?

The thirst will get you in the end.

Was he right? Was she going to turn into one of them? God, she hoped not. Lauren had to hold it together long enough to reverse this retched condition or to find some sort of cure. But could she trust this guy to stick to his word until then? Would he even stay alive long enough to do that?

Would she?

10 *The World You Knew*

Lauren reached under the lens and deactivated the starlight system. Looking back through the viewfinder, the lens still displayed everything in shades of green. She tried it again. Still green. She rapped it in frustration. Finally, the lens returned to normal. But now it was dirty.

"Cheap, Chinese crap," Lauren mumbled.

"What's that?" Ethan asked, focusing the binoculars.

She quickly unscrewed the lens from the mounted camera. The act would ruin the current section of film, but she had to clean the glass. Lauren removed her gloves and fished out a thin cloth from one of the bags. She noticed him spying her from the corner of her eye.

"Small problem with the camera lens. It's an easy fix, don't worry," she assured him.

"Expensive toys lead to expensive problems."

"Cute saying," she muttered, wiping both ends of the lens body. Reattaching the two pieces, she explained, "I bought this setup on the black market a little before I made friends with a proper supplier. There's no refunds, and you get what you get. Lesson learned, alright?"

"Good for you."

Lauren leaned on the tripod, studying him. His eyes still glowed with the same golden color from before. Their faint yellow reflected off the black metal casing of her binoculars.

"Tell me, does that glowing help you see any better?"

He worked the focusing ring again. "I can see that all of the guards here are thralls."

"Oh yeah? How?"

He lowered the binoculars. "They have pale spots in their aura. Signs of vampire blood in their system. If we have to engage, expect them to be stronger and tougher."

She shook her head in confusion. "Wait. You can see auras? What are you some kind of hippy?"

"Don't be stupid."

"Don't be a prick," Lauren shot back.

Ethan glared at her.

"Well? Why do they glow like that?" she asked.

"Not now."

"Oh c'mon! You know who I really am *and* what I do, and yet I know next to nothing about you."

"I don't care who you are or what you do. Consider your precious little secret safe," he rattled off.

"Oh, I feel so much better," she mocked. "If you're not one of them, then explain to me how the hell can you jump thirty feet in the air, see people's auras or whatever, and walk on gravel without leaving a footprint? How are we supposed to work together if I don't know what you're capable of?"

Ethan sighed, though to her, it sounded more like a growl. He put the binoculars down, his eyes blue again. "Fine. Ask."

Lauren sat down on the empty bag. "Alright. For starters, are you human?"

"What did I just say about being stupid?" he sneered.

Lauren rolled her eyes. "Seriously, what are you, then? Besides an asshole."

Ethan took a deep breath. "Remember all those monster stories you'd hear growing up?"

"Like Dracula?"

"Close enough. People don't believe monsters like that exist. They just go on with their lives like everything is normal. But sometimes, people learn they're real and have been forever. Maybe they survive an attack. Maybe they stumble into one of 'em during dinner time. Either way, a regular person always responds with fear and tries to ignore what they've seen; assuming they survive. But a rare few—one in a million or more—respond with anger and hate.

"Long ago, some of those rare people figured out how to fight back. How to turn their bodies and their faith into weapons and fight the monsters. Those that survived long enough picked out apprentices and handed down all their knowledge and techniques. Over time, those hunters spread out across the world, slowly doling out justice to every vile creature they met— sometimes punishment, sometimes death. They've been doing it for ages. I'm one of them."

"How imaginative," she scoffed.

"Don't believe me? Go look in a mirror."

Dick. "So what do you call yourselves?"

Ethan shrugged. "We're not a sports team; we don't have a name. The man who taught me thought of himself as a soldier for Amaterasu. He took me as his apprentice and passed his knowledge down to me. If I live long enough, it'll be my turn to do the same. But, I don't call myself anything. I just kill the parasites that prey on humanity."

Lauren squinted, her mind stuck on the strange word. "Who taught you?"

"An old Japanese man. He's been doing this for a really long time."

"How long have you been doing it?"

"Long enough."

"No, seriously, how long?"

The expression on his face screamed *Do not go there.* Lauren turned away, getting the message. "Okay," she said uneasily, "what exactly happens when your eyes glow?"

He grumbled again.

"By focusing the spirit in a specific way, it makes your body lighter than air. It enhances your vision, letting you see the spirit—aura—of others. It can also suppress pain. And, if your soul is pure enough, it disrupts the flesh of supernatural beings by touch alone. With enough training, those aspects can be combined and even extended into weapons like blades, clubs, and throwing weapons.

"But it requires lots of physical conditioning and meditation just to even begin the learning process. And, there's a trade off, too. All that focus burns through your body's energy fast. Do it for too long, and you'll pass out from exhaustion. Keep going past that, you can kill yourself."

Lauren looked back through the camera and checked for movement. She remembered the burning pain when he held her down last night. It felt like he had pressed a white-hot iron against her skin.

"My arm felt like it was going to melt off when you held me down last night," she said, sullen. "I guess that means I *am* one of them now, doesn't it?"

Ethan regarded her for a beat. "Maybe."

"Maybe?"

"Your aura is different."

"How? What does it look like?" she perked up, a hint of hope in her words.

His eyes began to glow, and he focused his gaze on her. She felt uncomfortable, as if her father was judging her again.

"Right now, you're surrounded in a halo of silver with orange highlights all filled with static like an old television set on the fritz, and it sparks at the edges. The colors are pale and muted. It also pulses with a heartbeat. A *living* heartbeat."

She looked down at her hands as if she could see the colors he just described dancing around them.

"What does all that mean?"

"For starters, it means you're sad and anxious. Also, slightly afraid."

"You need magical powers to figure that out?" she mumbled under her breath.

"The paleness indicates you're a vampire."

She winced. "Is that normal?"

"No. Vampires are dead. They have no heartbeat. That's why they're cold to the touch. But you still have one."

"How is that possible?"

He shrugged again. "I've heard of stories about half-breeds before. But they're just legends: a child of a vampire and a human and so on. I watched them make you like this. How, I don't know. I'm not a scholar. You don't learn shit like this in a school or a library. All I have is a collection of stories and experience, all handed down from master to apprentice: do this, don't do that, here's how, and—if you're lucky—why."

"How much *do* you know?"

"More than you. The things aren't exactly eager to tell us all their secrets."

"Do you know how a regular vampire is made, then?"

Ethan adjusted his footing.

"From what I've seen, vampires don't make more of themselves on a whim. More of them means more competition for food; more chances for exposure. But, when they do want to add someone to their ranks, they have to kill you first—the transformation will only work on a dead body. Once the heart stops, the vampire puts some of his own blood into the corpse. After that, the candidate wakes up the next night, a brand new parasite with all their strengths and weaknesses. And they are always very, *very* hungry."

Lauren's throat tightened. She remembered waking up after the mansion feeling dazed and completely parched. She had stumbled into the bathroom to splash some water on her face before noticing her reflection in the mirror. The memory still made her blood freeze.

"But you were alive when I pulled you off that altar," Ethan continued. "And you were still alive when I got you to your home. I watched over you and saw zero change—hell, I thought you were getting better. And unless I'm missing something, your heart never stopped beating the entire time. Yet, despite all that, you went into a massive seizure. When I held you down, you shot up and tried to drain me like any other vampire—fangs and all.

"Now, your aura is pale like theirs. It also sparks—something I've never seen before. And you still have a heartbeat, which like I said, vampires don't have. So, I've got no answer for what happened to you. Whatever that ritual was, it made you this way. For what purpose, I have no clue."

"Can it be reversed?" she venture hesitantly.

He shook his head. "If I knew what the hell they were doing, I don't know, maybe. But even then, who knows? There was a lot of funky stuff happening that night, and I know next to nothing about magic."

Lauren hung her head. This was all too much for her to take in. Never had she dreamed of vampires being real let alone getting turned into one against her will. Who would even want that?

She stared into the plant yard. The security truck slowly made another round of the perimeter, oblivious to them. It approached the path she and Ethan had taken, and she tensed up. When it rolled on, she let out a short sigh of relief. She didn't feel relieved, though. She wanted her life back. There had to be a way out of this. No situation was hopeless. Lauren thought her childhood was hopeless, and she had escaped that. All it took was time and planning. She just needed to understand what had happened.

With a deep breath, Lauren pushed out the despair. "So then . . . why do I look like this?" She pulled down a tuft of white hair.

Ethan shrugged. "You looked normal when you bit me."

Bit him. God, was that a precursor for the rest of her life now? "I meant it earlier when I apologized for that," she conceded.

He looked out to the depot. "I heard you the first time. You took a lot of my blood with that bite. Passed out right after I ripped you off me. It was noon when I came too, and even then I was still woozy. I needed food, and you had nothing but crap in your kitchen, so I grabbed your keys and wallet and went to a diner I knew. Barely made it to the garage without breaking my neck. I planned to check on you after, but you found me instead, and when I saw your aura, I figured it was too late. It wasn't until the rooftop that I noticed your heartbeat."

"But you left me at the diner and kept trying to run away. Why?"

Ethan opened his mouth to answer, but something at the bus depot grabbed his attention. He quickly snatched the binoculars. "Wait. Something's coming."

Down below, two unmarked cargo trucks pulled up to the main entrance. Three black Chevy Suburbans escorted them—two leading and one following. The security guard raised the barrier and waved the caravan inside. The vehicles came to a halt next to the main building and waited there for a minute before turning off their engines.

The doors on the black Suburbans opened, and twelve black clad men with submachine guns slung over their shoulders stepped out along with a single man in a dark suit. He was very pale and began directing half of them to spread out around the trucks and SUVs, while the rest stayed by the rear cargo doors. The man pulled out a cell phone and began speaking, and three men in transportation uniforms exited the main building seconds later. They walked over to the caravan, spoke to the suited man for a minute, and headed off towards the mass of parked buses.

Lauren snapped pictures of the entire exchange.

"Those men in black. My memory is still fuzzy, but, they look like the heavies from the mansion," she noted.

"They're thralls, all of them. The suit is a vampire."

As they watched, the vampire waved the parked red buses over. Three of them rumbled to life at once and pulled up next to the two trucks. The remaining heavies gathered next to the cargo doors. One of them raised the rear door of each truck while another rolled a set of yellow mobile stairs against them. Inside, people stood shoulder to shoulder like at the meat market. They looked dazed and inebriated. On a signal from the vampire, the heavies began herding the disheveled people into the waiting buses.

"What are they doing?" Lauren spoke.

"Best guess? Transferring feeding stock."

Lauren zoomed in on one of the people from the trucks. His clothes looked ragged and piled on with miss-matched shoes and baggy pants filled with holes. She saw at least two distressed jackets on the man, both full of large, different-colored stains from who-knows-what. Two heavies hauled him onto one of the waiting city buses. His head lolled around while a guard prodded him inside with his gun. The process was slow and degrading.

"They look drugged," she said.

"No need to damage the food that way. Look at 'em, they're all homeless. This is the first time I've seen so many of them in one place. So far I've only seen 'em on buses. They must be rounding them up from all over the area."

"Why would they do that?" she sneered, still snapping photos.

"Best guess? Meals on wheels." He glanced at her with a look of utter contempt that she hoped wasn't directed at her.

Over the years, Free Port had boasted a stellar record when it came to dealing with its homeless population. The city council had sponsored numerous soup kitchens and shelters for the homeless and derelicts. The police kept the streets clean of vagrants—only a handful of encampments existed, and they were notoriously small and tightly packed. Representatives from all over the eastern seaboard regularly visited the city to learn how it dealt with the homeless. Was this the secret of how it was handled? If Ethan's hypothesis was right, and these people were rounded up for food, then this operation had been going on for years.

Scorn twisted her face behind the camera. "This is heinous."

A ragged looking man suddenly jumped out one of the trucks and bolted for the exit. The homeless man was near the exit when a single shot rang out. The derelict collapsed, a dark splatter of blood pooling beneath his head. The vampire tucked a large pistol back into his suit as a banker did his wallet. Two heavies quickly stuffed the body into a trash bag and tossed it one of the trucks while another sopped up the blood with the homeless man's clothes.

"Guess not all of 'em are drugged," Ethan remarked callously.

They continued their surveillance as the process dragged on. Lauren checked her watch. It was half past midnight when the first bus finished loading up. She noticed that the homeless were being separated by sex. The males went to the first two buses and the females were stuffed into the third.

The camera suddenly reached the end of the film roll. Lauren quickly wound it up and ejected it. Sticking the roll in her coat pocket, she furiously sifted through the camera bag for a new one. Fresh film in hand, Lauren quickly loaded the camera and snapped a shot to cycle the first frame. From the side of her eye, she noticed Ethan shoot to his feet, rapidly adjusting the focusing ring. Lauren promptly tracked his view through the camera. A younger looking girl with a tangle of matted blonde hair had just been yanked from the trucks. A thin waif, her eyes were sunken and her skin was sallow with a distinctive mole just under her left cheek—a beauty mark. Lauren snapped a few pictures of her being loaded onto the third bus before looking back to Ethan. His jaw was tight, like his teeth were about to crack.

"Hey, are you alright?" she asked.

He answered her by dropping the binoculars and pulling the sack off his sword. The scabbard was black with a dirty red silk cord tightly wrapped around length of it. Ethan swiftly looped a loose leather strap connecting the top to the bottom of it over his torso and stuffed the bag inside his coat. He snatched up her piton launcher.

Surprised, Lauren blurted, "What're you doing?!"

Ethan fumbled with the gun for a second. "You

stay here."

He aimed at the catwalk directly beneath them and fired. A loud, metallic clang echoed off the rusted grating. Lauren immediately stood up.

"You said we were just going to watch them! What the hell are you doing?!?"

Ethan moved to the edge of the tower, gun in hand. He looked back at her. His eyes were glowing brightly now. "I said, stay here!" he commanded.

With that, he leaped off the tower. He plummeted past the spiraling stairs before pressing the button on the gun's winch and arresting his descent, arcing down towards the tall structure. He landed against one of the lower catwalks, compressed his body, and launched out horizontally. Letting go of the gun, Ethan sailed over the chain-link fence on the way down, tucking and rolling as he landed on the unforgiving pavement. Coming to his feet, he sprinted toward the bus depot.

Lauren watched her "partner" abandon their stakeout in a most spectacular fashion. Her launcher knocked against the hollow catwalk.

"How the hell am *I* supposed to get down!?" she shouted.

11 Howlin' for You

*I*n a single bound, Ethan perched atop of the brick wall overlooking the bus yard. The vampire lazily puffed his cigarette while watching the armed thralls continued to transfer the drugged chattel into the awaiting buses.

She's alive!

Ethan's mind was abuzz with thoughts. For years, he foolishly hoped that his sister hadn't died that night. Sensei had reminded him time and time again that she was gone. It was the last thing the old man told him: She is gone; you need to forget her.

But, deep down, Ethan refused to give up. That hope had kept him going through all those years of training. And that girl just now looked so much like her! He had always teased her about the mole under her left eye. And that girl had one just like it. In the same place, too! Same mole. Same hair.

He had to look into her eyes.

He *had* to know if it was her.

A strong breeze blew at Ethan's back. When the wind reached him, the vampire sniffed the air and went stiff. He looked out over the yard, alert. Shouting and movement erupted from the cargo trucks. Flashlights immediately danced as the black-clad thralls fanned out into the depot. The vampire started pointing in Ethan's direction quickly followed by sporadic gunfire.

He immediately froze. He was already made.

A handful of the homeless men broke for the parked buses. More gunfire. A few of them fell and the rest scattered into the grouped vehicles. Four of the black clad thralls chased a group into the grid of tightly packed buses to his right. Flashlights bounced between them, he thralls slowly making their way south, their beams occasionally shining through the windows and gaps. Three more armed thralls marched down the double-length buses sitting directly in front of Ethan. They played their lights through the windows for the other runaways.

More indistinct shouting came from up ahead. A thrall climbed onto one of the cargo trucks and swept his flashlight across the lot. A moment later, the vampire leaped up next to him and began directing the thrall's light. The white beam swept across the parked vehicles. Ethan dropped off the wall just before the flashlight revealed him. He landed next to a trio of squat, sand-colored shipping containers arrayed in front of the buses.

Bent low, he padded up to the nearest container and concentrated until all the thralls bloomed into his mind's eye. Across the central lane, four of them slowly searched through the lot of single buses. Surprisingly, only three of them were thralls—one was a fully fledged vampire, probably recently turned. Three more of them hunted through the double buses directly ahead. With none of the thralls looking in his direction, Ethan quickly crossed to the next container.

Moving up to the corner, he noticed a single flashlight beam bobbing on the ground behind him. It's owner was came from the north—the lone foot patrol. Silently sliding to the end of far container, Ethan readied his big hunting knife. As the thrall crossed into view, Ethan buried the blade under the security guard's jaw. The flashlight clattered on the ground. Surprise locked the man's eyes wide while life left him. He was the same man that had threatened to shoot him earlier.

Ethan pulled the dead guard behind the containers and kicked the flashlight behind him. Droplets of blood sprayed against the sandy metal box when he wrenched the knife free. He laid the body on the ground and deactivated the light.

"Holy shit!"

Ethan looked up to see Lauren drop from the stone wall. Outrage silently oozed from the woman seeing him wipe the knife on the dead guard's trouser sleeve. Expertly, she dodged the errant beams of light on her way to him. Soot smeared her knees, and disgust deformed her heart-shaped face. She gestured furiously at the dead body, chastising him with her eyes.

"What the fuck are you doing?!" she exclaimed, her voice barely hushed.

"I told you to stay on the tower," he scolded with the same hushed tone.

"And you said we were just going to watch this place and sneak in *later*!"

Ethan knelt down and searched the guard, retrieving a set of keys and his sidearm. He then rifled through the man's wallet and stuffed the handful of bills into his own pocket. He tucked the keys into his jacket and checked the gun's chamber.

"The plan changed."

Ethan handed Lauren the pistol, butt first.

She refused the weapon. "What do you mean *the plan changed*?!"

"I need to see those buses up close." He pushed it back into her hands, Take it."

"What am I supposed to do with this?!"

"You're the one who said you can't fight. Even the odds."

She looked at the pistol in his hand. It was an old Beretta 9mm. Lauren shook her head, but dropped the pistol in a jacket pocket.

"Did you have to kill the guy?" Lauren pointed to the dead security guard.

"He would have alerted the others. Besides, he's one of them."

"A vampire?"

"No. A thrall, remember?"

She scowled blackly at him, disgust still painting her face. "I heard gunfire while I was coming down. What did you do?"

"It wasn't me," Ethan shook his head. "Some more homeless escaped, and it looks like they're searching for the rest."

Ethan tucked the body next to the western-most container. The shadows were pretty thick there. It should help conceal it for as long as possible.

Lauren stood close behind him. "When I saw all those heavies spreading out into the lot, I thought they were looking for you."

"Is that why you chased after me? You were worried?"

"Don't get your hopes up, asshole." She held her hands on her hips. "I'd love nothing more than to be rid of you, but this?" she pointed to her eyes. "This is different. I can't just open up the yellow pages and look up *vampire whisperer*. You're all I've got. And, if you're going to charge into a nest of armed men, half-cocked with just a *fucking sword*, you're damned right I'm coming after you! Somebody has to make sure you don't get yourself killed before I can get rid of whatever the fuck is happening to me!"

Eyes glowing, Ethan thrust a finger at her furious look. "I am not babysitting you."

Lauren was about to fire off a comeback when her face twisted and she sniffed the air. Ethan sensed it a split second later—a thrall, and he was drawing close. One of the men in black tactical gear stepped out between the two containers. Ethan reached for his sword, but Lauren pushed him against the metal wall, nearly tripping him over the dead body. Grabbing his temples, she kissed him just when the thrall turned.

For the first time since leaving Sensei, Ethan was completely taken by surprise.

"What the hell?!" the thrall stopped short at the sight of the two, painting them with the flashlight on his gun. The guard's face scrunched while the filthy pair went at it.

"Crazy fucking addicts. Get back to the bus!" he barked, raising his weapon.

Ethan felt Lauren's canines grow as she forced herself on him. He winced when one of the razor sharp teeth tore his lip and drew blood. She moaned, but the noise sounded more like pain than pleasure. Concentrating hard against the paralyzing euphoria, he frantically dug his right hand underneath his jacket. Finding his rear pocket, Ethan pushed Lauren with full force. She stumbled back, and he flung a trio of razor sharp metal stars at the thrall. They thudded into the man's upper chest, throat, and eye with three spurts of blood. Shock immobilized his remaining eye. The guard fell to the ground, grabbing at the star wedged into his throat.

Stumbling off the container, Ethan spat out a wad of blood and saliva, slightly dazed. "Fucking, bitch. You bit me!"

Lauren feverishly wiped the red spittle off her mouth with her sleeve. "Oh, God!! I think I'm gonna puke!" she rasped, bent over, retching. Ethan dragged the body next to the other one.

"Never do that again!" Ethan thrust a finger at her. "Do you hear me!?"

"Ugh, what the fuck is wrong with you? You're like tasting acid!" Lauren gagged, ejecting more fluid.

He ignored her and pulled the stars from the

body. He noticed a fourth object embedded in the chest. Wiping the blood from it, he inspected the blade in the moonlight with an arched eyebrow. It was a long, flat knife, matte black and razor sharp. Looking back to the body, he noticed that the thing had pierced the thrall's kevlar combat vest and the sternum.

Lauren quickly snatched the knife out of his hand and returned it under her coat.

"I told you I can handle myself." she snapped, her voice still raspy.

The same belt from her fancy black suit wrapped snugly around her hips under her coat. Her blocky climbing gun dangled from a clip over her right leg, and multiple black pouches of differing shapes and sizes filled the belt all the way around.

The woman nervously felt her lips after buttoning her coat. Ethan hoped that act was just a one-off stunt to distract the guard. More so, he hoped her teeth was an accident, too, because the opposite worried him far more than the possibility of another infatuated tag-along.

"Is that how you can tell they're a thrall?" she murmured. "Blood in the iris?"

Ethan leaned against the corner facing the lane. Behind him, she goggled at the two bodies wedged against the container. Her hand tentatively reached for the black-clad thrall's eye but pulled back.

"Yes. But it's easier to just view their aura."

Lauren glared at him. "Hmpf. Easy for you to say . . ."

"What was that?" he remarked.

"Nothing."

"If you're gonna follow me around, then stick close and stay down."

Replacing the cleaned throwing stars back in his pocket, Ethan fished out his balaclava hanging from his belt. He flapped it out and pulled it over his head, covering everything from the neck up except a wide strip across his eyes. Watching him, Lauren popped off her knit cap and pierced two holes in it with one of her blades, covering her upper face like a makeshift mask. Her hair had to hang loose to make it fit, so she tucked the long white strands into her jacket.

Shouting erupted from the collection of red buses. Flashlights danced frantically between the vehicles before suddenly converging on one point. Moments later, two thralls appeared in the boulevard dragging a homeless man by the feet, shrieking and thrashing like a rabid animal. A third thrall whacked the man limp with the butt of his gun. The fourth one followed close behind, chuckling. The thrall standing on the truck trained his flashlight on the group returning to the loading area.

The vampire began shouting to the men searching through the lot of blue double buses. Their lights bobbed up and down faster, flashing underneath the vehicles. Two of them started forcing open doors and searching the interiors.

With all the attention focused on the captured runaway, now was the best time to move. Ethan waved Lauren forward and together they scurried across the open boulevard. A quick spot-check told him the coast clear. He made to move when Lauren slapped him on the shoulder.

"Hey, jackass!" She pointed across to the buses they just left. "That heavy hitter is about to find your handiwork. We need to do something, or we're screwed."

Across the way, a single thrall had broken off to the south. She was right—he would reach the containers with the two dead bodies soon, and their presence would be blown. The buses would drive away before he could confirm that girl's identity. Or the men would open fire and force him to abandon everything so far. Either way, Ethan needed to get to those loaded buses without being seen.

He needed distraction.

"That pistol I gave you. Fire a few shots into the air and run towards the chemical plant to the south. You should be able to loose them if you get back to the tower."

She heartily disagreed. "What?! No! That'll just put everyone on alert. They'll start searching even more aggressively."

"I need to distract them," he demanded.

"Watch and learn, Rambo."

Lauren drew the pneumatic pistol from her belt and shoved him aside. She aimed at a blue bus and fired. The piton spiraled over the boulevard and struck a side window on the center bus, shattering it into a hundred pieces. All the flashlights abruptly fixated on the sudden noise. Even the thrall that had split off whipped around at the sound. She quickly retracted the line before the men converged on the broken window. Lauren returned the gun under her coat.

"Done," she said with a satisfied grin. She brushed past him and headed into the empty bus lane.

Ethan sighed.

It was only the first night, and he was already regretting this little partnership.

12 Breaking and Entering

Lauren reached the end of the line of buses.

A large refueling station opened up in front of her. Its long awning extended all the way to the first set of garage doors. Dim fluorescent lights hummed and pulsed rapidly from malfunctioning ballasts attached to the ceiling. Liquid-filled ruts carved from countless bus tires marred the old black top around four smelly pumps. Everything had thick coat of exhaust soot, and the entire place reeked heavily of diesel vapor—metallic and bitter.

Over by the main building, the cargo trucks were nearly empty. Two heavies busily forced the last of the homeless into the final bus while another pair tossed two limp bodies wrapped in plastic into one of trucks. A different pair of heavies entered each bus and checked all the doped-up homeless inside. Behind them, two more hauled the last escapee onto the awaiting buses. Once they were all loaded, the man in the suit jumped off the cargo truck, with the heavy climbing down after him.

Ethan crept next to her and pointed upwards before swiftly vaulting onto the bus to his right. He then leapt across the huge gap onto the awning in an unearthly athletic display.

"Right. Okay. My turn," Lauren encouraged herself, rubbing her hands together.

After a couple of false starts, she bounded to the top of the bus. Seeing the distance to the awning first hand, she backed up to the middle of the roof and gave a good running start. Stepping off the edge, she flew high over the gap but, like the alleyway yesterday, fell short by a foot and slammed against the metal ledge. While she hung there, legs kicking wildly for purchase, the three loaded buses rumbled around for the exit. They slowly lurched forward, their headlights bathing entire swathes of the yard.

"Hey! Hey!!" she hissed. "Gimmie a hand, damnit!"

Ethan rushed over and dragged her onto the platform, kicking up a small dust cloud in her wake just as the lights swept across the awning.

Coughing, she peered through the cloud of dust to see Ethan crouched behind the awning's high lip. Avoiding all the electrical conduits and other trip hazards, she settled next to him. They watched the three buses drive down the boulevard below them. Next to her, Ethan quickly scribbled the numbers down in a small notebook while Lauren silently read them off: 2935, 4687, and 2046. Four of the heavies piled into an SUV and followed the big vehicles out of the depot with the two cargo trucks leaving shortly after.

Once all the vehicles had left, the vampire retrieved his cellphone from his coat pocket. He slowly idled towards the fuel station as he dialed. Lauren peeked over the edge. His pale face glowed a bluish-green from his phone, contrasting harshly against his dark gray suit. He wore a maroon tie and matching pocket square. His dark hair was close cropped and combed back. Through the thick odor of fuel, she caught a faint scent of ash from him. And something else, something old and musty like the butcher but leagues stronger.

The vampire came to a stop underneath them. She could almost hear the voice on the phone.

"Yes, it's done." His voice was smooth and sinister, with a smoker's rasp. "No. There were no complications."

A pause. It sounded like the person on the other end was shouting.

"We handled it."

More shouting.

"I said, we handled it! There's no one else here but our people. No one heard the shots. We're fine." Resentment laced his words.

Another pause, quieter this time. He looked out over the yard.

"I noticed that. Want me to take care of it?"

More quiet talking.

"Are you sure?"

Lauren glanced at Ethan. He was watching the phone conversation, too.

"What do you want to do about it?"

The vampire listened for a beat and then waved over one of his heavies. The armed hitter trotted over. The equipment stuffed in his vest ruffled softly with every step. He pocketed the cellphone and turned to the thrall.

"Two of you to come with me. The rest here and watch the building. Nobody comes in or out."

The man went back to the others, gave them their orders, and returned with a second one. The two then followed the vampire into the building. Ethan moved to the middle of the awning, pocketing his book and pen. Lauren followed.

"Well? You got your look at the buses. Are you satisfied now?"

Ethan shook his head. "Not yet. You said you can break into the building through the roof?"

"I said the security would be easier to bypass."

"But can you do it?"

Lauren blinked. "Wait. Now?"

"Can you get inside?" he asked pointedly.

"Haven't we done enough already?" she exasperated. "We have to plan this out and come back with proper tools."

"No time. I need to know where that bus is going, now. Are you a thief or not?"

She glared at him. This was definitely not what they had agreed on. Ethan looked out over the bus yard. The rest of the men lazily spread out, watching the depot. Some lit up cigarettes and began chatting. He looked back at her.

"Alright. No one's watching. If we move now, we can jump over there unnoticed."

She gazed at the building, judging the distance from the awning to the roof. The gap between the two looked even wider than the first jump. Ethan shuffled to the edge. He took a short running jump and launched high across the gap. He caught a window sill with both hands and pulled with such ease that he shot up a good ten feet, effortlessly clearing the roof. Reappearing over the edge, he signaled for her to follow.

Lauren had dedicated a large portion of her youth to gymnastics. Years of working on pommel horses and balance beams at schools and private gyms had perfected her grace and poise, and over a hundred jobs entering from rooftops and balconies had stripped her of any fear of heights. And this fucking guy casually made her look like a damn amateur.

"Show off," she breathed.

She drew her piton launcher, aimed, and shot. With a hiss of compressed gas and a *thwip* of uncoiling wire, the spike embedded itself inches below Ethan. She smirked, wondering what missing the wall would have looked like. She activated the winch and quietly mantled onto the old brick building in a matter of seconds.

The roof swelled before her like a snowy large hill. Years of weather faded the once white commercial shingles to a dull, dirty gray. A thick layer of weathered dust blanketed the building the same as the distillation tower. Ventilation units sat on rusted metal stilts at regular intervals across the building. Skylights lit up portions of the old tile a dull, milky orange.

Lauren trailed behind Ethan, stepping carefully not to slip on the loose shingle grains. Meanwhile, he trotted along unhindered, swiftly moving to the nearest darkened roof access. He stooped down and examined the raised metal panel. Halfway there, she spotted a collection of painted electrical wires snaking from it into a curved conduit pipe poking out the roof tiles.

It was an alarm.

And Ethan didn't see it.

"Stop that!" she whispered loudly, finally reaching him. Ethan froze, his fingers under the lip around the panel. She swatted his hands away and pointed to the wires snaking off into the distance. "There's an alarm on this thing. Give me a minute before you royally fuck up."

Lauren shooed him away and inspected the panel. It was long, about five feet by three feet and slightly raised—standard emergency hatch. Following the wires she found an infrared transfer beam tucked under the lip inches where his fingers just were. That damned oaf nearly tripped it! She pulled a neatly folded bundle of aluminum foil from her belt. Gingerly tearing off a strip, Lauren gently slid it between the beam sensors and then fastened it into place with a piece of tape.

Breath held, she waited a second for any sound of alarm from the garage down below. When nothing happened, she let out a soft sigh of relief. Under normal circumstances Lauren had a special tool for disabling electric alarms such like this, but Ethan's impatience forced her to improvise with older, less elegant tricks.

"Alright. That should take care of the alarm," she said to herself, standing up.

On the rim of the panel, a simple padlock hung from the handle. Straddling the thing, Lauren grasped the padlock and held her ear as close as she could manage. It had been years since she had cracked one of these. She spun the dial around a few times to reset it and then turned it slowly. She listened intently for the clack of metal. Feeling for the ever-so-slight bump each disk made had always given her problems. Not impossible, just slow going.

Not this time, however.

Even with the uncomfortable distraction of Ethan watching her, she felt each bump in the padlock as easily as walking barefoot over spilled rocks. She heard the disks loud and clear. In less than a minute, the padlock clicked open. Lauren shut her eyes, remembering the spilled cup—all this new sensitivity came with a terrifying price.

A small twist handle with a key slot was the last thing in her way. She unhooked a large pouch from her belt and unfurled her lock picks. Forcing open the dust cover over the key hole, Lauren went to work on the lock. As she felt for the subtle indents of the tumblers, a cluster of keys in a dirty hand wrapped in boxing tape appeared at the corner of her eye.

"Will any of these work?"

Lauren looked at the keys and then at Ethan. With a sharp breath, she snatched them from his palm and returned her picks to their pouch. One by one, she tested each key on the lock. After the seventh try, it turned and the access panel popped loose. She stood up and dumped the keyring back in Ethan's hand.

The hatch opened with a painful creak. The first

thing to hit her was the smell. The scent of acrid, dry-rotted rubber marched hand-in-hand with the sour tang of engine lubricants and fuel on top old, musty wood. Lauren pinched her nose, forcing herself not to gag. She wished she had a full face mask right now. She wished she had her suit right now.

A wooden ladder descended through dark rafters all the way to the garage floor below. Fluorescent panels hanging from long chains bathed the cavernous room with harsh white light, leaving the wooden beams above in shadow. A spider's web of red sprinkler pipes and gray galvanized conduits expanded out across the bottom of the rafters, occasionally dropping down and connecting to the stationary diagnostic machines or into the floor itself. Here and there, black vinyl vacuum hoses snaked around the matte gray steel pillars and lead to a loudly buzzing vacuum system nestled in a far corner.

CCTV cameras stood vigil high up on the front wall, one over each rollup door. Red and black tool chests and carts cluttered the lanes between five buses raised up on massive hydraulic jacks—each one at a different height. The western most lane was empty, its jacks flush with the ground. A long catwalk ran along the back wall connecting a few small mezzanines to a raised office that overlooked the empty space. Racks and racks of body panels, engine parts, spare seats, and massive tires lined the wall it. A handful of mechanics in dirty overalls busied themselves down below. The metallic rattle and clatter of wrenches and ratchets echoed throughout the open area, punctuated by the occasional chatter of pneumatic tools.

Ethan silently descended into the rafters first and lightly perched on the nearest wood beam. Behind him, Lauren mounted the old ladder. It looked ancient and brittle with a hardened layer of dust like a fuzzy coat of paint earned from years of neglect. She climbed down, careful not to put any weight on the center of the wooden rungs. With a short hop, she steadied herself on the beam next to him. Ethan didn't react to her, nor did he budge. His eyes were closed, locked in some kind of concentration. Sidling up to him, she wondered what the hell he was doing. Was now really the time to meditate again?

Lauren reached for his shoulder when Ethan opened his glowing eyes, startling her. She grabbed a vertical strut to steady herself and threw him a nasty look in response. He pointed to the office on the mezzanine on the other side of the garage. Nodding for her to follow, Ethan pushed off to the next set of rafters. He flew across the gap and easily latched onto the upright beam. To her amazement, the man made no sound at all. He didn't even disturb the layer of dust! Ethan climbed on and waved her forward.

Lauren stared at the gulf between them in disbelief.

Ever since she had struck out on her own, every job Lauren took, regardless of scope, was meticulously planned out ahead of time. Even her most impulsive personal escapades required some bit of forethought. From the layout of the target area, to construction records, to shift rotation, to police response times, there was always a specific tool to use or new technique to acquire or knowledge to learn to circumvent whatever security standing in her way. Dealing with personnel was no different: avoid or distract. And if that wasn't possible, there was always someone who could be bribed to look the other way.

But, she always had some sort of safety net to fall back on, be it her suit, a climbing harness, or just her piton launcher. Every job was a riddle to be solved with the right tool or skill, and she preferred it that way. Risks could always be mitigated with enough planning. Yet, here she was breaking into a garage with barely any prep or tools, and on top of that, she was about to make a suicidal leap between two distant sets of rafters.

The shit he was doing tonight was careless and stupid and reckless, and she loathed every second of it.

Hesitantly, Lauren edged to the lip of the beam. She looked down to see one of the mechanics digging through a toolbox directly below her. The distance to Ethan looked no further than seven or so yards—easy for a running jump—but one slip, one mishap, and she'd be broken over all those boxes and carts.

Ethan waved at her more vigorously.

Gripping the uprights, Lauren steeled herself.

This man will be the death of me.

With a deep inhale pushed off with all her strength. For one solid second, the world around her slowed to a breathless standstill, floating weightlessly through the twenty foot void. The mechanics below froze in place. Even a white-gray puff of cigarette smoke hovered in place. Her hands and feet stretched out in front of her with anxiously glacial speed.

Real-time instantly rushed back to normal when she grabbed the support struts next to Ethan. Astounded, Lauren pulled herself onto the beam, but her foot slipped, and she fell. In a flash Ethan snatched her wrist. Lauren hung there in his burning grasp. A loud metallic clang suddenly rang out, and her mind instantly jumped to the worst scenario.

Down below, a mechanic picked up the large crescent wrench at his feet with an audible grunt. Straining silently, Ethan hauled her back up. The mechanic went back to work.

Lauren blew a sigh of relief.

Rubbing the burning pain from her wrist, she looked back to Ethan to thank him. He was already jumping to the next rafter.

Beam by beam, the two stealthily hopped their way over to the mezzanine office. The two heavies from outside now stood guard on the catwalk that surrounded the raised room. One stood by the door, looking out over the work area, while the other slowly paced around the small building.

Ethan maneuvered around the vertical beams until he stood over the catwalk at the rear of the office. He waited for the guard to pass under, knife drawn. He was about to drop down, but Lauren stopped him with a hand on his shoulder. He glared at her impatiently. She pointed to the man and then tapped her chest. He shook his head and indicated the knife in his hands. Lauren shook her head forcefully and pointed to the armed man and then to herself again. He rolled his eyes and shuffled aside. By then the thrall had disappeared around the office wall.

Lauren removed her jacket and flopped it on Ethan's arm. She unhooked her launcher and shot at the ceiling directly above them. Attaching the gun to her belt buckle, she gently shoved off the beam and carefully inverted, wrapping one leg around the thin wire to steady herself. Her long hair drooped like a curtain of snow.

While waiting for the heavy to return, Lauren withdrew a small blue pellet from one of the pouches on her belt and cupped it in a fist. When the armed man drew closer, Lauren tapped a button on the gun's winch and descended. In one smooth motion, she crushed the pellet and pushed the guard's exposed face tightly into her cupped hand. Dense white smoke seeped through her gloved fingers. Within seconds he fell limp in her grasp, unconscious. Holding him with one hand, she lowered herself and laid the heavy man on the catwalk before deftly flipping into a crouch beside him.

Not a sound was made.

Grinning, she signaled Ethan. He immediately dropped down next to her. Lauren indicated her handiwork, pleased with herself.

"No blood, no fuss," she whispered.

He shook his head and tossed her her rolled up coat.

Donning her coat, Lauren holstered her launcher and followed Ethan along the grated catwalk. The area behind the office was dark. Tall windows wrapped around the office with beige metal blinds rolled down at different lengths, all blocking line of sight. All the interior lights were off. She stopped next to Ethan crouched by a lone window slightly cracked open with the blinds pulled up part way. She couldn't put her finger on it, but something felt off about the area. Lauren looked around for any hidden cameras. Satisfied that they were safe, she crossed over to the other corner of the window and peeked inside.

The office was a complete mess. Stacks upon stacks upon stacks of rumpled papers and bent files lay strewn about every raised surface in the small room. A simple metal tanker desk took up most of the room with a pair of battered blue pullup chairs in front of it. A single ancient computer monitor glowed green and black atop a matching two-in-one beige plastic computer case and keyboard sitting in a sea of paperwork on the desk. Along the walls stood mismatched metal filing cabinets—some black and tall, some beige and low. A worn out, almost shredded bus tire leaned against the cabinets under a bank of wall switches near the door. Damp and dirty ceiling tiles surrounded two strips of deactivated fluorescent lights, and a lop-sided wall clock dangled over the lone door.

Sitting on one of the metal cabinets, a small bank of tiny TV screens displayed black and white footage from all the security cameras in the depot. Along with the computer monitor, they provided the only light in the office. Tobacco smoke gave the faint light from the screens a toxic haze.

Two men occupied the room. One was the

vampire from the yard. He sat on the desk corner, lighting cigarette hanging from his lips. The other man in a similar dress reclined in a chair behind the desk with his feet propped on the opposite corner. Lauren studied the second man. He looked strangely familiar. The dried cream in his slicked back, dark blonde hair gleamed in the dim light. She noted that he smelled much like the vampire they had followed, only stronger. The white of the security monitors highlighted a thick scar over his lip when he reached for some papers behind him.

Eyes wide with realization, she quickly ducked down and frantically gestured for Ethan to come over. He cocked his head in confusion, and, after a few moments of going back and forth, she crawled under the window next to him.

"That's him!" she barely kept her voice hushed.

He tilted his head.

"Emile Berger."

Ethan shrugged.

"He owns the mansion!"

Ethan popped back up and glanced at the man reclining at the desk chair. He kept from activating his enhanced vision in case it gave them away. While they talked, neither of them breathed unless speaking. They ducked back down.

"He's the presence I felt earlier. Very old, very strong."

They peered through the window again. Ethan strained to hear their conversation. Lauren heard them clearly.

The first vampire took a drag from his cigarette, "Like I told you, no one heard any shots. We own everybody here and most of the security across the street is on our payroll anyway. We're fine."

"Alexander, I have never doubted your capabilities, but your rashness will be your downfall," the second vampire said. His deep voice held a faint hint of Welsh cadence. He flipped an antique pocket watch repeatedly between his fingers. The worn cover bore an engraved train roaring down a set of tracks. It opened and closed with a distinct *clip-clap* sound. "How many loses?"

"Three. Seven escaped. We reclaimed four of them."

The older vampire sneered. "You were careless. Didn't you administer the anesthetic?"

"We ran out near the end. A few of them had to go without."

"Hmm. We will need to procure more for the next shipment, then. I do not like losing product due to an oversight." *Clip-clap.* He continued, "No matter. The drivers have their instructions?"

Alexander exhaled a ball of smoke and withdrew a flipbook from his coat.

"Bus 2935 will deliver twenty-seven bags to the Bell Island ferry for storage and sorting. Number 4687 will send twenty-three bags to Ember for immediate distribution. And bus 2047 will take the remainder to the warehouse to get deloused and readied for Deacon Hill on Saturday."

Lauren glanced a question at Ethan. *Bags?* she mouthed. He waved her off.

"Excellent. That should make the old boy happy." *Clip-clap.*

"That crackpot really thinks he can do it again?" Alexander asked.

Clip— The second vampire narrowed his eyes. "What did I tell you about watching your tongue? He is an elder and a member of the council."

Alexander scoffed, "Those were your words, London."

—*Clap.* "Correct. My words, not yours. Council members are treated with the utmost respect.

That means you will afford him such respect, and me as well."

"Apologies, *master*," Alexander said in mock deference. He took another pull. "Do you think he'll succeed this time?"

London idly twirled his pocket watch some more.

"Unsure. But, he requested more bags for Saturday night. I do not know exactly what he has in mind, but we shall see."

Lauren shared a concerned look with Ethan. That was in two days.

"I heard his little party was ruined, and he got stuck. Just one guy did all that?"

"Yes. I just spoke with Oberon. He is still recovering from the wound."

"And this guy made off with his woman, too?"

Clip-clap. London nodded.

Alexander gestured behind him. "And you're sure that's who it is?"

London glanced at the bank of screens. "Looks about right."

"Huh. Not what I expected."

"The same. But he will be dealt with in time. However, Oberon will want that woman back, unharmed if possible. He expressed interest in studying her after what happened."

Lauren suppressed a sharp inhale. The two vampires were talking about them. This Oberon must be the one who had conducted the ritual. The one that turned her into this. Lauren's stomach twisted at the image of that hideous old freak studying her. His thin, sadistic smile leering over her while he prodded her like some science project.

She grimaced. She hated her imagination sometimes.

Looking back up, another thought popped into

her head: why was this the only open window? Was it just for the smoke? And why were the lights out inside? Scanning the room, she caught sight of three orange twinkles while Alexander sucked down the last drag of his cigarette. Her eyes hovered over the strange lights for a short moment until she saw it.

There, in the front corner, poking between a pair of banker boxes atop the tallest filing cabinet, lay a single camera. Light reflected off two smaller lenses underneath a main lens—a nightvision camera. She had dealt those expensive things before—they beamed out infrared light to see in the dark. Usually, her goggles highlighted their invisible cones, letting her avoid them with ease. And this one was pointed directly at them. Her blood froze.

Alexander stubbed out his cigarette and shifted slightly towards the window. "Why waste time, master? If we have the opportunity, why not just take it?"

Lauren ducked down and waved at Ethan. When she finally pulled his attention away from the window, Lauren mouthed the word *camera* and frantically pointed to the front corner of the office.

"Agreed, but—" London began.

Lauren and Ethan looked back in time to see Alexander draw the big pistol from his coat and aim it at the window, all with blinding speed. The vampire fired instantly, shattering the glass and shredding the blinds.

Ethan tackled Lauren to the ground, the rest of the shots cutting through the office wall above them. Rounds whizzed over his head, millimeters from his scalp. Before the gunfire stopped, he quickly rolled off her and screamed to move.

Driven by reflex, Lauren immediately smashed a large gray pellet from her belt on the grate between them. It burst with a loud crack and instantly enveloped them in a ten foot ball of thick gray smoke. Her hand momentarily went numb from the micro explosion. Gloves or not, Lauren knew better than to pop a smoke pellet in her hand, but they were caught and seconds counted.

The two jumped to their feet and hurtled down the catwalk. Blowing by the unconscious guard, Lauren heard his radio buzzing with chatter. The heavies outside had found the bodies stashed between the containers! And with the gunfire just now, they were seconds away from storming the building.

Her mind churned at top speed, processing what she needed to do. Get to the roof, check the position of the guards, and break line of sight—maybe cause a distraction to lead them in the opposite direction. With any luck, the heavies would head the wrong way long enough for her to get to her car unnoticed.

They sprinted down the catwalk for the wooden ladder. No matter how high they could jump, climbing would take too long. She primed her piton launcher amid more bullets punched through the windows after them. Reaching the ladder, Lauren fired at the ceiling. The piton lodged into the dark ceiling. With a nod, Ethan quickly grabbed hold, and they ascended to the roof access.

Alexander burst through the office door onto the mezzanine. With a freshly loaded magazine in his pistol, he aimed at the two interlopers flying upward. Bullets chased them, perforating the wooden ladder in their wake. One bullet overshot and snapped the micro-thin line of Lauren's gun.

Terror blossomed on her face as every fear of falling came gushing from the depths of her mind. The two of them tumbled through the rafters in slow motion. Her body rolled in a flat spin. Beside her, Ethan flopped hard on the metal catwalk with a bone-crunching sound.

As her face met the unmoving concrete, her last thought was how much she hated Ethan.

13  A Sinister Kid

London wrenched the pistol from his protege's hand, bending the metal barrel in the process.

"What the fuck was that for!?"

London tossed the warped weapon onto the mezzanine. "Oberon wants her alive, damnit! Not full of holes!"

Alexander stood his ground with the elder, not backing down even though he had angered his master. "I had the chance to take him out, so I took it! That's what you said, right?"

The elder swallowed his anger. Much like his members of his private security firm, London encouraged lateral thinking and individual initiative (along acceptable lines, of course), and Alexander was no different. But while he excelled at those aspects, the boy tended to go a touch too far at times. Oberon's comment about his protege's attitude instantly came galloping to the fore.

London opened his mouth when four of his men charged into the building through the middle roll up door. They immediately took up firing positions while the mechanics fled the garage. Another of his thralls trotted up behind Alexander and saluted.

Looking at the thrall, London pointed down the stairs, and growled, "Take the rest and secure that woman, now!"

Ethan blinked the fuzziness from his head to no avail.

Thick shapes criss-crossed the darkness in front of him. He reached out to touch one, but felt gravity pulling at his arm and realized he on his back. Turning his head to the side, Ethan squinted through a blurry set of lines and saw several equally blurry black blobs approaching in the distance. The shapes slowly undulated towards something below him.

A low droning hum filled his ears. Through that, he heard a muffled noise, like someone shouting through a thick wall. Ethan was sure he should be alarmed at the noise. He shuffled around and looked down. A dull ache clawed at him when he moved. Peering through the grated floor, Ethan saw another blurry blob laid out below him. It too was dark but smaller and with a big white streak on one half of it.

White streak?

Ethan squinted harder and his vision sharpened a little. It was a person, and the big white streak looked like hair.

Wait.

Didn't he talk to a woman with white hair the other day? Yes. And she had tagged along with him to watch a bus depot. What happened there? He had seen something alarming there. Someone he knew— someone he needed to find. And that white-haired woman incessantly nagged him the entire time. What was her name? Katherine? Laura? Is that her on the ground below him?

Pain exploded across his body, and the world suddenly surged into focus. Ethan had fallen from the ceiling. That was Lauren below him. The dark blobs were thralls. And they were heading straight for her.

"Oh, shit," he murmured.

Adrenaline pumping, Ethan sprang to his feet. He drew the o-katana from his back—the razor sharp blade gleamed in the white fluorescent light. He quickly gathered his spirit and flushed it through his system. Pure essence energized his body and the blade in his hand. Inner warmth radiated throughout him, washing away the pain and lifting his feet bare millimeters off the ground. None of the thralls had noticed him yet.

Eyes blazing with golden fury, Ethan leapt onto the thrall reaching for Lauren. He plunged the energized blade through the shoulder and into the torso. The guard collapsed under Ethan's weight with a wet gurgle. Keeping his momentum, Ethan rolled onto his feet, and with a heavy grunt, hurled the body over his head, twisting his blade free as it flew from his hands. The flying thrall crashed into the row of tool chests and scattered his advancing comrades.

A hail of suppressed submachine gun fire tore through the congested lane. Sparks showered off metal. Glass shattered into tiny fragments. Tires burst. Ethan flung himself under one of the buses, barely dodging the wall of angry lead. The group of thralls ceased their fire and sounded off, quickly assessing each other for damage. One of them checked the vitals of the recently thrown body while the rest crouched and scanned under the bus for any sight of Ethan.

Still glaring at his master, Alexander snapped around to see one of the security team bowl over a row of tool boxes and disperse the other men. They quickly gathered themselves and fired on the masked man while he disappeared under a raised bus. Their gunfire ended moments later once they saw he was gone.

Beside him, London yelled out to the regrouping fireteam, "Find that man, and kill him!" His master turned to him. "Let them handle the interloper. Bring me that girl!" Alexander went to vault the railing, but the elder grabbed him. "And no more losses this time. Oberon wants her *alive*."

The younger vampire met his master's eyes again, the unspoken implication if he failed hanging in the air. With a stern nod, the impetuous vampire swung over the railing. He marched under the catwalk straight for the woman. To his right the four thralls searched for the masked man in pairs, checking under the two buses and behind boxes.

Three lanes ahead, the girl lay spread out between a stack of boxes and a huge rolling tool chest. A large, misshapen pistol lay in front of her. She slowly stirred awake, pushing herself upright. Thick rivulets of blood ran down her nose and collected in a large pool. He didn't notice in office, but she wore a dark beanie as a makeshift mask. Patches of dust clung to the blood-soaked thing. Long blotches of red covered the torn knees of her pants. Rubbing her temple, she pulled the cap off, leaving red streaks on her face and hair.

The girl noticed Alexander bearing down on her. She instantly snapped to and scrambled away from him. He was almost on top of her when she pelted his chest with a salvo of blue marbles. They shattered on impact, creating a cloud of thick white smoke. Tears of blood welled up in his eyes from the tingling vapor. Semi-blind, he knocked over a cart of tools. The four thralls immediately halted and aimed at the loud clanging sound.

Through his tears, Alexander spied the armed men standing there, waiting.

"Don't look at me!" he coughed. "Kill that asshole!"

Whatever was in those marbles severely aggravated his eyes and throat and sent a dull, sluggish sensation slithering through his limbs. He waved the thick gas away in time to see the girl limping to the end of the bus lane. He pushed the cart aside and went after her.

Ethan watched four sets of black combat boots slowly walk by.

He clung tightly to the undercarriage of one of the lifted buses, hiding behind a lowered side panel running between the wheels. Oil and other lubricants from countless maintenance intervals soaked the floor below him. At least twice a beam from their tactical flashlights glinted on the dense puddle underneath. Seeing no footprints or any other evidence of his passage, the men continued on.

When the last set of boots passed, Ethan unhooked his legs from the exhaust pipe one at a time and silently dropped down.

Tools suddenly clanged on the ground nearby and grabbed the thralls' attention. The vampire from the yard—Alexander was his name?—immediately barked orders at them. With the thralls distracted, Ethan crept out behind a toolbox. They watched Alexander hurry under the catwalk towards the main offices. He quietly drew the sword from his back and plunged the razor sharp blade into the nearest thrall. The sword burst through his vest with a spurt of blood and a wet howl. The other three instantly spun around and fired.

Lead saturated the lane. Ethan ducked behind the skewered man and pulled the pin off a grenade clipped to his belt. He planted a heavy foot into the thrall's backside and kicked him off his sword and into the others. Bullets pelted bleeding thrall's ballistic vest but did nothing to stall his flailing momentum. Ethan vaulted over the bus right as the grenade exploded with a deafening clangor and a blinding flash of light. The blast shattered the surrounding windows and tossed the thralls off their feet.

More boxes crashed to the ground up ahead.

Dashing under the catwalk, he saw Alexander hounding Lauren through the steel posts supporting the elevated walkway. Her cap was gone, and her face and hair was streaked with red. Hobbling, she grasped one of the racks standing against the wall and, with a painful cry, tore the heavy thing down, shattering a pair of massive of windshields in her wake. With one hand, Alexander whipped the toppled rack to the side like so much balsa wood. Glass crunched under his expensive leather shoes.

Lauren tipped over another rack before hurrying down the next lane, spilling padded seats and chrome tubing. The parasite tossed them away without losing stride.

"Where the fuck do you think you're going?!" the fang exclaimed.

Ethan's jaw flexed hard. Their first night and Lauren was already in mortal danger. History was bound and determined to repeat itself.

Not this time.

Running full tilt, Ethan sliced diagonally across the parasite's back, ripping through the his expensive coat from shoulder to hip. Pale flesh split wide, revealing moist muscle and bone underneath. Bits of skin turned gray and flaked off, yet hardly any blood escaped. Yowling in pain, the fang staggered from the aggravated wound on his back.

Ethan promptly dodged the blind haymaker when the vampire whirled around. He deftly dodged Alexander's wild strikes again and again. Ethan spun under a flailing fist and knocked the vampire off balance and angled his sword at the unbleeding gash.

Auto-fire suddenly rattled the air, chasing Ethan out of his attack. He tucked into an awkward roll between a bus and the line of tool chests. Alexander jumped to the side, barely avoiding the hail of lead.

"Watch you're aim!" Alexander scolded loudly.

A thrall knocked the gunman's head with his elbow while he reloaded his weapon. The three of them ran up to Alexander.

Wincing, the vampire pointed under the bus. "He went under there! Go!"

They quickly split up and hustled around the vehicle, the leader going into the lane with the other two going around to the next one.

Alexander grabbed the lone thrall. "Wait! You, come with me." He took the pistol from the thrall's thigh holster and racked the slide. "Now, where the hell did that bitch go?"

London Bray observed the mayhem unfolding in his garage. He watched the masked man stab and fling one of his personnel and quickly disappear from view only to reappear moments later and kill another one. He watched the girl hobble away from his protege, desperately throwing heavy obstacles in his path.

When the masked man attacked Alexander, London tightened his grip on the railing. When the man landed a telling blow on his number two, he bent the steel bar.

He felt some relief when his men drove the swordsman off, but lost that feeling when they nearly shot his progeny—not that it would do anything. While Alexander shouted orders to the men, London spied the girl limping off towards one of the open rolling doors.

Without hesitation, he dashed into the office and nimbly ran through a bank of electrical switches on the wall. Originally installed as backups in case he needed to close the building from prying eyes, each one cut power to the massive doors. Outside, the heavy steel shutters rapidly slammed shut one by one. He craned his head through the doorway in time to see the girl skid to an ungainly halt, mashing her hands against her ears while the rest of the doors clanged shut one after the other.

That should keep her from getting away.

The deafening cacophony of six huge metal shutters slamming down in sequence reverberated throughout the cavernous garage. Alexander jogged ahead peering into each lane for the girl. He checked under each bus he passed in case she tried hiding in the undercarriage. After the second lane, he snapped a glimpse of her running along the bank of closed garage doors back towards London. She moved faster and wasn't limping anymore.

Must be scared shitless, he laughed to himself.

Alexander abruptly reversed course, retreading his steps past the last three lanes. The first one was empty and the two thralls searched the second one, but ducking, he spotted her in the third lane heading for the back of the shop. He silently signaled his thrall to go around and wait. When the girl reached the middle of the lane, Alexander rushed in, startling her stiff. Alexander grinned at her terrified reaction and strolled forward.

The girl pulled a pistol on him.

"Go ahead." He spread his arms wide, "Do it. I dare you."

The barrel shook. The girl took backed up and steadied the gun with the other hand, but did nothing. Alexander took another step. Behind her, his thrall crept around the bus.

"What's the matter? Scared?" Alexander extended his canines as he spoke. The girl's eyes grew large. *Her red eyes.* He blinked at the confusing sight. They were like a thrall's eyes, but more intense.

She fired.

The shot punched through his lower torso and out the back of his jacket. It stung . . . for a moment.

Alexander poked at the bullet hole, laughing.

"Think I'll need a new suit?" he cackled.

The girl fired again. And again. And again. The gun roared until the slide locked open, and nothing but smoke left the breech and barrel. Only a handful of rounds found their target—most of the shots struck random parts and barrels beyond him. One snapped off a rusty red pipe valve, spilling out a thick stream of stale water. Alexander laughed again. He focused on the handful of bullet holes and forced them closed in matter of seconds. A handful of 9mm mushrooms clinked on the floor.

The girl's jaw dropped, terrified.

Eyes wide, she fled, smacking right into the thrall. He grabbed the frightened woman and held her in a big bear hug. The girl furiously bucked against the thrall's grip, the empty pistol tumbling from her hand. He lifted her off the floor for control, but one of her mad kicks pushed against a bus panel and threw him off balance. He scrambled to stay upright only to thud against the other bus, loosening his hold. The girl immediately snatched the thrall's arm and sunk her teeth into it.

Alexander froze.

Did she just grow fangs?

Crimson seeped from her mouth. Shots from the next lane overtook the thrall's painful screams. Failing to rip his arm free, the thrall lifted the girl off her feet again. Alexander tried to grab her, but a flailing foot caught him square in the jaw with surprising strength. His eyes rolling up, the thrall struggle slowed. With his last bit of fight, he drove a fist into the girl's stomach, folding her over and dislodging her from him with a spray of blood. He groggily went to grab her again, but the girl instantly wheeled him flat on the hard concrete with a heavy grunt. She fell to her knees, clutching her midsection, ruby specs dripping from her mouth.

Alexander lunged, but the girl snapped her hand her hand out. Something smacked him in the chest with a heavy thud. He looked down to see a black metal knife handle jutting between his collar bones. He yanked it out and regarded the ruby-slick weapon.

"Fancy toy."

Tossing it over his shoulder, he lunged again. She threw another one. He deflected it with a quick wave of his hand. The girl threw another only to get batted out of the air with another laugh. She grimaced and threw one more. Alexander twisted his arm to swat the projectile, but tripped instead. Catching himself, he saw a knife sticking out of his shoe. He kicked it away with the other foot.

"You dumb bitch! Those are expens—!"

His head abruptly jerked back from a second blade *thunking* into his eye socket, spilling Alexander into an overturned tool cart. Gripping the flat handle, pain rippled from the metal shank. Bits of blood and cornea trailed the blade ripping out of his skull. He threw the blade on the ground, seething. Alexander whipped his head at the sound of light footsteps fading off to his right.

Two thralls slowly stalked down the empty lane, shinning their flashlights under both buses. Every two steps they looked through a window, checking the seats and floors inside. The one on the left felt a sudden rush of air from his teammate. He checked over his shoulder to see the masked man rising up between them.

"Look out!" he cried.

Shoulder to shoulder with the two thralls, Ethan moved fast to keep them off balance, because one slip up, one opening and any or all of those bullets would find their way into him.

Ethan snapped a powerful kick into the thrall's solar plexus, pushing him into the bus, and, with the same leg, thrust a heel into the second thrall behind him. He ruined the first thrall's aim with a quick elbow to the receiver and then threw a backhand the second thrall. Too slow, the second thrall took the hit in the face and bumbled into the bus—his trigger finger spasming bullets onto the concrete.

Capitalizing on the success, Ethan aimed the tip of his katana under the first man's chin. But the first thrall had already recovered. At the last second he deflected the thrust with his MP5 like a shield. The razor sharp blade punched into the bus panel next to him. Ethan ducked the rifle stock flying for his face. Sensing the second thrall behind him, Ethan elbowed the man in the face, disrupting his retaliation with a broken nose. Blood spilled onto the man's tactical vest. A lightning jab to the throat kept the first thrall at bay. Ripping his sword free, Ethan quickly spun, slashing across the second thrall's jugular with a thick arterial spray. Keeping with his spin, Ethan plunged the blade into the first thrall's rib cage.

Both men collapsed.

Flicking off the blood, Ethan snapped around at the sound of cackling from the other lane. Through the windows, he saw Alexander gloating at one end of the cluttered lane. At the other end, Lauren leaned against the vehicle, bloodied and haggard. Behind her, another thrall rolled on the ground, cradling a bloody forearm. The fang lunged at her.

With a powerful jump, Ethan vaulted onto the bus roof in time to witness Lauren throw a knife right into Alexander's face. The hit sent him reeling. Ethan paused. Though the distance was relatively short, hitting a target as small as an eye was no mean feat. The lack of surprise on her face told him she expected that to happen.

Guess she really can take care of herself.

As the vampire struggled to remove the knife,

Lauren slipped off the bus panel and hurried towards the office mezzanine. Ethan moonsaulted off the roof. Surprise flashed across the wounded vampire's remaining eye when he landed in front of him. Ethan immediately slashed upward as he rose, gouging a hideous rut from waist to shoulder. The fang screamed from the ashen trench splitting his skin in the blade's wake.

Alexander locked his one good eye with Ethan's golden pair. He threw a pair of angry punches at Ethan's dirty mask, but they struck only empty space. Dodging a desperate haymaker, Ethan raised his sword to finish off the fang when a sudden burst of gunfire sliced the air between them. A stray round drilled into the vampire's left shoulder, and another sheared off a small chunk of Ethan's right thigh. He gnashed his teeth, the pain bleeding through his energy infusing his body.

The thrall on the ground sat up, bracing his submachine gun, and fired.

Angry lead chased Ethan onto the bus behind him. The thrall climbed to his feet and loosed another burst. Bullets hounded Ethan down the raised vehicle and onto the catwalk above. Fluorescent lights shattered in his wake, drenching parts of the garage in darkness.

Cupping the gaping hole on his face, Alexander waved the thrall after the masked man. He glowered at his bloody palm. Complex organs always took a long time to reform no matter how hard he focused. It would be at least a full day until his eyesight would return to normal.

"Fucking cunt," he uttered.

The two cuts were a different story. They burned like firebrand pressed against his skin. He touched the edge of the cut on his chest. A chunk of flesh flaked off, disintegrating into nothingness. What the hell could make a wound like?? Alexander angrily pushed himself off the cart with a pained grunt and headed after the girl.

The last thrall hustled around the bus, playing the barrel-mounted flashlight on the darkened catwalk. He carefully picked his way through the fallen debris from Alexander's chase. Two lanes down, he spied movement: a single red sneaker on the railing. The thrall snapped off a quick burst. Sparks showered from the grating, and the gun's bolt locked empty. He ejected the spent magazine and slammed in a fresh one from his vest in a smooth, practiced motion.

The masked man soared overhead, leaping from the catwalk to the bus roof on his right. The thrall chased him into the next lane, barrel blazing. The swordsman ran to the front end of the bus and flipped over it, bullet holes trailing him. The thrall ran down the lane, quickly loading a new magazine as he went. He released the bolt just and leapt around the corner, blasting a quick volley of down the connecting aisle.

Nothing.

He scanned under the buses. To his right, fallen carts and chests and their spilled contents. To his left, the office mezzanine sat over pallets of boxes wrapped in plastic. Next to it he saw the girl frantically pulling a big crate aside while Alexander sneaked up behind her. The thrall shifted his focus upward. The bus roofs were empty and so were the interiors. He carefully walked down the lane, stepping over the first of his men the masked swordsman had slaughtered. Keeping an eye out for movement, he pocketed his fallen comrade's spare magazines before moving on.

As he reached the end of the lane, pistol fire rang out by the mezzanine. The thrall swung around at the sound. Alexander had the girl in his sights, laughing as she braced against a stack of crates.

The thrall went back to his search.

Something smacked his chest. He looked down to see a sword sticking out of his vest. His body grew cold, and his arms went limp. His body jerked when the masked man twisted the weapon free. With a spin the swordsman flashed the blade's tip just under the thrall's head. Everything suddenly went blurry and color started to fade. The last thing he saw was a whirling red heel.

14 Through the Fire . . .

*L*auren ran into the clearing by the mezzanine.

Her temples throbbed. Her vision swam. Her knees creaked and burned. Blood trickled from her smashed nose. She had never fallen from a height that great before. Three stories right onto hard packed concrete!

Damnit, she knew this was a bad idea. One night with that psychopath, and now she was about to die. How could she have gotten herself into this? She should have stayed home. She should have ignored that damn dream. She should have never gone into that mansion.

But no!

She couldn't let it go. Had to go inside. Had to know what was behind that stupid fucking door!

Five years!

Five years of successful jobs. No injuries. No deaths. Perfect plans. In and out like the wind. But one bout of demented curiosity, and look what happened! Her life was circling the drain, fast. And that beast of a man was hounding her the entire way. Nothing could stop him. Sleeping gas pellets didn't work. Bullets only made him laugh. Even a six inch blade in the skull—to the hilt!—only managed to piss him off!

She paused in the empty lane. A couple of carts

and tool chests lay about. Dried up patches of oil and other chemical stains marked where a bus normally sat. Pallets of boxes clogged the area underneath the raised office, and more boxes and crates lay stacked in rear the corner.

And beyond all that, the warm, inviting glow of an emergency exit sign.

The vampire suddenly screamed out in pain. She swiveled at the noise, her sweat-soaked hair flapping from the motion. Under the bus, she spied Ethan's red sneakers moving next to the vampire's bloody dress shoes.

Damn asshole! All this chaos is his fault!

Gunfire.

Shell casings sprinkled next to the heavy lying on the floor. Lauren stared at the man's bloody forearm gripping the chattering weapon. She refused to acknowledge what she had just done to him. She didn't even think to do it—it just happened. More disturbing, it didn't taste like the cup of pig's blood—it tasted like dirt.

The gunfire stopped and Ethan's red sneakers disappeared. For the first time in her life, Lauren dreaded the sound of silence. A split second later, he was on a bus roof, running and jumping away from more gunfire.

She released a heavy sigh.

My turn.

Lauren hurried towards the emergency exit. Her knees weren't stiff anymore. Lauren didn't know if she had fractured something in that fall. And she definitely didn't want to think about why it didn't hurt to move all of a sudden.

Reaching the heavy crates, she dragged the first one to the side, damn glad to have that extra bit of strength right now. She gripped the next crate when the wood at her fingers burst into splinters.

Alexander stood at the corner of the bus with a smoking pistol in his hand. A jagged red gash covered half his face. Eerily, no blood leaked from the hideous wound. A nasty tear separated his black jacket and shirt. The skin underneath was dried and desiccated, exposing his bones and other organs through the slit. Bits of charred flesh floated away as he limped closer.

"Trying to get away?" he sputtered with a violent cough.

She tried to mount the crate when he took his eyes off her, but another bullet ended that attempt. Unable to take her eyes off the approaching vampire, Lauren blindly groped for something—anything— behind her to use as a weapon. Her hand knocked into a heavy tool bag and chucked it. Alexander knocked the bag away with his shoulder, breaking his aim. Lauren quickly heaved a small metal tool box at the distracted vampire.   He twisted, and the heavy thing sailed harmlessly over him.

She grabbed another object, but Alexander shot it out of her grasp.

He was close now.

Lauren dove to the right, but Alexander was faster. He yanked her off her feet with a fistful of hair and spun her around mid-fall. She deflected the pistol butt aiming for her head, but missed the punch to her stomach. The ungodly force of it jack-knifed her body.

Tucking the pistol in his belt, Alexander lifted her off the ground by the throat with both hands.

"The old man said to take you alive, but he didn't say what condition!"

Ten bloody fingers squeezed. Lauren grabbed at his arms with all her new strength, but Alexander simply squeezed harder. She snapped her feet at his waist only to get the same result. He pushed his thumbs into her neck, tearing at the pale flesh below her chin. With her last bit of defiance, Lauren drove a knee into

Alexander's jaw, but the bastard didn't even register the hit. Her arms grew tired, and her eyesight darkened. Her lungs burned, and her face flushed deep red with trapped blood. Her legs ceased kicking. She heard muffled gunfire off in the distance.

The image of Ethan lying in a pool of blood flickered across her fading vision.

Everything suddenly shook.

Lauren opened her eyes to see Alexander twitching with shock. Precious air rushed into her lungs from his waning grip. She glanced down. Ethan—eyes burning—stood at Alexander's side with his sword buried deep in the vampire's torso.

Pressing both feet against Alexander's chest, Lauren shattered his grasp and fell. She clutched her throat gasping for breath. Ethan flipped Alexander onto his back, twisting the blade free as the vampire landed with a wet thud. Flecks of gray drifted from the gaping hole through his sides. Ethan raised his sword, ready to chop down on Alexander's neck.

Something dark dropped to the floor in the corner of Lauren's bleary eye. She swiveled her head to see a massive tire collide into Ethan, sending him careening into the bus across the empty lane. He flopped onto the floor like a ragdoll.

London stood next to the mezzanine stairs. He fixed his stone gaze on her and marched after her. Terrified, Lauren scrambled away on all fours, but the tall vampire plucked her off the ground with one arm. He ignored her frenetic struggle, curiously staring at her eyes. He pulled her close and inhaled deeply.

"Such a strange scent you have."

Dark blood blotted his clean shirt sleeve where her nails dug into his skin. The scar on his lip turned his sneer into a snarl.

"You insolent little girl."

In an instant, London hurled Lauren through the

air like a shotput. She tumbled head first, limbs flailing, through all the debris she had spilled under the catwalk minutes ago.

Her body ached with a new collection of pains now. Shaking, she rose up on her hands and knees. Through the blurry ringing, she saw London help Alexander to his feet.

"Leave", vampire said.

"But . . ."

"You're useless in this state. Go. And take this with you."

London handed Alexander a large billfold of paperwork with a VHS tape strapped to the side. The younger vampire took it, holding the large gray hole festering above his hip. He glowered at London for a moment and hobbled to the emergency exit.

Ethan hauled himself to his feet with a labored groan. The bus behind him teetered precariously on the hydraulic lift jacks from his impact. Across the lane, London checked his pocket watch.

"You've cost me more than just time, boy," he growled.

Lauren pulled herself together, hearing the flat packing sounds of fighting in the next lane. She had to get out of here, but how? The rolling doors were shut, and those two were blocking the emergency exit. She could try the offices, but her lockpicks would probably take too much time. Maybe she could try her luck with the roof?

A recently familiar smell interrupted her train of thought, but she couldn't quite place the aroma. It had a metallic twinge to it, like at the chemical plant. Or when she dangled over the fuel pumps.

Her eyes fell on a pair of plastic barrels to her right. One gushed greenish fluid from a trio of bullet holes near the base. She followed the flowing liquid to a large rippling puddle on the floor when she suddenly realized she was in that puddle, and both her hands and knees were soaked green. A half dozen labels plastered each barrel, but one stood out among them:

Caution! Flammable! Diesel Fuel.

As if things couldn't get any worse.

Lauren shook the liquid from her hands. Turning to run, she kicked something on the ground. It was her piton launcher. The wire had snapped, but everything else looked in working order. Next to it lay the body of a dead guard in a large pool of blood. She squatted down on the balls of her feet and hooked the launcher to her belt.

Curiously, she gazed under the bus. Ethan and the older vampire moved around rapidly. There was nothing she could do to help—the best thing she could do was stay out of the way.

Rising, Lauren caught her reflection in the pool of blood at her feet. She was an utter mess. Blood smeared her face and smashed nose and streaked down her hair. Deep welts ran down her right cheek and darkened both eye sockets. She looked away, the irony of the sight reflected in a pool of blood not lost on her.

Looking up, she noticed a pistol strapped to the dead heavy's thigh. She'd gone to shooting ranges and practiced with guns before. She even kept a small revolver in her nightstand in case of emergencies. But Lauren never liked firearms. Not due to some self-righteous, holier-than-thou principle; just that they were loud and obnoxious. Useful tools, especially for intimidation, but for her, resorting to a firearm meant she had failed at her job.

The image of Alexander's bloody face flashed before her. Bullets did almost nothing to these people, but right now she felt safer with a gun than without. She unhooked the strap and slid the pistol out.

The square Glock barely cleared the holster when the glass windows above her exploded outward.

A blizzard of shards sprayed into the lane followed closely by Ethan. The shock of the crash knocked her on her backside. He crashed into the large tool box, bouncing on the ground and sending it rolling into the next bus. He slowly righted himself, tools sliding off his back and clanged on the concrete.

Above her, London landed atop the tilted bus with a heavy *thunk*. Ripping off his torn vest, he dropped down and lifted Ethan off his feet. Lauren quickly crawled away. The vampire punched Ethan hard enough to shake his entire body—the sound was nauseating. The vampire punched him again, and blood from Ethan's mouth dampened his black ski mask.

Horrified, Lauren witnessed the vampire wrecked Ethan's body, one punch at a time. Her fingers tighten around the pistol, that strange anger from the diner swelling again from the dark recesses of her mind. She brought the gun up, remembering the advice of the shooting range instructor.

Focus on your target. London held Ethan limp in his hand.

Line up your sights. The vampire grinned maliciously in front of her barrel.

Exhale. He reared back for one final punch.

Fire!

The vampire's head whipped violently with a blossom of blood and bone. Her hands quivered. Smoke drifted from a gaping crater of gore that was his left temple, yet the vampire still stood. Straightening up, he cranked around, dropping Ethan like a discarded toy. The vampire's bloodshot gaze seized onto her, his already pale face now bone-white with bright red veins growing thicker closer to the hole. A blood-curdling growl poured from him like a starved beast.

Roaring, London dug his fingers into the big red tool box behind him and wheeled the impossibly heavy thing over his head. Lauren barely skittered away from the half ton of crunching steel. Sockets and drill bits exploded from the top compartment, smashing glass and puncturing side panels. Others ricocheted off the panels and into the hanging light panel above. Shadows drenched the lane with showering of electrical sparks. Through sheer, impossible luck, nothing touched her.

London tossed the capsized chest aside, knocking it back onto its wheels as he stomped after her. Lauren fired. Bullets harmlessly splattered tiny dots of red on his dirty dress shirt. The vampire moved like a stop-motion puppet in the flickering muzzle light. Nearly on her, he lunged.

Ethan's fist suddenly shot up under London's chin, rebounding him senselessly off the tilted bus. He shot to his feet, eyes blazing bright. Ethan wheeled his arms around and moved his hands in the same gestures she saw atop the diner. The air around him rippled slightly in the half light.

Yelling at the top of his lungs, Ethan launched a furious series of rapid punches and kicks at the staggered vampire. His limbs blended into black and blue blurs, and to Lauren's amazement, so did London. She watched the two men twist and bend, dodging rocketing fists and blurring feet. Some of Ethan's strikes whizzed through London's flashing arms, landing with the same sickening crunch that nearly crippled him earlier. She barely caught the spinning red sneaker arcing into London's bloody temple, splattering dark fluids onto the bus next to them.

Lauren scooted away, hating the gnawing feeling that she should do something with the gun still in her hand. But shooting the vampire was pointless, all it did was enrage the monster further. The best it would do was create another mild distraction. But she had to do something. Reluctantly drawing the pistol again, Lauren felt a curious warmth creeping up her back. She noticed the bitter metallic smell from earlier had mixed with a burning one now and dozens of orange twinkles on the glass chips in front of her. Keeping the pistol pointed at the fracas, she peeked behind. Growing flames danced along the puddle of diesel fuel.

Her eyes bulged out of their sockets.

Lauren jumped away, the flames licking at her grimy tennis shoes. She ducked under the bus and ran for the exit, clawing at the crates again.

A fiery explosion erupted from the wrecked bus. She whipped around to see flaming liquid burst into the air. A second barrel ignited. More liquid fire erupted, lighting up the bus, the catwalk, and even parts of the rafters.

Strangely, the sprinklers didn't activate, and Lauren wondered why. A flaming red valve handle landed on the crate next to her, and she suddenly remember blasting it off while shooting Alexander. More flaming debris fell, sending her tripping. Liquid fire splashed the surrounding boxes and barrels. Large stickers plastered each barrel, the largest of which read: *Gasoline*.

"Oh, c'mon!!" Lauren protested.

She ran for the rolling doors.

Ethan landed a few feet behind her, knocking Lauren on the floor. He was covered in sweat and blood and bits of broken glass still clinging to his mangled jacket. The bright golden radiance of his eyes had faded to a dull glow. His body shook with weariness, and he fought to keep his balance. Straining, he helped Lauren to her feet.

Slipping her hand free of his uncomfortable grasp, she met Ethan's tired gaze.

"Please tell me that thing is dead!"

A bestial roar answered her question.

London pounced over the teetering vehicle, oblivious to the flames licking at his feet. Ethan shoved her away from the enraged vampire's bloody white fist cracking the dense cement where she just stood. The frenzied vampire threw himself at Ethan while Lauren skidded across the floor. He struck the crazed vampire's good temple with a spinning red heel kick and swept his legs as he landed. The combo flipped London next to the fallen debris, his blonde skull bouncing on a dried patch of oil. Ethan snatched his sword off the ground. He took a heavy breath and charged the prone vampire.

With inhuman strength, London pushed himself onto to his feet, holding a ruptured piece of bracing ready to smash Ethan's head off.

Lauren inhaled sharply seeing Ethan tumble centimeters under the vicious steel. In the blink of an eye, he rebounded off the dented raised bus, rocking it further off kilter, and torpedoed into the vampire's exposed back. His blade sliced true as he landed, shearing a large trough down the elder's spine.

The bent strut clanked on the oily patch of cement. London shambled around, the frenzied rage draining from his eyes. Panting heavily, Ethan raised his sword.

Gasoline barrels erupted, flinging everyone in the air along with bits of wooden shrapnel and burning liquid. London spun off the stairs and into the pallets under the mezzanine. Ethan flew into the front of the bus, spider-webbing the glass door into a shallow crater. Farthest from the explosion, Lauren flipped head over heels, bouncing to a stop a few yards from Ethan.

Coughing, her head swirling, Lauren pushed up on her elbows and surveyed the carnage.

Fire engulfed the entire garage now. Guttering flames climbed higher and higher, further blackening the already dark rafters. The vortex of heat churned the smoke clinging to the ceiling. Through the roar and crackle, fluorescent bulbs burst under the extreme temperature. Behind her, the toppled boxes loudly settled under the creaking platform. The metal skeleton of the destroyed bus groaned loudly on the lift jacks.

Sprawled out in front of her with his sword still in hand, Ethan slowly stirred. Another series of explosions rocked the teetering vehicle. Metal squealed from the forward jack ripping into the undercarriage, slowly tipping the giant thing over.

No!

With a surge of adrenaline, Lauren tackled Ethan out the other side of the twelve tons of falling steel. Their tangled bodies rolled to a stop in the middle of the newly widened lane. Another fuel barrel ignited under the flaming catwalk and launched a wheeled tool chest down the crowded corridor.

The world around her inexplicably slowed to a crawl. Burning embers lay suspended in mid air. The flapping waves of the fire flowed like molasses. The rocketing chest crept forward at a glacial pace. Lauren pulled Ethan limp body and rolled into the bent lift jack. Real-time returned once the chest sped past. It punched through the corrugated metal rollup like so much tissue paper. Cold night air rushed in through the newly created hole.

Lauren sat up and pulled Ethan into her lap. She slipped off his mask to reveal a swollen mass of black bruises and spit skin. Sweat and worry dripped onto his face while she fervently patted his bloody cheek, willing him to wake up. Behind her, a rafter collapsed and knocked another bus off its jacks.

"Wake up, damnit! Wake up!" she yelled.

Ethan's blue eyes popped open after a hard slap.

He focused on the blurry face hovering inches above his. Lauren's troubled red eyes came into view, her long hair surrounding him like a grungy curtain of white and red. Her frightened expression soften slightly when he tested his body. Ethan's face twisted when every wound he took tonight protested all at once. Slowly, painfully, he dragged himself upright. He wiped the blood and ash from his sword and stiffly sheathed it, groaning the entire time.

"This place is falling apart." Lauren thrust his bloody mask into his hands, barely containing the panic in her voice.

The blaze engulfed the western wall of the building and was spreading fast. Flaming debris danced on the tipped over bus, increasing with each flap. Rafter beams splintered and crumpled one after the other. She pointed to the busted door and motioned for him to follow.

"C'mon!"

Gunfire ripped the panic off Lauren's face.

Her legs buckled. Ethan rushed forward, catching her before she collapsed. She looked up at him with complete surprise. Blood trickled from lips trying to form words, and she fell limp in his hands. Looking over her shoulder, Ethan saw blood oozing from a cluster of holes in her dirty coat.

On the catwalk in front of the blazing office, a lone thrall groggily braced his submachine gun against his shoulder. The rafters above the man shuddered and gave way before Ethan could react, crushing the catwalk and everything on it in a ball of flaming fury. The metal frame shrieked loudly from the impact.

Underneath, London burst out of the broken pallets. His white shirt was horribly shredded and his pants hung in tatters. The mezzanine collapsed in a heap of snapped beams and flaming scrap seconds after the vampire stepped out. He locked eyes with Ethan through the flames, ignoring the raging inferno around him until more falling rafters cut off their view.

Ethan hefted Lauren's limp body in his arms. Her chest heaved in short, labored breaths, and blood trickled from her jacket sleeve. He carried her through the destroyed rolling door and ran to the end of the bus yard.

Stopping at the vacant security gate, Ethan spared one last look behind. Smoke belched from broken office windows on the eastern side, and clouds of black smoke billowed from shattered skylights. Like too many others battles, he had almost died tonight. But, after decades of foolishly holding onto to hope, he was finally vindicated. His sister was still alive! And he finally had a solid lead on where to find her.

Sirens echoed in the distance.

Ethan ran south, cradling Lauren in his arms.

*T*he pain was still unbearable.

London sat in a large personal library, continuously flipping his pocket watch. Though the plush leather couch was soft and comfortable, he still found it difficult to relax. The cuts, the bruises, even the bullet hole on his temple all knitted themselves back together as usual. Drinking enough blood closed any wound, but this one was different. The aggravated lesion healed no faster than a burn from fire or sunlight no matter how much he drank.

Not since coming to America had London wore a bandage, if only to keep from ruining another set of clothes.

The library was dead silent. Only the steady ticking of the grandfather clock in the corner of the large room broke the room's silence. He hated idle waiting. Time was precious, and London needed to oversee processing the bags for this weekend. But the events at the garage were too important to ignore. The appearance of Oberon's progeny—if he could call her that—was too important not to discuss in person.

He checked his watch for the ninth time in the last half hour. Oberon was late. London should have left by now. He hated being off schedule.

London had already walked around the room

twice to allay his vexation. Three of the walls were lined with antique, hand-carved wooden shelves each brimming with leather bound books. A wrought iron spiral staircase with polished brass accents allowed access to a balcony with even more books. A checkered pattern of green and black marble tiles stretched out along the main floor. Two brown leather couches and a century old varnished coffee table sat on a luxurious black and green floral rug in the room's center. Ornate brass sconces hung from the walls around the room and a brass chandelier dropped from the center of the filigreed wood panel ceiling.

Wood carved pedestals with glass cases dotted the room. Each case held a weapon from a different era of history. A Roman gladius. An Egyptian khopesh. A French rapier from the reign of Louis 13th. One case contained an atlatl—a curious weapon from the Aztec civilization. Another held a Webley revolver from the late Victorian period, very similar to one London himself had once owned. On the console table behind him, a display case held three open books: an original Gutenberg Bible, a hand written Franciscan Bible, and a third book written in a runic language he did not recognize.

Every single item here had been lovingly transposed from their former home at the edges of the city.

London looked out the massive floor-to-ceiling window to his right. A near uniform sea of five to ten storey buildings stretched for miles east of the Appalachian Mountains. Much of the city had been built in the latter half of the eighteenth century, before the advent of central air and ventilation allowed for taller constructions. Beyond the line of low rise structures lay the affluent neighborhoods. Old estates and mansions dating back to the Colonial period looked down upon the old city from those hills. Numerous construction cranes rose closer to the coast, denoting where older buildings gave way to newer projects. The high rise he looked out of was one of them, built at the edge of the Old Town district by the bay.

Abraham's doing, London thought sourly.

The council had long argued against pushing too much new construction near the affluent parts of the city. The council did not want to interfere with the normal affairs in that region as disruption to its function and feel risked flight of the residents there. London himself had warned how massive traffic rerouting due to the construction would result in major problems in the distribution of feeding stock. And even though the council held sway over the major organized crime syndicates in the city, some members worried that random low level street crime would rise, further affecting the citizenry. All of these factors would seriously impair hunting in the area and create unrest with the more traditional minded undead residing within those districts.

Abraham had assured the rest of the council that the renovations would bring in more potential feeding stock to fuel the primarch's distribution operation.

Honeyed words.

Everyone knew that only Abraham's control had spread throughout the area. Rumors spread of all the bribes and secret deals he had made to get his way— both with council members and with various mortal institutions. He had also personally promised London that the installation of new subway lines accompanying the construction would increase the councilor's influence with the district. But despite the deals, many resident vampires complained nightly that others under Abraham's influence began moving in on their domains and competing for territory. A few fights had already broken out, and tensions between the rival groups grew by the night.

The double doors near the grandfather clock creaked open.

Oberon entered. Like all others of his advanced age, the vampire's skin was taught and pale. His yellow eyes receded somewhat into his face, with dark circles underneath them. His eyebrows were permanently arched into steep points, and his salt-and-pepper hair was combed back and curled slightly past his collar. He wore a gray three piece suit sans jacket. His thin lips wrapped around his yellowed teeth into a curled smile that no matter how genuine and inviting failed to conceal the malevolence just below the surface.

The aged vampire gently shut the door behind him.

London clapped his pocket watch closed and rose to his feet.

"Apologies for keeping you waiting, my friend. How are you?"

The two shook hands. The exertion disturbed London's wound, causing a visible spike of pain. The older vampire noticed the grimace on London's face.

"It hurts, doesn't it?"

"Yes," he nodded, pocketing his watch.

"The same for me." Oberon lightly patted his chest, just beside the heart, flinching slightly from the touch. "Well, regardless of the circumstances, I am glad you survived."

Oberon walked over to a heavy wooden console behind one of the couches and opened one of the cabinet doors on the side. Clouds of chilled air rolled onto the ground. He pulled out a bottle with finely filigreed gold carvings sleeved onto the base. Removing the bottle's stopper with a wet squeak, the elder poured out a thick red liquid into a pair of small crystal goblets. He returned the bottle to the cabinet, and handed a goblet to London.

"To our recovery."

They clinked glasses and sipped.

"Good flavor," London regarded the goblet. "Is that a hint of cinnamon I detect?"

The two vampires sat down across from each other. The elder pulled a pair of leather embossed coasters and slid one to London.

"Indeed. The donor was specially prepared with alcohol before harvesting. My man also added in a few spices in the final mix. I find it creates a wonderful aftertaste. Helps soothe the nerves, too."

London took another sip. He found the spices easy enough. And his friend was right, they did help the cinnamon linger on his tongue.

"So. How have you been?" the elder asked.

"You can say I have seen better nights. I had to drink quite a lot to mend this wound along with the others."

Oberon nodded. "It seems our mutual friend has some very dangerous abilities."

London agreed, trying not to disturb his bandage.

"How is your man, Alexander?"

"He fared far worse than I did, but he will recover. He is a tenacious sort."

Oberon took a short sip. "What exactly happened last night?"

London gathering his thoughts after a deep draught.

"The night started out well enough. Alexander supervised the transfer of a shipment for the normal delivery along with extras gathered for your special request. There were a couple of hiccups during the process, but everything went well."

Oberon creased his brow. "What sort of hiccups?"

London gently waved him off. "Nothing to worry about. Some of the bags tried to run, but my men were able to retrieve most of them unharmed. Your shipment will arrive tomorrow evening unabated."

The older vampire's face relaxed. "Do go on."

"Near the end of the loading, Alexander noticed something strange in the air. A peculiar scent. Like a newly created vampire, but slightly off."

"Off? How so?"

"I am not entirely sure. Remember how you first explained the nature of our blood to me? How it has a certain mystic charge to it?"

"Of course I remember," Oberon nodded, tipping his goblet to London, "That was quite a long time ago when we had that conversation."

"Yes. You had told me that the charge combined with the digestive potency gained over the centuries is what gives our humours its identifiable odor. The same applies to our thralls as well, though they lack the potency."

Oberon smiled. That was the first conversation they had concerning the ways of magic. He had tried to initiate London into the mystic arts then, but his friend was a man of action and had showed no aptitude for it. Still, he remembered the lessons well.

"The scent that Alexander had encountered last night smelled like both: the warm blood of a thrall and the potent charge of a full vampire."

The elder's sunken eyes narrowed. "So she *is* alive."

London nodded.

Oberon pressed an index finger to his chin. "I was certain the interruption of the ritual would have destroyed her body. But here she is, skulking around your operation. How interesting."

"Indeed. More troubling, though, is that *he* was with her."

Thin arched eyebrows dropped suddenly. "Our masked menace?"

"They looked to be working together."

Oberon contemplated the idea. "I wonder, were they in league before the ritual? He showed up out of nowhere, killed several of your security personnel, violently interrupted the ceremony, and made off with my subject. He even evaded the patrols I sent into the surrounding forests. Perhaps it is possible our friend was protecting her?"

"I have no idea," London shook his head. "Who was this woman, by the way?"

"Unfortunately, I do not know."

Oberon finished his drink and stood up. He took London's empty goblet and refilled them at the cooler. "You recall that a special subject is needed to complete the ritual, right? A woman with a specific metaphysical requirement?"

"Yes."

Returning with the goblets, Oberon said, "The ritual is millennia old—deciphering it took many years. Through my efforts, I learned it will only work properly if the subject is 'created by death and defined by defiance'."

The two clinked glasses.

"How cryptic."

"Very. Given its age, vague phrasing is to be expected. I believe the first part indicates that the subject's existence must be one born through the death of another, and the second references the subject's temperament. Unfortunately, I could not glean exact explanations."

"A riddle perhaps?"

"That was my thought."

"Then what was the smaller ritual in your laboratory for?"

"That was a small rite of my own creation— something I use when I wish to manipulate a specific mortal. It target's the subconscious and creates a recurring dream of my construction that grows in intensity with each night. By the seventh night, the dream is so powerful that it compels the target to seek out the subject of the dream, be it a location or object. Once they are close enough, I create a temporary mental link with him—or her in this case. Once established, I can guide the subject with more precision. The target merely thinks it is just another dream. There is an interesting side affect, though: the mental link allows me to see into the target's thoughts."

Oberon frowned. "Unfortunately, that woman's mind was an absolute maze, difficult to penetrate. I was unable to learn anything from her at all, let alone a name. Whoever she is, she mourned someone named Kathleen. A sister or a mother? A close friend perhaps? Regardless, that was the only bit of information I took in the short window provided. And given her peculiar mode of dress that night, I doubt she would have carried any form of personal identification."

He took another sip, "Though, come to think of it, it might explain her sneaking around your operation."

"An interesting tool, your rite. That still does not explain how you found her, though."

"Quite simple, really. I took a few pieces from the ancient ritual and added them into the subject portion of my luring rite, allowing it to home in on the nearest woman with the desired spiritual attributes. It took a few test tries to perfect, however. In the end, the little trick worked."

His frown returned. "But none of that matters at the moment. Right now we need to learn exactly what *he* is. I was not afforded the opportunity to see much of him when he attacked. What can you tell me about the man?"

London closed his eyes. The presence of the masked man troubled him. For as long as vampires existed, they have lived in parallel symbiosis with mortals. In the early days of human civilization, they lived on the outside, hidden away from the small settlements. Like a shepherd managing a herd, they culled the weak and tended their flock from other predators. And like shepherds, they depended on the herd for sustenance. With the march of time and the development of cities, vampires traded living in caves and hovels far from mortals to living amongst them using the same structures they built.

But, regardless of what vampires did for their flock, there were always those mortals who could not tolerate being managed. While the general view among vampires was that when one of their own culls too much, the affected mortals will mourn and move on, but sometimes, the response travels too far in the opposite direction—usually taking the form of a lone mortal lashing out and hunting their erstwhile shepherds. Nothing that a seasoned vampire couldn't deal with on his own.

Worse is when these so-called mortal hunters banded together. At the height of the Catholic church's power, the Inquisition did much to harm the vampire community in Europe. But that was centuries ago—the hunters of the Inquisition were merely a shadow of their former power these nights. And regardless of origin, vampire hunters always used normal weapons to enact their petty vengeance. Rarely did such instruments overpower a vampire's innate resilience. This masked man left biting wounds that refused to heal.

"Whatever ability this man wields, it is lethal to us. When my medical expert inspected Alexander's wounds, he found they were consistent with cauterization. The affected tissues needed to be removed before the wounds would close. And even then the process was slow. The stab wound he sustained was worse, as we could not properly excise the corrupted flesh. He drained an entire bag in order to close it"

"Unfortunately, I learned that first hand."

"On both Alexander and myself, the lesions looked as if a torch had been used on us."

Oberon waved an arm, indicating the weapons encased in glass. "Though I may dabble in such things, I am by no means an expert, London. What manner of sword could do such a thing?"

"I have a few theories, but no solid conclusions. At first I thought the weapon might be alloyed with silver. Though the metal causes severe allergic reactions to us similar to burns, it is much too soft and malleable to hold a proper edge. And we both can attest to the sharpness of his weapon."

Oberon shifted uncomfortably in agreement.

"And when worked into a suitably strong alloy, the concentration of silver is so weak as to be trivial. So with the rejection of that idea, I thought maybe it secreted a strong acid. Sufficient quantities of the chemical can replicate similar wounds on a vampire's body. I remember many decades ago a particularly industrious hunter utilized a longsword with minute holes drilled along the spine where acid could be secreted. The blade of the modified longsword had to be very thick in order to accommodate the delivery system, though, and I noticed the katana the masked man wielded has a rather deep fuller running along its spine, so I ruled that out. Furthermore, wounds from acid do not persist as long as the ones he inflicted on us. Given his glowing eyes, I believe he may be mystical in nature, which is your expertise."

The elder placed his goblet on the table and crossed his legs, resting his hands over the bent knee.

"There exists only a small handful of mystical orders that have potent martial elements. The Society of Black Scrolls comes to mind, but those madmen typically operate in and around the Middle East and the Mediterranean states, and as such, they don't use katana swords. However, they do frequently battle with vampire society at large, so I would not rule them out completely."

London stroked his shaved chin. "Do they have a particular ethnic makeup?"

"Oh yes. The Black Scrolls exclusively recruit from the local communities in that area."

"Hmm. I caught sight of him unmasked right before he escaped. His face had been misshape from our fight, but he was decidedly of Caucasian stock."

"He might be part of the old foe," Oberon offered.

"The Inquisition?"

"Yes, but the Inquisition has not been active for over a century," London countered. "They have been dormant since the beginning of the last century."

"Yes," Oberon gazed into his goblet. "Come to think of it, they too prefer to arm themselves with thoroughly western implements, be they modern or otherwise and have never been observed utilizing any unusual athletic abilities like our friend. Regardless, I have heard of isolated sightings of vampire hunters in Europe with golden eyes, but I never substantiated any of those rumors beyond a mortal mage attacking our kind or gypsy hearsay."

London sipped from his goblet. "Do you know of any Japanese orders that might fit this man, given his choice of weaponry?"

"Only two. Their names escape me at the moment, but they focus on elemental magics, and only one has a martial practice. That one focuses on reviving the spirit of the samurai. Their chosen weapon fits the description, but like the Black Scrolls, they recruit exclusively from Japanese stock, which excludes the man we encountered. But that still doesn't explain the strange flames he deployed against our followers."

"Flames?"

Oberon nodded gravely.

"Though I did not see them, he attacked some of my followers with blue flames capable of incinerating them in an instant. If their descriptions are correct, not even our old foes in the Inquisition are capable of such things."

London tilted his head, "Then our new friend is an unknown. A new player perhaps?"

"Perhaps. I will have to research more into this. It may be that those sightings in Europe were more than just rumors."

"Then you should need this."

London reached into his jacket and retrieved a compact disk in an unmarked jewel case. He handed the CD over to Oberon. "Surveillance footage from the garage before the fire destroyed it. I had a specialist clean it up as best he could earlier today. You might find it useful."

Oberon regarded the disk and placed it on the coffee table between them.

"Thank you. But enough about this interloper. You said my ritual subject was in league with him?"

London inclined his head. "That appears to be so. As I said, it was she whom Alexander had detected. They had stolen into the garage facility together, and they left together."

"And her scent was similar to that of a vampire and a thrall combined?"

"Exactly." London checked his watch again.

Oberon recognized the gold time piece. It was a conductor's pocket watch, a gift after they had first worked together—the man's timing had been impeccable. "When Alexander notified me of the presence of another vampire lurking in the area, I figured that the council had sent them there to commit sabotage."

Years ago, Free Port was home to a dedicated

occult community dating back to it's founding. Back then, Darius Bennett, the council's new primarch, had banned magical practices within Free Port after a negotiation between him and the elected leader of the local mages devolved into a shooting match. Mystics within the city's limits—of which Oberon was one—objected to the proclamation, claiming Bennett's move had created hostile tensions between vampires and mages. The mages fought back. Dissidents in the vampire community joined them and took up arms against the council. The primarch had launched a vicious pogrom against the coalition and forced Oberon to cut ties with his arcane confederates and give up his mystical practices. He refused and was forced to curtail his practices since.

Oberon never forgave the primarch for that.

London went on, "But, when nothing happened and the buses left the depot unmolested, I gambled that the interloper was there simply to spy on us instead. So, I set up a bit of a honey trap with a hidden camera." London glanced at his time piece. *Clip-clap.*

"A bit of a long shot, but it paid off."

Oberon smiled and nodded, noticing London fiddle with his watch. In the years since the pogrom, Bennett's influence had spread everywhere, and his minions had became known for their fanaticism. Even a few members of the councilor were his former attack dogs—survivors of the pogrom. The man was an expert at twisting people and turning them to his cause. More than once Oberon had foiled one of Bennett's spies from snooping around his private affairs. Bennett had even turned one of Oberon's most trusted lieutenants during the pogrom, prompting an immediate and harsh response and replacement.

The primarch had grown increasingly overbearing in his dealings with Oberon of late. London warned his friend that he was being rather paranoid, but the old mage had become quite adept at sniffing out Bennett's schemes. It was only a matter of time that someone would catch on that he and London were using Bennett's blood distribution network for their own needs. The old mage swore that he would be ready when that night came.

London rubbed his thumb on the watch and continued.

"We captured footage of them listening in on us. When I recognized them from the descriptions you had given me, I planned to hunt them down later for you. But, Alexander bungled that up quite badly."

"I warned you you should discipline that boy," Oberon said darkly.

"I believe the wounds he incurred afterwards were punishment enough."

"Complete obedience should be maintained at all times, London. I have told you that time and again. You should not tolerate failure."

"I understand that, Oberon, but too much control squashes independent thinking." The two had clashed many times over the subject of loyalty. It had always been a sticking point between them. "I encourage my people to take initiative when they see it. It makes for better soldiers. Regardless, a fight ensued. I ordered Alexander to capture her while my men dealt with the masked individual. Sadly, the security force died to a man."

"From what happened at the mansion, I am not surprised."

"During the scrap, Alexander noticed something very peculiar, though. The girl expressed more than one vampiric trait."

"Really? How so?" Oberon raised an eyebrow.

"To begin with, she tried to drain the blood from one of my thralls."

"You must be joking!"

"Alexander witnessed it himself, fangs and all. Not only that, she also expressed a level of strength commensurate with that of a newly created vampire as well. Though we were able to overcome her, she had resisted to a degree far beyond her slender frame."

"Interesting."

"I thought as much. But there was something else we noticed. Her eyes were bright red, like an ancient thrall with a high blood saturation."

The old mage fell back into the couch, pondering the description. "You were right to try to capture her for me. The fact that she is still alive is unusual, but these expressions are very intriguing. It seems the first half of the ritual succeeded after all. I shall assign some of my men to return her to me."

London held up a hand.

"You may not need to. I purposefully let slip the details of our deliveries while they were spying on us. This masked man seemed intent on disrupting the primarch's delivery operation, and if the girl is indeed in league with him, then they should show up for your delivery. If so, he will find us prepared. My men will be lying in wait for them. I will arrive with the rest ahead of the delivery, and together we will box them in with overwhelming firepower. If my luck continues, you will have your delivery and your subject. and, we can be rid of this masked man before he truly becomes a nuisance."

"Thank you."

"Think nothing of it," London said, looking down at his watch, frowning.

"Oh, one more thing about the girl. This is merely speculation, but, if she has expressed vampiric qualities like fangs and so on, it is possible she also shares our resilience. I mention this because she took a few rounds before the masked man escaped with her again. If she does not have our resilience, then you might have to look for a new subject for the ritual. You are planning to attempt it again, correct?" *Clip-clap.*

"Of course." Oberon quietly noted the watch spinning faster in London's hand.

"When will you restart, if I may ask?" *Clip-clap.* "I would like to prepare tighter security for it."

"Soon," Oberon's eyes creased slightly. "I already have plans in motion."

"Good. But . . . if my auditorium is still viable, what are the bags for?"

The elder pressed his thin lips hard, regarding his old friend with veiled suspicion.

"The wards I laid will retain their power for many months to come, so that should not pose a problem. The vessel for the second half of the ritual, however, will. It can only hold it's charge for a few days. If we can capture the subject before Tuesday, then the ritual could be resumed without delay. If not, I shall have to scour your bus full of females for viable candidates to refill it before attempting the ritual again. What preparations do you need to make, might I ask?"

"Preparations?" *Clip-clap.* London rolled his eyes around in thought. "I believe the manor needs to be redressed. I must maintain the building's image as a haunted mansion lest the local government try to take control of it again. You understand?"

Oberon steepled his fingers. "Of course. No prying eyes and such."

"Exactly. Bennett has eyes everywhere. Were he to find out about our operation, he would bring down a very harsh response to a violation like this."

The mage's eyes hovered over the gold watch twirling faster and faster.

"A *harsh* response indeed."

Clip-clap. "You will be on hand to receive the delivery, yes?" London asked.

Oberon fell silent for a moment before uttering

a falsely hearty chuckle. "Not to worry, I shall personally be there to support your plan."

"Good. When should I expect you?"

He looked out the window to the mountains. "Ten P.M.."

London promptly pocketed the watch and stood up with a relieved smile, leaving his goblet unfinished. "Well, then. I should be off."

The elder immediately rose and shook London's hand. "This has all been very illuminating, old friend. Thank you."

"Think nothing of it, Oberon," London smiled. "The resurrection will resume tomorrow night."

Oberon's grin fell into a scowl once London shut the doors behind him.

He stood there, silently glowering at the empty couch. The grandfather clock echoed loudly throughout the empty parlor, it's incessant ticking growing on his nerves. Oberon finished his goblet in one quick gulp and walked over to a phone sitting atop the chilled cabinet. He picked up the brass receiver and dialed. It rang several times before the other side picked up.

"Armand? Activate the hit on Don Sancho. Tomorrow night. No, the time table has moved up. Remember to make sure it fails. Also, I want you to send a contingent of your men to Undergrove Manor tomorrow evening at ten o'clock. Expect augmented resistance, so make sure they use the *proper* ammunition. Correct. No survivors."

Oberon replaced the receiver and moved to the window, gazing out to the dark hills in the distance. It pained him to make that call. He always believed London above Bennett's influence. But he was wrong. And if that was the case, then so be it. Spies needed to be dealt with swiftly and harshly. A new ritual subject would have to be found, but that was merely a temporary setback.

His friend's betrayal was not.

Electronic dance music pulsed like the rhythm of her heart.

Red and purple lights throbbed from the dark, high ceiling, painting the writhing sea of bare shoulders and gelled hair with an evil glow. Small spotlights on swivels traced circles of white over the sweaty, gyrating dancers. Tables under-lit with neon purple lined the sunken dance floor. A patchwork of booths and tables topped with black lights encased in tiny glass cages radiated walled-off dance floor, each crowded with more hedonists. Velvety purple and black wallpaper embossed with stylized pentagrams and pitchforks crawled up every wall.

A pair of long, black lacquered bars with frosted, glowing white tops dominated the rear of the main floor. A lone entryway covered with strips of old distressed leather separated them. And a sinister looking bouncer in an equally sinister looking black suit stood vigil over the entrance. Panel after panel of mirrors with carved geodesic designs loomed behind the bar, held back by an extensive collection of liquor bottles arranged on clear plastic runners.

The second floor balcony looked down on the debauchery, accessible only by a single, double wide staircase. Miniature lights shaped like stars accented each step. Smaller booths and tables sat against walls full of swirling black clouds and twinkling constellations.

The scent of perfumed sweat and flavored liquor parted as Lauren stalked onto the main floor. A thin silk top hung from her neck, leaving little to the imagination. Tight black leather wrapped her legs like wet paint. Her long white hair was done up in a delicate twist, and smokey black eye shadow rimmed her bright red eyes. Pearls hung from her ears, gold ringed her wrists, and red tipped her fingers. The neon light gave Lauren's pale skin a baleful radiance.

Men stared at her, and women watched her.

She strolled up to the bar between a pair of men with their backs turned and snatched a shot of liquor that both were too busy to notice, downing it with a quick flip of her head. The drink was harsh, yet unfulfilling. Lauren faced the dance pit, thirsty for more.

Scanning over the wriggling bodies on the dance floor, she clocked a couple entering a recently vacated booth. They dressed simpler than the rest of the crowd. The man wore a plain dress shirt and khakis with horribly worn sneakers. The girl had on an ill-fitting dress and constantly stumbled on a pair of low heeled shoes. They looked painfully out of place and uncomfortable. Normal.

Innocent.

Weaving her way over, she leaned against a pillar, observing the two arguing in the booth. The woman accused her man of ignoring her. He blamed her for not putting out. She thought coming to the club was a mistake. He came here to loosen her up. They sat there in silence. Lauren grinned.

She approached the booth, immediately catching the love-birds' attention.

"Can I help you?" the man droned.

Lauren bent forward on the table, pulling her elbows in to emphasize her cleavage. The neon underlit her face with purple shadow and highlighted the subtle glow of her crimson eyes.

"I couldn't help but notice you two could use a good drink."

The woman instantly stared daggers at her. The man glanced at the lump of contempt sitting next to him and back to Lauren. With her eyes the girl insisted he do something.

"Lady, we're kind of busy. Maybe someone else would like to drink with you?"

Lauren gently turned the man's face away from his woman's angry glare. "Tell you what, Junior. You meet me at the bar, and I'll show you things she would never dream of."

He blinked, transfixed by the promise of her lips. With a wink, Lauren left, letting her invitation hang in the air. The girl slapped him across the face, but he was too busy watching Lauren disappear into the crowd to notice.

Minutes later, the man found Lauren, sipping a glass of dark red wine at the bar with her legs crossed lightly on the stool next to her. Spying him, she sat up and patted the cushion. He uneasily climbed onto the high seat. Lauren handed him a red drink just like hers.

Inspecting the glass, the man looked at her, "This has a ruphie in it, doesn't it?"

She snatched the wine from him and sipped it before thrusting it back in his hands. "Do I look like the kind of girl who needs drugs to get what I want?"

"Umm, no?"

"Good answer. Now, about that drink?"

He stared at the liquid before finally giving in with a shrug. He reached the bottom of the glass in one go with a hungry smile growing when he finished. He looked at her with a desire that didn't exist moments ago.

Grinning, she took him by the hand to the leather curtain between the bars. The bouncer's skin was pale like hers and glowed just the same. The man's salt and pepper hair had a nasty widow's peak and was combed back, curling up at the collar. Dark circles ringed his sunken eyes, and his thin lips curled upwards into a wicked smile when saw her.

"Right this way," the bouncer said, parting the brown leather straps.

Lauren lead the man through a hall lined top and bottom with dark red neon. Pressed against the walls, more club-goers sucked face, snorted drugs, and groped bodyparts in various combinations. She waded through the narrow corridor with her new man in tow, passing up room after room occupied by people doing the same things only more vigorously. Finally, she found an empty room at the end, and shoved him inside.

The room was lit like the hallway with a long table shaped like a black glass coffin filigreed with gold. Glowing red lines circled the dark stone floor with matching designs on the black couch.

Lauren threw the door shut and pushed him into the cushions. She straddled the man and wasted no time with him. Worming her tongue into his mouth, she ripped off his shirt one button at a time. After a few moments of stunned confusion, he joined in, feeling his way up her torso. Before he found anything forbidden, Lauren pinned his hands above his head.

"You're stronger than you look!" he exclaimed with an awkward laugh.

"I'm a lot of things."

She parted her lips while he tried to kiss the top of her breasts. Sharp fangs gleamed in the red neon. With her free hand, she grabbed a fist-full of the man's hair and wrenched his head to the side. His neck exposed, Lauren sunk her teeth into the pulsating flesh.

The man struggled for a breath before giving in to her.

Blood flowed through the two punctures, and she drank slowly and deeply, savoring the warm sweetness coursing over her tongue. She felt his heartbeat fade slower and fainter with each swallow. When there was nothing left of him, Lauren let the body collapsed into a heap on the couch.

Lauren exhaled slowly, licking the red liquid from her stained teeth and lips. She stared into the man's lifeless eyes, frozen in painful ecstasy.

She felt sated and whole.

Complete.

Lauren jolted awake.

Her body was stiff and her face felt numb. She stared stupidly at the gray wall in front of her until she realized she was face down in bed. The dark, silvery sheets had been thrown aside, and all the pillows were gone. With a pained grunt, Lauren rolled over and lost herself in the plain white ceiling.

"Another nightmare," she sighed.

She sat up at the edge of the mattress and rubbed her aching head. After ten straight days of disturbing dreams, Lauren had forgot what a good night's sleep felt like.

As the rest of her bedroom came into focus, Lauren noticed the vertical blinds were open and her apartment was bright and warm. Did she forget to close them again? She reached over to the switch on her nightstand only to realize her shirt was gone. In fact, she wasn't wearing a top at all. Alarmed, Lauren looked down to see a thick layer of gauze covering her torso from collar to sternum. Her pants, gloves, sneakers, and equipment belt lay on the rug at the foot of her bed, all covered in dust and chemical soot.

And blood.

Lauren rushed to the vanity mirror in her bathroom. The bandage was hastily wrapped, thick in some sections while thin in others. The back of her shoulders was rigid with dried blood. More crusted crimson caked her hair and smeared her face and nose. She wiped the stains away with a few splashes of water. Shockingly, she found no scars, and her nose had been set. She frantically unraveled the gauze and presented her back to the mirror. Craning her neck around, Lauren saw no wounds there either. No scars. No scratches. No nothing. Her body looked exactly like it did the day she met Ethan.

"What the hell?"

Tossing the gauze in the waste bin, Lauren threw on her bathrobe and stepped into a pair of slippers. It was about that time she noticed a curious noise floating through the door. It sounded like something scraping metal, long, slow, and repeating every two seconds. Coming to the head of the stairs, she saw where the noise came from.

Years ago, Lauren had a twelve by fifteen foot section of carpet installed on the raised floor behind her couch. She used it for her daily exercises. Stashed in the corner next to it lay all her weights and athletic equipment along with her writing desk.

Kneeling in the center of that carpet, Ethan carefully dragged a small square stone across the edge of his sword wearing nothing but a pair of old gym shorts. His big green duffel bag rested against her weights, along with a rolled up sleeping bag. Piled beside it lay a few thin sheets of steel, a file, a rusted pair of tin snips, and a loose stack of those throwing stars of his. A green beaded necklace with a shiny cross sat on a small black book with red pages at the corner of the carpet beside another pair of books with old library tags.

The cross glinted in the sunlight shining down

through the windows behind him. It was early in the afternoon.

She had slept late again.

Slowly descending the stairs, Lauren sniffed at the faint scent of cooked beef and spices in the air. Following the smell, she saw dirty plates in the sink and a warm frying pan left on the stove. Half a pot of slightly fresh coffee sat on the counter. In the corner, draped on the brushed metal garbage can lay the bloodied remains of her shirt and coat. She picked up the clothes and inspected them. The shirt was ruined. Holes riddled the back and still-moist blood completely soaked the rest of it. Her jacket was slightly better off, but still just as done for. She held the black pea coat up to the light. The midday sun poked through six small holes just below the shoulders.

She looked over to Ethan. He ignored her, silently working on his sword.

Well, at least you're still alive, she thought to herself.

Sighing, Lauren took the two rolls of film from the pocket and stuffed the bloody garment back in the trash. Being alive wasn't making her feel any better right now. She put the rolls on the kitchen counter next to a bowl. Inside were six squashed lead bullets covered in dried blood. The last thing she remembered last night was gunfire.

"I got shot last night, didn't I?"

"Yes."

Lauren hung her head. "What happened?"

Ethan dragged the stone down the blade's edge. His movements were smooth and precise. "Remember that guard you insisted on knocking out? He woke up." He paused and turned to her. "Never leave a gun at your back."

Lauren silently cursed herself. This was the second time she almost died in as many nights. She nodded to the bowl, "I suppose I should thank you for healing me, then?"

He shook his head, "I didn't heal you."

"You didn't use some weird magical mumbo-jumbo you haven't told me about yet?"

He paused with his sword again, "Nope. You did that on your own."

"I did *what* now?"

"You were bleeding pretty badly when I got you to your car. Had to use my shirt to stop it before driving back. By the time I got you here, the bullets started coming out on their own. Your wounds were still open, though—had to bandage you up. Figured you wouldn't want to bleed all over the place."

"Wait, you mean the bullet holes were closing on their own?"

"Vampires heal wounds much faster than regular people. Recovery time depends on the level of injury. Small ones heal in seconds. Larger injuries, multiple bullet wounds for instance, take longer. They typically have to feed before they can heal those. I had a feeling you shared that ability with them."

Ethan resumed sharpening his weapon. Lauren stared into the bowl. The memory of biting the guard's arm flashed across her mind. She had actually bit into someone and drank their blood last night! She wasn't sure if she should be horrified or grateful considering what happened next.

Her stomach growled hungrily.

She detested that sensation.

Lauren opened her fridge. Of the steaks she left out yesterday, only five remained. A snappy remark at Ethan crossed her mind, but she didn't have the energy. She took one out and tossed it in the pan, cooking it barely long enough to sear the outside. Plopping it on a plate, she threw on whatever seasoning was left on the counter, fixed a cup of coffee, and sat down on a stool.

Ethan passed his stone twice while she debated eating her meal. With a final sigh, she gave in.

Cutting through the bloody, almost raw meat, Lauren observed the extent of wear and tear on Ethan's body. He was corded with muscle with barely an ounce of fat or flab on him, but she suspected that wasn't by choice. If not for the muscles, Lauren would have thought him malnourished. However, the lattice work of scars stretching over his skin fascinated her. Patches of gnarled burns, deep scratches, and long cuts crawled across his body. Small, bullet-sized dots, some alone, some in groups, peppered his limbs and torso. She tried to count them all, but gave up in the mid teens.

One scar stood out from the rest, though. A set of four thick troughs dragged diagonally down his chest. The scars looked as if entire chunks of flesh had been scooped out. Curiously, the massive bruises on his face had receded. No discoloration or inflammation, only a few faint lines marked that they ever existed.

"So, if I heal fast because of . . . um, my circumstances, what's your excuse?"

He looked up at her. "Meditation."

"And here I thought only Buddhists and weirdos who collect crystals did that."

He returned to his sword. "Through meditation, one can align the mind, the body, and the spirit. Once aligned, the body can be commanded to perform incredible feats."

"Oh, really? Like what?"

"Enhancing performance. Purging diseases and toxins. Forcing wounds to close. Reknitting bones and nerve tissue."

"Yeah? I'll bet you can walk on water, too," she said with her mug on her lips.

"Yes."

She rolled her eyes. "What are 'bags'?"

"What?" he inspected the edge.

"Those two in the office talked about bags. Is that what they call people?"

"Slang. Short for blood-bags." He rubbed the stone down the blade some more. "As in 'a walking bag of blood'."

"That's disgusting."

"Yep."

Ethan continued working on the weapon. He looked oddly at peace considering the events of last night, as if being pummeled and thrown across the room like a ragdoll hadn't fazed him. He looked calm. Serene. Meanwhile, her hands trembled so much she had trouble cutting her steak. The crazed look on Emile Berger's face after she shot him sent shivers up her spine. How he moved with unearthly strength and speed even with that massive hole in his head. Or how her knife did nothing to the other vampire even after sinking it six inches through his skull.

Lauren shivered, still feeling Alexander's hands around her neck. She had to take her mind off last night.

"Are you religious?" she pointed her knife at the book at the corner of the carpet.

Ethan nodded. He doused the stone with a cup of water and continued sharpening the blade.

"I never really got into that. My family wasn't very religious."

"Then start," he said.

Lauren sliced off a piece of meat. It was horribly oblong and very red. She regarded it for a moment. "I think it might be too late for that."

He paused and looked her over as she popped the piece of meat in her mouth. Lauren fought the urge to smile from the taste.

"It's never too late to reach for faith."

"Maybe," Lauren swallowed. "So. Where'd you get that scar?"

Ethan turned to her fully, one eyebrow raised.

"That big one on your chest," she indicated it with her fork. "Did a vampire do that?"

"No."

"A bear?" she guessed.

"There are more dangerous things out there than vampires and bears."

She watched him return to his sword.

The sound of stone scraping on metal filled the apartment again. What kind of creature could leave marks that big and be a greater threat than what she saw last night? Could a vampire turn into some immense clawed beast? She envisioned a twisted, hulking mass of muscle and bone galloping after her. Claw-filled limbs smashed through concrete like play-sand. It's heavy footfalls sent tremors, knocking her off her feet and forcing her to scurry away on all fours. After a minute, Lauren forced the hellish vision away.

"Why did you run into the bus depot last night?"

He wiped his sword with a damp cloth, giving it an oily sheen, before sheathing it and placing it in the long cloth bag next to the barbell rack.

He stretched. She sighed.

"You're a wiz with conversation, you know that?"

"What?"

"The bus depot!" she raised her voice. "You ditched me on that tower and ran into that place! What the hell were you thinking?"

He stared at her, measuring his words. "I saw something."

"Oh really?" She leaned back on the stool, arms crossed. "Like what?"

"It doesn't concern you."

"Doesn't concern me?" She marched around the counter. "You left me on that tower and charged into a den of armed killers without any knowledge or prep. They had machine guns, and all you had was that fucking sword. Of course it fucking concerns me!"

He glared at her, his jaw set. "Leave it alone."

"No!" she jabbed a finger at him. "You brought me along to watch the depot. Fine, done, no problem. We watched the place and planned for entry—like we agreed—but then you decided, 'Fuck the stakeout!' and immediately stormed the place. We got ambushed last night, Ethan! Those two in that office left a single window open with a night vision camera pointed directly at it. They set a fucking trap for us! I can't believe I didn't pick up on it earlier. Hell, they want to dissect me like some sick experiment! You might be okay with that, but I'm not!"

His eyes hardened. "I thought sneaking into places is what you're good at."

She bit back her tongue. Those were her words alright.

"I know what I do is dangerous," she looked at him sharply. "But when I do it, I prepare for it. I am calm. I am quiet. And I damn well don't leave dead bodies lying around! What you did last night was stupid and reckless! You're going to get yourself killed, and because I have no one to turn to for this shit, you're gonna get me killed too!"

"I tried to keep you safe," he seethed.

"Bullshit. You tried to abandon me."

"No. You told me you don't like violence. I told you to stay in the tower, not follow me," he said, holding back scorn.

"I had to protect my investment!" Lauren barked, shoving a finger at him. When he said nothing in return, she added. "We had a deal. I help you break into places, you help me find a cure. You promised me—!"

"I promised you nothing!" he thundered.

She stepped back at his sudden outburst.

"I didn't make any promises to you, and I don't owe you a damn thing," he shouted. "You walked into that fucking mansion on your own. You got yourself captured. If not for me, you'd be one of them now or worse. And you begged me to let you help."

Something deep down inside her began to simmer. "'Cause you were about to cut my head off! What was I supposed to do, sit there and let you do it? I didn't wanna fucking die! It was the best idea I could come up with in the moment."

"And I accepted the offer. You're the thief, so when it comes to breaking and entering, I'll consider your input, but—"

"Oh, like you did when you tried to pry off that roof hatch?" she interrupted. "You almost tripped a fucking alarm! I didn't see you consider me then. We agreed to watch the place and come back later, not take a few pictures and waltz right in."

"I didn't ask you to follow me. I gave you every chance to walk away, but you didn't. You say you can handle yourself, but you damn well don't act like it."

"Don't even start with me like that! I plan out everything I do. I consider every move, game out every angle. I don't put my life in danger just because *I saw something*!" she retorted, dressing her last words in a mocking tone.

Ethan ripped the bowl of bullets off the counter and thrust it under her face, the little bits of copper clicking wildly from the motion.

"*This* isn't a Goddammed game! These parasites will kill you without hesitation if they so much as *think* you know anything about them! If you're so afraid of dying, then why did you keep following me? I told you to stay away at the diner. I told you not to follow me into the depot. I tried to give you an out, but you ran after me every single-fucking-time! You even *blamed* me for what they did to you and *demanded* I do something about it! You have bitched about this little partnership of yours at every turn! If you don't like how

I do things, *then walk the fuck away*!!"

An angry tear rolled down her cheek.

"I've been doing this for far longer than you can imagine, so don't lecture me about how I do my job, especially if you're gonna stick to me like some lost, fucking child!"

Her jaw clenched tight enough to grind her teeth to dust. She wanted to put those bruises back on his cheeks, to unleash every rotten thought that had been festering inside her since that horrible night . . .

But, he was right.

She kept following him—even when he tried to shoo her away. And if he still wanted to put her down like he said, he simply could have left her in that burning building.

Tears fell, but not from anger.

Ethan slid the bowl back on the counter and disappeared into the utility closet near the front door. He rummaged around loudly inside before returning with a pile of clothes in a basket. She watched wanly as he dressed with the same jacket and jeans he always wore along with a blue shirt and quickly stuffed the rest of his belongings into his big duffel bag.

"I'm going back to the mansion before they show up," he said, his voice holding only a hint of anger now. "They're going to deliver those people tonight, and I'm going to stop them. If you still wanna help, then help. Otherwise, stay the fuck out of my way."

Lauren wiped her cheeks. "You know it's a trap, right?"

Ethan looked her square in eyes. "It probably is. But if I do nothing, innocent people will die."

"Don't you think those vamp—people are prepared for that?"

"They don't know what I'm capable of."

She belted out a sardonic laugh. "Who do you think you are? Rambo?"

"Who?"

Lauren blinked, stunned out of her gloom. "You've never seen *Rambo*?"

He shook his head.

"You're kidding me, right? Sylvester Stallone? Giant knife? 'I'm your worst nightmare'? You never heard of it??"

"I don't watch television."

"God, have you been living under a rock all your life?"

He looked at her blankly.

"Never mind," she sniffled. "It doesn't matter anyway. Today's Friday. Emile said they were going to be there tomorrow."

"Today is Saturday."

"Bullshit. It's Friday."

"You slept through Friday."

Confused, Lauren looked at the digital clock above the garbage can. He was right, it was Saturday. She had lost an entire day resting. She glanced over at the empty clothes basket and the pile of dirty dishes in the sink. The puzzle on the coffee table was complete. A few new pieces of origami littered the couch.

Her moist eyes went wide.

He had watched over her. He had let her tag along and even saved her life, twice, without complaint. He had every chance to abandon her—like her father— but he didn't. In fact, she couldn't recall if he had ever asked for any kind of compensation.

Holy shit. I'm the asshole!

Lauren walked onto the carpet under the afternoon sun. Her lips screwed under the natural light. She wanted to back away from it, but refused to acknowledge the pain. Her nose twitched, and she realized he had showered. For the first time since meeting him, his scent didn't make her gag. Surprisingly, it was almost pleasant. Her scowl melted despite her tingling skin.

Taking a deep breath, she looked up. "I'm sorry I've been acting like a—"

"A what?" His brow remained furrowed and his jaw set.

"I don't know. I'm just," she fumbled, trying not to look into his eyes. Apologizing never was her strong suit. "I know it sounds stupid, but, I haven't been myself lately."

Her gaze fell on the long, grisly claw marks running down his chest. She went to touch them but pulled her hand away. How could he be standing after all that? Ethan watched her, puzzled.

"Look, you saved my life. I owe you for that. If you want, you can leave your stuff here, I don't mind. If you're still up for it, we can help each other, but I can't go with you tonight. What you do is way too dangerous. I . . . I just can't."

Hesitantly, Lauren picked up the necklace and pooled the jade beads into her hand.

"Here. You'll probably want this—"

As she handed it to him, the crucifix fell into her palm, and her skin instantly sizzled. Lauren recoiled, dropping the necklace, and cradled her smoking hand to her chest.

"What the hell was that?!" she gaped incredulously. A blackened cross was burned into her flesh. "Felt like my hand was going to burn off!"

Ethan looped the necklace over his neck and tucked it under his shirt. "Vampires are severely allergic to pure silver."

"Great, another thing I have to worry about," she mumbled, rubbing her hand.

He met her gaze. The hardness in his eyes had faded. They weren't disapproving like her father's, but they bored into her just the same. He took her burned hand and held it. For a moment she expected him to do something intimate, but instead, he just put it back by her side.

"I need paper."

"What?" she said, taken out of the moment.

"Something thick I can write on. Like a note card."

She sighed, dejected. "Umm, sure. In the desk, right next to your bag. Top drawer."

Ethan checked the desk and took out a brick of note cards wrapped in cellophane. He ripped off the plastic with his big survival knife and laid out a bunch of them on the carpet. She winced when poked his left palm with the sharp blade. Dipping his finger with the blood, he began chanting in Latin similar to what little she remembered from that night in the auditorium. He traced his blood on each card, filling them with words she couldn't read.

He wrote out the same intricate red script fifteen times, chanted some more, and then, making a symbol with one hand, passed it over the wound. The blood receded back into the cut before her eyes, and the tiny gash closed, leaving a small scar on top of similar ones. Ethan stood up, pocketed the cards, and took a fresh roll of boxing tape from his bag. He then withdrew a small drawstring sack and hung it from his shoulder along with his sword.

"What was all that for?" she asked.

"Preparations."

With that, he walked out of the apartment., the heavy wooden door reverberating behind him.

Lauren stood in the middle of her carpet in silence. She tried not to think about tonight. He was going to fight who knows how many of those men to stop a bunch of people from being used for food. She admired his courage, but deep down, she knew he was going to die. And if she followed him like before, she would die along with him. She couldn't go. Lauren was a thief, not a fighter.

Going with him was suicide.

It was better this way.

She tried to finish her breakfast, but had since lost her appetite. Her eyes instead hovered over the bowl. She rolled one of the bullets between her fingers, idly inspecting the tiny specs of blood still clinging to it. She recalled it not hurting. But then again, she had passed out right after, so maybe that really didn't matter.

"Why did all this happen to me?"

Lauren blew a dirty lock of hair from her face. When it fell back on her cheek, she pinched the small bundle away. Bits of dried blood flaked onto the cutting board. The sight disgusted her. Trudging upstairs, Lauren prepped her tub for a long, hot bath. When everything was ready, she climbed in and let the steaming hot water envelope her. She drifted off in the soothing heat, and fragments of that night under the mansion floated across her mind. The disembodiment. The evil chanting. That vampire's vile grin. Was she really chosen to be one of them? She shuddered when the incomplete memory reached its climax. Though she didn't see it, Ethan said that the big arena had lit up when the vampire bit her. But he also said that vampires weren't made that way, so why all the fanfare?

Drying off, she caught herself in the mirror. Were those strange lights the reason why all her color was gone?

She went down to the kitchen and started cleaning. With all she had been through since then, she still had no idea how they had discovered her identity. Kathleen Baxter was long gone. That woman only existed in dreams now.

Was she chosen because of her inheritance?

Lauren chuckled to herself. If that's what the vampire was after, he was shit out of luck. Lauren couldn't pass for her old self anyway now that her eyes had changed. She probably couldn't even pass a retinal scan. Hell, that homeless girl at the depot would do a better job looking like Kathleen Baxter.

She reached for the frying pan and froze. She slowly turned to the two film rolls still on the counter.

Was she *why Ethan ditched the stakeout?*

Lauren snatched the film and quickly climbed into her workroom. The lights flickered on. She pulled her dirty suit off the work bench and tossed it over the chair. One of the sleeves nudged the computer mouse, waking the still slumbering machine. Ignoring the humming computer, she pulled down a jug of developing fluid from the shelf and began preparing the basin. While reaching for the darkroom light switch, the computer monitor blinked to life, displaying her last session. Lauren went to shut it off when she saw the portrait of Emile Berger filling the screen. His foreboding gray eyes stared down at her, capturing her attention.

Her head fell, and she gazed at the bloody collar of her suit. Who knows what would have happened that night if not for Ethan? But that wasn't the first time she had a brush with death. Her eyes drifted to the obituary on the cork board. Five years ago Kathleen Baxter chose to die alone, alienated from a world that had ignored her. Now, Lauren Fox chose to live alone, keeping everyone at arm's length for her own safety. Both women had no real family. No real friends. No one that cared for them. And they both ran from their problems.

What was it Emile had called her? *Insolent child.*

Her father had called her that the day she left for good. Those words plagued her for years no matter how hard she tried to forget. Even now, after all these years, his contempt still chipped at her foundation. Her fingers tightened on the bloody outfit.

"Goddammit," she breathed.

Throwing the suit over her shoulder, Lauren hurried to the ladder. She ripped the knives from the paper target and climbed down.

17 Undergrove Manor

The shadow of Undergrove Manor loomed long over Ethan in the late afternoon sun.

Riding atop city buses had taken him longer than expected to get to Deacon Hills. He had to jump over to another bus four times—two more than the last time. And more than once some pedestrian gawked at him sitting cross-legged on the dusty roof. A child in a stroller even waved as he transferred between vehicles.

When he finally made it to the right neighborhood, he hopped off and walked the rest of the way. The entrance to the abandoned mansion lay a good mile past the sparse upscale community. Even after reaching the dirt path leading to the old residence, he still had to walk for at least a quarter mile to reach his destination.

Towering oak trees dating back before the nation's founding shrouded the overgrown path. Errant strips of moss hung from their entwined tree limbs. Tall grass and brush from the forest had crept into much of the old road. Rotten boards of what was once picket fencing littered the sides of the route, their original paint long lost to the ages. The afternoon sun broke through the thick tree canopy at irregular intervals, tiny shafts of light stabbed through the gloomy view.

At the edge of the treeline, the crumbled remains

of the property's ancient stone wall lining the property separated the ocean of tall grass that was the mansion's courtyard. Though the grass was just as overgrown there as it was along the dirt road, the area was devoid of any giant oaks. A few worn statues jutted out from the tall grasses on either side of the mansion. Errant bushes and a few small trees dotted the yard. At the end of the dirt road, the remains of a large iron gate greeted him, more or less intact. Bent and warped, many decades of rust had fused its hinges open, leaving just enough room that a semi-trailer could slip through if angled just right.

Twenty yards from the main doors sat the crumbling copper armillary. In the sunlight, Ethan saw that it's metal structure had been corroded into a moldy, mottled green from the march of time. The large skeletal globe was bent and misshapen all around, but the large arrow piercing it still pointed true. It sat in the middle of a defunct, round fountain connected to a long reflecting pool extending out into the yard. The entire thing was fashioned from weather-worn chunks of white marble. Thickets of weeds sprouted along the edges of the old structure. Dark green water stood silent with lily pads and clumps of algae floating on the still surface. If not for the cool weather, insects would be swarming over the murk.

And in the center of the courtyard spread the rotting carcass of the mansion. Built on gradual slope, the first floor rose six feet from the ground with a wide stone staircase leading to the main entrance. The original brick structure of the building lay exposed like bleeding sores beneath the colossal wreck's crumbling white wash skin. All the windows were either boarded up or smashed in with nothing but the broken lattice-work of their frames left to show they even existed. To the south and north, the newer wings of the mansion were made of decaying wood. The siding had lost all its paint over the countless years of neglect, leaving them dark and crumbling. Its original roof was missing many shingles, too, and large swathes of it had been ripped open, exposing portions of the top floor and attic to the sky.

Ethan climbed up to the main entrance. Sick brown moss and lichen covered the awning stretching over the huge front doors. Strings of brown and gray dangled from the rotted eve. The front door was locked. He should have known that. If this was a secret meeting place for vampires, of course they'd want it secured. Though looks alone would deter people from snooping around, keeping the place locked up made sense, especially given the wild spectacle he saw the other night.

He stretched out with his senses. The surface was devoid of any presence, save for the trees in the nearby forest. Some of them were so old and established, they had powerful energy signatures of their own. He felt scant signs of animal life in the area, but no signs of vampire activity. When he pushed his senses down the surface, he felt it: that unnatural, festering coldness from before. It was different this time, smaller and more concentrated. There was something else there, too. Something ominous lurked underneath, waiting, like its purpose had not yet been fulfilled.

Ethan backed up and checked the floors above. To his surprise, the window in the south wing was still open from his last visit. For a moment he debated if it was part of that trap Lauren had predicted, but his senses told him everything supernatural about the building lay beneath the foundation, so, he decided to hazard a try anyway. Heading over he noticed that the grass became decayed and malformed the closer it got to the foundation. Gnarly black vines climbed the walls, encasing the lower floor in a cage of sharp black thorns. The ugly vines dug into forced their way into the mansion, creating hideous cracks in the edifice.

Was that there last time?

Under the open window, Ethan infused his body with energy. His grubby, thrice-repaired sneakers lifted bare millimeters off the ground, and he jumped, soaring past the thorny first floor. Grabbing hold of the escarpment under a second floor window, he pushed off and launched even higher to the roof overhang. Dangling from the lip, he shimmied across to the left until he reached the window and swung inside.

With the sun still out, Ethan got a good look of the place this time. Faded wallpaper that may or may not have been blue peeled away from the damaged lath and plaster walls. The ceiling had caved in on the left side long ago, revealing dry-rotted rafters. Shattered fragments of ceiling plaster and two centuries of debris and dirt covered an old feather mattress under the cave-in. Multiple sections of it had been ripped open and turned into nests over the years with the mattress's innards spilled out over the destroyed bed frame. Directly in front of him, the door to the outside hall still hung by a single rusted hinge. And among all the dust, he saw Lauren's slim footprints.

Ethan shook his head.

There was something about that woman he couldn't quite put his finger on; the odd tartness of her aura. He hadn't encountered that before. The lady deputy came close, but nowhere near the same potency. And when she wasn't busy mouthing off, her tenacity impressed him. She was one of two people he'd ever met who could keep up with him. Not a small feat.

Standing up, Ethan froze. The sound of an approaching engine echoed faintly through the trees. He quickly ducked behind the wall next to the window sill. He checked his watch.

They couldn't be here already? Unless they sent

scouts.

With a hand on his sword, Ethan carefully peeked through the open window. The sound grew louder and steadier. Interestingly, it didn't sound like one of those large trucks he saw at the depot. Too high pitched and full of treble, it sounded like a small car. With a loud exhaust.

As the vehicle drew closer, its tenor sounded more familiar. When the source of the noise finally broke through the tunnel of trees, Ethan let go of his sword.

There across the overgrown courtyard, a red convertible carefully rolled through the rusty gate. Lauren pulled stop at the end of the reflecting pool. Her expensive car idled there for a long minute, her head glued to the mansion. Ethan stepped fully into the window frame and whistled. Black sunglasses and a wide brimmed hat snapped to his position, and she promptly continued down dirt path along the pool. She navigated through the decayed grasses and disappeared behind a huge copse of overgrowth past the south wing. The engine shut off, and she reappeared a minute later.

Walking over to the open window, Lauren aimed her piton launcher and fired at the overhang a few feet from his head. Ethan stepped back while she zipped into the room. She wore a long tan trench coat tied up at the waist and her fancy black suit underneath. Her parted hair framed the stern frown on her face and dangled behind her in a long, thick braid.

Lauren removed her sunglasses and regarded him coolly. Silhouetted by the setting light, her irises gave off a subtle luminosity. Neither spoke as if daring each other to break the silence first.

Exhaling softly, she relented.

"I'm not here to fight anybody. I just want to know why they did this to me. Once I'm satisfied, I'm gone. Are we clear?"

Ethan checked his watch again and nodded to the door.

"Lead the way," he said.

The rest of the mansion was more deteriorated than either had remembered. Broken tiles and chunks of plaster competed with destroyed furniture and shattered glass for floor space. They passed through a ballroom that housed the remains of a hollowed out grand piano, covered in dust and leaning on one leg like an abandoned car in a bad neighborhood. Dust and cobwebs coated everything in sight disturbed only by animal tracks leading to nests built in hidden corners. Shadows clung to the walls, chased away only by errant shafts of waning daylight filled with twinkling motes of dust. The bodies of the two sentries Ethan had killed were gone, their blood mopped up and floorboards redressed with more dirt and debris.

They navigated through broken stairs and around gaping holes in the floor until reaching the cool and musty basement. Though she didn't need it, Lauren brandished a small but powerful flashlight, illuminating areas that probably hadn't seen electric light in over a century. Nearing the wine cellar, she noticed the moldy aroma of old fermented grapes still hanging in the air, far stronger to her this time. In fact, everything in the mansion smelled stronger. She found herself covering her mouth and nose with a gloved hand more often than not.

The wine cellar was pitch black. She swept the flashlight over the collection of empty, cross hatched shelves, each one thick with cobwebs. In the very rear of the room, she found the shelf that covered the hidden tunnel. Sections of it were cut through, outlining the vague outline of a door. Funny, she didn't noticed that last time.

Lauren slowly approached the false wall.

Hesitantly, she reached up to the iron sconce and pulled down. Ancient gears engaged behind the walls, and the shelf coughed open. She handed Ethan the flashlight and pushed against the heavy shelf. Cold, stale air blasted her. The false wall revealed the same long, rough-carved hallway from her nightmares.

This was it. This was where her life started to fall apart.

She looked back to Ethan, her eyes screaming to turn back. He returned the flashlight and gave her another nod. Swallowing hard, Lauren stepped into the passage.

Neither one had said anything since entering the mansion. Only the sound of their footsteps crunching rubble disturbed the quiet. She was content to hold her tongue around Ethan, but being back in the mansion pulled at her every nerve.

"You know, you kinda look like him," she finally broke the silence. Her voice traveled far down the tunnel.

"What?" he echoed back.

"*Rambo*. The first movie."

"This again?"

"Seriously."

"You are annoying, you know that?"

"You kind of remind me of him, too. With all the scars and the pensive quietness."

Ethan groaned wordlessly.

Lauren stopped and turned to him. "Look, I'm scared shitless right now. Help me get my mind off it, will you?" she pleaded.

He grumbled something under his breath. She took that for a yes and started walking again. "I won't ask you why you do this, but . . . it has to be lonely, right?"

He said nothing.

"Told you, just like him."

Ethan dragged a hand over his face. A smile crept onto hers.

"People get in the way," he spoke. "Friends or family only provide a weakness for them to exploit. Anyone I get close to could be used against me. They could be threatened, kidnapped, killed, or worse: turned. It's better to work alone. Less complications that way."

It sounded bleak, but she knew the logic behind it. "Can't let anybody know what you do in case it comes back to haunt you, right?"

"Yes," he agreed distantly.

"I know what you mean. Sounds like you've experienced that first hand, huh? You don't have to answer that by the way," she quickly followed up.

He didn't. She expected as much.

A moment later, Ethan continued.

"People can't handle the truth about the supernatural. It's not something you really talk about with anybody. Normal people won't believe you, and if they do ever witness it, they either rationalize or completely ignore what they saw. And those that don't are usually unhinged to begin with. Only a rare few understand what I do for them."

"You sound like a cop."

"Cops have families to go home to. Coworkers they can relate to about the horrors of their job."

The flashlight beam bobbed up and down with Lauren's shrug.

"For what it's worth, I can't talk about what I do, either," she said. "Too much chance of being caught by the police. Or worse: criminals—they don't have ethics to hold them back. But, it's like you said, relationships can be exploited and used against you. Can't have a life or a family. The job is your life. Your contacts are your family. Gotta hold everything inside if you wanna survive. Not many people in my line of work last long if they can't handle that reality."

Ethan mumbled something that sounded like an agreement. "If it's any consolation, you've handled the last few days better than I expected."

"Really?" the complement took Lauren by surprise. "Thanks."

They walked on for another beat until, Ethan asked a question: "How did you know I was at that diner?"

"I didn't."

"You're kidding me."

"It's true. When I woke up and saw myself in the mirror, I nearly lost my mind. I had to get out of my apartment before I went crazy, but my keys and my car were gone, and . . . I don't know . . . I just started walking. I wasn't even paying attention to where I was heading. Did that for hours. Then, all of a sudden, there was my car, parked on the side of the road."

"You found me by dumb luck?"

The beam bobbed again. "Kinda? When I checked it out, I smelled something on the shifter. The same smell that was all over my sheets." A guilty chuckle escaped her lips, "Didn't know it at the time, but it was your—"

"Yeah, I know," he finished her sentence.

"I followed the smell into the diner and right to your booth." They went on for a little longer before Lauren stopped again. "Can I ask you something?"

"Is this about another movie?"

"No," she suppressed a tiny smile.

"Good."

"Were you really going to kill me that night?"

He hesitated. "Maybe."

"Maybe?"

Ethan exhaled roughly. "Look at it from my perspective. I just saved a woman from being turned into a vampire by some strange ritual that I've never seen before, only to have her try to drink my blood hours later—a transformation time far faster than normal. And while I'm trying to recuperate and figure out what to do next, she tracks me down and confronts me in broad daylight." He looked into her eyes. "Seeing all your changes when you sat down in the booth, I thought it was too late. But later, when I saw the terror on your face, I figured the best I could do for you is give you a quick death. Spare you from a life of misery as painlessly as possible."

Lauren's chin twitched. "You really were going to do it, were you?"

He looked away. "No one deserves what you had gone through."

"But, would you still do it?"

He inhaled slowly. "I don't know. Maybe. I suppose, if you ever gave in to the thirst, I'd be forced to."

"Oh."

Lauren shuffled around, crestfallen, and continued down the bleak tunnel.

18 Scene of the Crime

Ethan and Lauren continued further down the tunnel.

The rickety spiral staircase creaked and crackled but never gave under their combined weight. Piles of ash blanketed the tunnel floor barely a yard from the foot of the stairs. Lauren shined the flashlight on a pant sleeve from a pair of dirty jeans, and glanced a question at Ethan.

"They chased me after I grabbed you," he answered.

"How many were there?"

"Enough to fill the room."

She kicked the pile out of the way and resumed walking.

Reaching the end of the tunnel, they came to the massive double doors from before. Six recessed panels made up each towering door with a strange arcane symbol intricately carved into all twelve sections. The dark doors bore no knobs or handles, only a pair of heavy iron rings that looked like they had been stubbornly hammered into the wood. Its baleful energy was palpable, even to Lauren. Her spellbound eyes traced the carved frames. She squeezed them shut, pleading for the nightmare to let her go.

"For days, I dreamed of this door." Sorrow tinged her voice. "Every time I closed my eyes, there it was, and it always opened inward. Behind it was a red room, like a darkroom for photographers. I never saw what was inside, though. I would always wake up before they fully parted."

Her shoulders sunk a little. "Every night, the dream grew longer and more vivid, showing me more of this place each time until the whole mansion eventually revealed itself. I couldn't get it out of my mind. Even when I was awake, I kept seeing it." Lauren let out a sad chuckle, "I nearly blew a job interview because of it. By the eighth night, I woke up in the middle of the dream. I felt . . . I don't know, drawn here. Compelled? I couldn't shake the image, so I suited up and took a cab."

She held her head, embarrassed, "God, I shouldn't have done that! It was such a stupid move even wrapped up in a coat like this. I searched the place, but when I got to the first floor, something came over me. It was like I was in a trance. Like my body just moved on it's own. The last thing I remembered clearly was this door."

Lauren turned to him. "You know the rest."

Ethan walked up to the doors. He placed a hand on each one and pushed. Neither budged. Puzzled, he pushed again. Nothing happened. "What the hell?"

"What's wrong?"

He gave it a third try, his feet dragging dirt. "It's not moving."

"Locked?"

He stepped back. "It's like trying to push an oak tree."

Lauren highlighted the iron loops with her flashlight. "Try twisting the handle, maybe?"

With a shrug, Ethan gripped one and twisted hard, but the thick ring refused to move. He put his back into the other one with both hands. Nothing. He tried both at once, but again, the door resisted his efforts.

Ethan faced her. "How did you get in last time?"

She shook her head. "I don't know. I can't remember anything once I saw the door. All I see are fragments."

"Think hard."

Lauren didn't want to think about that night. But she came this far . . . She closed her eyes and concentrated, the fragmented memories twisting her face. After a few moments, she looked up and said, "I think . . . I just pushed it."

Ethan focused his senses on the door. All twelve panels contained a separate, distinct magical aura, each one overlapping with the others. But the auras felt muted, dormant. He traced tendrils of energy interlacing between each section reaching out and entangling with each other. The tendrils snaked into the tunnel walls on either side. He thought for a moment. Seeing them with better light, the carved patterns looked identical to the ones traced onto her skin that night. He regarded Lauren with a raised eyebrow.

She gave him a wary look.

"Push it," he said.

"What?!"

"Go on."

"Hell no! I'm not touching that thing!" Lauren backed up, waving her hands.

He gestured to the doors. "Do it."

"If you can't push it open, then how the hell am I supposed to do it?" Terror seeped into her voice.

"Humor me."

Ethan held his gaze until her shoulders sagged.

"Asshole," she muttered through gritted teeth.

Lauren stepped up to the scary doors, her trembling hand hovering in front of the nearest panel. She looked back at Ethan expecting guidance, but he simply nodded for her to continue. Taking a deep breath, she pressed her palm on the carved wood, ready to retreat at any moment. A soft red light spread under her fingers, and she immediately recoiled. The sorcerous light quickly rippled outward, tracing through the symbols of all twelve panels. A heavy muffled *thunk* came from the other side. Ethan gripped his sword, eyes glowing.

When nothing happened, Lauren looked to him. "So . . . now what?"

He drew his weapon and flicked his head at her. Cautiously, Lauren pushed the doors inward on ancient hinges. The room beyond was shrouded in darkness thick enough to touch. She stepped back and aimed the flashlight into it, but the inky blackness swallowed the beam. Even her heightened vision couldn't penetrate the thick shadow.

"What is it?" she asked, dumbfounded.

He pushed his senses into the darkness. After a moment, he said, "It's an illusion."

"Illusion?" Lauren cocked her head to the side.

"Just stay here." Ethan crept through the curtain of shadow, sword ready.

"Yeah. Sure. I'll just stay here. Alone. With my nightmare," she mumbled.

Lauren strained her ears for any sound, but nothing escaped the black wall. Seconds stretched into an eternity. Her mind raced with all sorts of horrible possibilities. Was the room beyond teeming with vampires lying in wait for them? Was he dead already, suffocated by the tangible shadow?

Hell, was the watery blackness a portal to another world like that movie with Kurt Russell a few years back?

Suddenly, a pair of ghostly blue flames winked into existence just beyond the doors. The blackness dissipated, and Ethan appeared a few yards ahead, one foot on a slightly depressed stone tile. One by one, braziers along the curved wall ignited in the same otherworldly blue. The auditorium was vast, easily a hundred yards in diameter. Across the chamber, a wide iron gate barred a set of carved stairs, ascending into darkness. More flames burst to life on torchieres ringing the pulpit at the bottom. Four hanging braziers with orange fire surrounded a large iron spike laced with thorns on the ceiling. It hovered over a black altar in the center of the arena.

Lauren's heart froze when she saw it, and her hand unconsciously drifted to her neck. Ethan sheathed his sword and motioned for her to follow, but when she didn't budge from the door, he came back for her.

"C'mon."

His voice tore her eyes off the altar. Ethan stood in front of her, eyes blue, hand extended. Shaking, Lauren took it. She crossed the threshold with a sharp inhale. Fragments of that night assaulted her mind's eye in rapid fire. The image of the arena filled with hooded monsters all hungrily gazing at her superimposed over the empty theater before her. Lauren's legs refused to go further. Her hand slipped from his.

Ethan turned around. Lauren trembled at the head of the stairs, her eyes trapped at the bottom of the arena.

"You alright?"

She didn't respond. When he came back, she swallowed. "Give me a minute." Her eyes met his for a brief second, and she murmured, "Please?"

"Sure."

Letting her go, Ethan walked along the perimeter to the gate. Its bars were inches thick, and it probably weighed multiple tons. The gate was pitch black and coated with a fine layer of rust and grime. He saw no pull chain or handle or anything that could open the massive barrier. Nor did he see the same on the other side.

Moving on, he made his way down to the dais. The four dead thralls from before were gone, but their blood stains were still there. Ethan knelt in front of the stone altar and traced a finger along one of the thin red lines carved into the glassy black rock. They all looked and smelled like blood, but something kept it from oxidizing. Each line spread out from the altar at the center and arced off the platform into the raised seating area. He chose one and followed it over plinths and up the seats. The lines created circular patterns around the whole auditorium with a few hard angles here and there. Latin and Greek script accompanied them where they intersected with each other.

Back at the top of the auditorium, Ethan surveyed the room with his golden vision. Wisps of mystical energy rose from the large diagram just like he saw that night. The giant spire drew that energy and shunted it into the altar below.

This was the evil presence Ethan had felt outside the mansion. It's power was tremendous at this distance. He had to let go of his senses before the aura overwhelmed him. He pulled out his pocket book and started drawing.

While Ethan traced the mystical pattern, Lauren remained transfixed with the altar down below. With monumental effort, she took a single step onto the stone stairs. She fought a losing battle with the tears welling up in her eyes. She took another step. Her heart thudded harder and harder in her chest, and her hands trembled at her side, gradually. Another step. Her hands balled into fists. Each step took less effort than the last, until she found herself at the foot of the dais.

An odd shape drew her eyes to the base of the platform. It was her black hood and goggles. They were exactly where those armed bastards had tossed them. Absently, she stuffed them into a coat pocket.

A whisper of anger brushed Lauren while she

watched herself get carried onto the platform. No matter how hard she thrashed that night, the men's grasp was too great.

She stepped up onto the dais. She exhaled, suddenly remembering to breathe. Taking in the black altar's shape, she saw numerous severed straps hung from the slab—Ethan's doing. The red lines from around the chamber snaked their way up the aged black thing. She blinked, momentarily seeing pulse in tandem with her own heartbeat like thick veins.

Her heart jumped into the back of her throat, and the sound of rushing blood filled her sensitive ears. Dregs of anger left over from her argument with Ethan boiled over, this time without shame to hold it in check. Grinding her teeth, she drove her heel into the hard stone. The impact vibrated through her leg and up her spine. She ignored the pain and kicked it again. A small piece of it cracked off. Growling, Lauren dropped the flashlight and ripped the nearest torchiere out of a stone plinth. The blue flame winked out once she wrenched the iron pole free. With both hands Lauren speared the altar with the crooked rod. Days of bottled-up fury echoed throughout the chamber.

Lauren's outcry snatched Ethan's attention from his drawing. Below, she savagely tore at the altar, breaking off piece after piece of worked stone. Pocketing the book, he made his way over to the stairs. As he descended, he noticed the floor under her begin to shake. She repeatedly speared the altar, oblivious to the vibrations. The shaking grew violent.

Ethan moved faster, bounding the final two rows onto the platform. He caught the pole before she struck again and whisked her off the dais. Her anger instantly turned to tears in his arms. They watched a strip of floor underneath the altar suddenly drag back a section of the stone platform to reveal a steep set of stone-carved stairs leading down. Faint red light flashed to life underneath. They exchanged looks of surprise.

He released her and inspected the remains of the fractured altar. Bits of black rubble lay strewn about from her assault. Checking the crumbled slab, he found a small hole with a round bit of stone lodged inside. It looked like a hidden switch. She must have tagged it by accident. He concentrated on the immediate area. Despite the damage, the altar's aura remained intact. Energy from the spire poured into the altar and continued down beneath it. Grabbing the flashlight, Ethan poked is head down the opening. The stairs were shallow and continued down a good ways.

"Looks like there's another room down there."

She stared at him expectantly, still panting.

"This whole place has some sort of magical diagram carved into it. It draws in energy and funnels it into the spire. The spire shunts that energy into the altar which then goes down into this room. Whatever they had planned to do with you—or more likely *to* you—looks like it ends down here."

The rage had fully left Lauren now. The blunted torchiere clanged heavily on the stone platform, echoing throughout the cavernous room.

"And I suppose you want to go down there, don't you?" she asked, flatly.

"You're the one who wanted to know."

"I'm having serious second thoughts right now."

Ethan straightened up. Flashlight in hand, he descended the narrow stairs. A few seconds later, Lauren reluctantly followed.

The new room looked like a small crypt. Red and black bricks formed the walls and the low curved ceiling. A handful of small alcoves surrounded the room, each one stuffed with melted candles. They burned bright red and gave off no heat. On the ceiling, directly beneath the altar, descended an iron spike like the one above, only smaller. More red lines spiraled down, glowing like the candles.

And underneath the glowing spike, lay a huge sarcophagus.

It was wide and long, easily large enough to fit two people with room to spare. Fashioned from solid black glass like the altar, it glinted ominously in the candle light. Long iron bars lined the edges, and thick gold filigree laced the entire surface. The scent of copper was sickeningly thick in the room. Lauren felt her fangs instantly grow and covered her mouth.

Ethan closed his eyes and slowly passed his hand over the stone casket. He glanced at Lauren hovering close behind him. Giving her a quick nod, he put his hands on the cover and pushed.

"What are you doing?!" Lauren blurted through her fingers.

"Help me with this, will you?"

"Are you fucking crazy?! One of them could be in there!"

"There's no presence inside it."

Lauren didn't believe him, but right now, she didn't know what to believe anymore. This was so far out of her wheelhouse, she could barely keep herself together. The creepy crypt looked like something out of a cheap late-night horror movie, yet it was real and right in front of her. She didn't like it here, but, Ethan hunted these vampires for a living and seemed to know what he was doing.

Looking from the massive coffin to him, Lauren hesitantly put her hands on the top, and on his count, they pushed together. The heavy glass scraped to the side, opening what she guessed was the head of the thing. Ethan stood up and shined the flashlight inside.

"It's blood."

"Huh?"

Lauren dared a look. The sarcophagus was filled to the brim with thick viscous fluid, unmoving and deep,

deep red. Its pungent metallic odor floated up, and she immediately and backed away, dizzy from the overwhelming stench.

"Oh my God!" she gagged through her fingers.

Ethan knelt down.

"There's an inscription here."

Words were chiseled into the sarcophagus's dark mirror finish. They looked like the same ones used in the diagrams criss-crossing the room above. "It's in the same mixture of Latin and Greek they spoke that night."

"Do I want to know what it says?"

He slid his hand across the words while he read them aloud. "As the first . . . child of the night . . . bestowed the power . . . of blood . . . upon his—no, *her*—progeny . . . through . . . the power of blood . . . shall she be . . . "

Ethan looked to her and recited the last word: "Reborn."

"Reborn?! What the hell is that supposed to mean?"

He rose to his feet. "Remember when I said you'd be one of them or worse?"

She nodded nervously.

"I think we found worse."

Lauren let out a desperate laugh. "Well, I suppose we can rule out Baxter Logistics from all this, right? Right??"

The sun had finally disappeared over the treeline.

The skies above had turned orange and red with a hint of violet. A caravan of five black SUVs slowly rolled through the gate. They came to a stop in a loose semi-circle around the dilapidated fountain. As each vehicle shut off, four men stepped out. Twenty men gathered next to the old fountain. Each man was clad in black tactical gear. Submachine guns hung from bungee straps across their chests, automatic pistols hung from their belts, and black cylindrical grenades filled their vests.

Each man went through his weapons. They checked magazines, extended stocks, attached suppressors, and slid bolts into place. They adjusted their ear pieces and synchronized radio frequencies. One by one, each man pulled on a black balaclava with two holes for eyes and affixed a set of nightvision goggles over their masks.

Four pairs split off and quickly searched north and south. One group radioed in that they had found a red convertible hidden near the south wing. Everyone regrouped soon after. One of the men, a pale one with steel colored eyes, took a cellphone from his pocket and dialed.

"Alpha team here. We've arrived at the mansion entrance, sir." His voice was low and gravelly.

London spoke on the other end of the line. "Good. Bravo team has secured the secondary entrance."

"We've found a car hidden to the south, sir. There's a camo net on it."

"Then they took the bait. Spread out and cover the area. If you find them, do not engage unless you absolutely have to. Just keep them from leaving the building. Bravo team and I will join you in thirty-five minutes. Understood?"

"Yes, sir."

The team leader turned to the others and relayed the orders. The men paired up and dispersed around the mansion. Most hid behind broken statues or large bushes sprouting in the open area. A few moved around back and covered the rear of the building. The rest of them crouched down in the tall grasses.

All of them watched the mansion for movement.

Waiting.

19  Stop Stop

*T*he scent of blood still clogged Lauren's nose.

They had left the auditorium, unsure what to make of everything there. Lauren hadn't uttered a word since leaving the room with the sarcophagus. She simply stared at the ground and followed Ethan up the tunnel. Arms wrapped around her waist, she stepped through the secret door, oblivious to the world. The false wall locked shut with a thick *clunk*.

Holding the flashlight, Ethan lead the way out of the basement to the upper floors. They had just climbed the second flight of broken stairs when Lauren broke her silence.

"What do you think it means?" Her voice was small.

Ethan steered her around a tangle of broken floorboards. "Not sure. I don't know much about their internal mythology."

"Was I supposed to be some sort of sacrifice?"

Ethan shoved a fallen door to the side. It crashed onto the floor, kicking up a dark cloud of dust and splinters. Before he could respond, Lauren continued with her worry.

"They were going to put me in that thing, weren't they?"

"I don't know. And neither do you," he

reassured her.

"They had a spike on the ceiling of that small room, just like the one above that altar. What else could it have been for?"

"It could've been for anything. Don't worry about it."

"But what did that inscription mean: 'shall be reborn'?"

"You don't know what that thing down there is for," he told her, his voice growing firmer. "I don't know what it's for. Stop thinking about it. It'll only make things worse."

"Ethan, they were going to drown me in that thing!"

He suddenly took her by the shoulders. Startled, Lauren quickly looked away. She didn't want him to see the fear and anxiety gripping her. But even in the shadows of the dark mansion, Lauren knew there was no way she could hide it.

"Lauren, you are not in that thing. You are right here," he pointed to the ground between them, "alive and on your own two feet—of your own free will. Whatever was supposed to happen that night didn't. So stop dwelling on what-ifs and could-have-beens. All that will do is drive you crazy."

He let her go. "Trust me on that."

"You heard what he said in the garage, they're still looking for me," she mumbled. Her watery gaze wandered to the floor, "And even if they don't succeed, you'll probably kill me."

Ethan lifted her head back up. "I'm not going to do that."

Her red eyes trembled. "Why?"

"I changed my mind. Just leave it at that." He checked his watch. "C'mon, we need to move."

A minute later, they reached the window on the third floor.

Ethan shut off the flashlight and returned it to Lauren. He crept forward and peered out from the corner of the window. Above the treeline, the orange sky grew darker and the moon rose higher by the second. Dusk had shrouded the grounds in darkness. Behind him, Lauren sat against the wall, still withdrawn. After a minute, Ethan stepped back from the window and motioned her over.

"They're here," he said, his voice hushed.

"Figures," she sulked.

"There are five cars down there. The thralls are spread out, but I can't see them."

"Let me see."

Lauren dug out her goggles. She knelt behind the window and pulled the thick lenses over her eyes. With the press of a button, the device lit the world with a soft, electric whine. The grass and reflecting pool walls turned to a flat shade of bright gray as did the trees, the bushes, and the armillary, all with slightly brighter outlines. The dirty water was pitch black like the sky above. Next to the fountain, she saw five SUVs like from the bus yard, each with glowing white blotches on their hoods and tires.

"They haven't been here that long—their engines are still warm."

"What are those things?"

Lauren continued her scan. "Thermal vision. The military and police have been using stuff like this for years. This is an experimental model I got from my supplier a few years back. They're lighter and smaller than standard issue goggles, which helps to keep them from falling off while moving around. The battery life is shit, though. You've got an hour, maybe, before needing a recharge."

Panning around to the other section of the yard, she stopped. Two small, fuzzy dots poked out above the tall grass. She worked the focus rings until the dots sharpened into a pair of heads attached to bright gray shoulders. They faced the mansion, completely still.

"I see two of them."

"What are they doing?"

"I don't know. Looks like they're watching the mansion."

"They know we're here, then."

Sighing, Lauren pushed the goggles onto her forehead. "If we can get to the roof, we can—"

"We?" Ethan interrupted.

Lauren held up a hand, turning to him with a weary look on her face. "Don't make a thing of this, please? If I can get to a better viewpoint, I can see how many are out there."

Creeping back into the mansion, Ethan looked for one of the roof holes he had seen earlier. They searched far into the north wing before finding one in a guest bedroom. There, a massive tree limb had punched a hole through the ceiling ages ago. It drooped through the opening onto the decayed remains of a massive bed. Rotten leaves and other moldy detritus coated every surface in the room. They carefully clambered up the rotted limb and onto the roof. Hunkered down, Lauren sidled next to Ethan by the northeast corner and pulled the goggles back over her eyes.

The mansion roof gave her the better view she needed. Peering over the grounds, Lauren spotted more of them. They were spread out across the grand courtyard in pairs. The two she saw earlier weren't the only ones hiding among the tall grasses. Others hid behind some sort of cover: a broken statue, bushes, a lone tree, the reflecting pool, and all of them watched the mansion. Lauren counted eight in total, but with five vehicles, there had to be more.

"Well?" he asked.

She removed the goggles from her head, "Eight of them spread out in pairs."

Ethan flapped out his ratty mask in response. Lauren grabbed his arm. "What are you doing?"

He stopped with the mask half over his forehead. "What do you think? I'm going to go down there and take them out before any more arrive."

"You don't know how many of them are out there!" she said, her voice barely hushed. "Those men will shoot you dead the moment they see you."

He let go of the mask and fixed her with a hard look. "I have been trained to fight things that can rip a man's head off in one swipe. I can keep going after being mauled by shit that can eat people alive. I can do things that normal people think are Goddamned impossible. Do you *really* think a bunch of guys with some guns are going to scare me?"

"But you could die if you go down there!"

"Of course I could fucking die!" Ethan spat out. "Damnit, woman, I told you this isn't some fucking game! To them, we are food. Cattle to be harvested or culled. You either join the fight, or pray they don't put you on a dinner plate."

"Ethan, if you die, I die! Besides, I can't do what you do," she protested.

"That didn't stop you from following me into that garage! You know how to be silent, and you know how to take someone out from behind. I've seen what you can do with those knives of yours. You're better at this than you think."

"But . . ."

He looked out into the courtyard in frustration.

"Look. Once I clear a path, you make a break for your car at the first opportunity. But if you do that, we are done. After I free those people, I'll grab my shit, and that'll be the last time I do anything for you, got it? I have no time for cowards."

She turned her head to the courtyard. What he was suggesting was insane. Lauren was a thief, not some holy warrior. Even if she helped him rescue those people here, what good would they do? There were three buses to deal with and who knows how many more people beyond that. Free Port was a big city with lots of old bolt holes to hide in. They could be anywhere by now.

"You are fucking crazy, you know that?"

"I call it righteousness. Where would you be now if I wasn't?"

That was the question she had been asking herself everyday since she met him. And she knew the answer. She'd be dead or one of them. Or worse: locked in that hellish coffin. But lucky for her, he had been around to save her that night. A knight in shining armor—only stunk like hell with a mood to match.

How many people out there had someone to help them?

She gazed up at the night sky. The moon had completely risen now. It wasn't full anymore, but it still shone brightly. In the soft light, she saw the courtyard clear as day. Remembering where the armed men were, she could easily pick them out despite their attempts to hide. They were here to kill him and capture her. And she knew what they would do to her if they succeeded.

"I'd be on a plate," Lauren exhaled harshly. "What's your plan?"

Ethan pointed to the courtyard. "The grass out there is pretty tall. If we stay low, we can take them out one at a time. We make a full circuit around the building and clear the area. When that's done, we hide until the bus shows up. But, we have to do this quietly. They could signal for backup or something if they spot us, which would make things a hell of a lot worse. We'll have to play the rest by ear depending on how many men they bring with the delivery."

"Play it by ear? How the hell have you survived this long?"

"Killing parasites is what I'm good at. It's what I do."

Lauren shook her head. Her eyes fell on the stark white braid draped over her shoulder, no longer the warm, vibrant yellow memory of her late mother. They did this to her. Those vampires shattered everything she had built for herself in one night.

Insolent child, London's words echoed again. Once more, she had been used and discarded like an unwanted child. And for what—some crazy ritual sacrifice?

"There!" Ethan pointed to the flash of resentment pouring from her eyes. "Use that anger. Pretend they're the one that bit you, and hit 'em like you did that altar. Hell, pretend they're me if it helps—I don't care. Remind these blood-sucking freaks that we have teeth, and take some fucking revenge!"

She laughed inwardly. Ethan was right. It did feel good to wreck that altar. Thanks to him, she was lucky enough to survive this long. This wasn't going to end well, but fuck it, go for broke.

Lauren met Ethan's eyes, resolved. "Okay. Let's do this."

He nodded and finished pulling on his mask. He took the drawstring bag off his shoulder and removed an old military belt with three hand grenades clipped to it. Pocketing the bag, Ethan hung the belt next to his scabbard. He took his big knife and rubbed a handful of dust on the blade after spitting on it, dulling the polished steel.

Lauren disrobed her trench coat, revealing her sneaking suit underneath. The black rubbery outfit absorbed the dim moonlight, reflecting nothing. A violet rope belt with golden tips tied across her sternum held her cut suit in place. Following Ethan's lead, she dulled the gold tips with a handful of dust and rubbed the rest of it on her exposed body, obscuring the sliver of pale skin above and below her black undershirt. She beat the dust off her hood and slipped it on. It covered her entire head and neck save for a thin strip across the eyes. Normally, Lauren carefully wrapped her hair down with a series of special bobby pins, but without them, her braid simply hung out the back.

As ready as she could be, Lauren turned to Ethan with a thumbs up. He gave her a quick once-over and a hard pat on the shoulder. Moving to the edge of the sloped roof, he made to jump down, but she grabbed his shoulder.

"Wait. Use these," she handed him the goggles. "Ever since the depot, I've been able to see better in the dark. You probably need this more than I do now."

Holding the expensive optics, he pressed the button on the bridge. The goggles emitted the same high pitched whine again. He settled the device over his mask, slivers of dim light bleeding through the black fabric. Ethan slowly waved his hands in front of his face, like he was having an out of body experience.

"Thanks."

Lauren unhooked her piton launcher and shifted over to the edge. She anchored the tip with a *pop-hiss* and swung out, waiting for him. Once Ethan grabbed hold, the two silently descended to the ground.

Crouched, Ethan spotted the first pair of sentries out to his right. The two men were knelt down behind a large bush sprouting out in the open. He pointed them to Lauren, and she nodded. He stalked through the thick field on a wide arc to the north, leading her behind the first pair. Ethan prowled up behind the scout on the right and signaled Lauren to the one on the left. Knife in hand, he grabbed the man by the jaw and plunged the darkened blade down the side of his neck. Blood spurt when he ripped the blade out. At the same time, Lauren crushed a pair of blue pellets in her fist. She cupped her hand over the thrall's mouth and nose while simultaneously pulling him over her knee. The man struggled silently in her grip until the gas did it's job. Once he fell limp, she rolled him onto the ground.

She gave Ethan another thumbs up, and they moved on to the next pair.

Two scouts crouched beside the remains of a Roman soldier on a horse. Time had reduced it to the a pair of legs and hindquarters with the tail snapped off. Worming their way around, the two split off to either side of the statue on Ethan's signal. He yanked the left thrall's feet out from under him and came down with his knife right between the collar bone. Seeing his partner suddenly disappear, the other thrall spun around in time for Lauren to pin him against the statue with a fist full of smashed pellets. He quickly lost consciousness and fell from her grasp.

The two regrouped a few yards from the statue.

She peeked over the grass line for the next pair of men. This was going surprisingly well. Readying another pair of pellets, Ethan pushed her hand back to her belt.

"Those pills of yours won't last long on thralls," he whispered. "Remember the garage!"

Lauren pictured the heavy she had taken out that night. The same one who woke up and shot her when they tried to escape the burning building. She could try to strangle the next thrall, but that would take time, and silence couldn't be guaranteed. Ethan offered her his knife. She stared at the bloody weapon for a long moment. It was one thing to kill in self defense—she had made peace with that after leaving her second mentor—but it was another thing entirely to kill in cold blood.

Lauren pushed the blade away. If she was going to do this, she'd do it her own way. She returned the pellets to their pouch and drew one of her throwing knives. They weren't as long or as intimidating as

Ethan's Rambo-knife, but they were just as sharp. And a strike to the vitals wouldn't require a large blade anyway.

Continuing south, they found the next pair of sentries hiding by a tree defiantly growing out of the courtyard. Slithering in from behind, one of the guards turned towards them. They immediately hunkered into the grass. When no shout of alarm came from the thrall, Lauren delicately parted the tall stalks to find the scout facing the tree. She heard water splattering the bark and caught a strong whiff of ammonia. Lauren stifled a gag as another sentry obliviously urinated in front of her.

Ethan crept up behind the man and, in one smooth motion, pulled the hapless thrall's head back and sliced his throat. He restrained the flailing man until he choked on his own blood before laying him down. Ethan waved her up.

Taking a deep breath, Lauren yanked the thrall onto her knee just like the first one, cupping his mouth. She hesitated. The man fought against her grip grasping for his gun. She quickly smacked the weapon from his hand and dragged her knife across his exposed neck. His red-ringed eyes bulged as dark blood poured from the gaping slit.

Lauren stared at the stained blade in her hand—she was a killer now, and there was no going back. In the back of her mind, she understood why it was necessary, but she loathed herself for doing it. But worst of all, the thick crimson didn't nauseate her like she thought it would—in fact it exited her. She tried to ignore the gentle twitching inside her mouth.

Ethan put a hand on her shoulder, ripping Lauren from her thoughts.

She didn't jump this time.

He pointed to a pair of scouts by the middle of the reflecting pool. Following his lead, they crept to the edge of the tall grass across from them. Ethan gestured that they rush the two men. Lauren shook her head, extending her arm like a throw. He disagreed, stabbing at the air with his knife. She shook her head more vigorously and made like a noose hung her by the neck. He waved her off, rustling a few grass stalks with the motion.

As they wordlessly argued, the rear sentry shifted his position toward the rustling sound. The man saw the movement and shot to his feet. Ethan burst through the grass, pinning the scout to the low fountain wall and plunged his knife through the man's sternum before the thrall could call out. His flailing arms loudly splashed the dirty water and alerted the other sentry. The thrall snapped his gun up to fire, but a gun-metal-black knife struck him just below his chin.

Lauren stepped out of the grass, another knife in hand. Stunned by the attack, the sentry spun into the pool, finger tight on the trigger. A hail of lead sprayed into the air, peppering the mansion, the armillary, and one of the SUVs. Suppressed bullets punctured the vehicle's rear quarter panel and shattering the adjoining glass.

A curious thing about modern cars. Since the 1970s, more and more new vehicles had car alarms pre-installed from the factory during construction. And the five brand new, Chevy Suburbans parked in front of Undergrove Manor were such vehicles. Headlights lit up the mansion, and its horn blared repeatedly, announcing to every living being around that something had happened.

A pair of thralls at the opposite end of the reflecting pool traced the angle of the bullets and fired. At the northern end of the mansion, another pair of thralls rounded the corner. At first they only walked, but once the alarm went off, they broke into a full run. The two men fired at Lauren and Ethan, forcing them to the ground. She heard shouts of alarm from the dislodged earpiece of one the two dead scouts.

Every muscle stiffened. Lauren's worst professional fear quickly spiraled into reality. By reflex, she winged a smoke pellet at Ethan's feet, instantly shrouding both of them with thick gray. She levered off the ground, and together, they ran for the armillary fountain. Before they reached the safety of cover, Lauren glimpsed something black and round the size of a soda can bounce off the stone wall next to them.

Eyes wide, she immediately tackled Ethan behind the first SUV. As they hit the ground, the black object exploded and the world went white and silent.

London's pocket watch clapped shut.

"Time to leave."

A wide stone slab stood up at a perfect 45° angle, held in place by multiple hydraulic pistons. Over a century ago, during the corrupt aftermath of the American Civil War, London—still going by his human name, Emile—had an alternate entrance to Undergrove Manor's hidden auditorium constructed. The stone slab had been hollowed out and a lattice work of steel bars reinforced the shape of the big rock. Underneath, the tunnel lead on forever, the length of small sporadic cage lights converging into a single twinkle in the distance. Decades ago a modern hydraulic lift system replaced the original heavy-duty gear assemblies. The electric motors ran on buried power lines snaked in from an isolated ranger station at the edge of the nearby Neepawa Wildlife Reserve.

At Oberon's insistence, London created the disguised entrance as a means of easily accessing the massive underground arena, allowing their people to worship without any sort of outside interference. The decision paid off over the years, especially with the growing human population in the nearby city of Free Port. Since the vampire's numbers rose alongside their human flock, so too did Oberon's worshipers. And on nights like the one earlier this week, the tunnel allowed all their people to safely exit without disturbing the mansion's facade.

London kicked a football-sized rock next to the raised slab. It slowly sunk into the ground before returning to its original position. The big flat stone retracted with a heavy dull whir. He looked out into the tiny clearing spreading out from the hidden entrance. A handful of his men stood watch.

He had formed his private security force in the 1930s in order to safeguard Oberon's flock. The original recruits came from various walks of life: former army, disgraced police, even criminals. He had personally trained that first batch—augmenting those with promise to thralls and even elevating the best to full vampires. After the turn of the century, London turned his personal force into a private company named Monarch Security and leased them to various mortal institutions for additional income and legitimacy. Over the years, the group had grown into a small army of well trained, well equipped, blood-augmented troops, each man loyal to London himself.

"Let's pack it in," Alexander spoke into the radio hanging over his ear. "Drivers, get ready. We're twenty minutes out."

The younger vampire stood next to his master in the open tract. Thralls wearing black uniforms and automatic weapons crept in from the woods all around them. A few of them were full vampires, sporting sidearms and truncheons—close combat specialists brought in just for tonight. Twenty men in total gathered around the clearing. Barrel mounted flashlights provided the only illumination.

London looked out at his men standing before

him, proud.

"Alright. Our quarry has taken the bait. Double-time it to the trucks. Move!"

As one, the men quietly trotted east through the forest with London and Alexander right behind them. Everyone navigated the forest quickly, only their lights betraying their presence. After nineteen minutes, the dark cadre emerged from the thick treeline where two large unmarked cargo trucks were parked, their big diesel engines idling with the lights off. The rolling doors each opened up from the inside. Small lights bathed the cargo area with a faint bluish glow. A pair of large, battery-powered flood lights on collapsed tripods were strapped to the rear of each truck. In the back of the lead truck, a large green crate and a smaller one of similar make sat against the side wall. The emerging group split in two and filed into each vehicle.

London and Alexander each entered the passenger side of the truck cabs. A pounding noise from the thin rear wall of the cab signaled that they had finished loading. Done, both trucks trundled down a dirt road. Their headlights turned on once they turned onto a paved country highway.

He checked his watch.

Thirty minutes.

London's phone vibrated in his combat vest. Alexander was on the other line.

"Go."

"What's the plan, London."

London glanced out the window, perturbed. "Manners."

He heard an elaborate sigh on the other line.

"What's the plan, *master*?"

"Better." London paused. "Once we link up with Alpha team, you and I will split Bravo team and hunt for the targets, room by room, floor by floor. You will take half the men to the north wing, and I will take the south wing with the rest. Alpha team with remain in place and keep them from escaping."

"If we're going hunting, shouldn't we be carrying something more potent, like shotguns?"

"Out of the question. Remember, Oberon wants the girl for the ritual unharmed."

"If you're right that this girl can heal like the rest of us, it shouldn't matter what we use."

"Correct. But, that level of trauma would take too long to heal, and time is of essence. Also, I do not want my mansion damaged."

"Why? Look what happened to the garage. The entire place burned down because of those two."

London frowned. His young lieutenant was right, but the boy still refused to appreciate the necessity of the manor's cover story. London had maintained its state and image for over a century. The populous at large believed it to be haunted, and outside of the doggedly curious—of whom he dealt with personally— it remained the perfect location for Oberon's worshipers to gather and practice.

"Undergrove cannot be harmed. Ordinance and heavy weapons are not to be used."

"You've seen what that guy can do."

"I have. I reviewed the security footage from the garage. The girl will prove easy to neutralize. All we have to do is separate them, nothing more. Once she has been secured, both teams will converge on the masked man. If necessary, I can deal with him myself. He may be strong, but he is still human."

Alexander was silent.

"How many men do you expect to lose?"

London rolled the thought around, calculating the attrition. Every battle had it's losses. Only a soft-hearted fool expected to win a conflict unscathed. Zero casualties was always the exception to the rule, going back to his earliest days.

"Forty-six percent. It will be tight confines inside the manor, which favors his chosen style of combat. But, that is why we brought flash grenades, nightvision, and specialists. That should tip the scales in our favor. Also, that girl is vulnerable to loud noises. At the garage, I watched her double over when all the doors came down at once. That is a weakness we can exploit."

Traffic grew thicker reaching the outskirts of Deacon Hill. Tall, galvanized light posts beamed down blue light from the medians at regular intervals. Lights from sporadic mansions and their expansive grounds poked through the pine trees walling off the thoroughfare.

"If we're expecting a close quarters fight, then what's the MG for?"

"Insurance."

20 . . . And the Fury

Bullets perforated the vehicle while Ethan hefted Lauren behind the center truck.

His ears still rang from the blast, but fortunately, the goggles had protected his eyes from the blinding light. He leaned Lauren against the passenger door and yanked the goggles down. She slid to the ground, her chest rising with quick, panicked breaths. Her eyes, still luminous, were locked in terror, and her hands were firmly clamped over her ears.

Ethan reflexively ducked the bullets *plunking* into the truck and rained chips of glass on them. He drew his katana and inched closer to the rear end. When he leaned out to check the situation, another volley of bullets rattled the vehicle, cracking the plastic taillights and shattering more glass. He knelt down behind the rear wheel, feeling the bullets pelt the Chevy rather than hear them. Focusing through the chaos, Ethan threw his senses out in a wide net. The thralls' tainted auras bloomed against the cold, emptiness of the courtyard. Their signatures converged into a nebulous cloud on both sides of the fountain. Half of them split off and approached the vehicles.

Ethan ran up to Lauren, and feverishly fumbled through the pouches on her belt. Her hands hadn't left her ears, her eyes still distant. The signatures were getting closer. He yelled at her to wake up, unable to hear his own words. Just as the first submachine gun peeked around the truck, he found the right pouch and slammed a pair of her gray pellets on the ground. Feeling the muted double pop, a fifteen foot radius of thick vapor instantly enveloped Ethan, Lauren, the SUV, and everything around them. The thralls halted at the corners of the vehicle, cautiously entering the spreading miasma. Beams of light swept left and right, unable to pierce the dense cloud.

But, thanks to Lauren's goggles, Ethan saw them clearly.

With a devilish grin, he attacked.

Ethan cleaved through the first scout's neck and shoulders with a quick overhead chop, severing arteries, muscles, and even bone. The warm blood sprayed bright white through the googles when he yanked the blade free. He followed up with a hard kick to the abdomen, folding the man in two.

His senses still active, Ethan quickly spun around and thrust, catching the thrall behind him before the man could fire. The gun dangled on it's sling, and the scout reflexively gripped the blade in his belly with both hands. Ethan twisted it out, spilling guts and fingers on the ground.

Another pair of London's men rounded either side of the vehicle, weapons ready. Ethan quickly closed the distance to the nearest thrall and slashed up under the submachine gun, disarming the man at the shoulder. The fourth scout fired into the smoke cloud behind him. Sensing the eminent attack, Ethan shifted the dismembered thrall into the deadly burst. With his free hand, Ethan flung a handful of throwing stars in a tight group at the shooter. The landed just above the collar, one of them embedding diagonally in the neck. The man choked, his finger still on the trigger.

The radios on the dead sentries sputtered out a

retreat signal.

Ethan paused. His hearing had returned.

Something hard and solid suddenly whacked the back of Ethan's head. Tripping on a body, he fell on the hard-packed dirt. He twisted to see the blurry white outline of a suppressor muzzle aimed at his face.

The two trucks holding Bravo Team finally reached the road to Undergrove. London checked his watch again. *Ten minutes.* As the two trucks mounted the broken curb of the old dirt path, the elder vampire's phone rang.

"London."

The gravelly voice of Alpha team's leader barked through the phone's speaker.

"Sir! We've made contact!"

London shot forward in his seat.

"Report!"

"We have them pinned down by the fountain, but I'm down to just seven men and we're running low on ammo."

"What!? You had a team of twenty! How in blazes could you be down to less then half?"

Suppressed gunfire came over the phone. *Clip-clap.*

"They used stealth, sir. They took out four fireteams before we found them. When we rallied, the two found cover by our vehicles and dug in. They repelled the squad I sent to flush them out"

London squeezed his hands into fists. He stopped when he heard a crack and looked down. A nasty fissure ran through the glass of his pocket watch.

"Keep them pinned. We are," he stared at the broken watch face. Though the hands still ticked, he couldn't see the time clearly anymore. His jaw tightened. "We're a few minutes out!"

"Yes, sir."

The call abruptly ended. London shoved the phone back in his pocket. That cursed swordsman had already reduced his force to sixty-six percent before he had even arrived. Never in two centuries had he encountered a lone hunter so damned troublesome. Staring at his damaged time piece, London punched the door, driving a large dent in the frame and shattering the glass between the panels. The driver swerved from the sound.

"Fuck!"

Staring at the thick barrel, Ethan braced himself for the inevitable. It wasn't the first time he'd stared down a gun barrel, but it felt like the last. A thin dark blur abruptly zipped into the thrall's face. The man wobbled and collapsed in a rigid heap, feet twitching as he landed. Behind him, a black silhouette blended in with the rapidly cooling car with only a thin bright strip down the torso betraying it.

Ethan yanked the goggles down. Lauren leaned against the door with her right hand outstretched. The smoke had fully dissipated now.

"Are you okay!" he yelled, climbing to his feet. The ringing in his ears had faded.

"What?!"

Hers was still shot. Ethan moved over and checked her for any damage. She looked haggard despite her mask, and her breathing was labored. He gave her a quick pat and peeked through the broken SUV.

The rest of London's men had pulled back to the end of the reflecting pool. Beyond, a small speck of light appeared down the dirt road. It gradually grew larger and then split into a pair of lights and then two more. The sound of diesel engines echoed through the trees when a pair of white five-ton cargo trucks smashed through the rusted gates, spinning the two hunks of iron into the air.

The trucks halted behind the remaining thralls. More thralls in similar tactical gear hopped out the back of each vehicle along with a handful of men armed with machine pistols and extendable batons. Ethan focused his vision on them. Vampires.

He'd dealt with vampires who controlled police or gangs before, but a militarized force?

The passenger doors swung open, and the two parasites from the depot exited the cab of each truck. London scowled at something in his hand and angrily barked orders at the rapidly assembling men. A pistol hung holstered under his arms. Alexander stood next to him in similar armament—his eye had regrown. Both wore black fatigues like the thralls still scampering out of the trucks. Some of the men began angling portable flood lights at the mansion. The rest formed into groups along the truck including the remaining scouts.

Ethan ducked back down to find Lauren blackly staring at him.

"Well? How royally did you fuck this up?" she barked.

"Me? You're the one they heard!"

"Like hell! We wouldn't be in this shit, if you would've done like I said!" she jammed an accusatory finger in his chest.

"Will you shut up and quit bitching for once?!" Ethan whipped another squint behind them. "You want the good news or the bad news?"

"Bad news," she grumbled.

"Your friend Emile is here, and he brought backup. A lot."

She muttered something under her breath. "And the good news?"

"The bus isn't here."

Lauren pulled a double take. "How is that good news?!"

"One thing less to worry about."

She glared at him furiously through her hood. "Is this your idea of *playing it by ear*?! Why don't you try playing patty-cake with them next?! Throw 'em off guard!"

"Fuck off. How many of those smoke things do you have left?"

She quickly checked her belt. "Enough."

"Good," he spared another glimpse beyond the fountain. "It looks like they're gonna try and rush us from both sides again. If we toss a couple of those smoke bombs, I can get in close to one of the groups and take them on."

He tapped the goggles around his neck.

"What about the other side? I can't fight like you—I'm a sitting duck here!"

He shook his head. "I'll be the distraction. While they're focused on me, use these."

He pulled off the belt with the hand grenades and handed it to her. Her eyes grew large holding the deadly explosives.

"I've never used these things before!"

"Simple: pull the pin, toss the spoon, and throw. You got a five second fuse. Once we throw the smokes, I'll go left. Use one of those on the group to the right. That should scatter them and give you time to sneak to your car and get the hell out of here."

Lauren looped the belt over her shoulder. The radios at their feet began chattering again. They were coming.

"What about you?"

"Don't worry about me. If we split up, they'll

have to divide their forces to go after us. You should be able to shake them with that fancy car of yours. I'll lose them in the trees and meet you at your place later."

"And then you're gonna leave me . . . "

Ethan turned back. A twinge of gray crept into her aura, edging its way into her angry red halo.

"No."

Spotlights bathed the mansion with blinding white light. Ethan squinted through the broken glass while Lauren fumed. He was right, eight men moved up on each side of the pool, weapons ready. They were prepping grenades from their vests this time—they wouldn't fall for the same trick twice.

"Smokes, now!"

Lauren dumped a handful of smoke pellets into Ethan's hand. The things were small, but they had heft. The two turned and threw the pellets together. The little gray things soared far over the Suburbans and black waters and, one by one, hit the ground or a thrall, enveloping the two assault groups in massive plumes of smoke. The thick miasmas swallowed parts of the spotlight beams, shrouding the SUVs and mansion in partial shadow.

Ethan resettled the goggles over his eyes while he gathered his strength. He launched high over the black vehicles onto the crusty green armillary. His sudden appearance in the partial light attracted a large volley of submachine gun fire from the trucks. As the first bullets pinged off the rusted metal frame, Ethan plunged into the giant ball of gray to his left.

He landed on a thrall trying to exit the tarry haze, stomping him into the ground with audible cry. Six armed thralls, some scouts, some from the trucks, and one of the vampires whipped around loosely in his direction. Riding the momentum, Ethan hurtled off the thrall and thrust his sword into the nearest thrall. The tip dug into the man's shoulder bone and painfully drove him back. Ethan pulled the sword and quickly hacked the man sprawled out behind him. The blade sliced into his neck, not enough to sever the head, but more than enough to kill him. Shouts and call-outs erupted though the murky cloud.

Ethan quickly ducked and turned, gunfire ripping through the air. The shots came from the pistol-wielding vampire at the rear of the group. He couldn't see where Ethan was, but he heard him through the confusion. Ethan loosed a trio of throwing stars before the fang's weapon zeroed in on him. One landed on his chest, cutting deeply with a burst of ash and blood, but other two knocked the fang's weapon aside, firing blindly searching for the shuriken's origin.

Ethan rolled left. A hail of submachine gun rounds tossed up loose soil chasing him. He came up with a rising cut through a thrall's vest from hip to shoulder. The man's knees gave, and he fell on his back, shrieking. Ethan charged the thrall standing in front of the vampire, half a step ahead of the barking pistol. He spilled the man's intestines with a savage cut under his combat vest. The thrall abruptly forgot about Ethan and desperately grabbed at his falling organs. The vampire hadn't forgotten him, though, and snapped searching fire Ethan's way. He dove and tumbled, the winnowing lead nipping at his heels until the gun's slide slammed empty. Despite his acrobatics, the last shot grazed Ethan below his left armpit and pushed a tiny spray of blood through the exit hole in his jacket. Catching Ethan's scent through the chemical smoke, the fang flicked out his baton, and the two lengths of metal clashed above them.

A frag grenade detonated across the reflecting pool, instantly followed by multiple simultaneous flash bangs in the same location—likely the thralls' own ordinance touching off. The Ethan smiled under his mask, imagining Lauren sprinting for her car.

A big black combat boot to the gut knocked him back to reality, separating him from the vampire. The fang quickly followed up with his baton, but Ethan pulled his sword in close at the last moment, catching the truncheon at his side. The vampire whipped his boot around, smacking Ethan solidly on the jaw with the heel, and sent him spinning. He quickly swapped magazines while Ethan thudding the ground.

Loaded, the vampire found Ethan clawing to his feet through the thinning smoke and fired. The last two thralls promptly added their weapons to the vampire's fusillade. The cloud lit up with the gouting flame-flash of the combined muzzles.

Rolling to his feet, Ethan moonsaulted high over the massed barrage. He landed behind the men and thrust his sword through the nearest thrall, shielding himself from the tracking fire. With the body still on his sword, Ethan clamped down on the man's trigger finger. The vampire dove for cover, automatic fire climbing up the last thrall's his vest. Wild shots punctured the white plywood paneling of the cargo truck. The gun clicked dry. At once a dozen MP5s aimed at Ethan.

Suppressed gunfire rang out just then, but none of it found him. Risking a peek, he saw the line of thralls by the trucks had scattered.

The fang had finished reloading again and snap-fired at Ethan. Heavy pistol rounds drilled through the thrall's torso, winging Ethan. He yanked his blade free and kicked the corpse into the gunfire. When bullets robbed the thrall's body of its momentum, Ethan lunged. The vampire dodged the horizontal slash, and spun around with his baton. In a single, swift motion, Ethan intercepted the metal rod and sliced into the vampire's torso with a puff of ash and blood. Ethan pressed the assault with a trio of rapid rising cuts. The first slid off the baton, but the second severed his gun hand, and the third removed the baton from the elbow.

Ethan swung once more, decapitating the fang and reducing both head and body to dust before either hit the ground.

Exhausted, Ethan stood among the scattered bodies, covered in sweat, blood, and dust.

He yanked the goggles down. The smoke screen was completely gone now. The other side of the reflecting pool was cleared as well. Bodies were strewn about, some crawling, the rest limp. He strained his ears for the telltale sound of Lauren's expensive car, but heard nothing but shouting.

Shit, did she make it?!

Flurries of shrieking bullets tore through the air around him. Ethan threw himself against the fountain wall, pulling his legs close. More gunfire buzzed overhead. One of London's thugs called out a grenade. Twin explosions erupted, and Ethan felt nothing.

Alexander trotted over to London.

The old soldier watched both fire teams advance along the reflecting pool when two smoke bombs detonated right on them. To his right, that fucking asshole with the sword appeared on the armillary, attracting a wave of gunfire. London ground his jaw when the shots missed and peppered his precious mansion. The swordsman dove into the cloud surrounding the right hand fireteam. Gunshots and death screams punctuated flickers of the masked man's weapon. Moments later, a short volley of blindfire from the brawl rippled through the cargo truck, sending the entire firing line diving for cover.

"Why aren't we firing?!" Alexander picked himself off the trammeled grass.

London, already on his feet, shot a glance at Alexander, his jaw flexed hard enough to crack bone. A rapid trio of explosions tore through the other smoke cloud. The blasts blew away most of the thick haze to reveal a shallow crater of blackened gore.

"That asshole is slaughtering our men! We need suppressing fire," Alexander pointed to the cargo trucks behind him.

"I will not sacrifice my manor to kill one man!" the older vampire snapped.

Using the MG would do the trick, but heavy rounds would overpenetrate right into the mansion's facade. Flashes of gunfire lit up the thinning smoke cloud. Twisting vortices of gray trailed the masked man's sword as he decimated the assault group.

"Fuck the building! We won't have anyone left at this rate!"

London glared at him with anxious rage. In the years since the old man had taken him under his wing, the young vampire had never seen him this disturbed. The older vampire turned to the men recovering from the errant shots.

"Bravo Team! Firing line, now!"

Twenty men hustled into two lines in front of London with practiced speed.

Pointing to the shrouded brawl, he shouted, "Ready weapons!"

Twenty submachine guns braced at once.

"Aim!"

Every barrel mounted flashlight highlighted the slowly appearing fight.

London inhaled to speak, but suppressed autofire chewed a checkerboard of holes into the cargo truck. One of the men flew back, the contents of his head splattered against the tall wheel. Another spun to the ground with a spray of red from his right shoulder. The rest of the firing line scattered, with Alexander and London dropping to avoid the incoming bullets.

The guns stopped, Alexander snapped up to see one of the newer lieutenants reduced to ash. Dorian was a promising thrall who had been turned weeks prior.

Now he was nothing. The smoke had fully cleared now, exposing the masked man surrounded by dead bodies and a pile of ash.

"There he is!" one of the men shouted out. "Shoot him!

The broken line was still recovering when the first submachine gun opened up. Soon more joined it, filling the air with angry lead. But the delay allowed the masked asshole to scramble behind the heavy stone wall of the reflecting pool. Hundreds of small caliber rounds chopped dirt or chipped marble, hitting nothing.

London grabbed the nearest thralls and shouted, "Prepare the MG! On the double!" Two men quickly disengaged and disappeared inside the rear cargo truck.

"Time for that insurance?" Alexander demanded.

"Yes," the old soldier growled.

Down the line, someone yelled out "Grenade!" Both vampires looked up, and the night exploded.

Ethan opened his eyes.

He had felt no blast and his hearing was still intact. There was no blast residue at his feet or any evidence of an explosion at all. Suddenly, muffled gunfire stitched the air above him. A cloud of smoke swallowed him up with a loud crack. His mind immediately jumped to Lauren getting gunned down, and he ran full speed towards the vehicles, pulling the goggles back in place. A single flashing muzzle sprayed shots down the length of the reflecting pool, seemingly ignoring his advance. Sword in hand, Ethan reached the curved wall of the armillary, ready to tear whatever fangs threatened Lauren to pieces.

He stopped short.

Braced against the marble on one knee, Lauren's black silhouette fired one of the fallen submachine guns across the reflecting pool. Four more of the weapons lay in two piles next to her. Tufts of white belched from the bucking suppressed gun, its sliced bungie cord swinging wildly from the stock.

Bullets flew down range. Countless tiny holes in the cargo truck showered white chips of wood like snow on the pinned thralls. Despite the chattering vibration, she kept the big firearm steady in her enhanced grip. When the bolt locked empty, she tossed the spent gun into one pile and snatched a replacement from the other, repeating the process. After the fifth and final weapon clicked dry, she dropped it and turned to Ethan falling into cover next to her.

"What the hell are you still doing here?!" he said, wrenching the goggles down.

"The plan changed!" Her mask barely muffled her anger.

He heard shouts from the trucks as the men regrouped. In response, Lauren grabbed a pair of flash bangs from a collection at her feet. Pulling the pin off a pair, she flung them out to the end of the reflecting pool. The grenades sailed high over the long stretch of water and let out a deafening double-bang scant seconds later, rescattering London's men.

"What?!" he yelled.

She glared at him, her ruby eyes burning intensely. "I finish what I fucking start, Goddamnit! Even if that means keeping your psychotic ass alive!"

"Now who's crazy!?"

Ethan spared a glance back at the truck. London continued barking out orders. Two of his men unpacked a large, belt fed machine gun. The rest were shaking off the stun.

Not good.

"How many of those flashy things do you have left?"

"Two."

"Get 'em ready."

Ethan reached into his jacket and pulled out a

bunch of his notecards. Fanning them in his hands, he chanted in Latin. The blood-inked words activated with a bluish-gold light when he spoke, pulsing brighter with every syllable. Lauren watched, wide-eyed by the mystical display of faith. The blue light increased enough to bathe the surrounding area blue. Finished, he nodded at Lauren.

She stared at them, still awestruck.

"Do it!"

Startled, Lauren immediately ripped the pins from the flash grenades, chucked them, and ducked down, closing her eyes and plugging her ears.

Before they detonated, Ethan spun to his feet, cards in each hand. The two thralls were nearly finished setting up the large gun, and the rest instantly opened fire when he showed himself. A wall of lead whizzed passed, tearing into his shoulder and splintering his right hip. Bits of his blood and tissue sprayed against the damaged black Suburban behind him while more shots perforated the vehicle.

Ethan grimaced. He had misjudged the timing by a single second.

The submachine guns halted once the flash bangs finally detonated in rapid succession. Ethan shunted his remaining energy into the glowing prayer cards, and blue flames sprang. He threw his arms wide and cast the mystic papers at the trucks.

Lauren peeked over the fountain wall at his feet. The burning papers trailed ribbons of blue light over the black water. They fanned out, striking the ground and the men in a wide arc each card exploding with a blinding, blue-gold corona of fire. A deafening peal of thunder accompanied each burst like consecutive bolts of lightning from the heavens. Thralls burned and vampires disintegrated. Lauren gaped, completely mesmerized by the awful display.

The attack obliterated much of London's security

team, but not all. Alexander ran up to the large gun and pulled the burning corpses off. He slammed the bolt into place, feeding the large weapon, and clamped his finger around the trigger.

The heavy mechanical *chunk, chunk, chunk* of the big machine gun cut through the rolling thunder. Large caliber bullets chewed the stonework at the end of the reflecting pool and punched large holes and larger craters into the five black Suburbans. Bits of plaster and brick exploded off the face of the mansion. The base of the huge green armillary burst into a cloud of metal splinters, and the rusted globe collapsed under its own weight into the black waters.

The crash shook Lauren from her awe. She quickly grabbed Ethan's belt and yanked him out of the deadly storm of lead. Dirty water splashed over them while the big machine gun continued to saturate the air. Ethan's eyes looked distant under his mask, their golden hue fading. Lauren shook him from his daze with a sharp slap to the cheek.

"What the hell was that?!" she yelled.

He blinked. "Remember those notecards!?"

Lauren's gaze trailed off before coming back to him wide as saucers. "That's what those were for?!? Why didn't you do that at the depot?!"

"Out of paper!" he shook his head.

"You're fucking kidding me!? That almost got them all! Can you do that again?"

The skin around his eyes tightened, betraying the pain hidden under his mask. "Not enough left."

The remaining submachine guns joined Alexander's chattering weapon. The SUVs ceased to be vehicles and more like blocks of metallic swiss-cheese on wheels. Lead punched hole after hole into the SUV directly in front of Lauren. A tire exploded sending a sharp quiver of panic through her spine. Bullets shredded the fender in two, sending each half spinning into the dirt by their feet. The stone wall behind them steadily lost more and more pieces.

Ethan looked over to her. Her hand crawled to the pair of grenades dangling across her chest. He watched her gloved fingers loop through both pins.

"What are you doing?"

Lauren turned, fright creeping into her eyes. "I am not going into that coffin."

"Don't you have any more of those smoke bombs left?"

She ducked down lower as a bullet ricocheted off the stone inches from her head. Lauren gave a nervous look at the thralls behind them. "We wouldn't make it there anyway."

Ethan caught the defeat in her voice. The machine gun focused on the thick wall by their heads, forcing them both to hunker down further. Bullets steadily chipped away at the dense stone, and dirty water seeped onto their shoulders through cracks forming in the wall. The constant stream of hot lead vibrated their backs.

He looked around. There was no place to go— two of the black SUVs had caught fire, and the rest were already smoking. They might make it to her car once the gunner stopped to reload, but he sensed another group of thralls just past the courtyard.

More reinforcements.

Lauren's finger tightened around the grenade pins. Ethan put a hand over hers, grabbing her attention. Despair tugged at the edge of her eyes. He told her to have faith, but the earsplitting gunfire drowned out his voice.

Out of nowhere, a string of explosions abruptly silenced the machine gun.

Poking their heads over the ruined fountain wall, Ethan and Lauren saw something unbelievable.

A dozen swarthy-looking men in loose fitting

street clothes piled out of older, custom-looking Buick and Chevy sedans and fired on London's team. Two of the security detail instantly burst into ash from the gunfire. The remainder dove for cover, including London and Alexander. Some of the swarthy men threw grenades and flaming bottles.

Explosions tipped the nearest truck over in a flaming heap. Every bullet sent brilliant showers of sparks, starting small patches of fire in the tall grass. Alexander ripped the machine gun off its tripod and fired at the newcomers.

The courtyard erupted into chaos.

"Who the hell are they?" Lauren wondered aloud.

Ethan shrugged. Blood gushed from his shoulder.

"You're bleeding!"

Lauren immediately climbed over and pulled down Ethan's jacket, revealing a gnarly bullet hole in his shoulder. Putting pressure on the wound, Lauren paused, putting a hand to her mouth. Shaking a look of disgust and despair from her eyes, she frantically went from pouch to pouch on her belt for anything useful when Ethan grabbed her hand. Catching her worried gaze, he shook his head.

Ethan slowed his breathing, calming his heart and blood flow. He closed his eyes and made a short series of hand gestures at his waist. Her eyes bulged at the grisly hole slowly sealing shut, leaving a fresh, bloody scar on his shoulder. She looked down to see his hip repeat the same process. Two bloody metal mushrooms fell from the freshly healed wounds.

She dropped back on his legs, dumbfounded.

Through the gunfire, a large engine thundered to life. They both looked back. London, Alexander, and what was left of his men climbed into the second truck. Black smog churned, and the big vehicle lumbered for the gate. Bullets rained down on it, shredding any stragglers. The swarthy men continued to fire on the truck while some of them retreated to their vehicles.

"Damnit, they're getting away!" Ethan exclaimed with renewed strength.

He jumped to his feet, knocking Lauren to the side, and mounted the bullet-worn fountain wall. She climbed to her knees, gawking, as Ethan jumped off and sprinted full tilt on the water like it was pavement. Small ripples appeared with each footfall, but he didn't sink, not even an inch.

"That son of a bitch can walk on water!"

Realizing what he was doing, Lauren quickly followed around the fountain. When Ethan reached the edge of the pool, he catapulted high over the flaming hellscape and landed in the enclosed cargo bed right before the truck slammed through the line of cars. A thrall tried to kick him out, but Ethan caught the boot and tossed the man back into the courtyard. Alexander and the last two of London's men immediately jumped onto him.

Lauren had reached the end of the reflecting pool, when the truck plowed through a green Buick blocking the gate. In her haste she failed to see a one-in-a-million shot from London strike one of the swarthy grenadiers square in the chest—mid toss. The man's surplus grenade sailed backwards and bounced off the stone wall of the reflecting pool. It bounced once more on the dirt and detonated a handful of yards in front of Lauren, throwing her head over heels into the jagged stone.

Blood pooled under her body while the vehicles disappeared down the tunnel of trees.

21 Lonely Boy

Her head felt muzzy and warm. Very warm.

Lauren's eyes fluttered open. The tall grass in front of her swam like rough waters. Her head hurt, and her ears throbbed. Nauseous, she forced herself onto her hands and knees. Through her mask, she smelled bitter, chemical smoke but didn't see any fire around her. Strangely, all the swaying blades of grass subtly glowed orange. Lauren put a hand to her forehead to steady the world, and it felt like a hot poker.

"D'ah!" she cried and ripped her hood off in a panic.

Flames melted the crown of the black polymide hood. She stared at the dancing flames. Sweaty strands of white-gray flopped onto her face. Sitting up, Lauren wailed through gnashed teeth, the pain suddenly radiating from her torso. A thick slice of marble jutted above her left hip, blood slowly trickling from the edges. It was wide and every twitch grated against her hip bone with an electric jolt.

Without thinking, Lauren wrapped her hands around the stone and pulled. Each bur sent white-hot stabs arcing up and down her body until the thing slid out with a thick spurt of blood. Finally free, she held it up to the moonlight. The needle-sharp wedge was as wide as her hand and slick with red. She tossed it next to the flaming hood.

Lauren gazed at the dark spot pooling between her knees. Blood. Her blood—lots of it. Gloved hands pressed against the wound, futilely holding the massive gash shut. She immediately regretted removing the big stone chip. Her eyes fell back on her mask burning next to it.

This was it.

She was going to die.

Lauren knew Ethan was going to be the end of her. Why did she have to be right? Bleeding out after a firefight was not how she expected to go out, but, as her first mentor used to say: "Such is life".

Odd.

She expected it to be colder. She looked at the gushing wound out of morbid curiosity. Miraculously, the bloody lesion diligently knitted itself closed.

"That's handy," she huffed, wobbling from the blood loss.

Lauren peered down the dirt road. The cargo truck was a distant speck of red light under the long tunnel of oak trees. Those other men quickly chased after it in their cars. She wanted to chase after them to give Ethan what for, but all vehicles left were destroyed.

If only she had her car.

Her body went rigid with realization, blowing out the muzziness. Lauren jumped to her feet with a sudden burst of adrenaline and sprinted to the south wing of the mansion faster than her legs could handle. She rounded the large copse of bushes and ripped the camo netting off her Daytona Spyder.

Lauren jumped into the driver's seat and frantically searched her belt for her keys. For a split second, she darkly wondered if she left them in her trench coat on the roof. Grinning from ear to ear, she found the keys and slammed them into the ignition switch on the dashboard. The big V12 awoke with a metallic roar. Pulsing the throttle twice, she dropped the hand brake and peeled off, fishtailing through the tall grass spewing twin tails of dirt and grass behind it. She steered around the carnage at the end of the reflecting pool. The other cargo truck laid on its side, flaming and broken with burning corpses arrayed around it like some sort of sacrifice. Lauren briefly wondered what would happen if or when someone found everything here, and what they would think. It didn't matter. She would never return to this place as long as she lived.

Headlights flipped up and illuminated the tangled tree limbs as she rocketed out of the courtyard. Up ahead, the truck and cars remained specs of red and white. Lauren bit her lip. The terrain refused to give her a break. She fought hard to keep the Ferrari from spinning out—her car had lots of power and plenty speed, but on the dirt, it had very little traction. To make matters worse, the roughness of the ride exacerbated the nauseous feeling in her stomach, and she felt her vision blurring at the edges. She gripped the wheel tightly, focusing past the growing wooziness.

At last the endless canopy of tree limbs ended. The street wasn't far now.

The chase turned sharply onto the main road. Sparks burst from each vehicle bouncing off the high curb, and a couple of the cars spun out from the sudden transition. Though slowed from the transition, the high speed caravan quickly vanished south past the row of tall pine trees lining the road.

Five agonizing seconds later, Lauren's car jumped the curb onto the street. She braked hard, barely dodging a motorcycle driving south. The rider beeped his pathetic horn, swinging his fist at her. On any other night, traffic should have been sparse on the old back road, but this was a Saturday, and people wanted to get out—especially out here near the rich, old mansions.

Finally on solid pavement, the Daytona shined.

The engine revved smoother and higher speeding after Ethan. Her frazzled braid whipped wildly in the rushing air. Small flashes of light winked from the cars' side windows accompanied with distant pops. More than once the tall cargo box swayed dangerously weaving through traffic. Gaining on the chase, Lauren saw the truck distinctly now. Inside the cargo area, Ethan engaged the survivors from the mansion. They fought each other almost as much as they fought to keep their balance in the pitching vehicle. Occasionally, the men in the custom lowriders found their aim amid all the bobbing and weaving. Bullets sparked off the heavy steel frame of the truck or the box skeleton inside. One lucky shot penetrated one of the truck's rear wheels. The hot rubber rapidly shredded off the spinning rim and scattered into the air.

A large chunk of steel-belted rubber struck the lead car tailing the five-ton, smashing its windshield into a massive white cataract. The driver swerved violently and dropped to the rear of the pack. Lauren jinked, dodging the flying debris at the last second.

All the gunfire and the explosions at the mansion had done a number on her sensitive ears—especially those flash grenades. The stuffy white noise had never fully stopped until moments ago. The high pitch roar of her Ferrari melded with the loudly rushing wind as she raced on. She heard the heavy diesel whine of the cargo truck, the growling V8s of the lowriders, the sudden cracks of the gunfire, and the panicked beeps of traffic desperately trying to avoid the whole crazy procession, all with full clarity.

But in all that, she heard a new sound. A wailing sound.

Snapping a glance behind, she saw the flashing blue and red of an old Crown Victoria police cruiser chasing after them. At some point they must have passed a parked cop car. Lauren wanted to laugh, that the cop was getting himself into something he was woefully unprepared for, but she remembered the warning from her first mentor: *where there is one police officer, more are sure to follow.*

It was only a matter of time before backup joined in.

The cargo truck abruptly screeched around a street corner under a freeway overpass. The pursuing vehicles stopped short. A pair of them overshot the turn. A small, lighter commuter car ping-ponged off one of the lowriders and into other vehicles, jamming the entire intersection with the resulting pileup.

Barreling through a row of cars lined up under the freeway, the five-ton wheeled around again, screeching left up the on ramp. A huge puff of grayish-black dust blasted out the cargo door and showered the nearest lowrider's windshield. The car missed the on ramp and shot over the guardrail, tumbling into a line of trees. The three other cars picked their way around the waiting vehicles as fast as they dared before thundering after the truck. Scant seconds later, Lauren, her car far more agile, handily carved through the tossed automobiles. She pulled into the ramp and hammered the throttle.

In the passenger bench, London scowled at these mysterious assailants dogged him, killing his men and shooting holes through his truck. Damnit, if not for them, he would have finished off that damned swordsman! They had dark brown skin, and their cars looked modified with small tires, flaming paint jobs, and lots of garish chrome. To London, they looked like Mexican gang bangers. But what in the world were cartel scum doing attacking his men?

He dug out his watch to check the time but immediately closed it. The glass was cracked badly—like it would tell him anything. Instead, he fished out his cellphone and quickly dialed. Oberon oversaw the cartels. He might shed some light on this situation. The phone rang twice before the other end picked up. The elder's butler answered and promptly transferred the call.

"Yes?" his friend picked up.

"Oberon!"

"Ah, London. Everything is going to plan, I hope? I'm sorry to say I will not be free to join you tonight. Something came up, unfortunately."

"Never mind that!" London growled. "What the devil are your people doing?!"

"Excuse me?"

"A group of cartel thugs showed up and attacked me and my men at the mansion! They're chasing us on the highway right now!"

"Oh, my. That sounds dreadful. Are you sure those people are with the cartel?"

London looked out the side mirror again. Catholic symbols and old Latin script decorated the windshields on each car along with other strange symbols that only Oberon would recognize. He saw a pop of light from the nearest one just before the mirror exploded.

"Of course they are!"

"Hmm. I see. I can make a few calls, but I should warn you. There has been a rather nasty upset within the San Carcos. Apparently, a civil war has broken out amongst the leadership. I believe the don survived the initial assault, but he is still sorting out the usurpers."

"Well, do something! Call them off!"

"Not to worry, my friend. I shall speak with them immediately."

Oberon hung up and went back to his book.

The Ferrari launched onto the freeway, skipping

an inch off the ground. The tires angrily chirped when they touched the asphalt. Lauren gripped the wheel with all her strength, refusing to lose control of her precious convertible. Towering street lamps beaming down blue light shot by at regular intervals. High stone walls lined the outside lanes, enclosing the elevated interstate from the rest of the world.

Far less traffic congested the eight lane road, allowing the truck and the three tailing cars to drive on unmolested. With the road clear, Lauren buried the gas pedal into the carpet, and the mighty V12 screamed in response. The needles in the gauge cluster danced and twitched with every gear shift. Though her car was old, it was built in a time when safety regulations were far more lax or outright nonexistent. There was no restricted emissions nor any pesky governor limiting its top speed.

Lauren kept the throttle wide open and kept an eye on the steadily climbing speedometer. Eighty miles per hour, ninety, one hundred, hundred-ten, hundred-twenty and still climbing! The wind flapped her braid so savagely, she had to tuck it between her shoulders and the seat. Behind her the tailing police cruiser struggled to keep up.

Thundering forward, Lauren finally caught up to the three gang cars. She braked too late and ended up between them and the five-ton, bullets whizzing over head. In front of her, Ethan still fought with the vampires inside, though there was only two now. She recognized Alexander. Her hands tightened on the steering wheel. She wished the worst on him. A dark grin took shape when Ethan kicked the pompous vampire into the back of the cargo area.

A pair of holes punched through the windshield by her head. She reflexively ducked and risked an angry look back. The lowriders started splitting their attention between her and the truck. Ahead, Ethan grappled the other vampire while Alexander struggled to his feet. Lauren looked back again. The gangers were lining up more shots on them.

She had to do something.

One hand on the wheel, Lauren dug into her belt for a small handful of smoke pellets. Wedging herself into her seat, Lauren twisted and flung the entire fistful at the cars behind her. The majority of the pellets bounced harmlessly off hoods or the rushing concrete, bursting uselessly in the distance. Two, however, embedded in the grille of one of the lowriders. Dark smoke fluted from the engine bay and obscured the windshield. The engine sputtered from the thick chemical vapor clogging the air filter. The car swerved into another lowrider before over-correcting into the heavy concrete barrier. The metallic blue Buick toppled into the oncoming lane, quickly becoming a distant spec of smoke.

The two remaining gang cars ignored the truck and started firing at her. She heard the metallic thunks of bullets piercing her car's bodywork.

"Well. That really got their attention!" she said to herself.

From the side of her eye, Lauren saw Ethan break the grapple. He threw his opponent to the wood floor and stabbed the prone vampire. He withdrew the sword, reared back, and slammed the blade into the bastard's neck. Wind sucked out the resulting burst of ash. Lauren immediately ducked and held her breath as the cinders quickly flew over her windshield.

Her car bucked violently. The two remaining gang cars had each pulled along either side. The right-hand car slammed into her. The red convertible rocked again from the impact. Not missing a beat, the left car rammed into her, too, sending the lighter Ferrari rebounding back into the first one. They both rammed at once, sandwiching her precious vehicle in a shower of sparks and crunching metal. She fought the wheel in vain trying to break their hold.

"Get off my car, you fucking assholes!" she exclaimed into the wind.

The passenger in the lowrider to her right aimed an AK-47 at her head. Catching sight of the big rifle at the last second, Lauren scrunched into her seat. Bullets chattered overhead, shattering part of the windshield on the other lowrider. The second car immediately peeled off, releasing her in the process.

The first vehicle promptly swerved to avoid an oblivious station wagon right as the gunman pulled the trigger again. The sudden movement flung rifle against the door, and it fell out of his hands, bullets sparking the pavement.

Grinning at her fortune, Lauren jerked the wheel and slammed into the car, crunching the door panel— and the passenger's arm. He screamed and fell into his seat, clutching the ruined limb. Her grin disappeared when another heavy in the rear seat replaced him with a short-barreled shotgun outside of the window. She reflexively threw a fistful of her smoke pellets. Most harmlessly broke on the passenger door, but the other skimmed under the shotgunner's nose and detonated inside the cab. Smoke instantly belched out of every orifice in the vehicle. The man coughed violently, nearly losing his grip on the weapon. The driver swerved into her car once more.

The other lowrider had dropped back and rammed the Ferrari's rear bumper, whipping Lauren's head back from the jarring collision.

This is getting impossible!

She reached to belt for more pellets, but froze. The pouch was empty. In a panic, her eyes fell on Ethan's hand grenades.

"Fuck it."

Lauren ripped one off the belt and pulled the pin

with her teeth. She'd seen it done countless times in the movies, but never realized how much it would hurt her mouth. The spring-loaded spoon flew from the pineapple. She reared up to throw at the smoking car, but the other one suddenly rammed the Ferrari again. The grenade flew from her hand the opposite way. It exploded harmlessly on the empty pavement in a burst of flaming black smoke.

Pissed, she grabbed the other grenade.

"Last one," she reminded herself.

She pulled the pin. The lowrider smashed her rear bumper again, and the grenade slipped into the Ferrari's footwell.

London leaned out the passenger window and took aim at one of the gang cars. He fired twice before its windshield shattered and swerved out of sight. He thought about climbing up to the roof, but froze when a giant spotlight enveloped his truck. A helicopter bathed the truck with its searchlight while a second one kept pace higher up. Underneath them, he spied multiple police cruisers trailing at a decent distance. London swore and climbed back inside. He reached for his cellphone and dialed a different number this time. It picked up immediately.

"Roman!"

"Who the hell is this?" the voice on the other line demanded with a thick New York accent.

"This is London! I need a favor!"

"Why?"

"A group of San Carcos thugs are shoot at my men and I along Highway 65. The police have joined the chase."

"You're fucking with me, right?"

"There are two helicopters chasing us along with a group of police vehicles! I need you to call off their pursuit!"

"Hold on." There was a pause. In the background, London heard a television news reporter. "You're all over the fuckin' news, London. I can't do anything about this. You've got three cars on your tail. Looks like they're fighting each other, too."

"I need time to get away from them. Call off the police!"

"This is gonna backfire bad, London. I can't do that."

"Just have them pull back on the truck, then. I need time to get away!"

There was a longer pause on Roman's end. "You got a traffic jam coming up. Looks like the highway patrol are about to deploy spike strips before you reach it."

"Roman, this could affect the deliveries across the city. Call. Them. Off!"

"This is gonna cost you."

Behind the truck, an explosion sounded off. London poked his head out the window. A black cloud quickly shrunk in the distance.

"Christ, you're friends back there are poppin' off dynamite."

"I can give you twenty percent control of the Deacon Hill district."

Roman paused again. "Fifty percent."

"Thirty!" London responded.

"Forty."

London sneered silently. "Fine! Make the call."

"Stay on the line."

London vainly checked his watch and waited for a few moments. Through the broken glass, the second hand ticked at glacial speeds. The scuffling in the cargo compartment grew louder.

He was not about to give up his control of Deacon Hill. The area was sparsely populated and held little variety for sustenance, but control of the residents' moneyed power more than made up for it. The ability to influence the habits and views in Deacon Hill gave London the clout to push back against the machinations of the rest of the council. His control of the district maintained the delicate balance of power across Free Port City. More importantly, it kept the primarch from looking into Oberon's activities. He would be damned if he gave it to that thug, Roman.

And he would be even more damned if he let go of Undergrove Manor. For Oberon's sake, and his bid to remove the primarch, London could not lose that mansion.

Roman rejoined the call.

"The highway patrol is standing down. You've got three minutes, tops. And you'd better ditch that truck soon. They think you're carrying explosives."

"Thank you!"

"You can thank me by paying up."

The call went dead. The helicopter spotlight suddenly turned off. London poked his head out the window in time to see the police chopper peel away. The cruisers behind them hung back even further. A series of explosions rang out from behind.

Lauren frantically felt under her legs for the grenade, mentally counting down. *One.* She moved her hand faster, feeling left and right. *Two.* Her panic growing she felt around closer to her feet. *Three.* The rear car slammed her again.

Something round and dense bumped against her hand, and she instantly snatched it up. The gunman in the rear seat, having regained control of his shotgun, leveled the barrel just above her driver's-side door. Lauren chucked the grenade. The little green bomb bounced right under the lowrider.

Four.

Smoke and fire blossomed beneath the custom

vehicle, lifting it off the ground with a swirling mushroom of flame. The shockwave slapped her face with its split-second of searing heat-wash. Time abruptly jerked to a stand still around Lauren. The lowrider arced over her covered in a kaleidoscope of frozen flame. Tongues of orange heat leapt off the hovering ballet of carnage, surrounded by shorn pieces of glass and steel like tiny meteorites orbiting a celestial body.

Lauren shifted down and mashed the gas pedal while the car fell. The tachometer needle whipped around the dial and the red convertible surged. The flaming ball of metal kissed the pavement inches away from her rear bumper, the impact rippling through the disintegrating frame. It bounced and rolled into the other lowrider, crushing it instantly.

Time reasserted itself and the wreck quickly faded in her rear view mirror.

The sandwiched hunk of fiery debris skidded along the road, keeping up with Lauren through sheer momentum. The police cruisers ground to a halt next to the flaming junk.

It was just Ethan now.

Ethan jerked his head at the sound of an explosion. The blue Buick chasing them suddenly burst into flames and flipped onto the white Chevy with the flame job, barely missing Lauren's fancy red convertible in the process.

Alexander's yell snapped him back to the truck in time to see a heavy punch followed by a quick pair of jabs. Ethan barely dodged the streaking fist by an inch. He deflected the second punch with his free hand, but the third crunched a rib, knocking Ethan off balance in the process. Alexander capitalized on the hit and knocked Ethan flat on his back with a heavy right cross. The o-katana slipped from his grip and bounced out the open cargo door. It tumbled through the night air and lodged into one of the bullet holes in Lauren's windshield. In a panic, she slammed the brakes, swerving and losing pace.

"No more knife, asshole!" the vampire gloated, stomping on Ethan.

Ethan rolled right. The floor splintered under the heavy boot, throwing up shards of wood. He caught the next stomp inches from his chest. The sneering fang put all his weight behind the boot. Struggling under the weight, Ethan started when the muzzle of Alexander's pistol appeared inches from his face. He wrenched the boot to the side just as the gun roared. The deafening bullet punched through the splintered wood right next to his temple.

Alexander cursed and unloaded a barrage of fire. Ethan quickly twisted the foot further, knocking the vampire's knee into his weapon. He jerked his head to avoid the misaligned shots, pulverizing the wood floor next to him, but one bullet sheared a bloody path down the length of his skull. White heat pierced through the spiritual energy coursing through his body.

"Sit-fucking-still, you little shit!"

Alexander whipped down with the butt of his pistol, but Ethan pulled the captured boot onto his chest—the sudden weight forcing the air from his lungs. The pistol butt missed his head and struck the ground.

Ethan wrapped a leg around the captured limb and slammed the vampire onto the floor. Had he air in his lungs, it would have winded him. The gun flew from Alexander's hand into the back of the cargo compartment. With a quick breath, Ethan kicked to his feet, ignoring his damaged rib and bleeding temple. Eyes blazing with renewed vigor, he rushed Alexander. Fists wrapped in tattered boxing tape smashed ashen welts on the fang's newly regenerated face, driving the parasite deeper into the cargo room, dampening the knuckles with dark and viscous blood.

"Where are the buses!" Ethan roared.

"Right where I fucked your mother last night, shithead!" Alexander chuckled a spittle of blood.

As Ethan wound up for another strike, Alexander thrust his knee into Ethan's groin. He kicked the dazed man off, sending him stumbling. The vampire rose. He immediately lashed out with a flurry of quick shots to the body shots. Each hit shook Ethan, but he clamped his left arm around the third punch. He lifted up, locking Alexander's joint in place, and retaliated with rapid strikes to the fang's chest and a quick elbow across his chin.

The vampire's arm burned in Ethan's grip. Grimacing through the pain, he caught the fourth strike and twisted hard. Ethan resisted Alexander's vice-grip by ratcheting the locked limb higher, releasing his fist. Before he could punish the fang with a straight shot to the head, Alexander slammed a black boot into Ethan's damaged rib, tearing the two apart.

Alexander chased him, trading punches and parries. He landed a heavy uppercut under Ethan's chin. The sweat-soaked mask further darkened from burst lip. Ethan smashed the vampire's nose with a reverse roundhouse. Blood trailed from Ethan's sneaker. He quickly swept his other leg behind the vampire's unsteady feet. The fang flopped on the hard wooden floor.

Ethan fell on the prone vampire and grabbed the collar of his combat vest.

"You sent bus 2047 to a warehouse! Where the fuck is it?!" he thundered, punching the parasite's face after every noun.

Alexander spat a tooth and cackled, "Like you could do anything about it, blood bag!"

The vampire whipped a fist into Ethan's bloody temple. The shock bowled him over, his hand ripping the zipper part way down his vest. Alexander rolled on top and grabbed a chunk of Ethan's leather jacket. He head-butted the masked hunter and rose, flinging him sideways out the corner of the cargo door. Ethan latched onto the edge, his legs kicking over the rushing pavement under him. He fought for purchase and carefully hooked his feet into the truck.

A high pitched horn rapidly beeped behind of him.

Lauren pointed wildly ahead of the vehicle. Peering around the corner, he glimpsed a fast approaching sea of red lights in the distance with a big one dead center. Before he could see more, Alexander dragged him back inside by the feet. Ethan clawed at the collection of bullet holes, briefly halting the vampire's progress. The board snapped in his hand, and the vampire whipped him into the back wall, knocking the air out of his lungs.

Gasping for breath, Ethan dragged himself off the floor. He froze when he saw Alexander's pistol aimed at him. The hammer snapped, and he immediately jerked to the side, the bullet grazing his chest.

"Squirrelly little fucker!"

Alexander steadied his aim with both hands and fired. Ethan dove, rolled, and flipped off the wall while the barrage smashed through the cab, chasing his every move until the gun's slide locked empty. Swearing, Alexander went to pistol whip him, but the truck abruptly tilted, throwing both of them off balance. The big vehicle lurched again and gained speed.

Ethan flung a group of throwing stars at Alexander, knocking the pistol out of his hand. He dove under the incoming haymaker, rolling over the smashed wooden floor. Alexander twisted around, following him with another heavy punch—

—And suddenly went limp on Ethan's shoulder

with a wet grunt.

Ethan stepped back and let the vampire crumple to the floor. A splintered piece of floorboard poked through the tear in Alexander's vest. Dark blood dribbled from it and his mouth. He lay still as ice.

Ethan ran to the door.

London dropped his watch to steady the wheel.

The driver was dead in his seat. Blood oozed from multiple holes on his back and one through his forehead. A giant patch of bloody bone fragments dripped down the cracked windshield. London tried to wrench the steering wheel back on course, but the man's foot was wedged against the throttle. Unable to slow down, the truck tipped over, still barreling down the freeway at full speed.

The toppled truck skidded into the rapidly approaching silver tanker in the center of the traffic jam. Standing on the driver's body, London punched out the passenger door. He gripped the frame to climb out but stopped.

His watch!

Looking to his feet, he noticed his precious trinket glinting next the door handle. He quickly reached for his friend's gift just when the truck collided with the tanker.

Exquisite pain tore through Alexander's very being, but he couldn't move, not even to scream. He helplessly watched the masked man fly out the truck. His body bashed the trailing convertible's windshield, cracking the passenger side into a spider's web of clear-white.

The driver—that white-haired bitch from the garage—slammed on the brakes and the truck violently rolled over. Alexander painfully ragdolled onto the new floor. The ground underneath him quickly grew hot.

The car rapidly shrunk behind a wall of sparks.

Suddenly, the truck crashed into something big, flinging him into the perforated back wall. A split second later, an explosion swallowed Alexander and everything around him in a ball of white-hot flame.

Ethan struggled to grab the top of the windshield.

Screeching to a halt, Lauren stood up in her seat and pulled him up by his jacket. Steadied, she looked down at him. Her jaw clenched hard, and her heart pounded in her chest. She wanted to scream at him. She wanted to slap his mask off—no punch it off.

But all that came out was laughter. Together on the still functioning wreck of her precious car, Lauren couldn't help but laugh at it all. The mansion, the crypt, the bloody courtyard, and a flat-out sprint to catch up with him, as she could do was laugh. Her laughter spread to Ethan. The two rejoiced in front of the rising conflagration. Black chemical smoke plumed skyward, outlined by city's ambient light pollution, and consumed the last of the vampires from the mansion. Against all odds, they were victorious.

Ethan suddenly sat up.

"Look!"

He pointed to a city bus taking off in the HOV lane. A man stood on top of it. Her jaw fell when she saw it.

"Get me on that thing!" he barked, golden energy swirling back into his eyes.

She stared at him incredulously. "You've gotta be kidding me!"

"He's the only one who knows where the bus went to!"

Lauren didn't argue this time. She fell back into her seat and gunned the engine. Ethan felt the hot motor buzz angrily under dented hood. He braced himself as the tires smoked and the car fishtailed past the burning wreckage. Lauren steered through the throngs of people still running from the fire. None of them looked to be hurt, by his estimation.

Small miracle.

Another car exploded, spinning abandoned vehicles further into the rest of the lanes, blocking off the road behind them.

The Ferrari picked up speed, quickly catching up to the bus with ease. Ethan noticed the big vehicle was empty. It was probably heading a different bus yard. Above, London strode atop the roof like some kind of circus performer straddling a trained elephant.

Ethan let go of the windshield and steadied himself on the hood. His jacket flapped wildly in the rushing wind. Lauren edged her car as close as she could manage without getting caught under the bus's huge wheels. When she was close enough, Ethan wrenched his sword out of the window with a sprinkle of glass. Gathering his strength, Ethan vaulted onto the massive transport.

London spun around, surprised. Ethan rose to his feet, staring at the older vampire with menacing golden eyes. Sections of the vampire's fluttering black uniform were singed and frayed.

Sharp winds buffeted the two of them.

"You just don't give up, do you, boy?" London called out.

Ethan held his sword up, ready and silent.

"Do you really want to do this here?" the parasite exclaimed.

"Where's 2047?" Ethan demanded.

London shook his head with disgust. "I have killed more obstinate vampire hunters than you time and again. You are nothing new."

Ethan settled into his stance, the passing street lights gleaming off the sword's edge. "If you you won't tell me where, then I'll carve the answers out of you."

London quickly checked his pocket watch. The glass was completely cracked and the dial frozen. Rage welled up on his face.

"Fine!" he roared. "Have it your way!"

Ethan charged. London sidestepped the downward slash and again with the upward uppercut. He planted a boot squarely on Ethan's chest and pushed. Ethan flew back from the heavy thrust, rolling to the edge of the curved roof. He caught one of the vents before he went over. Lauren's car pulled under him, watching in case he fell.

Climbing back up, Ethan readied another attack.

As he approached the vampire, London knelt down and ripped a long panel from the roof, the twisted metal sheet went flying into the night. London tore a thick length of conduit pipe from the gap with a cloud of ozone and sparking wires. Light spilled from jagged hole. Holding the pipe in front with a hand on his hip, the vampire beckoned his masked opponent forward.

Ethan met the challenge, swinging the o-katana down against the rushing air. With a flick of his wrist, London flashed the pipe up, guiding the curved blade away. Ethan rolled with the parry, spinning his weapon around and under. The pipe intercepted him again with ease, pushing Ethan back a step. London chased him with a quick series of jabs, twirling the pipe in a tight arcs. Ethan swung his sword out, barely catching the jagged lead shaft before it took his head each time.

The vampire gloated, and pressed the attack with another rapid assault. His weapon held close, Ethan struggled to keep up with the fast overhead strikes. He swung down on London's fourth attack, forcing the pipe low and thrusting the blade of a red sneaker into London's chest. The kick sent the fang back a few steps.

With a sizable gap between them, Ethan spun his sword in reverse and wheeled his arms around. Spiritual energy surged into his muscles and ligaments, drawing every fiber and tendon taut. The wind whipping by his body broke for a split second of silence before resuming its flow.

It was a gamble.

He knew supercharging his body like this would quickly deplete what was left of his stamina, but this parasite was strong. Only one of his prepared notecards remained, and with the wind blasting him on the roof, it was certain to miss. Ethan had no choice but to meet strength with strength. After a deep, centering breath, he charged.

London thrust. Ethan caught the metal shaft with incredible speed, sliding it off his sword in a small burst of sparks. He wheeled the metal club down and sliced up, cutting through the vampire's combat vest and driving a shallow gash across his chest. The vampire quickly retreated, fearing the burning pain from the last time Ethan cut him. He gnashed his teeth and glared at him with a mixture of fury and bewilderment. Ethan stood unaffected by the buffeting winds, waiting.

Bellowing, London rushed. His pipe rained down again and again, yet Ethan batted each strike aside with ease. He snapped a front kick to the vampire's chin, sending him off balance. Ethan immediately chased him with a heavy slash, cutting a deep trough that created an X with his previous strike. Shaved bits of black fabric and kevlar disappeared into the night.

London recoiled from the telling blow. Growling in frustration, he ripped off the useless vest and tossed it into the wind. For well over a century,

London had protected Oberon's dealings from prying vampires and foolhardy hunters. He would not be bested by some filthy miscreant with a sword. With a snarl London jumped, letting the wind carry him, and chopped down with both hands. Ethan brought his sword up to block, but the force of the hammer-blow crushed his parry and drove the sword against his body. The jagged head of the pipe bit into his torso, cracking more ribs. Even with the supercharged effects of the spiritual energy, he screamed from the pain.

Elated from the sound of Ethan's cry, London struck again, knocking the masked man backwards. His sneaker caught on a raised air vent, and he spilled onto his back. London reared up to smash the prone hunter, but his pipe met sharp steel desperately parrying the vampire's savagery. He angrily swung at Ethan's sword hand instead, knocking the weapon over the side before raising his weapon again.

Ethan quickly rolled backwards at the last second, the pipe smashing into the white sheet metal. He reached into his back pocket for more throwing stars, but it was empty—he had used them all. He rolled, and London struck again. The roof buckled from the blow, and a thick tangle of live wires snaked around the bent end.

While the elder stubbornly struggled to free the sparking weapon, Ethan heard his name over the deafening wind shear. Peering over the side, Lauren kept pace with the bus, her car's high pitched exhaust roaring through the rushing air. Next to her, his sword stood upright in the passenger seat, swaying in the wind. She ripped the blade out and hurled the weapon. The blade spun through the air and stuck into the side of the roof. Ethan wrapped his bloody fingers around the worn red handle and yanked it free.

With a giant spray of sparks, London finally ripped his pipe loose. Live wires flopped out of the smashed roof like wounded snakes. Snarling, the vampire charged with his weapon held high like caveman's club. Ethan brought his blade up as the angry vampire smashed down. The sharp blade bit deeply into the lead, binding both weapons together.

"Where's 2047!?" Ethan rumbled under the strain.

"What does that have to do with you?" London spat.

Ethan's eyes blazed bright. He pushed back with twenty-three years of pent up pain, sorrow, fury, and hope. Rage turned to confusion and then to alarm the more ground London lost. With a burst of speed, Ethan hooked the pipe to the side, broke the bind, and sliced horizontally along London's torso. Wisps of ash trailed from the glistening edge, leaving a thin reddish-gray gash over the parasite's hips. He quickly followed with a cascade of slashes from all four axis, pouring every last drop of fury into the attack.

London barely kept up with the assault, loosing more of his footing and shirt and skin with each slash. He caught the sword on the last swing, wheeling the katana into the ground. The hunter's strength was immense now, nearly rivaling his. The masked man pushed against him, slowly raising the pipe off the roof. London's teeth cracked under the strained, blood pooling in his mouth. He spat in his adversary's face, causing him to blink. Seizing the moment, he released the pipe and thrust a hand at Ethan's chest, faster than the hunter could intercept, and hurled him through the jagged hole. One of the torn metal sheets ripped Ethan's jacket sleeve and tore into his left arm and shoulder. He banged off one of the support poles and collided into the dirty floor. His sword clattered behind him.

The driver looked over his shoulder and shouted, but his voice sounded so small and distant to Ethan's ears. Shaking, he latched onto one of the vertical posts and pulled himself to his feet. Blood ran down his left arm. He tried flexing, but it simply hung there, dribbling red on the floor.

London dropped into the bus with a heavy thud. His scarred lip curled into a satisfied sneer when he saw Ethan struggling to stay upright. He strode forward with confidence, patiently picking his way from seat to seat. He gingerly stooped down and picked up Ethan's sword. The driver looked back in stunned silence.

"I must commend you, boy. It's been well over a century since someone has wrecked so much havoc upon me and my dealings."

Ethan slid his good hand into his jacket.

Now or never.

"Last chance . . . asshole . . . to tell me where she is," he wheezed. Exhaustion strained his voice.

London sniffed the air and chuckled. "Why? So a disgusting vagrant can save his people? Spare me."

Ethan withdrew his last prayer card. Its letters were already glowing. London flipped the sword, switching his grip in one smooth motion, and hurled the blade like a javelin. Ethan tried to dodge but instead slipped on his own blood and fell to the floor. The sword careened over him, piercing the driver at the far end of the bus. The man collapsed on the blade stapling him to the wheel.

The chuntering engine surged, and the bus barreled through traffic. Each impact rocked the driver, Ethan, and London. The driver's body lurched to the side and brought the steering wheel with him. The bus teetered the wrong way into a turn and punched through the stone divider. Twenty-five tons of metal and glass arced into a city intersection in a rain of smashed stone and gravel. The massive vehicle crunched on the pavement. The wheels buckled and every window broke. Cascades of sparks shot up until friction finally forced the colossal hunk of steel to a grinding halt.

The damaged Ferrari screeched to an ungainly stop right when the bus rammed through the tan barrier. Behind her, speeding cars honked their horns at her vehicle sitting in the middle of the road.

Lauren jumped out and to the opening. Standing at the edge, the big vehicle lay in the middle of a wide intersection below. Cars and trucks scattered from the hunk of steel and glass violently interrupting the busy street. Drivers and pedestrians alike cautiously stood nearby, pointing and staring at the still settling wreck. Some of them were on their phones, calling friends or alerting emergency services.

Lauren's blood ran cold.

No one could survive a crash like that. Ethan was dead and with him any hope of curing herself. The cops had fallen back for some reason, but they wouldn't stay away for long. She had to get out of here and figure out her next steps.

She turned to leave but halted mid stride. The image of Ethan closing the bullet wounds on his body popped into her head.

Could he?

She went back to the edge. Down inside the wreckage, she saw movement. A blue light suddenly flashed through the broken windows. Her hand instantly fell to the grip of her piton launcher. The drop wasn't so far that she couldn't make it down with the gun. But no, she couldn't just abandon her car. The cops would eventually find it and trace it back to her. Lauren looked down the length of the freeway. The next off ramp was three quarters of a mile up.

She hopped behind the wheel and sped off.

Ethan's eyes burst open with a hoarse gasp.

Every part of him felt numb and weightless. He leaned against one of the posts at the front of the bus. The bus was dark except for the occasional shower of sparks from the ceiling and street lights angling through the shattered windows. The driver hung dead on the wheel next to him, his sword still sticking out of his back. Broken seats and snapped railings piled up near the rear doors.

With his second breath, every wound since the mansion suddenly came rushing back. The muscles in his legs burned from exertion. His knees refused to budge. Looking down, a bloody shunt of bone poked out of his left shin. His torn shirt revealed a thick sheen of crimson covering his chest. Ironically, Lauren's fancy goggles were still around his neck, dirty as all hell, but undamaged.

He reached for the pole above him, but his arm refused to lift over his shoulder.

The pile of seats settled in the back when a pair of men in uniforms with medical patches clambered through the damaged doors. When they saw Ethan, they ran over to him. The first man checked his wounds with practiced precision while the other unpacked a first-aid kit and assured him he'd be okay.

The pile rumbled again.

Ethan rolled his head around to the men. He tried to form words like "Danger", or "Run", or "Get the fuck out of here", but only a rasping whistle left his lips.

Suddenly, London burst through the collapsed mound. A slurry of grease, soot, and blood smeared his upper body, and what was left of his tattered shirt. Deep gray gashes traced across his chest. Stepping from the pile, a short length of broken conduit sticking out of his left kidney caught on a bit of railing. Registering the object, the vampire ripped it out and winged the tube to the side. The hole didn't bleed, nor did it close.

The second EMS stood up and ran over to help.

Bad idea, Ethan tried to say.

Two red eyes fell on the man, and London snarled. Before the hapless first responder could react, the vampire grabbed his neck and arm. Fangs out, he chomped on the man's shoulder, nearly tearing the meat off of him. Blood gushed, and London thirstily guzzled the warm red fountain. The gaping hole in his mid section sealed shut as he drank, and the red drained from his eyes. The gashes from Ethan's sword refused to seal all the way. London threw the desiccated corpse like a doll on a toppled seat back.

The other med-tech shot up, consumed by abject horror from London stomping his way over. He looked down at the catatonic human and quickly backhanded him. The man's head spun around completely, snapping his neck with an ugly crunch.

The parasite gazed at Ethan with contempt. He wrapped his fingers around the hunter's neck and lifted him off the floor. Ethan howled, his bones rubbed in ways not meant by nature. London ripped the damp hood from his head, revealing all the wet cuts and fresh bruises riddling his face. A jagged tear ran down his temple, and deep black rings hung under both his eyes. Red stained everything below his smashed nose.

"Not so special looking are you," London observed. "Where does a man get abilities like yours?"

"Wyoming," Ethan wheezed through clenched teeth. He squeezed London's wrist with his good arm. His eyes flickered gold for a second but quickly faded to blue.

"Still putting up a fight, eh?"

"I put demons like you in the ground," he uttered, still holding on to his hate.

"Demons!?" London scoffed. "I think you have your mythologies mixed up, boy. I am a fucking vampire."

"You're all parasites on humanity."

The elder sighed, "And you are just another angry sheep trying to bite its shepherd." London pulled the o-katana from the driver. No longer pinned to the wheel, the corpse folded onto the floor in a heap.

The vampire looked the weapon over. "A fine sword. A few chips and dents, but nothing a good sharpening could not easily remedy. Tell me, sheep," he said, casually inspecting the blade. "How does a vagrant from Wyoming get a hold of a weapon of this quality?"

"A gift . . . from Sensei," Ethan coughed.

The elder promptly thrust it through Ethan's lower torso. Blood spurt from his mouth when the vampire wrenched it out. His hand fell from London's wrist.

"Consider that a gift from Oberon." London reached back with the sword, angling the tip at Ethan's heart, "And this is from me."

With his last bit of defiance, Ethan snapped the crucifix off his rosary and shoved the silver Icon between London's eyes. The vampire screamed while the pure silver burned through his skull. He dropped Ethan and the sword and staggered backwards, gripping his smoking face in utter agony. Bright blue flames crackled loudly when Ethan's blood-stained fingers fell on the prayer card. London snapped his head up at the sound, revealing a concave brow of flaking gray.

Ethan flicked the prayer card. It whizzed forward on a ribbon of blue light and golden cinders, weaving over and through the bent railings. The card impacted London right on his lifeless heart where it burst with a thunderous clamor. A corona of blue and gold engulfed the blinded vampire. He howled and exploded into a shower of dust and debris.

"Consider that a gift from God."

Coughing, a bitter smile formed on Ethan's face. He lay there on the floor, completely drained. He didn't get the bus 2047's destination. But at least he ended a powerful vampire. Multiple in fact.

The blue flames gradually died down. Slowly, Ethan steadied his breathing and stilled his heartbeat. Ethan knew forcing the wounds closed might be dangerous, exhausted as he was, but he would bleed out if he didn't do something now. He focused on his limp arm and punctured torso, pouring what was left of his stamina into mending the bone and sinew. His ribs fused back together. His arm moved again. And his lungs breathed freely.

Now for the big one.

Achingly, Ethan rolled over and reached for his leg. Biting down on a thick clump of jacket, he punched the protruding bone back into place. He cried out through the bunched leather from the explosion of pain. Fighting the creeping unconsciousness, he drew from his dwindling pool of energy and forced the bone together and the skin to reform, leaving a fresh, jagged lump of pink tissue next to countless others.

After the pain subsided, he pulled himself to his feet. He grabbed the katana off the floor. The two repaired limbs were still raw and inflexible. Stiff arms reached over his shoulder and sheathed the sword. Still unsteady, he bent down and pocketed the broken rosary and mask. He hobbled out of the bus, his freshly healed leg refusing to bend all the way.

Dozens of people had gathered all around the wreck, silenced by the strange light show that happened minutes earlier. He stood there wobbling in front of the staring crowd.

"Dude, what happened?!" asked one man with dreadlocks.

Ethan opened his mouth to answer but collapsed on the ground, face first.

23 Mind Eraser

The world passed over Ethan.

Dragging his eyes to the right, he saw buildings whizz by on either side, and blackness filled the wide gap between. Small pin pricks of light and the waning moon broke the darkness. Every few seconds, something bright blue or green floated overhead with the occasional yellow or red. A giant white spiderweb crept out of the dark and fuzzy earth. Below the ground, Ethan saw his sword wedged next to his leg. Its beaten leather strap swung lazily tapped his bloody knee. He reached for the weapon, but his arm collapsed, too heavy to move even an inch. The dirt next to it was tan and spongy like a carpet.

Ethan blinked.

He was in a car. It was moving.

His head rested on a piece of tan leather next to red metal. Beyond it, people walked back and forth in front of buildings. A few looked at him strangely. Ethan tried to move again but moaned from the exertion. Pain wracked his body with every heartbeat. He heard the muted bleating of a horn. He heard multiple horns, all with different tones. He heard cars. He heard trucks. He heard shouting.

Familiar shouting.

A woman's shouting.

Something black and rubbery grabbed his shoulder. It was a hand. His vision swam when it shook him, and his head rolled left. The attached arm was just as black and connected to a body also covered in the same rubbery darkness. A tangle of white in the vague shape of a head sat on top of it. It kept turning back and forth between him and the spiderweb.

"Ethan!!"

His name jolted him awake. Car horns and squeaking brakes suddenly blasted his ears. His vision sharpened. He was in Lauren's car. Half the windshield was shattered into a thousand bits. Her gloved hand vigorously shook again him while she drove. A fuzzy white scarf concealed her long, heart-shaped face from the nose down, its tasseled ends hanging over her scraped and bloodied bodysuit.

"Ethan! Wake up, damnit!"

Panic warped her big red eyes. She snapped her head forward and yelled, mashing her expensive convertible's pathetic horn. Her frazzled braid flopped around with every movement.

"I'm taking you to the hospital, okay! Stay with me!"

Ethan hadn't been to a hospital since he was a child. He remembered his mother and father always fought about going there. Too expensive, Dad used to gripe. Sensei Takuan hated them, too. Why was that?

That's right, the things prowled around hospitals all the time.

"No . . . hospital . . . " he managed.

"What? Why?" Lauren leaned closer, keeping one eye on the traffic, "Why can't we go there??"

Ethan felt muzzy. His vision darkened around the edges, and his eyes started to roll up. He felt so tired.

Lauren panicked and shook him harder. "Ethan! C'mon Don't do this to me!"

The world came back with a sharp breath, kicking the muzziness away. His head rolled to a rest facing her.

"They . . . control . . . hospitals."

Lauren looked at him, her eyes frantic. "Right. O-okay. What do I do then?!"

Ethan remembered the time he broke his leg as a little boy. His mother sat with him in the truck while his father drove them to the hospital in town. She kept crying out, "What do we do, what do we do!?" His father comforted her: "It's just a broken bone, he'll be all right. Don't worry," he had said, patting her knee.

"Don't . . . worry. It'll . . . be alright."

"Don't worry?! Damnit, Ethan, you're dying! What the hell do we do?!?" she cried.

Sensei Takuan always knew what to do. They never went to the hospital. He showed Ethan how to focus the mind and purge pain. How to close wounds and set bones. He always repeated the same mantra with each lesson and every time afterwards: "Fight on empty belly, die on empty belly. Empty stomach heal nothing!"

"Need . . . food . . . "

"Food!?"

"Lost . . . too much blood. Need . . . food . . . to heal." he said.

Lauren went quiet for a moment. "I can take you through a drive-thru?" she offered.

"Good food," he breathed out.

"Oh. Yeah." She thought for a second. "Then where?"

Ethan struggled to lift his hand over the center console. It fell on her knee.

"Home."

Lauren glanced at his hand. Strips of the torn boxing tape drooped over, revealing flat, gnarled knuckles covered with ash and blood. The skin was torn and mashed, looking like so much ground beef.

"Steak!" she suddenly blurted. "I have all that steak at home?"

"Perfect," he exhaled.

She rested her hand on his, nervously squeezing his fingers. "Okay, okay. I'll get you home. You're gonna be alright. Just don't die on me!"

Lauren jerked the wheel in a sudden u-turn. Horns honked as she spun the car around. Its engine sputtered in protest and its tires squealed. She sped through a red light, angering more drivers.

Ethan swallowed and scraped the depths of his being for whatever dregs of strength remained, like eating soup with a broken fork. The entire car jolted from a pothole, eliciting a vicious swear from Lauren and rocking Ethan in his seat. His eyes flashed golden for a moment from the jarring bump. Lauren's rapidly pulsing aura flared in front of him. It was still pale and orange with sparks like before, but the silver was replaced with a thick, steady pink.

Pink. That explains . . . all the 'we's' just now.

His eyelids grew heavy again, and his golden vision faded, but just before her aura completely dissipated, he noticed a thin ring of blue seeping in at the edges when her hand rested on his again.

Ethan knew what blue meant. Blue complicated things. Blue led to distraction. And just like it did six months ago, it always led to tragedy.

As consciousness slipped away, Ethan saw the mangled form of the lady deputy.

But this time, her hair was white.

Lauren kicked open the door to her apartment so hard it left a small crack in the stone wall.

After nearly causing a traffic accident with her wild u-turn, she took every back alley and side street she knew getting back to her home on 82 South Baker St. Twice, she doubled back to make sure no cars were tailing her, and she changed streets every time she saw a hint of the police. She had even stopped once to rip off the license plate before continuing on.

Confident she had made it back without being spotted, Lauren hid her beat-up car in the furthest, deepest section of the building's parking garage and hastily shrouded it under a massive car cover. She had originally purchased it to protect her precious Ferrari from dust and particulates, but now it protected it from unwanted eyes. She helped Ethan to the stairs. With both of them covered in dirt and blood, she didn't dare risk getting seen by some random tenant on the elevator. Carefully, she scaled the towering stairwell using her piton launcher.

Gripping Ethan's arm over her shoulder, Lauren hefted him into the living area. Despite her strength he was heavier than he looked. She swiftly shoved the coffee table aside. The wooden puzzle he had rebuilt rolled off the edge and burst apart on the hard floor. Ethan groaned even though Lauren lowered him onto the couch as gently as she could. She quickly ripped off her white stole and tossed it and his sword on the cushion next to him before running into the kitchen.

Jerking the fridge door open, Lauren fished out one of the wrapped steaks and tossed it onto the counter. She then threw a giant wad of butter into the frying pan. Returning to the steak, spatula in hand, she turned on the stove. She stared at butter bubbling around the slab of meat. Their first meeting burst into mind.

What did that waitress say about him the other day?

Lauren threw another steak into the pan.

"Umm, how do you like your steak?" she called out.

"Cooked," he croaked.

"Really? I'm kinda partial to rare," she responded with a nervous laugh.

"Freak . . . " she heard him say. An awkward smile pulled at her lips. He wasn't completely gone.

Once the butter fully melted, Lauren flipped the meat. When one side began to sizzle, she flipped them over. And then flipped them again. And again. And again. After two anxious minutes, Lauren realized she had no idea what the hell she was doing.

When the meat smelled less like food and more like firewood, she immediately plopped them onto the cutting board. She hastily diced the two burnt hunks into small, uneven cubes and tossed the pile into a bowl.

She paused to assess her creation.

It was the most pathetic looking meal she had ever made.

Lauren grabbed whatever spices were left out from the morning and sprinkled them over the blackened beef. Snagging a fork, she bounded back into the living room. Ethan was drifting in and out of consciousness by then. Lauren thrust the bowl into his hands.

"Here!"

Startled, Ethan looked at the bowl of char and back to her perched on the edge of the coffee table, catching the embarrassment desperately hiding behind her crooked smile. He took it with shaky arms, almost spilling the meal from his lack of strength. She attentively watched him stab a chunk of charred meat and chew. He forced the bite down with a grimace and gave her a weak thumbs up.

"Uh, water?"

Her eyes lit up. "Right!"

Lauren bounded back into the kitchen. If there

was one thing she had plenty of in her home, it was bottled water. Next to the garbage can, she popped open a cabinet revealing a beverage cooler brimming with rows and rows of fancy bottled water. She snatched a couple and hurried back, twisting one open as she returned.

Ethan emptied half a bottle in one labored gulp.

"Thanks for pulling me from the bus."

"You saved my life—twice. And you watched over me when I got shot. I honor my debts."

Ethan slowly worked through the bowl of beef. Lauren hovered on the table corner, spare water bottle in hand, hopeful her meal was enough. When he looked up, Lauren blinked—suddenly self conscious—and fumbled behind her for the TV remote. An infomercial appeared on the big screen, droning on about some sort of brand-new cleaning product. She quickly flipped through the channels until finding the late night news. Their car chase plastered the whole screen surrounded by the station's logo graphics.

"Holy shit! Look!"

She cranked up the volume. Ethan stopped eating, and they both watched.

" . . . Just joining us, a deadly car chase between rival gangs erupted earlier this evening with multiple reported fatalities. The chase ended when one of the vehicles collided with a tanker truck on the I-65 Freeway near downtown. The police are still evacuating a one mile radius around the explosion as investigators say a biological agent may have been transported in one of the vehicles. Fortunately, no civilians were hurt during the shootout."

Behind the anchor, a clip from the news helicopter played out, showing one of the cars flipping over Lauren's convertible. Her stomach instantly tightened.

The anchor continued: "Moments ago, FPPD

Commisioner Thomas Harrison issued a statement, identifying the perpetrators as members of the San Carcos drug cartel. Sources within the department believe the chase is connected to the violent shootout at a mansion on Glenfort Island earlier in the evening. In other news . . . "

"Lies," Ethan muttered.

Lauren muted the television. She expected as much. In her line of work, she knew how easily corruption spread through bureaucracies. But she never would have guessed it came from vampires. Never in a million years.

"I guess they control the media, too, huh?"

"Yeah," he said, taking another bite.

"So, did you get him?"

Ethan swallowed. "He's ash."

"But you got the bus location from him, right?"

"No," he sighed.

Lauren frowned. She rest the remote on the table.

"Well . . . we know where the other two buses went. It's a start at least."

"A start?"

"We have to help them. They're people, not food."

Ethan stared at her.

"We're partners, remember?" she added.

"Right," he replied, cautiously.

"Alexander said they were going to Ember and Bell Island. Ember is a fancy nightclub near Oldtown. I've been there on business a couple times—very garish and very exclusive. You gotta dress up to the nines, and we'll probably have to bribe the bouncers to guarantee entrance. Definitely the kind of a place where *they* would hang out. The other place, Bell Island, is a geothermal plant in the middle of the bay. Some sort of environmentalist project from back in the seventies. It's closed to the public. I'll have to look more into it."

Lauren caught his stare and cracked an awkward smile.

"Sorry. You probably realized that I like to plan things out."

"I've noticed."

"I'm just . . . I'm just a little wired, still, I guess. I mean, I've never driven like that before! I took lessons at a track one time after I bought my car, but—"

"You did well," he interrupted.

"Thanks," she beamed, relieved.

"Why didn't you leave the mansion when you had the chance?"

Lauren averting her eyes, shamefaced. "I . . . I wanted him dead."

"Emile?"

"And that little toadie of his."

He said nothing.

"I . . . I can't run away from this." She turned back to him, hard and sober. "I want to help you."

"Even after all that?"

An imperceptible smirk crept through her somberness. "Even Rambo had help."

Ethan rolled his eyes. "What is it with you and that damned movie?"

Lauren blushed, her grin growing wider.

"Yeah. Okay. So, it's a little embarrassing, but when I was a little girl, I would sneak around all the time. Hard to believe, right? Well, the first time I snuck into the theater, the second Rambo movie was playing. It was fun and all, with the guns and the helicopter chase and everything, but . . . well, I thought he was really cute," her voice trailed off.

Ethan blinked.

"I watched all of Stallone's movies and had posters of him in my room. I really liked the second one where he's holding that big gun with his shirt off and the headband and he's all sweaty—"

The fork clanked against the bowl. "Aww, shit," he muttered.

Her white cheeks instantly blushed beat red. Why the hell did she even mention that?

"Can we drop that subject?"

"Yes! Yes, totally!" she blurted, willing her face to relax.

Ethan returned to his food while the television silently replayed the chase footage. Lauren watched the lowrider explode and flip over, missing her car by inches as she sped up. She replayed the moment in her mind—the big blue Buick tumbling overhead in slow motion. Stomping on the clutch and throttle in tandem, working the shift lever, her car shooting out just before the wreck landed. No way she could have reacted that fast.

But she did.

"We should be dead, shouldn't we?"

"Yep."

"I've done some wild things before, but tonight was the absolute craziest thing by a longshot. We went up against a whole army of heavies and kicked their ass! And the way you fought him on the bus? Holy shit!" I don't know where you learned to do all that, but you were amazing.

Ethan gazed down at the bowl in his hands and sighed. "Go to my bag."

"Huh?" she tilted her head.

"There's a small pocket on the side. Look in it."

Puzzled, Lauren went to the bag and felt around until she found the pocket and opened the flap. Inside was an old Polaroid photo, battered and faded. On it, a family of four stood together, waving at the camera, smiling. A husband, tall and sturdy, held his wife who in turn held a slightly bulging belly, and two children— a brown-haired boy and a girl with bright blonde hair like Lauren's. A team of rough-looking men sat at a wood table behind them, laughing and eating from a whole spread of barbecue laid out between them. Everyone wore simple dress clothes. Behind them an old barn with faded blue paint stood vigil over a large wheat field. In the far distance, jagged mountains rose up with a hint of snow at the top. On the bottom strip was a handwritten note: Ward Farm. Independence Day, 1980.

She returned to Ethan and handed it to him.

"Not long after this was taken, a group of parasites attacked the farm. They didn't want anything. They didn't take anything. They just started killing. Bastards toyed with and tortured everyone for hours."

"Everyone?"

"Mom. Dad. My uncle and his girlfriend. The farmhands. Earlier that day, a drifter had passed through. An old Japanese guy. He stayed for dinner and talked with my father and uncle well into the night. I don't know what they talked about, but he left before the parasites showed up. He returned during the attack and drove off the vampires, killing a few in the process. When everything was over, I was the only one left. The old man helped me bury what remained of my family."

He looked down, "My sister and I managed to hide in the barn while they were killing everyone. After all the shooting stopped, she poked her head out the door. One of them grabbed her. I still hear her screams sometimes when I sleep."

Lauren looked away, begging her imagination not to run wild.

"After the old man drove them off, he grabbed whatever supplies he could carry from the house and took me with him into the mountains. I didn't have any other friends or family that could take me in, so he taught me everything he knew like I was his own. I killed my first fang when I was eighteen. That's when he gave me this," Ethan patted the sword resting next to him. "When there was nothing left to learn, we went our separate ways. That was six years ago."

She quickly did the math. "You've been doing this for twenty-three years?"

He nodded.

"There's not many of us out there. The training is very long and very harsh, and our life expectancy is short. I don't do this because I like it, or for the thrill of it. I do this because someone should, and because I can. No child should have to go through what I did."

Ethan's eyes grew heavy. The bowl fell from his grasp, but Lauren shot out a hand and caught it with surprising speed. She placed it next to the remote.

"Thanks," he managed.

Lauren leaned in, worried. He smelled heavily of blood and sweat. Both scents made her light-headed. She backed off the instant her she felt her mouth twitch.

"Are you gonna be okay?"

Ethan rested his head against the couch. "I'll be fine. Long nights like this . . . They take a lot out of me."

She gazed at the massive claw mark on his chest. The slick blood made it glow in the soft the apartment's soft orange light. She tried not to think of what made that scar.

"Let me get you a blanket."

He didn't protest. Lauren went upstairs and dug through her closet. She hurried back down with a blanket and a set of sheets but found Ethan sound asleep, the picture still in his hand. She put the photo on the table along with the stole and his sword and unfurled the blanket over him. The moist blood on his chest would probably ruin the expensive fabric, but she didn't care.

Unbuckling the belt under her chest, Lauren peeled off her gloves and the top of her suit, letting the sweaty thing hang from her waist. She billowed her black undershirt, airing out the damp fabric. Quietly, she headed for bed. Hand on the railing, Lauren stopped and went back to the Polaroid of Ethan's family. Something about the little girl in it looked oddly familiar. She suddenly remembered the two rolls of film from the stakeout. It was late, and she was growing tired as well, but curiosity clawed at her. Surrendering, she opened the hatch to her workshop. Sparing a quick glance at Ethan, Lauren climbed up and got to work.

There were about forty pictures in all. Most of them were useless now that the depot had burned down—but all she wanted was just one: that blonde homeless girl that kicked off the entire night. Lauren was right. With a little bit of cleanup—and a lot of rehab—the girl might pass for Kathleen Baxter.

But that wasn't what had caught her interest.

She returned to the living room. Ethan was still dead to the world. Lauren knelt in front of the coffee table and held the Polaroid beside the freshly developed photo. The homeless girl was older and haggard, but her cheeks were sharp, just like the Polaroid. And both of them had a small mole below her left eye.

A beauty mark.

Lauren gazed at Ethan slumbering on the couch. He had found his sister.

Lauren awoke to stillness.

Her covers were still on and the pillows thankfully under her head. Peering at the nightstand, the clock read 11:49am with the same bright, bloody numbers. The apartment was silent and dark.

He must be sleeping still.

She had slept hard again last night, but this time she didn't dream. It was the first night of uninterrupted sleep since this all started. She debated whether to wake Ethan and ask him about the photos, but decided against it. They had both gone through hell yesterday, and rest was more important. She had left the photos on the table and slinked up to her bed, exhausted once the events of the day had finally caught up with her. Lauren didn't even have the energy to shower—only enough to peel off the rest of her sneaking suit and throw on a clean shirt before collapsing into bed.

Shuffling into the bathroom, she went through her usual morning routine as quietly as possible. Showering never felt so good. Drying off, Lauren inspected her hip. The giant gash over her kidney was completely gone with not even a shadow of a scar. For the first time, she felt grateful for the changes.

Wiping the condensation from the mirror, Lauren stared at the woman in front of her. She rubbed her tongue around her canines. They were normal right now, but for how long? The pearl-like flects in her red irises glinted in the vanity light. Was that the reason for her sensitive vision?

Lauren balling her fists on the beige stone counter.

They did this to her.

She was going to find out what exactly had happened and reverse it. Somehow.

While she brushed her teeth, Lauren gazed at her sneaking suit heaped on the floor. The thing was thoroughly damaged. The cut down the center, the big puncture over the hip, and all the other scrapes and tears. Like her body, it needed fixing. And if they were going to track down those buses, Lauren needed to be in top form.

She would call to Vassily about repairing it today.

Refreshed and robed, Lauren climbed downstairs while she dried her hair. She wondered what she could prepare for breakfast. She knew Ethan liked steak and eggs, but what else? Stepping into the living room, the damp towel slipped through her hands.

The apartment was empty.

Ethan was gone.

The couch was vacant and the bloody blanket folded. The bowl of steak was empty and in the sink. His bag in the back corner was missing. Both the photos were gone, too. Even the wooden puzzle she had knocked over was rebuilt and back on the coffee table by the remote.

And next to it lay her thermal goggles.

She held the device. His blood and sweat had been wiped away, but it still smelled faintly of him. A single, orange origami fox with a long, fat tail sat neatly in the dim shadow of the puzzle. She stared forlornly at the little paper animal, sinking slowly into the couch.

Lauren was back in her world again.

It was empty, and she was unhappy with it.

Epilogue

Sunday, March 9th, 2003. 11:01pm

The dark room was thick with tobacco smoke and impatience.

A test pattern blinked onto a large screen before displaying aerial video of a wrecked city bus lying in a crowded intersection. The image wobbled silently while dust slowly settled around the vehicle. One by one, tiny bystanders approached the wreckage. After a few moments, an ambulance drove up, and a pair medical techs entered it. A minute later, bright blue light flashed through the shattered windows. After the light faded, a man in a black jacket hobbled off the bus and fell on the ground in front of the still gathering crowd. A few people hesitantly prodded him. Not long after, a damaged red convertible pulled up beyond the ring of bystanders. A white-haired woman dressed in black shouldered her way through the pedestrians. After warding off the people next to the man with a large pistol, she dragged him into the car before driving off.

The video paused. Cigarette smoke wafted into the shaft of light from the ceiling projector, distorting the car frozen in mid escape. A tall, stately-looking man stepped in front of the screen holding a sleek television remote. The image on the screen reflected off his flawless ebony skin. His crisp three piece suit fit him impeccably.

"This was taken last night. Anyone care to explain what happened?" He spoke with a deep and clipped voice with perfect enunciation and a hint of malice.

The tall man moved an empty chair and leaned against the long, glossy black conference table in front of him. Nine other chairs accompanied the table, all but one filled with sharply dressed men and women of all stripes and ethnicities. The dark man observed the occupants gazing at one another with well-masked suspicion. Oberon sat in deep shadow at the far end of the table and spared a minute, almost imperceptible, knowing glance at the empty seat.

The stately black man tossed a burnt pocket watch onto the table. The cover flipped up as the charred object slid down the polished lacquer veneer. Everyone clocked it gliding past them, and come to a halt before Oberon. The glass face was cracked, and its hands frozen.

Oberon hid his grimace.

"My people found ashes in that bus. They tell me they belonged to Councilor Bray. Has anyone spoken with him in the last few nights?" the tall man demanded.

A thick set man with a thicker five o'clock shadow leaned forward. His voice held an equally thick New York accent. "Councilor Bray called me right before that crash. Told me a bunch of San Carcos gang bangers were chasing him and his men. He wanted the police called offa him so he could deal with the scum."

"Thank you Councilor Balar." The dark man turned to Oberon. "Councilor Petrelis, do you have any words concerning the San Carcos?"

Oberon felt Darrius Bennett's gaze hovering

over him. His thin lips curled into the slightest of sneers under the primarch's demanding gaze. He leaned forward, his hands flat on the table.

"There was . . . a bit of a commotion within the San Carcos last night. Some of the senior members revolted in a rather violent fashion. Multiple traitor cells attacked key parts of the cartel's infrastructure culminating with a massive assault on the don's home on Glenfort. My people are still tallying the damage to the organization, but the estimates so far are quite large. Fortunately, the coup failed, and *our* control still stands. The main organizers have been neutralized, but many of the lower rung traitors escaped. I have reason to believe that what we just witnessed was connected to the coup attempt."

Bennett tightened his accusatory stare. "I found their attack on Councilor Bray to be somewhat suspect. On a hunch I sent a few men to Undergrove Manor late last night."

Oberon leaned back, his fingers curling into fists. He was waiting for this.

"They found dozens of dead bodies and a few burning vehicles when they arrived. Most of them belonged to Councilor Bray's private security firm along with a handful of your San Carcos *traitors*, but they also found the remains of vampires as well. And evidence of silver use."

"Yes, well, as I said, the San Car—"

Bennett interrupted, "What was the gathering last week for, Councilor?"

"I beg your pardon?" Oberon hid his stammer well.

"I had heard strange rumors of an unsanctioned gathering there last week. You know that any public assemblage of our people over a dozen expressly requires council authorization. That rule was created to prevent the public bringing unnecessary attention to our existence. I expect to have such problems with the nightclubs, but the rumors indicate there were *five times* the legal amount present at Undergrove."

Oberon bared his yellowed teeth in a wide grin. "With all do respect, Primarch, I do not know the full extent of Councilor Bray's private affairs. While I am not privy to everything he may—"

"Councilor Petrelis," Bennett halted Oberon with a raised hand. "It is well known that you and Councilor Bray have been fast allies for over a century. Do you mean to tell me you had no idea what your *friend* was up to last week?"

The two elders locked eyes for an frigid second until Oberon spoke with a perfectly measured voice and a hint of scorn. "That is correct, Primarch. Councilor Bray's private affairs were just that: private."

Bennett lingered on Oberon before turning to the rest of the group. "What are we doing about this?"

One of the women present spoke up. Her skin was paler than the rest, and her dark hair had been pulled into an uncomfortably tight bun over the crown of her skull. The red lipstick she wore was indistinguishable from fresh blood. Her nose hooked slightly, and her face carried a perpetual scowl with a thick layer of mascara. She took a long drag from a cigarette affixed to a thin black stick.

"I've already instructed the news outlets to bury everything concerning councilor Bray. The footage we just saw is the only physical copy left of the aftermath. All others have been destroyed." The woman's voice wore her contempt like a second skin.

"Thank you Councilor Naverre."

Roman piped in. "My thralls in the police are personally directing investigations into the San Carcos. During the chase, patrol units were held back due to the possible threat of biological agents and explosives stored in the truck. The official statement on the incident will confirm that the bio-agents were incinerated when it crashed into the fuel tanker. All further investigations will find evidence that backs this up."

"Good. Next?"

Oberon tamped down his indignation when Bennett's gaze turned on him.

"Within the week, police and news outlets should receive information regarding the rogue elements of the San Carcos. The police will find them dead from an apparent quarrel within their ranks that grew out of hand."

"Excellent," Bennett smiled. He loved it when a well oiled machine worked its magic—his kind of magic. "The last thing to discuss is these two." He rewound the video to the woman carrying the man. He faced the rest of the council. "Who are they?"

"Unknown," Naverre uttered through a ring of smoke.

"Any information on the vehicle?"

"The red car was seen chasing Councilor Bray's truck along with the cartel scum," Roman added. "Witness statements make it a Ferrari. Nothing else is known."

"There can't be many of them in this city. Find out who it belongs to," Bennett ordered.

Roman nodded. Oberon watched him from the side of his eye.

"What about the man? That blue light is likely what destroyed Councilor Bray. Councilor Petrelis, you were a member of the occult community. Any thoughts on the incident?"

Oberon regarded Bennett coldly before answering. "There are so many different ways to utilize the mystic arts to replicate the effects of fire. It would be hard to pin down exactly what happened, or who precisely was responsible."

Bennett leaned closer, his head hung like a vulture. "Is the occult community up to it's old tricks again, Councilor?"

Oberon narrowed his eyes across the table. "Hardly, Primarch. They are a scattered shell of their former numbers and have not recovered from your pogrom two decades ago. Their kind has not been seen within the city limits since."

The primarch cast his gaze to the rest of the councilors present. "What about the Inquisition?"

A few of the vampires exchanged worried glances. A woman of eastern European origin leaned forward, unperturbed by the word. The waves of her long red hair shimmered in the projector light. She spoke in a thick slavic drawl. "Contacts within the Vatican have reported no movement of late. The Inquisition has not mobilized in many years."

Bennett pointed to the screen. "Whoever those two are, I want them found. I want to know everything about them: who they are, where they're from, what they were up to, and why. Remove all mention of them from the media. I want this hunt quiet and internal. Once we have everything, liquidate them."

"Consider it done, sir," Roman said.

Naverre's lips parted with a forced grin.

The primarch looked at everyone, "Meeting adjourned."

"There is . . . one other matter," Oberon interjected before everyone stood up.

Bennett eyed the emaciated councilor. "Which is?"

"While we are all present, I think we should consider the fate of the late councilor's holdings," Oberon said behind steepled fingers.

Roman leaned in, glaring at Oberon, "Yeah, let's consider."

Bennett looked at the two councilors.

Roman continued, "The last time I spoke to the *late councilor* he agreed to sign over half his Deacon Hill holdings to me. I believe those are mine by right."

"I *believe* there should be a proper accounting of all the properties, holdings, etc. before we begin doling them out among us," Oberon clarified. "Especially any transfers based on unverified verbal agreements."

The thick councilor clasped his meaty hands with a scowl coming over his hooded eyes. "Ya know, I learned a long time ago to record every phone call I make. Never know when it might come in handy. Would you like me to bring you proof of this *unverified verbal agreement*?"

Oberon turned to Bennett. "Primarch, as the previously mentioned long-time compatriot of the late councilor, I think it is best for all of us here that I oversee the dissemination of the properties and responsibilities in question so that they are handed out to those best qualified to manage them."

Roman thrust a thick finger at Oberon. "You can hand out whatever the hell you want, so long as I get my fifty percent!"

"I can assure you, councilor, you will receive all that you bargained for," Oberon sneered.

"Enough!" Bennett roared.

The two councilors hushed and turned to the Primarch.

"We will not discuss such things at this time," Bennett proclaimed. "The holdings of London Bray will be held until the two responsible for this chaos have been dealt with. Further I have already instructed Councilors Stephenson and al Mustaim to handle the delivery operation left vacant by Councilor Bray until such time as a replacement can be decided.Do I make myself clear?"

Two men in the middle nodded. One, a small, scruffy looking caucasian gentlemen. The other a larger, overly manicured middle eastern fellow with a light complexion. Oberon regarded both with quiet disdain. Everyone nodded in agreement. Even Oberon and Roman.

"Good. This meeting is over."

All the council members stood up and left along with Bennett. The projector shut off and the lights came on. A soft orange glow lit the now empty conference room. Oberon remained at the table. The prospect of the mansion falling into the hands of that oaf, Roman, would complicate his long term plans. But, if Bennett kept it off limits for the meantime, that concern could at least be put to one side—so long as no one went exploring in the cellar.

The girl, however, presented a more immediate problem. Oberon had already dispatched minions to find her. He only hoped they could locate her before Roman's people could get their filthy hands on his ritual subject.

The masked swordsman, however, posed a more interesting complication.

London was one of the more capable combatants on the council. He had acquitted himself well during the pogrom—much to Oberon's dismay at the time. Opposing him physically was reckless and dangerous, but, the masked man had actually succeeded in destroying the old soldier.

Surely, something had to be done about him. Like the girl, he too was a witness to the ritual. Oberon had tasked his people to hunt the swordsman down, too, but if Bennett could somehow successfully interrogate either of them, the nature of his plans would be revealed before he could unleash them on the council.

He stood up from the chair.

But . . .

What if this masked swordsman could be pointed in the right direction? With the proper incentives, his antics could distract the council long enough for Oberon to prepare his ritual again. He might even eliminate a few council members along the way.

Oberon's thin lips curled into a wide grin.